The Driftcap Inn

Kate Valent

Valiant Ink

THE REALM OF ITHAROS
THE FORLORN SEA
GATRAI BROTHERHOOD
THE NORTHMAW
COCEPS
VEVERNAS
GRAND DUCHY OF HERALIA
CACOSSHIAN TETRARCHY
CORSANA CHANNEL
ATRENEM
DIVINE KINGDOM OF VINATERIA
DUCHY OF RAANGNANVULIA
STORMDOCK
PELEPH
SCRUMBOGAST
PRINCIPALITY OF NEPHLAS
LOST ISLAND OF PALGIA
KINGDOM OF HEROTOGAST
URUNTA
CORCAL
GATHIA
NESET BAY
PANLANG BAY
DUCHY OF BRUMANTIS
CACHEVERMAL
PRINCIPALITY OF STRANIA
AHRIQOSAI EMPIRE
NELENE
NEPHENE
STRANACH CHANNEL
LEVENHAM
THE GREAT DIVIDE
POUTISE
HERATICA
GRAND DUCHY OF POROCAR
BUSANI
UNIFIED KINGDOM OF SINIA
KOPARAM
GULF OF MYCARADE
TETEBARECH MOUNTAINS
MT. CHILBRIN
APTHRAS
VILBAR
MT. NADEGARRE
TETECHETECH
YEL MOR
MIASMIC OCEAN
MUNA
KOHAR
KARAVAL
SANVILEAU

1

"Why did you make it look like a mushroom?" a husky voice asked.

Eino sat up, shutting his eyes against the bright sunlight streaming in through the crack in the curtains. There was no better way to spend the early morning than sharing sweet pillow talk with a new lover. But as soon as he sat up, his head began to thrum and ache from last night's revelry. "What are you talking about?"

"Your inn, of course." The Sinian man beside him rolled over and propped his head up with his hand. His long, dark hair was tied back in a ponytail that cascaded over his shoulder. He wasn't wearing the traditional manaque beads that marked one's status in the kingdoms of Sinia. Rather, all three beads had been replaced with a single spiral ornament in honor of last night's Sarbakh festival.

Eino rubbed his temples. "Well, because it's a mushroom. Why else?" A spiral dangled from a lock of his own curly red hair. He didn't remember putting it there. Then again, he didn't remember much of the previous night.

"Yes, but it's not really a mushroom, is it? Most people think it's just some sort of airship, but I think I've figured it out," he said with a smug expression. "It's an old Xiphang balloon, isn't it?"

Eino snorted. "Now if I ever got my hands on an old Dominion relic like that and brought it all the way back here, do you really think I'd be letting strangers sleep in it?"

"You don't seem opposed to sleeping with strangers." His lover smiled, tracing his finger in a circle over Eino's chest. "But if it's not a balloon, then what is it?"

Eino chuckled to himself. This wasn't the first time someone had asked about his peculiar inn. Far from it. Although most people didn't wait to bed him first before asking. "Fact is, it's just a bunch of big ol' driftcaps lashed together. Carved 'em out myself."

His lover frowned. "You're not going to fool me with another of your tall tales. We get driftcaps here in Poutise, you know. Even the ones too old and stale to eat are only about this big." He held his hands out at about shoulder width.

"Well, of course they don't get that big around these parts. There's only one place in all of Itharos where they do."

"And where exactly might that be?"

Eino winked. "Can't give away all my secrets."

"Of course." His lover rolled over and smirked. "I should have known better than to expect a straight answer out of you."

"It's the truth I'm telling you! Them mushrooms are much more comfortable than you'd think. Comfier than any ol' Dominion balloon, that's for sure." Eino glanced around the room, spotting the trail of clothes they'd left behind. He climbed out of bed and tugged his pants on. "You can see for yourself if you don't believe me."

"Really?" Interest lit up the man's eyes. "I've always wanted to ride in an airship."

Eino scoffed. "Airships are cramped and cold. But the Driftcap Inn? You won't find a cozier place in all the skies. A warm fire in every cabin, and home-cooked meals every day with fresh caught scramblers straight from the aura stream." Eino put on his most dazzling smile and offered his lover a hand. "Why don't you come on up and book yourself a stay?"

The man laughed. "You're just hoping for another customer, aren't you?"

"Normally I'd charge for a cabin, but for you…" He leaned across the bed and planted a kiss on his lover's neck. "You can stay with me in my quarters."

"That's quite the offer." He rubbed his chin.

"The offer won't stay on the table for long." Eino poked through the remaining pile of clothes for his shirt, but came up empty-handed. "We're leaving for Brumantis this afternoon."

His lover pouted. "You mean you can't stay a little longer? Not even for me?"

Eino grimaced. He so badly wanted to say yes, even though he couldn't quite remember the man's name. "I'm sorry. Wish I could, but the inn keeps her own schedule. The ol' girl just drifts wherever the aura streams take her."

"You're just floating around on the winds?" A bewildered look crawled across the Sinian's face. "Then how in Soleivar's name do you get where you want to go? Isn't there a better way?"

"It ain't about where you're going. It's about how you get there. And believe me, there's no better way to get where you're going. Even if you're not goin' anywhere at all." He threw the curtains open and held out his hands toward the window in a dramatic swish.

His lover shielded his eyes from the light of the morning suns. "What are you doing?"

"Showing you the inn." Eino glanced out the window, then did a double take. He scanned the sky, but there was no sign of his mushroom over the tiled roofs of the Poutise town center. It should have been just to the left of the temple's tall, twisting spire. The sky, however, was empty. He cursed under his breath, patting the pockets of his trousers. "What time is it?"

"I don't know." The man climbed out of bed and tripped over Eino's shirt. Eino grabbed it off him and slid it over his head.

"Strak! I overslept." He pulled his long coat off the doorknob. He checked three of its many pockets to ensure he had his most important items, including what was left of the coins he'd brought down with him. "I need to go."

"Already?" The man covered himself with his silken sash and stood up from the bed. "When will I see you again?"

"Today if you like." Eino pulled the man into a close embrace. "Come with me on the inn." He dropped his voice. "Please." His voice cracked on the word "please", unable to handle his desperate longing.

"Come with you? All the way to Brumantis? I—" The man stammered. "I can't do that."

"Sure you can. I promise you've never seen anything as gorgeous as the flowering meadows outside of Corçal."

"But I don't know what to pack! And I'd have to tell everyone I'd left. And I wouldn't be back until—" The man looked up, "When would I even be back?"

"A...a half-year." Eino grimaced, but tried once more to pour all of his charm into his words. "But it'll be the most unbelievable half-year of your life."

He shook his head. "I'm sorry, but I can't just leave for another country at the very start of harvest season. I can't do that to my family."

"Oh." Eino's smile faded, but he managed to put on a brave face to guard against the pain. "Then I guess maybe I'll see you again around planting time."

"We'll see." The man looked away.

Eino gave him one last bittersweet kiss, and then he darted out of the door, ignoring the tightness in his chest.

None of his lovers ever took him up on his offer to come to the inn. No matter how badly they seemed to want to join Eino, everyone always had ties keeping them home. It was a sentiment he couldn't share. As a young man, he'd left his home in Porocar to join the newly formed Sinian Air Legion and serve aboard an airship. He hadn't looked back since.

The Driftcap Inn was his home now. A home that never stopped moving, and always offered new views of the most beautiful places in all of Itharos. But without someone to share those views with, the loneliness left him feeling hollow during quiet nights.

As he ran down the street toward the main square, he raised his hand to his head to keep his hat from falling off. His stomach lurched. There was no hat. He'd left it behind.

Eino rushed back to the little house. Hoping to avoid an awkward encounter with his lover, or rather his now former lover, he decided to sneak in through the window and retrieve his hat without being noticed. As he clumsily clambered through the window, however, he found himself face to face with the man, clad only in a sash and Eino's hat.

It had a wide brim, like the simple straw hats worn by farmers and ranchers in the mountainous south of Porocar. But Eino's hat had more of a north coast Porocari flair, shaped from stiff felt and draped with fine patterned linen to give it the appearance of a mushroom cap. Neither northerners nor southerners would have considered it authentic, but wherever Eino went, it helped him to stand out from the crowd.

The man looked up from his hand mirror, meeting Eino's eyes with a sheepish smile.

Eino cleared his throat to keep from bursting out laughing. "It looks good on you."

"I was just curious." The man pulled the hat off and handed it back, looking away to hide his embarrassment. "It wasn't my style, anyway."

There was a long, uncomfortable silence as Eino took his hat, trying to think of an elegant way to crawl back out the window. With a deep breath, he broke the silence by reaching into his pocket and producing a small wooden idol. "Here. Something to remember me by."

"What is it?"

"It's Dilgaa, the mountain god. Hand carved by one of the greatest artisans in Porocar. It's kept me safe all this time." He placed it in the man's hand. "And now I want you to have it."

The man ran his fingers over it in awe. "It's beautiful. Thank you."

Eino gave him a soft smile. "Dilgaa watches over all of us from atop the mountains. He'll watch over you too." With that, he plopped the hat on his head, tipped it, and climbed back out through the window.

The "great artisan" who'd carved the idol was Eino himself. People loved gifts, making them an easy way to get out of awkward situations. He always kept a few Dilgaa idols on hand to help him out in a pinch.

He dashed through the quiet streets of Poutise. Mornings were always quiet and slow after the Sarbakh festival, but soon the humble town would be as busy as the capital.

The aroma of fresh bread drifted down the road from the nearby bakery. The smell made his mouth water. He paused in front of it, his stomach grumbling, but the sign was still turned to "closed." Beside the door, two drunken townsfolk slept off the festival. They weren't the only ones. The streets were littered with people who had passed out or were only now hobbling home after a night of celebrating.

The spiral trunks of the poutamme trees rose high above the streets, their large canopies casting great swaths of shade over the town. Even after the previous night's harvest, their branches were still laden with large, plump reddish orange fruits. These trees were the very reason for the Sarbakh festival, which marked the start of the spring harvest season. At the base of each tree was a small spiral shaped shrine to the city's patron goddess, Poutessa. Each shrine was covered with offerings thanking the goddess for a bountiful harvest. As Eino dashed past, he made the sign of the sacred spiral at each shrine.

Eino always made a point to visit the festival each year, and he never grew tired of it. He'd done his fair share of traveling and of sampling local cuisines from all over Itharos, but nothing was quite as sweet and refreshing as a freshly plucked poutamme fruit. As he darted around the piles of drunken locals and the havoc they had wrought, He spotted a branch full of fruit hanging low between buildings. He just couldn't help but pluck a few fruits, jamming them into his pockets before dashing off once more.

For one tavern, the festivities had not yet subsided, the dull sound of slurred singing and laughter emanating from inside its walls. Several men unloaded barrels from a wagon parked by the tavern. One man stumbled under the weight of a barrel and let go. The man at the bottom of the ramp darted out of the way in surprise, letting the barrel roll down the road.

"Stop that barrel!" The man in the wagon shouted, shaking a fist at the man on the ground.

It had to be full of poutamme wine, likely aged in the barrel since last year's festival. Eino wished he could snatch up the rolling barrel and take it with him to the inn, but he wasn't strong enough to lift it on his own, and his auramancy was nowhere near capable enough to achieve such a feat. Seeing no other alternative, he vaulted over the barrel, stumbling on the landing before righting himself and continuing his mad dash back to the inn.

At the next street, he made a right, dodging past the group of half asleep children on their way to the well. He ducked down a narrow alleyway into one of the older districts of the city. The simple, squat mud brick structures were a stark contrast to the bright colors and ornate architecture commonplace throughout Sinia since unification. It was a fascinating vision into a time not only from before the Unified Kingdom came into being, but of the early founding of Poutise as well.

Eino shook his head, trying not to let the quaint old structures distract him. The short buildings gave him a far better view of the sky and made it easier to find his inn. He had to squint against the morning suns, but he could see that it wasn't far past the town. Close enough for him to catch up to it.

His legs burned as he dashed through the town gates. Travelers and other locals were already lining up to get their fill of another day of drinking and feasting. But not everyone was partaking in the festivities. Up ahead, he spotted a fisherman driving a wagon loaded with fishing supplies. He rushed to catch up.

"Sir, excuse me! Can I ride along with you?" With the charm of a showman, Eino bartered with the man for passage. He pulled another Dilgaa idol from his pocket and offered it as payment.

Convinced by the handiwork of the "great artisan", the man accepted. He jerked a thumb over his shoulder, and Eino clambered aboard. The road led them out of town and to his inn, their speed picking up as they cleared the crowd.

Finally, a chance to catch his breath and check the time. He searched through his pockets, finding various trinkets and tools, some of which he didn't remember putting there. After trying three pockets, he found his watch. He squinted at the time.

Not as late as he'd guessed with how far the inn had gotten. It never stopped moving, but it always kept the same pace without his interference. This was the second time he'd noticed it moving a little faster along the aura streams than usual this year. Then again, maybe his watch was running slow. With all the wine he'd been drinking the night before, he suspected he hadn't wound it.

When he got close enough to the inn, Eino jumped off the wagon and trudged up to the top of a grassy hill. He pulled on his goggles, allowing him to peer up at the inn without the two suns hurting his eyes. Then he grabbed the whistle hanging around his neck and blew it. It made no sound, but after a moment, a large black shadow backlit by the morning suns unfurled from the top of his inn.

It descended, not in a sudden rapid dive, but in a controlled, gentle glide. As it drew closer, the bird's white feathers came into view, as did the tall red crest on the top of its head. As the creature landed, the wind from her tremendous wings was nearly enough to knock Eino from his feet.

"There's a good girl, Blue," said Eino, reaching up to rub the head of the creature, his crested greatwing. While their massive size lent them to use as beasts of burden, it was rare to see one outfitted with a saddle like Blue's.

Eino reached up for the saddle, but Blue squawked, craning her long neck around and nudging at Eino's jacket with her wide beak. She stood tall, preventing him from mounting the saddle.

He sighed. "Alright, alright." Eino pulled a small crushed cake from his pocket. Yesterday the pastry had stood in a spiral shape like so many other festival foods, but now it was just a pile of mashed cake and poutamme jam. Blue, however, didn't seem to mind the messy presentation. She eyed the pile intently.

"Now this was supposed to be a treat for when we got back." He tossed the wad of cake to her and she caught it, holding it aloft and swallowing it in one gulp. He rubbed her neck. "But you're my baby and I love you."

Blue let out a coo of delight as she swallowed down the cake.

Eino chuckled. The last time he'd forgotten to bring Blue a treat, she flew off and almost left him stranded on a small Cacosshian island. He had to sprint to a bakery and paid double to buy her the last savory honey roll.

This time, however, Blue seemed sated. She folded her wings in, making it easier for him to swing up and onto her back. He held on as her powerful wings sent them upward, keeping his goggles on to protect his eyes from the wind and sunlight. Their tint made it easier to spot the aura updrafts. Blue soared into one and drifted upward, riding the stream of invisible energy back into the sky. It took a few minutes to reach the aura stream, but as long as he took it slow, the old injury on Blue's left wing didn't seem to bother her.

His attention slid back toward Poutise while he ascended, taking in the full magnificent view of the city bathed in the morning light. It was a sight he relished every time he visited. Except for the Grand Spiral at the Great Temple of Poutessa. It jutted up through the treetops, and from up here he could see how the spiral was slightly off center from the town hall and market square. He pursed his lips. The longer he looked at it, the more the sight irritated him.

The city would grow rowdier as the day went on. As much as he'd miss all the dancing and music later, the mild ache in his head told him he was due for a quieter night at home in his inn.

2

Riding atop Blue, Eino slowly rose toward The Driftcap Inn. The main mushroom of the inn hung in the sky like a Heralian parasol. Pale spots dotted its orange cap, matching its white underbelly. Rope bridges tethered six smaller mushrooms to the main inn. They swayed in the air, dancing around the main body like a festival pole. Five of the smaller mushrooms served as guest cabins, providing a private sitting area with a fireplace and a loft bed. The sixth was Eino's most prized possession, his smokehouse.

Inside the stem of the main mushroom was his pantry and storage. The cap housed a shared kitchen, dining area, and common room, as well as a second-floor loft, which connected to Eino's private quarters. A wooden promenade circled the mushroom beneath the cap, giving guests space to stretch their legs.

Come autumn, driftcap season would begin in the mountains of Porocar. The wild mushrooms would detach from the ground and take to the skies in droves, floating as far west as the Great Divide. A driftcap plucked straight from the ground never quite tasted right, so savvy farmers and foragers would have their crop netted or roped down to keep them from wandering away. Until then, Eino's inn would be the only driftcap in the sky.

Blue landed on the cap of the smokehouse. Wisps of smoke danced in the air from the narrow chimney, carrying with them the scent of smoked mushrooms and mountain ibex bacon. Eino's mouth watered. Porocari cuisine had a reputation for being survival food, relying on smoking, salting and drying for long journeys up steep mountains. But even posh northern coastal cities used smoked meats and vegetables in dishes fit for nobility. No matter how far Eino drifted from Porocar, he always had the taste of home right outside his door. And more importantly, he could share it with his guests.

Two wool hens darted away with indignant squawks. Once more, Blue's beak poked at one of Eino's pockets, shaking him loose from his hungry daydreaming.

"Sorry, girl. I ain't got nothing for you. This here fruit is for Betta."

Interest lost, Blue turned her attention to preening herself. Eino jumped down onto the bridge that connected the two mushrooms, using aura to slow his descent. Because the inn was always roaming around just below the aura streams, it gave him access to an endless supply of aura to keep the inn adrift in the air, and more than a little to play around with.

When he reached the promenade, his stomach growled again. It was too late for breakfast, but he hoped Betta had saved some for him. She was the reason he so loved his smokehouse, because she smoked meats and mushrooms and then turned them into some of the most delicious Porocari dishes he'd ever had. Eino dabbled in cooking, but he didn't know how she made such wonderful food in his limited kitchen. Betta came to the inn as the cook two years ago in exchange for her own cabin. Every day since her cooking reminded him he was lucky to have her aboard.

He opened the door and the smell of Betta's breakfast hash made his mouth water. She always used the previous night's leftovers to make her signature hash, so it was never the same dish twice. Yet no matter what was in it, it was always delicious. He followed the scent through the sitting room and to the small kitchen tucked against the back of the mushroom, where the wooden counters followed the gentle curve of the mushroom's cap.

Betta bustled about, cleaning up. She wore her long, gray hair tucked into a neat bun, and her embroidered apron hung around her neck. The elaborate embroidered design showcasing several varieties of mushroom, though it matched perfectly with the curtains and hand towels, seemed almost out of place on a gruff woman like Betta.

It had been the handiwork of a seamstress who had stayed at the inn the previous year. When she was unable to pay for her stay, she offered her services to decorate the inn, and Eino graciously accepted. Now her touch was all over the inn, from little tapestries on the walls, her decorative embroidery, and even the soft silken lining of Eino's jacket.

"Smells amazing in here."

"Well, look who finally joined us." Betta looked up from the dishes. "I saved you a plate. Figured you'd get in late today."

She gestured to the table. It'd been his original table before he expanded his house into an inn. Since it was only big enough for two, the guests ate in the dining room. A plate sat at the ready at his favorite seat beside the window, a towel over top to keep it warm.

"Thanks. Here, I brought you something." He emptied his pockets of fruit out onto the table.

She quirked an eyebrow as she watched him pull more fruit than his jacket ought to have fit. "Well, cast me to the Wynds. Did you bring a whole damn tree back with you?"

He sat down. "I wish." Eino flashed her a sly smile as he dug into his hash. The soft, buttery cobbleroots melded together with mushrooms, vegetables and spiced breakfast sausage. It made for a hearty meal that eased his headache. "I mean, somebody's gotta restock our supplies since you called it an early night."

She snorted. "Them Sinians are a rowdy folk. One dance was more than enough for me. We don't all have the energy to stay out until morning." She picked up one of the fruits, weighing it in her hand. "I reckon I'll turn these into a pie."

Eino chewed loudly, smacking his lips. "My second favorite way to have a poutamme!"

"You can bet I'm not waiting around to turn 'em into wine." Betta gave Eino a suspicious look. "You didn't jam a barrel of wine into those pockets too, now did you?"

"I wanted to, but the barrels we have should be enough. Stranians love the stuff. They'll pay big for a barrel. Assuming there's any of it left when we get there." He sat down and eagerly dug into the food. "Did Joren come by for breakfast?" Joren was the only other guest currently staying at the inn.

"He did. He gave me that silent little head bow he does and took off with his food back to his cabin." She piled the fruit into a bowl. "That boy's been here since the start of winter and bless him, but I could count on one hand every word I've heard him say."

Eino shrugged. "Some people are quiet like that. I've been wondering where he's heading. He hasn't said."

"It ain't about where he's heading that worries me. That fella is jumpier than a pebble toad." She frowned, turning her attention to the window as she finished stacking the dishes. "It's like he's running from something."

Eino laughed. "If he's running, it's from everyone. I've never met someone as terrified of other people as him."

Betta stacked up the clean dishes and poured two cups of tea. "Ain't nobody that scared without good reason. But I think I know why."

"Oh yeah? Why's that?"

"See, he's always coming back with plants and herbs. And he always has that shoulder bag and those glass vials hanging off it." Betta leaned over conspiratorially. "That boy's a smuggler. You mark my words."

"Ain't no way. A smuggler's gotta keep a cool head about him, and the last time I tapped him on the shoulder, he damn near jumped right off the promenade." Eino sipped at his tea. "I reckon he's just a normal fella who's a little jumpy. Probably an apothecary. He must be taking them plants and vials and mixing up all kinds of medicine back in his cabin."

"I'll bet you he's cooking up 'medicine,' alright." Betta smirked.

Eino raised an eyebrow. "You willing to bet on it? Loser cooks the winner's favorite dish."

"Boy, if you could make a stuffed sea gourd worth squat, I'd take you up on that." She laughed, joining him at the table with a fresh pot of tea. "But I'm telling you, he's a smuggler. I reckon he's trading in dreamleaf."

"To who? Sinians?" Eino raised an eyebrow. "That stuff ain't exactly hard to come by." Eino himself had partaken of some the night before. Sinians were almost always eager to pass around their stick pipes, particularly during festivals.

"Somewhere in the Tetrarchy, I bet. You know how stuck up them Cacosshian folks can be." Betta held up a hand. "Not that it's any of our business. If he's that jumpy, might be best to leave him be."

"Sounds like you're just scared you'll lose our little wager." Eino grinned. "The hard part's gonna be getting him to talk."

"Well, food doesn't loosen his tongue any. Dilgaa knows I've tried."

"He's definitely not a people person. But now that all the other guests left for Sarbakh, we might get him to open up."

"We'd better. It's too quiet around here with only one guest." She pulled a list out of the apron's large pocket. "But now that you're fed, how about you make yourself useful and fetch me a few things from the pantry and garden?"

"Yes, ma'am." Eino pounded his chest and bowed, mocking a military salute. "It'll be a few days before we reach Brumantis. Are we running low on anything?"

"Nothing that can't wait. As long as the weather's this nice, I'm going to wash the linens today and hang them out to dry. It'd be a shame to waste such a beautiful day." She tilted her head toward the window. "My knees tell me it won't last long. There'll be a spring rain before we know it."

"Then I'd better check on the garden. And the core."

Betta gave a concerned look. "What's wrong with the core?"

"Nothing. At least I don't think there is. But well..." Eino trailed off as he tapped his chin. "You haven't noticed the inn moving faster than usual, have you?"

"Can't say I have." She squinted down at the floor in the direction of where the core was stored. "Have you?"

He nodded. "This is the first time we've gotten off schedule since I set one. But if you haven't noticed it, then it can't be too much to worry about."

Her concerned expression deepened. "If something's wrong with the core, then I'm worried. When's the last time anybody looked at that thing anyhow?"

He ran a hand through his messy wind-swept hair. "I suppose it's been a year or two…"

"Don't you lie to me, Eino. You ain't looked at that thing once since you first got it put in, did you?" She wagged a finger at him. "Now you listen to me. I am not falling out of the sky because you were too lazy to get the core checked out."

"It's a driftcap, Betta. The worst that could happen is we drift down out of the stream nice and gentle like." He flattened his hand, demonstrating the motion. "But I'll tell you what. When we get to port in Sanvileau, I'll pay a visit to my auramancer. If anything's off, he'll patch it right up."

Betta grumbled, but her expression softened. "We won't be back on that end of Sinia until summer."

"And by the time we get there, I'm sure it'll sort itself out." He stood up and took his plate to the sink. "Now, if you'll excuse me, some old nag gave me a list of things to gather."

She snorted. "Then you'd better get to it. Don't wanna keep that old nag waiting, do you?"

"No, ma'am."

"Before you go, there's one more thing you oughta know."

He paused. "Yeah?"

"Your shirt is inside out." She smiled as she lifted her cup. "Might want to fix that."

Eino glanced down. Sure enough, his seams were showing. He rushed out of the kitchen. He glanced around the common room to make sure he was alone before fixing the shirt.

Betta could be sassy with a razor sharp tongue, but there was something about her that reminded him of his grandmother, who had passed a few years before he left home. Both had a direct way of speaking. While Betta wasn't nearly as sweet, she was every bit as kind in her own way. It made him feel like he ought to hide his indiscretions from her, lest she think him a troublemaker and heartbreaker. Or rather, more of a troublemaker than he already was. The heart that he broke the most was his own.

He ignored the pang in his chest. He had too much work to do to get distracted by his latest rejection. There was also Joren to deal with. While he didn't think the man was dangerous, Betta was right about him running from something. Although it was more like he was hiding from the world. Even a gentle soul could lash out when pushed to the edge.

Eino would have to keep an eye on him. First, he'd prove the quiet man was an apothecary. Then he'd work on finding out what he was running from. On the other hand, if he was wrong and Betta was right, then he'd work on getting himself a good price on some dreamleaf.

3

EINO HEADED TO THE door next to the kitchen. The door's lock glowed with a pale purple thrumming with aura from the core. He pressed his palm to the locked door, and it sprang open, revealing a narrow spiral staircase leading downward.

Even though the lock was keyed to his specific aura, Eino still looked around to make sure he was alone before slipping inside and closing the door behind him. One incident with a child sneaking inside and hiding in the storage shelves for a whole day was enough to make him paranoid for life.

The stairs led down into the stem of the inn, with shelves lining every bit of wall space. When Eino first took to the skies in his giant mushroom, he had intended to use it to transport mail or other goods across Itharos. However, he quickly learned that the leisurely pace of a driftcap was no match for the speed of an airship, or even a greatwing courier. These days, he still transported some goods to trade, but most of his storage space now served as his pantry.

He wound his way down the spiral stairs, passing the door that led to the loading dock. At the bottom of the staircase, a small, unremarkable door rested between the shelves. In the dim light, it was easy to miss amidst all the stored food and supplies. But he knew his inn by heart and didn't need to search to find it.

He opened the door, revealing a small, glowing sigil. He pressed his palm against it. Aura flowed from his hand into the sigil, and the false back dropped, revealing the core.

On land, inns used their cores to power various amenities. A well-made core could direct aura to do all manner of basic tasks, like washing linens and making beds. Some performed grander feats, like creating fountains in the desert or animating entire shows of puppets. Most cores were hewn of stone or glass, with Decrian crystal being regarded as the highest quality. The larger the core, the more aura an innkeeper could wield. Some more exclusive establishments boasted cores even taller than a grown man.

Eino's core, however, was made of hardwood, shaped roughly like a seed and no bigger than his fist. Years ago, he'd carved it himself and presented it to an auramancer in Sinia as it was all he could afford at the time. Despite the auramancer's skepticism, he imbued the carving with aura. They'd both been surprised at how well the hardwood maintained and distributed the energy. Much of the core's power was used to maintain the mushroom's altitude, to keep it from rotting, and to hold a protective barrier around the inn. There was very little aura left to power any conveniences around the inn, but it had served its purpose well for years, and Eino hadn't seen any reason to replace it.

He examined the core, watching the thick purple band of aura swirling around its middle. Bright green coronas flashed and settled back down just as they did on the natural aura streams. He bit his bottom lip as he watched it. The aura was spinning faster than usual around the core. Holding out his palm, Eino drew out some of the core's energy. After a moment, it slowed down to a speed he thought seemed more normal.

"That ought to do it," he said, more to convince himself than anything else. Eino was by no means a master of auramancy, but as far as he could tell, nothing else seemed to be out of the ordinary. He shut the door and used his aura to lift the hidden door and re-seal the sigil.

Satisfied that he'd resolved the core issue, Eino dusted his hands and turned his attention to the list Betta had given him. If she was right about the rain, he needed to get their food sorted for the day before it hit.

His mouth watered as he read off the ingredients needed to prepare Betta's mushroom bake. After all the rich festival food, he needed something gentler on his stomach. He grabbed a sack from a hook by the door and gathered up the salt, spices, flour, and woodnuts. Then he made his way out of the stem to gather some mushrooms.

He stepped out onto the narrow wooden platform he used as a loading dock and gazed out at the countryside, dotted with neat rows of farmland. Soon they'd drift over the dense forests of northern Sinia, then across the crystal clear blue waters just south of Brumantis. No matter the weather or season, he never grew tired of the view. Every day gave him something new to admire.

To the east, dark clouds hung in the distance. They'd catch up to the inn within the hour. Did he leave the window in his room open again? He couldn't remember. Last time a storm hit, it soaked his pillows. In those moments he cursed his humble underpowered core. It wasn't powerful enough to completely seal his inn's protective aura barrier against the rain. It couldn't even close cabin windows.

His gaze wandered back toward Poutise. Even with the distance they'd covered, the harsh Grand Spiral still towered over the landscape. It reminded him of all the fun he'd had celebrating Sarbakh. And of his handsome Sinian lover.

He forced his attention forward. There was no use dwelling on his rejection. Not while he still had his inn to take care of. There were still plenty of things that needed to be done. In times like these, Eino reverted to his Air Legion training, keeping a strict schedule and routine. If he kept his mind busy, he'd be too distracted to keep wallowing in his heartache.

He pulled his goggles back on as he peered up at the stem. It was pockmarked with little patches of dirt and abandoned bird nests, which served as a fertile breeding ground for plump clusters of all sorts of mushrooms. There were a few smaller drift caps which had taken root, but also silver shelfs, hen's ears, and even a few plump herald's trumpets were growing in abundance. Something about the inn's aura made mushrooms grow fast. Often faster than his guests could eat them.

Eino climbed the knobby stem, using wooden boards haphazardly wedged into the stem as rest landings. His mouth watered as he plucked a few mushrooms and tossed them into his sack. What he didn't eat today, he'd trade for supplies in Brumantis or dry for later use.

He reached for a broad, meaty-looking silver shelf above his head, but as he plucked it, the rotting mushroom squished between his fingers, covering his hand in a brown, slimy film.

"Huh?" He climbed up higher to get a better look. There was a whole cluster of rotting silver shelfs clinging to the stem. He yanked them all off and tossed them away from the inn, inspecting the stem for any damage. Yet the stem looked fine, as did the nearby clusters of mushrooms. Still, it was odd. He'd never seen a rotten mushroom on his stem before. Things growing in the aura streams almost never rotted. It was why the Driftcap Inn was able to stay afloat for so long.

A distant boom of thunder echoed across the sky. Knowing his time was short, he let the mystery go and climbed higher. There would be time to investigate the cause later.

When he found a larger patch of rotten mushrooms, a cluster of hen's ears this time, unease tightened his gut. He plucked them and tossed them down, a few of them landing on the wooden boards below. Small yellow birds emerged from their nests and swooped down, snatching up the rotten hen's ears. Two of the birds fought over a large piece, and when the victor flew away with it, Eino took pity on the loser and tossed him a fresh mushroom from his bag.

Cold raindrops hit his face, and he moved faster as he rushed to finish his harvest before the storm hit. During his second pass up the backside of the stem, Blue appeared. She lazily drifted beside him, craning her long neck to tap at his shoulder as she flew past. Over the last six years, Blue had adapted to Eino's schedule. She knew harvest time meant easy food. When she didn't get a mushroom right away, she drifted back around and tapped him again.

"Yeah, yeah. I see you, you big ol' lummox." He tossed her a mushroom. She caught it, swallowed it down, and then clacked her beak for another. "Sheesh, you're getting greedy. You're lucky I love you." He tossed her another, using the distraction to climb onto her back before she could demand more.

"Up." He let out a low whistle. With a beat of her wings, she soared to the top of the inn. She landed in a flat open area between the common room's chimney and the spot where the longberry tree had taken root. He climbed off and patted the side of her neck, tossing the greatwing another mushroom. "Thanks for the lift."

Blue let out a purring coo, sounding more like a house cat than massive predator of the skies. The first time he'd ever seen a flock of crested greatwings up close was while serving aboard the Sinian airship *The Sun Chaser*, and even all these years later, it surprised him to hear how quiet they were. Rather than communicating in loud screeches like most other birds, they could change the color of the crests on the tops of their heads to coordinate with their flocks and convey their moods.

Despite a few attempts to research the subject in libraries across Itharos, Eino never found much information on what the colors and patterns of their crests meant. Through trial and error, he'd conducted his own studies on Blue. He'd come to understand that the current pale yellow of her crest meant she was satisfied. For now, at least.

He turned to the garden on the top of the inn's cap. The tall fence posts were spaced close together to keep Blue from stealing from the garden, while the netting over the top and sides kept the smaller pests at bay. He pulled open the gate and took a minute to admire his produce.

There was more than enough space on the inn's roof for vegetables, herbs, and even a few berry bushes. The longberry tree cast shade over part of the cap and garden, its branches already growing heavy with the coming spring harvest. There'd be plenty for pies, tarts, and jam as long as Blue kept the smaller birds away.

He'd taken up gardening to keep himself well fed between ports. As the inn grew, so too had the garden, now more than double the size of the first humble lot he'd placed on the cap. Though tending the garden was now a necessity to feed all of his guests, he never found it to be a stressful job. In fact, it was one of the activities he looked forward to the most while drifting across the sky. Harvesting his own food and cooking it up for his guests gave him a satisfaction like nothing else.

He plucked the vegetables needed for supper and stuffed them into his bag, ticking off everything from Betta's list as he went. As he gathered up the last items, raindrops pattered down on him. He finished just as the rain began blotting the writing on the list. Food shopping complete, he headed for the hatch in the roof near the front of the mushroom.

He climbed down the ladder into his personal quarters, closing the hatch behind him. His bedroom had been the first room he'd carved out when he first took to the skies, long before converting the mushroom into an inn. In retrospect, having to walk through his bedroom to get to the roof gardens was a bit of a design oversight. But then again, it did help to keep nosy guests and rambunctious children away from his carefully cultivated garden.

His quarters were humble compared to the size of the mushroom. With his hat on, his head only barely cleared the low ceiling. Still, his room never felt too small. He had enough room for a cozy bed, a small sitting area, and a private washroom. He'd decorated one wall with a painting of the tallest mountain in Itharos, Mount Chilbrin. There was a map of Porocar hanging above his desk, and several carved idols of Dilgaa the mountain god sat on a shelf beside it.

He appreciated having a comfortable place to retire to after a long day's work, though the one thing he was most certainly lacking was someone to share it with. Sadly, those who stayed the night seldom stayed for much longer.

Eino shut the skylight against the intensifying rains. Roots from the trees and bushes twined over his ceiling before disappearing back into the mushroom. When he first noticed the roots creeping through his ceiling, he'd been worried they would leak, or worse, that they would tear the cap of the mushroom apart. But after several years, they never did, and once he was certain he wouldn't get rained on in his sleep, he decided he rather liked them. They reminded him of the thick and sprawling roots of the trees clinging to the mountainsides where he had grown up.

He squeezed around his desk, which was just a little too big for the space, scattering a few of his rolled up antique maps on the floor. Eino groaned and took a moment to reorganize them. Satisfied, he hoisted the heavy bag laden with ingredients onto his shoulder, then pushed open his door and stepped out onto the loft above the common room.

Apart from his quarters, the loft was Eino's favorite part of the inn. He'd furnished it with a low table and floor cushions like the ones he'd seen while traveling through the territories of the Ahriqosai Empire. The large round window beside the staircase made it a comfortable spot to lounge and watch the sky during stormy days.

After a quick peek to make sure he hadn't left any dirty dishes lying around, he headed down the narrow staircase to the common room. Shelves full of books lined the walls, and a fire crackled in the hearth. Betta must have already cleaned the ashes from the fireplace and added fresh wood for the next chilly night. Eino shook his head. With only one guest, it hardly seemed important to keep the common room fireplace going. But for a lifelong south Porocari mushroom farmer like Betta, it was hard to stay still.

He passed between the waist-high railings that separated the dining area, heading for the door to the kitchen. As he reached for the door, it suddenly opened, and there, staring at him like a frightened maple doe, was Joren.

4

JOREN STARTLED, RECOILING AS if he'd been hit. He carried his breakfast plate, holding it up as if to shield himself. The thick scent of various herbs clung to him, smelling strong and medicinal. It was the scent of someone who spent his days mixing, drying, and mashing together elixirs and potions, Eino thought. Then again, a smuggler might use such aromas to mask the scent of his contraband, particularly for pungent intoxicants like dreamleaf.

His wavy, dark hair was shorter than the last time Eino saw him, now only reaching to about his shoulders. The jagged edges weren't quite even, making him wonder if Joren had cut it himself. Not surprising, thought Eino. He didn't seem like the type to trust someone else with scissors anywhere near his head. His chin, by contrast, was cleanly shaven. Eino snickered to himself, surprised that a man that jumpy somehow managed to hold a razor steady.

Based on his dark hair and dusky complexion, Joren was almost certainly a native Sinian, but when Eino checked the side of the man's head, he saw neither the spiral ornament from Sarbakh nor the beads of his manaque. From the highest nobles to the lowliest vagabonds, most Sinians regarded the manaque as a necessity of life, save those few isolated kingdoms that still hadn't embraced the practice. The beads indicated one's marital status, career, and where they were from based on their colors and designs. Those without the manaque were regarded with pity and suspicion in equal measure. Eino racked his brain, but he couldn't recall what Joren's manaque looked like. Or if he had ever worn them at all.

"Mornin'," Eino greeted cheerfully. Bumping into Joren always felt like crossing paths with a pebble toad. And just like when he used to catch pebble toads as a young boy, he did his best to avoid any sudden movements or loud noises.

"Oh," Joren stared at him, his gaze darting around from nerves. For a moment he said nothing before replying, "Morning."

Eino smiled, taking it in stride. "Enjoyed your breakfast?"

"Yes." Joren thrust his plate at Eino, poking him in the chest with it.

Surprised, Eino grabbed it.

Joren bowed his head and mumbled something that sounded halfway between "Thank you," and "Sorry." He then turned and darted out the door to the promenade.

"Figures," Eino muttered. "Can't hardly squeeze more than two words out of that fella." He shifted the plate and something slimy rolled into his thumb. He frowned at the small pile of mushrooms that had been pushed to the side of the plate.

A frightened pebble toad who didn't seem to have an appetite for mushrooms, Eino thought. Yet he had been staying in a giant mushroom since the start of winter, eating mostly mushroom-based meals. Betta was right. Joren was an odd one.

Eino peered out of the window, catching a view of Joren at the bridge to his cabin. The man paused a moment, his hand wrapped around the promenade railing, seemingly unaware of the rain pouring down on him. Reaching into his satchel, he produced what looked like a handful of leaves. He stuffed them into his mouth before taking a deep breath and dashing across the bridge and into his cabin. Eino caught the soft glow of a fire before the man closed the door behind himself.

Eino grimaced. Maybe Betta was right that he was a dreamleaf smuggler. Not only that, but one that consumed from his own supply. He shook his head and carried the plate into the kitchen.

Rain beat against the glass windows. A good day to clean inside and prepare for the next guests. Once the weather cleared, he'd continue harvesting the latest batch of mushrooms. He'd need to find out if the rot had spread anywhere.

Eino unloaded the sack of ingredients onto the counter, then went back to the common room to look for Betta. It was a brief search, as he found her in the common room folding a basket of linens. "You ain't seen our mysterious friend around, have you?"

"As a matter of fact, I have. Found out something about him, too." He held out the plate, gesturing to it. "He doesn't eat mushrooms."

"Oh, I already knew that. Poor fella always leaves a pile of 'em on his plate. What he don't eat, I toss to the wool hens."

Eino scratched his head. "You mean he's been here that long, and he doesn't even like the food?"

"It's like I told you. He ain't here for the food or views. The man's smuggling something."

Eino gave a sly nod. "Either that or your cooking is so good he doesn't mind eating around a few mushies in passing."

"Boy, you're just tryin' to butter me up, ain't you?" Betta smiled. "I ain't gonna pull any punches when you lose our little wager. You're gonna be making me that stuffed sea gourd. You mark my words."

"I thought I 'couldn't make a sea gourd worth squat'?" Eino said, his voice playfully mocking.

"Then I'm gonna have to teach you how to make it. But not tonight. Tonight's mushroom hotpot."

Eino's mouth watered. "Ain't had hotpot in a good long while."

"It was always Clofen's favorite. He was always such a picky boy…" Betta trailed off, her gaze focusing in the distance as if remembering something. It happened often whenever she brought up her son. She cleared her throat and blinked, shaking herself out of her daze. "The flavors ain't exactly refined, but even those with more genteel, coastie appetites should be able to stomach it."

"And just who are you callin' a coastie there, missy?" The term was a pejorative used by those from the southern mountains of Porocar to refer to those from the northern coast. It had been a couple of centuries since the old Heralian League states had first established colonies in the north, and though the league had collapsed over a century prior, it had left an undeniable mark on the Porocari culture. Most notably in the fairer hair and complexions of those who had Heralian blood in their lineages. Those like Eino, whose reddish hair and fairer skin contrasted sharply with Betta's dark brown hair and olive skin.

"Why I was referring to our picky friend, of course," Betta said with a smile too innocent to hide her mischief. "Besides, hotpot is only good when you have it fresh out of the pot. It don't travel well."

"Baiting him out to the table, huh? You sly ol' mountain goat."

Betta chuckled. "It'll come together quick. I reckon I'll start cooking in two hours. Until then, I'm going to have some tea and watch the storm."

"Give a holler if you need a hand chopping everything up." Eino strolled out the door and onto the promenade. He had plenty of time to relax, and he knew just how to fill that time. He dug around in his pockets, finding coins from various countries, and even a poutamme he'd forgotten to give Betta. Finally, his hand landed on what he was looking for, and he pulled out his most prized musical instrument.

The tarnaaq was deceptively simple-looking, appearing to be little more than a small, twisted black animal horn. With a twist of a knob at the bottom, the slide arm extended out and the finger holes became easier to see. It was simple to learn, and so compact that Eino carried it with him everywhere he went. It made it that much easier to travel over the endless seas and open plains and long stormy nights.

The heavy burst of rain settled into a steady drizzle as he took a seat, resting his feet on the promenade railing. Days like today made him glad he'd decided to build the promenade during his second year on the mushroom. At the time, it'd been a big expense, but as he sat and watched the storm clouds rolling across the horizon, offering peeks at the sea that lay ahead of them, he knew it had been well worth it.

He pressed his mouth to the horn and played his favorite warm-up song. It was a short ditty, one that was played at every festival and wedding back home.

Sitting under a mushroom cap in the rain made him feel like he was back in the forests outside of the tiny village of Tetechetech where he had grown up. Even on rainy days, he used to take refuge under the massive, broad-capped mushrooms of the forest to play with his siblings and cousins. Nostalgia tugged at his heart in a bittersweet way.

Even so, not once had he regretted leaving his old home behind. As Eino of Tetechetech, he was destined to live the dull and lonely life of a humble mushroom farmer, simultaneously isolated in a remote village and lost in the crowd of his own massive family. As Eino the Wanderer, he was still lonely, but now he at least had the freedom to become his own man.

The song started slow and got faster and faster until his fingers were racing to keep up by the end. The fast pace was what made the otherwise easy song a challenge. At parties, dancers did their best to keep up with the ever-increasing pace of the song, often stumbling and falling in a pile of laughter.

When he finished the song, Eino caught movement out of the corner of his eye. The curtains in the window of Joren's cabin shifted, and he caught a glimpse of the man peeking out at him. Eino adjusted his grip to wave, but realizing he'd been spotted, Joren darted out of sight. The curtain swished back into place.

"You're going to be one tough nut to crack," Eino mumbled to himself. Joren was becoming more than just something for him to gossip with Betta about. There was something truly fascinating about the mysterious man. Something enticing. He'd need to find excuses to bump into Joren more often. A difficult task when the man stuck to his cabin most of the time. But Eino had never been one to quit at the prospect of a challenge.

5

THE RAINY DAYS CLEARED away in time for Eino's next stop. Judging by the clear skies at dawn, there'd be no rain to ruin his port call. He inspected the stem before breakfast, finding no new patches of rot. In fact, the areas where the rot had been were now growing fresh, plump mushrooms. He wasn't certain if he should be relieved or more concerned.

He shook his worries loose as he sat down to breakfast with Betta. "You sure you don't wanna come down for a spell?"

"I'll be just fine watching it all pass by from the promenade," said Betta with a shake of her head. "Besides, we've been shut in since the rain started falling. I'm gonna air out all the empty cabins. Won't have too many more chances before rainy season picks up."

Eino adjusted the goggles hanging around his neck. "You're allowed to take a day off every now and again, you know. Won't do yourself any good workin' yourself to death around here."

"Oh, quit your worrying. Some time sittin' out here sipping tea is all the break I need." Betta cleared their breakfast dishes from the table. "And I certainly won't be getting any relaxation done around them Brumanti folk. They can be real contentious."

Eino sighed, disappointed, but unsurprised that Betta had yet another excuse to avoid coming to the surface. "Aww, come on now. You had fun at the Sarbakh festival, didn't you?" He'd hoped her visit to the festival would get her to leave the inn more often.

"You seen one town full of drunks, you've seen 'em all." Betta smirked. "Besides, somebody's gotta keep an eye on this place while you're out gallivanting across them pubs."

"I ain't gallivanting. I'm drumming up business." He rubbed his chin and shot back a smirk of his own. "But then again, maybe you should stay up here. I'd have a hard time convincing people to join your sour face up here in the skies."

Betta laughed. "Go on and git, you. And you'd better come back with some rich new customers."

He smiled back at her. "If you feel like joining in on the fun, you know where to find the basket."

Eino struggled to understand Betta's distaste for new places. A thirst for the new and exciting was what drove him to enlist in the newly formed Sinian Air Legion. By the time he was eighteen years old, he was already serving aboard the massive new airship *The Sun Chaser* on its maiden voyage west across the Great Divide. He'd given up his country's forests and mountains for deserts, oceans, and cities unlike any he could imagine. Between his time as a sailor and as an innkeeper, he'd spent over a decade in the sky, and he couldn't imagine ever leaving it behind.

Betta was much more set in her ways. She'd have stayed in Porocar forever if it hadn't been for her husband's tragic passing. With her son away serving in the Heralian guard, no one was around to help with the spring and fall harvests, and she was forced to sell her mushroom farm. When Eino found her, she was running a food cart in a small town near the Sinian border. They'd known each other for nearly two years now, exploring the skies of Itharos, laughing and sharing in both struggles and good times. But in all that time, he never doubted that she'd rather be back at her old home. Some Porocari were like that. They dug their roots deep and refused to let go of the mountains.

Eino headed out to the promenade. His breath hung in the air as he stretched his arms. The chill would disappear as the yellow sun rose higher, and any day now the smaller white sun would peek out from behind it, marking the official start of spring. By the end of spring, he would miss the crisp cool of the morning air.

Joren waited on the promenade, a muffin from breakfast in one hand as he peered down at the village below. He wore a long, dark jacket that contrasted sharply with the bright green wrap shirt beneath it. With his traveler's pack and bedroll slung over his back, he looked ready to travel, but nothing on him hinted at a destination. It was the exact same way he'd looked the day he showed up at the inn.

Eino had seen travelers of all types pass through his inn. Each one had a sense of where they were from and where they were heading next. Each of them except Joren. The man was uniquely difficult to read since the very first day he appeared, and he was certain that one day, without warning, Joren would simply walk away, never to be seen again.

"All aboard," Eino said as he stepped into the basket. Joren followed him without making a single noise. Eino glanced over his shoulder to make sure Joren was in before rolling the small aura stone embedded in the control pillar. The basket shuddered and slowly began to descend.

"Won't be long now till we touch down in the Duchy of Brumantis. Ever been before?" Eino asked.

Joren held a hand over his mouth as he chewed, uttering, "I haven't."

Eino wore a smile, but grit his teeth. Extracting any sort of information from Joren was never easy. He had a knack for giving answers that didn't invite more questions. Eino stopped the basket at the loading dock on the bottom of the stem. "This'll only take a second. I've gotta load some cargo."

Joren crammed himself into the far corner while Eino stacked several boxes into the basket. Despite the curiosity written across his face, he didn't ask about them.

"Alright, then. Next stop, Nelene Village." Eino hit the stone again, and the basket shuddered once more, gliding down toward the ground. As they left the inn behind, the rolling green hills of Brumantis stretched out beneath them. The distant crashing of the waves along the coasts grew louder.

Despite the sound of the wind and the ocean, the only thing Eino could hear was the silence between himself and Joren. He cleared his throat. "So, tomorrow come midday, I'll be one town over in Nephene. I'll pick up guests in the town square."

"Yes," Joren mumbled. "I memorized the schedule."

"Just figured I'd double check. Wouldn't be the first time the town names got somebody all mixed up." He shot Joren another big smile. "Just remember to be at the forest line outside Nephene by next evening if you want to catch the last basket out of town."

Joren simply nodded and continued eating his muffin. He kept his eyes straight ahead, rather than looking down.

The basket landed in what counted as the market square in the small village of Nelene. The sleepy hamlet was still waking up, leaving the square empty. No new guests were waiting at the landing site, which wasn't much of a surprise. Small towns seldom offered him much business, particularly this early in the morning. The only one waiting for them was a merchant, lounging on the seat of her wagon.

Like most citizens of former Heralian League states, Brumanti locals tended toward fair complexions. Both their skin and their hair, however, were typically bleached to a pale, almost white hue by the equatorial suns. The merchant wore a plain, off-white shirt that showed her midriff and the painted blue and red crisscrossed pattern across her stomach. A brightly colored silk headband kept her chin-length hair out of her eyes, and a decorative belt of woven grass and dried flowers added a splash of color across her tan knee-length skirt. The local fashion favored plain, comfortable clothing to mitigate the hot climate, but even the poorest Brumanti people decorated themselves with bright flowers, body paint, and other accessories. The rest of Itharos regarded Brumanti fashion as particularly scandalous, but after so many years, Eino was no longer shocked by it.

The merchant waved the floppy hat in her hand in greeting. "Welcome back, Mr. Wanderer."

"Thaena!" He jumped out of the basket. "Joren, I'd like you to meet—"

Eino turned around, but Joren had already darted away, making his way toward the forest.

"He seems nice." Thaena snickered and hopped down from her wagon. "So, who's your friend?"

"I sure wish I could tell you. All I know for certain is he's a guest at my inn." Eino shook his head. "If you can tell me the first thing about him, you can have all my cargo free of charge."

Thaena rubbed her chin and cast an eye toward the forest path. Joren had nearly made it to the tree line, his dark jacket already making him blend in to the shadowy underbrush. "That jacket..." A sudden realization dawned on her face. "You said his name was Joren, right?"

"Yes?" Eino quirked an eyebrow.

She pointed at the path and stammered. "That's the name of the duke's long-lost son!"

He whirled his head back to the tree line, scanning for any sign of Joren. "What?"

"It's true! They say he was born of an affair with the Grand Duchess herself, and that he's the true heir to the throne of Brumantis!" Thaena stammered as she spoke. "Why, he might even be the one to finally reunite the League!"

Eino looked back in shock before catching the glint of mirth in her eye. He sighed. "You know, you probably could've kept me going there if you'd have paced yourself."

Thaena laughed. "I'm just an amateur liar. Not a professional like you."

"Now I've never once told a lie in all my life," he said with a wide smile. "At most, I have possibly embellished the truth on occasion. Sometimes."

"Well, nobody 'embellishes the truth' like you." She gave a wistful smile. It was the same smile she'd given him years ago the first time he'd left her bedroom. The same smile his Sinian lover had given him when he too declined Eino's offer to see the world. And the same smile Eino had given her when she announced her engagement two years ago.

He pulled her into a tight embrace. "It's good to see you again, Thaena." He'd given little pieces of his heart to his lovers, hoping someday that someone would want the rest. No one ever did. His face wore a nonchalant mask, but deep down he wondered how much he had left to give before his heart cracked completely apart.

"It's good to see you too, Eino." She squeezed him back. "But you are a little early. You're lucky the skies have been so clear lately. I only barely caught sight of you on the horizon last night."

"Then it sounds like I'm just in time." Eino broke the hug and began unloading cargo from his basket onto the wagon. "I usually miss the first few days of the Founder's Festival."

Thaena rolled a few barrels from her wagon into the basket. "You're thinking of Nephene. Nelene's festival isn't for another two weeks."

According to local legend, both towns were founded by two brothers, Nelho and Nepho. Each town insisted that their namesake was the older brother, and consequently had been established first. It was a largely friendly dispute, but every year around festival time, there was always at least one tavern brawl over which town came first.

"So tell me the gossip. Has there been any festival bloodshed yet?"

Thaena laughed. "Not till the ale starts flowing. But the alderman did boast that our festival would have twice as many hand pies as Nephene's. Everyone in town is helping to draw in all the fish we need. Even me!"

"Sounds like you folks will need all the spices you can get your hands on. Lucky for you, I've got spice pods straight from the fields of northern Sinia ready to be ground up." He slapped one of the wooden crates. "They're even better before they're fully dried, you know."

"You should keep quiet about where those spices are from." She cast a suspicious eye around the empty marketplace, then drew Eino in conspiratorially. "Sinians aren't too popular around here these days. The unification of the kingdoms has some people a little worried."

Eino laughed. "Oh, the Sinians are harmless. The only thing keeping them unified is King Chandarre's money. As soon as his feathersteel fortune dries up, won't nobody be calling him 'King of Kings' no more." He gave a mocking royal flourish. "Them folks in Nephene are more likely to cause you trouble."

"Nephene is even more worried than we are. I've heard they're even seeing Sinian airships in the sky." Thaena loaded up the last of Eino's barrels onto his basket and wiped her brow.

"Legion airships? In a town that small? Now that I'd like to see." He secured the goods down on the basket, then tapped the aura stone on his necklace. The basket slowly lifted back up into the sky, chasing after the Driftcap Inn overhead.

Thaena climbed up into her wagon. "Well, I have to meet up with some traders there this afternoon. You can ride over with me if you like."

"I reckon I will," said Eino, glancing around the market square. "I just want to make a quick detour to the mystic's shrine first."

Thaena snorted. "You can try the shrine, but the mystic is probably out fishing with the rest of the village."

"Strak," cursed Eino. "I was hoping I could get a blessing."

Thaena smiled, putting her hand on her chin. "What, have you lost all faith in your mountain god?"

"I've got plenty of faith," said Eino, smirking, "but it don't hurt to have a backup plan."

"You'll have better luck at the shrine in Nephene." She patted the seat beside her at the front of the wagon. "Think you can survive the trip there without a blessing from the ancients?"

"If I've got you to keep my mind busy," he said, climbing up and taking a seat beside her. "Besides, we've got plenty of catchin' up to do. You were still expecting last time I saw you. The diviners said it was gonna be a boy, right?"

"They got it wrong, if you can imagine," said Thaena sarcastically as she cracked the reins. "Right now, my husband is watching our little girl. He insists on taking her out on the water to get her used to the waves."

The two chatted the whole way to Nephene, trading stories and laughing at old jokes. The old ache of his heart never truly went away, but he was truly happy to see Thaena doing so well. After the weeks of tense silence when speaking to Joren, it was a refreshing change of pace to just sit and talk with an old friend while watching the suns come up over the rolling green hills.

6

WHEN THEY ARRIVED AT the Nephene market square, he and Thaena embraced and parted ways. Here beneath the late morning suns, the Founder's Festival celebrations were already in full swing. Vendors grilled fresh fish along with other street foods, filling the air with a wonderful aroma. An auramancer performed, and all the while a small ensemble of buskers played a cheerful tune. The normally sleepy hamlet seemed much bigger and more lively this time of year. Eino looked up, discovering that the festival even had some unexpected visitors.

Overhead hovered a massive Sinian airship, clad in gold and glistening white feathersteel, bearing vibrant magenta banners with the heraldry of King Chandarre. It was long and cylindrical like a stickpipe, with a single antenna keeping it anchored to the aura stream. The paddle wheel at the back of the ship had stilled, so clearly, the ship planned to stick around for a while. It looked to be a newer, smaller vessel than *The Sun Chaser*. Eino, however, seemed to be the only one impressed by the ship. The Brumanti people all kept their eyes down, as if pretending to ignore it, or stared up in contempt as they complained to their friends.

Eino jangled the shiny new coins in his pocket, eager to spend the spoils of his trade with Thaena at the local taverns. After the past few days of calm in the sky, he was ready for some excitement, and so he found himself at the front door of a particularly raucous tavern, the sounds of laughter and revelry echoing from inside. He adjusted his mushroom hat and pushed the doors open.

Ever a conspicuous figure, Eino's entrance drew the attention of many of the patrons. A table near the front cheered when they caught sight of him. "The mushroom man's back in town!"

Eino waved to the bartender, then posted an advertisement for his inn on the notice board. Before he could even make his way to the bar counter, a woman had already thrust a foamy flagon of ale into his hand. "Welcome back, Mr. Wanderer. What news from abroad?"

The crowd grew thicker around him, spewing out a chorus of questions.

"Any word of the war in the north?" asked one villager.

"I heard the Vinaterians are suing Heralia for peace!" said another, his voice rising with excitement. "It's because Queen Vinat was slain, isn't it?"

A gruff voice in the crowd responded, "Vinat's a goddess, you idiot. She can't be slain."

"She was too! By Vennick of the Thousand Weapons himself," the excited man insisted. "The man's a god in his own right. He'll be the one to reunite the league. I'm sure of it!"

Before Eino could say a single word in response, the crowd erupted in a cacophony of opinions regarding the future of the league and the divinity of both Vinat and Vennick. He smiled and drank down his ale. As soon as he finished his drink, he found another flagon thrust into his hand. This was why he loved visiting small towns.

"Nevermind all that," said an older woman, quieting down the crowd. She directed their attention back toward Eino. "I wanna know what those damned Sinians are doing in our country."

The crowd cheered. Another voice chimed in. "And when they're gonna get out!" Another loud cheer. "To Strak with the lot of them!"

One desperate voice chimed in. "Chandarre is trying to buy out the duke. He's going to add Brumantis to the Unified Kingdom, isn't he?"

"Chandarre is dead!" another villager called out. "The Kingslayer struck him down in front of a huge crowd. A dockworker from Corçal told me so."

"If he's dead, why do you think there's a warship perched over our heads? It's an invasion, I tell you!"

All eyes were suddenly on Eino, mouths agape in anticipation of an explanation. He was no stranger to being the center of attention, but determining international politics based on rumors and gossip wasn't one of Eino's specialties. Least of all, with a mouthful of ale.

He gulped down the cool beverage, coughing to buy himself time. "Well, I don't—" Color caught his eye. At a corner table, he spied a handful of men in vibrant magenta uniforms. Even away from the bright sunlit windows, the gold trim and red sashes of their outfits stood out against the more muted colors of the villagers' clothing. They wore their manaque beads in the military style, with their single braids tied back in a bun with the rest of their hair to keep the beads from obstructing their vision. There was no mistaking that they were members of the Sinian Air Legion, sitting around and sharing a few pitchers of ale.

Eino pointed a finger at the table. "You could ask them ones why they're here. I reckon they're not drinkin' in the middle of an invasion."

The crowd dispersed in a chorus of disappointed groans and grunts. Finally able to move freely, he headed for the outcast legionaries. He hoped they might be able to tell him about some of his old friends from *The Sun Chaser*. At the very least, give him some of the answers to the crowd's questions. While he didn't share in the villagers' suspicion, he did share in their curiosity.

As he approached the table, he saw that most of the men sported large, curled mustaches. Two of the mustachioed faces looked up, their eyes lighting up at the sight of Eino. After a moment of squinting and glancing between the faces, Eino's eyes lit up as well.

"Well now, if it ain't the Sinian sky boys!" Eino approached the table, holding out his hand. "To what does the fair town of Nephene owe the pleasure?"

"Stand back, sir." A young-faced legionnaire stood up, blocking Eino's path. The man's sudden appearance startled Eino, a drop of ale sloshing out of his cup. Sparse hairs dotted the young man's upper lip. "We are here on a diplomatic mission under the authority of Chandarre, King of Kings, with permission from Sharreigh, Duke of Brumantis. "

Eino gave the young man an incredulous look, then turned to face a severe-looking man with graying hair at the sides of his head. "Hey, Daif. Who's the new kid?"

The man, who was old enough to be Eino's father, gave a sly smile. "Go easy on him, Eino. I remember when you were just as green."

"Aye, sir." Eino gave Daif a salute. "Cast me, I must've been around his age when I enlisted."

"Sir? How does this man know—"

"At ease, Mani," said Daif, waving a dismissive hand to the young legionary. "He's a friend."

"Eino the Wanderer is what they call me." He offered his hand for a shake.

Mani ignored his outstretched hand. "The mushroom guy?" Mani turned to the other legionary. "Pavan, is this another of your jokes? How much are you paying this man?"

Pavan had been Eino's bunkmate back aboard *The Sun Chaser*. He looked largely the same as he had back then, save for his sporting of the largest and most elaborately groomed mustache of the three. "Pay him? He still owes *me* money from a game of fool's gambit."

Eino scoffed. "That game must've been five years ago! You've gotta be part Gatrai to remember a debt that small."

Mani shook his head. "Nice try, but I'm not falling for it. I know there's no such man as Eino. You made up all of those stories."

"Still talking about me, huh?" Eino turned to Mani. "What sorta lies has ol' Pavan been fillin' your head with?"

Mani sighed. "He told me you ate a whole plate of rotten scramblers and that the next day a mushroom grew out of your head." He looked up at Eino's hat. "I'm not a child. I can tell that's just a hat. A poorly made one too."

"Now you listen here, son. First, this hat is most certainly not poorly made." He locked eyes with Pavan, the man giving him a subtle nod. "And second, it wasn't just one mushroom that grew out of my head. It was several."

"I'm not falling for it."

"It's true! Why do you think I'm wearing this big ol' thing anyhow?" Eino drew in closer. "You can take a peek underneath if you don't believe me. Just be discreet. I don't wanna frighten the locals."

Mani sighed and slowly lifted Eino's hat. As he did so, Pavan sidled up behind the ensign. At his cue, Eino feigned wincing in pain, and Pavan made a loud squelching sound in Mani's ear. The young ensign yelped, and the pair of pranksters erupted in laughter.

"Oh, it's good to see you again," said Eino, slapping Pavan on the shoulder. He looked around the bar. "Bashann isn't with you, is he?"

"No, your old boyfriend is still on *The Sun Chaser*," said Pavan. "And don't get any ideas about young Mani here. He's got a girl waiting for him back in Koparam." He playfully tapped the betrothal bead in Mani's manaque.

"Captain," said Mani, crossing his arms with a sneer. "Permission to crack their heads together?"

"Denied, ensign." Daif cracked a smile. "These two never learn. You'll only hurt yourself trying to knock any sense into their thick skulls."

"Did I hear you say 'captain?'" Eino asked. "So that's your boat outside? Congratulations on the promotion."

"Acting captain," clarified Daif as he took another swig. "The *Ray of Soleivar* is a fine ship, but unfortunately, Jiso's still at the helm."

"That old sky dog is still flying? I thought he would have retired by now." Jiso had been captain of *The Sun Chaser* over a decade ago. Even back then, rumors spread among the crewmates each voyage that he'd finally be announcing his retirement this time. "Where is he anyhow?"

"He's back in Corçal for a trade conference. He'll be sipping raangnectar and trying to suck up to the Duke for the rest of the week. Till then, I'm supposed to float around Brumantis and look pretty. 'Missions of good will,' they're calling it. What a steaming pile."

"Sir, I don't believe we should be discussing these things with an outsider."

"Relax, Mani. Eino here served dutifully aboard *The Sun Chaser* for what...five years or so?" Daif turned to Eino. "Besides. He swears to keep all of this information a secret. Isn't that right?"

Eino held his fist to his heart. "By Soleivar's light and the Crown of the Seven Kingdoms, I do so swear."

Pavan snorted. "It hasn't been 'Seven Kingdoms' for years. We're up to about thirty."

"Thirty-three counting Bhaleia," corrected Mani.

"Those Bhaleians are up to something. They've fought unification for years, then suddenly the Kingslayer incident happens, and now they want to join?" Pavan shook his head. "I don't think so."

Eino's ears perked up. "What's this Kingslayer thing I keep hearing about?" All winter long, He'd been hearing rumors about masked bandit slaying kings across Sinia, but many of the stories he'd heard conflicted one another, and most of them were clearly exaggerated.

"There's not much to say," said Daif, taking a swig of his ale. "Someone poisoned the king of Bhaleia during the unification feast in Karaval, so they're calling him the Karaval Kingslayer. I'm pretty sure he was already caught and executed, though."

"Ah, so that's what this is about." Eino tapped his chin. "So, do you reckon the Duke is gonna get the axe and then Brumantis is getting pulled into the Unified Kingdom?"

Daif chuckled. "I doubt it. Last I heard, Heralia and Vinateria were still hammering out peace negotiations, and there's even talk of the two of them coming together and re-establishing the Heralian League. I'm guessing the Duke just wants it to look like he's close with Sinia so he can negotiate for a higher position in the new league."

"Heralia and Vinateria working together? Not a chance." Eino snorted. "They've been at each other's throats as long as I can remember. There ain't no way they're gonna start being friendly."

"That's what I'm saying," said Pavan as he reached for the pitcher. "It's all just one big waste of time. For all of our 'missions of good will,' we're still not very popular with the locals. Perhaps you've noticed." Pavan gestured around the table. All the Brumanti townsfolk kept their distance, most avoiding looking in their direction, while some stared at them with contempt. "We'd get a warmer reception in the icy depths of Nerca."

"Be that as it may, we have our orders." Daif finished his ale and slammed the flagon on the table. "And as members of the Sinian Air Legion, we will follow our orders to the letter. No matter how stupid they may be."

"Aww, don't be all gloomy. It could be worse. "Eino playfully flicked Pavan's mustache, "You could have a ridiculous looking mustache!"

"You may laugh, but the ladies back in Muna love it. Ever since Chandarre started wearing a big mustache, all the nobles started doing it too. Now if you want to look like you have money, you need a big mustache."

"Well, it looks like you spent all your jingles on that thing." Eino patted Pavan on the shoulder. "How 'bout I buy the next round of ale?"

"I'll drink to that." Pavan hoisted his flagon. "To Eino the Wanderer!"

Even Mani smiled and raised his flagon. Buying a round of drinks never failed to get people to warm up. Suddenly, a hand grabbed Eino's shoulder, digging his fingers into his skin through his jacket. "You."

Eino turned around to meet the gaze of a furious local. The man's red face was familiar, though he couldn't place where he'd seen him before. "Howdy there, friend," he replied, squirming under the man's firm grip.

"Don't call me friend, you cheat." He gave Eino a shove. Two other villagers flanked the man, both of them staring daggers at Eino. "You thought we'd forget you after only a half-year?"

A cold jolt shot up his spine as he realized why the three men looked so familiar. On his last visit to this village, he'd played a few games of fool's gambit. One of the players, the shifty-eyed villager to the left of his assailant, had been using a set of dice with hidden aura crystals to cheat. When Eino realized it, he'd palmed the loaded dice, and used them to take the pot for himself. There was nothing wrong with cheating a cheater, he remembered thinking. How foolish that idea seemed now.

Eino was no stranger to a bar fight, but even on his best day, he wouldn't be able to handle all three of them. "Gosh, fellas. I'd love to reminisce about old times, but as you can see, I'm catching up with some friends right now. So if you'd kindly excuse me…"

The man bumped shoulders with Pavan, and yanked Eino right out of his seat. With help from a second man, he shoved Eino against the wall. "You'll be excused when you pay back what you owe. Every last jingle. With interest."

Pavan tapped the man on the shoulder. "The man said he's busy. And he owes me an ale. You can wait your turn."

The man turned his angry gaze to Pavan. "Mind your own business, spice weevil."

Pavan's usual vacant expression hardened. A hard edge entered his tone. "What did you just say?" Mani and Daif squared up alongside their crewmate, facing down the trio of villagers.

"I guess he's hard of hearing, lads," said the man, giving a mocking laugh to his comrades. His henchmen chuckled. With a smirk, he flicked Pavan's mustache. "I'll say it again. Slow this time. I said get out of this tavern and onto your ship, then scurry back across the channel where you belong, you ugly, stinking spice weev—"

The man didn't finish his insult before Pavan reached up and grabbed the man's finger, wrenching it to the side. He gave a wry smile at the man's pained yelp. "What was that? Speak up, please."

The other two men lunged at Pavan, only to be caught by Mani and Daif. A few other Brumanti villagers joined in the brawl, but their numbers were no match for the skill of the Sinian legionaries. On *The Sun Chaser*, Eino had spent long weeks training in close quarters combat with his fellow crewmates. They claimed it was to repel attacks from bandits or the dreaded Didinbo pirates, but really, it was just a way to pass the time. Consequently, his fellow air legionaries became quite skilled in hand-to-hand fighting, but having never encountered an actual enemy, they often got themselves into trouble at taverns just like this one.

Daif flawlessly executed a heel kick to the gut of a portly villager, and even Mani with his small frame managed to hurl a much larger man over his shoulder and through a table.

Many locals fled out the front door as the mayhem spread. Small disagreements became fistfights all around the tavern.

Eino stood back to back with Pavan, keeping his guard up and watching for any more charging villagers. "We should get out of here before things get ugly."

"And miss all the fun?" Pavan deflected a local's wild punch, repaying the man with a fierce uppercut. He let out a hearty laugh. "Not on your life!"

"Then don't let me hold you back." He patted Pavan on the shoulder. "Good to see you."

Having lit the tinderbox, Eino felt it would be wise to make himself scarce before he caused any more damage. As he ducked and weaved through the chaos, he made a mental note to avoid this tavern the next time he was in Nephene. Which was a shame, because this particular tavern made such wonderful pies.

As his luck would have it, a plate of pies, abandoned in the fracas, sat on a table beside two men locked in a fierce grapple. Eino lunged forward and snatched up the plate, saving it from being smashed as the losing man tumbled into the table.

At last, Eino slipped out of the door, a small pie in hand. It would have gone to waste had he not intervened, he thought. He deserved the chance to savor it. Never mind that he hadn't paid for it. As he bit into the soft flaky crust, the warm filling hit his tongue. The distinct, slightly sweet flavor of fresh shellfish, likely caught that morning off the southern coast of Brumantis, was elevated by a blend of rich and comforting spices common in northern Sinian cuisine. It was a beautiful testament to what the two nations could achieve if only they could stand to cooperate with one another.

Behind him, a man crashed through a window. Eino picked up his pace and headed toward the town square. He'd catch up with his old crewmates another time. For now, he'd find a place to spend the night. Somewhere that wouldn't want him dead by morning.

7

As a precaution against encountering any further trouble, Eino spent the night at a small inn near Nephene's Northern gate, close to where the town peacekeepers were stationed. As he'd hoped, his night was free of interruptions from any unsavory people from his past. Still, he thought it might be best to return to his own inn as soon as possible.

Waking up early the next morning, he scanned the skies for any sign of the Driftcap Inn. Despite the towns being less than a day's walk apart, the winding path the aura stream took meant that the inn could take a day or so to get from Nelene to Nephene. There'd been years when the stream had shifted so far that it detoured the inn all the way to the northern coast of the country before drifting back.

Normally, he didn't mind the detours, as they gave him wonderful opportunities to explore new places. But with how quickly the inn had been moving as of late, he risked missing his scheduled pickup for more guests. Most of all, he worried about leaving Joren behind. The man was quiet and standoffish, but something about him made Eino sad at the thought of not seeing him again. It'd be nice to figure out at least a few of the mysteries surrounding the man first.

Fortunately, he saw the Driftcap Inn off in the distance, floating along the aura stream right where it should be. With a sigh of relief, Eino got dressed and headed to the bustling town market. He'd posted advertisements in a few of the local taverns the day before, and with all the visitors from the festival, he expected he might get a few new guests.

Vendors were already setting up their shops in the town square, with some squabbling over the most prime locations. With all the best spots already taken, there was no place to land his basket, leaving him with nowhere to bring up any new guests.

Eino, however, had a plan to deal with situations like this. After almost getting into a fistfight with a vendor who refused to move his wagon aside during one ill-fated visit to a small village, Eino had spent the next year establishing a series of contacts to help him secure a landing site for his basket. He stood near the fountain in the middle of the square, adjusting his hat to make sure it was visible, and waited for one of his local contacts to arrive. It was only a few minutes before she emerged from the crowd and called out to him.

"Mushroom Man!" came the voice of a little girl. Her long tunic dragged through the dirt tripping her up as she ran to greet him. "I knew you'd be here! I just knew it!"

Eino crossed his arms, feigning offense as he stuck his nose in the air. "Well, of course I did. Don't tell me you doubted me!"

"It's him!" a young boy called out as he too dashed out of the crowd to meet Eino. He looked to be two or three years older than the girl, clad in the same style of tunic, though his didn't drag on the ground. Eino guessed the girl was his sister, and that she was wearing her brother's tunic. "When I saw your mushroom in the sky yesterday, I told all my friends, just like you said!"

"Atta boy. I knew I could count on you." He ruffled the boy's hair, trying to remember if he'd ever met this child before. The boy knew who Eino was, so it might have been the same young boy he'd spoken with the last time he visited. They grew fast in a half-year, and new, almost familiar faces seemed to crop up every time he visited. More and more children emerged from the streets and gathered around him until they numbered about a dozen.

"So um. Mr. Mushroom man," came the voice of another stammering child. "Um, do you have any new toys?"

"Straight to business! I like that, kid." Eino reached into his jacket and produced a pair of small sticks joined by what looked like a scroll. The top of each stick was adorned with a hand carved mushroom painted with the same orange and yellow of the Driftcap Inn. He produced another pair of sticks and, with his usual flourishing showmanship, he presented them to the children. "Have a look at these."

"What are they?" asked a curious voice.

"There's a game they play down in Strania called snatchbounce, and these are the nets." Eino took one pair of sticks and imbued them with a drop of his aura. With a loud snap, they grew to about twice Eino's height, joined with a net and adorned with small banners beneath the carved mushroom toppers. "Now come on and help me set these up."

With help from some of the taller children, Eino set up the two nets opposite one another beside the fountain, while the younger children drew out a playing court between them in the dirt. He gathered them around and explained the rules of the game. "Alright, you kids are about ready to play."

He reached into another pocket and pulled out a small stone encased in tree resin. With another droplet of his aura, the stone glowed, and the resin expanded into a light but sturdy ball. He bounced the ball to the crowd of squealing children and watched them play for a moment.

The children divided themselves into two teams, each trying to bounce the ball off of the other team's side of the court and into their net, scoring more points the higher the ball went. Their movements were cautious and uncoordinated at first, but it didn't take them long to catch onto the game, swapping out with kids on the sidelines and discussing new rules to keep the game fair.

He smiled as he watched the children play. Growing up in rural Tetechetech, Eino never had access to such well-crafted games. He and his cousins had to make do with what they had, creating their own games using sticks, pinecones, and old netting meant to catch driftcaps.

Eino had received the snatchbounce nets from a Stranian toymaker he'd had as a guest earlier that year. The man had no money to pay for a stay at the inn, but had offered to barter several sets of toys, puzzles, and games instead. Eino leapt at the opportunity, adding his own carved decorations and embellishments to a few of the toys.

"You kids remember to play nice now." He turned to leave, but with a dramatic flourish, turned back once more. "But before I go, do you all remember the most important rule?"

The children on the sidelines droned in unison, "Someone always watches for the basket."

"That's right. You remember to clear out when the basket drops. Now have fun!" Of course, Eino's actions weren't altruistic. With the makeshift snatch-bounce court set up, the children would not only reserve a prime location for his basket to land, but also draw in potential guests with their joyful cheering and laughing.

With his landing spot secured, he was free to wander about the market square. Despite the early hour, many food vendors were already hawking their goods. The scent of spices and grilled meat made his mouth water and his stomach grumble. Porocari cuisine tended to be rich and hearty, but sometimes plain in flavor. The same could not be said for dishes from neighboring countries. The first time he left Porocar, he'd ate himself sick on south Sinian spiced chasante stew. While Eino had learned to control his appetite since then, that fascination with new and exciting flavors never left him.

The aroma of fresh grilled fish drew Eino's attention, leading him to a flatbread vendor. Unable to resist, he ordered a traditional quickwrap in the local style, and watched enraptured as the vendor prepared it. It was humble fare, consisting only of grilled fish, vegetables, and sauce wrapped in a fried flatbread shell. Every nation in the former league states had some variant of quickwrap, with each one claiming theirs to be the original. Yet the simplicity of its presentation belied the wonderful complexity of the wrap's flavors.

As Eino bit in, the flavor of the fish washed over him, its succulent juices sealed in with a rich char. The vegetables added some crunch and a subtle sweetness, which was only enhanced by the sweet, sour, and spicy sauce. As much as he wanted to savor each bite, he couldn't help but gobble the quickwrap down.

He licked the sauce from his fingers and continued exploring the market-place, craving something sweet to close his appetite. As he perused the vendors, he caught sight of a man wearing a hooded cloak despite the heat of the morning suns. Eino stopped, squinting as the man walked. He spied a familiar, bright green shirt beneath the cloak. As the man turned his head to scan the square, he recognized the dark hair and suspicious gaze of Joren.

Eino ducked behind a food stall, regretting his choice of unique and conspic-uous headwear. He pulled off his mushroom hat and held it low before peeking out again. Joren didn't look his way, and he let out a breath of relief.

Considering the way the Brumanti people felt toward Sinians, he wasn't surprised to see Joren hiding his identity with such an unseasonable cloak. He was, however, surprised to see how much less nervous the man appeared. His steps through the marketplace came off as purposeful, almost confident. Still, his look was far from relaxed with the way his head turned this way and that, scanning the market with the suspicious eyes of a bodyguard. Or perhaps those of a criminal. He strolled over to a vendor's stall and presented a string of small fish, exchanging them for a small bag of coins. Then Joren left the market, making his way toward a back alleyway.

A few weeks before stopping in Poutise, Joren had started paying a visit to every town along the inn's route, no matter how small. Yet whenever Eino came down, he could never find him anywhere. He never saw him at any of the taverns or holy sites. He never crossed paths with him during any festivals. Save for the few times they'd ridden the baskets up or down together, this was the first time Eino had run into Joren outside of the inn.

Eino craned his neck, trying to figure out exactly where the man was going. The only information he could glean was that Joren had been fishing and gathering plants, but based on his unimpressive haul of fish, it likely wasn't his passion. Perhaps Betta was right about him, and the fish he sold had more to them than met the eye.

As a rule, he tried to avoid prying into the private lives of his guests, but Eino's curiosity got the better of him whenever it came to Joren. With how the man kept to himself, Eino couldn't count on getting another chance to learn about his mysterious guest. He followed him toward the alleyway, quickening his pace before he lost his target in the crowd.

"Why am I doing this?" Eino muttered to himself. What was it about this man that so captured his attention? It couldn't just be his good looks. He'd encountered plenty of handsome men and beautiful women in his travels, but most were hardly worth a second glance. Perhaps it was because other people were so easy to understand. Eino prided himself on being able to read people, but Joren confounded him at every turn. The man was unlike any guest he'd ever had before.

Most of the Driftcap Inn's guests were traveling just to see the world, lazily drifting along with no particular destination in mind. Or if they had one, they were in no hurry to get there. Some simply gawked at the novelty of the inn, while others needed the time spent drifting through the clouds to unwind and prepare themselves for arriving at wherever their next chapter waited.

But with how tense and paranoid Joren seemed, there was no way he was there to relax on a meandering sky cruise. It was possible that he was using the inn to travel to somewhere specific, but if he was, he was certainly being secretive about it. He was also taking a long and circuitous route to get there. Spring was just starting, and before the season was over, the inn would be right back where he'd first boarded the inn.

A small wagon trundled by in front of him, and Eino almost lost sight of his target. He squinted against the shade of the dark alley, but once his eyes adjusted, he found Joren speaking to a trader beneath a rather inconspicuous stand.

The trader fanned herself as Joren offered her something from his pouch. With rich dark skin and naturally silver white hair, she undoubtedly hailed from the icy lands of the Gatrai. From their tribal lands in the southern tundra to the colonial shipyards in the northern glaciers, nearly everyone in Gatrai society was involved with trade, and while they were a common sight across Itharos, it was rare to see them outside of their airships.

The trader peered at Joren's offering, coyly hiding her face behind her fan. Joren gestured angrily, but the noise of the crowd drowned out whatever he was saying. Eino would have to get far too close to overhear.

The trader shrugged, the motion causing the sleeves of her light cream-colored robe dress to slide farther down her shoulders. Joren pocketed his offering, threw a hand up in exasperation, and stormed off. When he was certain Joren was out of sight, Eino approached the trader's stall.

"Welcome, my friend, and may Querrina's winds bless you," she said, beaming as she spread her hands out above her goods. "What is it you are seeking today?"

Eino looked over the trader's wares. There were baskets of herbs, some fresh and some dried, and several vials filled with brightly colored tinctures. All things which wouldn't be out of place in an apothecary's shop. "All I'm after today is information."

"Information? That can be more valuable than gold."

"It surely can be." Eino tossed a small coin to the trader, and she caught it with a deft hand. "I was hoping you'd tell me a bit about that spirited discussion you and that Sinian fella were having."

She kept her expression neutral, making her impossible to read. "We were discussing business, of course."

"I figured as much. It also looked to me like whatever he was selling, you weren't buying. What I wanna know is, what was it he was trying to sell you?" He swept his gaze over her offerings again, hoping to find any clues.

"I am sorry, my friend, but to tell you that would surely break the Codes of the Brotherhood. A transaction is a sacred thing. Even one where no goods are exchanged." She offered the coin back to Eino.

Eino took the coin back. If she wouldn't give him information directly, he'd have to try another route. "One more thing," he said, leaning in and dropping his voice. "Got any dreamleaf?"

The trader raised an eyebrow. "You are a guardsman of some sort?"

Eino shook his head. "Just trying to relax and enjoy the festival."

"Well, if you are not a guardsman, then perhaps you would not know that dreamleaf is outlawed in Brumantis. By the Codes of the Brotherhood, I'm forbidden to sell it to you." She gave a sly smile. "If I had any, of course."

Eino rolled the coin over his knuckles, plucking two more from his pouch and fanning them out with as charming a grin as he could manage. "What is it the Brotherhood likes to say... 'Everything can be bought for a price?'"

The trader offered only an amused giggle in response. "Everything can indeed be bought for a price. But that, my friend, you must buy elsewhere. Now good day to you, and may Querrina's winds guide you."

Eino offered a polite nod and walked away. He should have known better than to try bribing a Gatrai. Their codes were more than just guidelines for business. They were a fundamental part of their culture's religious teachings. Their adherence to the Codes of the Brotherhood meant they were always trustworthy business partners. Unfortunately for him, it also meant there were never any shortcuts to be found when dealing with them.

Eino's investigation had proven inconclusive, to say the least. If Joren truly was the transnational contraband smuggler Betta believed him to be, he certainly wasn't doing a very good job of it. Then again, why would he and the trader be acting so suspiciously if their discussions had been something legal? Was he really just a socially anxious fisherman slowly making his way around Itharos?

Either way it hardly mattered. Even if he was a smuggler, the fine for something as innocuous as dreamleaf was less than what Eino had been willing to pay the Gatrai for information. He doubted the peacekeepers would cause him any trouble over the matter.

Besides, he had more important things to worry about. There were still a few hours before his inn would be overhead, and then he'd likely have new guests to deal with. Until then, there was still plenty more to explore about the festival. Plenty of dances to watch and music to hear. And plenty more delicious foods to savor.

8

A PAIR OF FIRE dancers had cleared a section of the market square for their performance, drawing in a crowd of onlookers. A young woman balanced herself upside down, supported only by her finger on the palm of her partner's outstretched hand. The other dancer then lifted her above his head, supporting her entire weight on his own finger. The aura coalesced between their fingers into a flame which grew brighter and brighter until at last it burst, launching the young woman high into the air. Elegant streams of flame swirled around her as she flipped and twisted. Her partner leapt after her, and the two danced together in midair, their feet leaving streaks of fire as they descended.

Eino nudged his way to the front, drawn in by the spectacle. He removed his hat for the sake of those behind him, though it was hardly necessary for the high-flying performance.

For their finale, the two jumped up once more, wreathing themselves in fire, and their aura burst in a bright explosion. Swooping into one another's arms as they fell, they descended toward a grill Eino hadn't noticed. With their aura focused into their outstretched hands, they set the grill alight, and the crowd's attention was now drawn to the sizzle of the grill, the aroma of grilled herbs filling the air.

Eino's mouth watered as he watched the dancers-turned-cooks grill up thick slices of bread, serving them topped with creamy butterfruit spread and a fried egg. He had spent the whole day eating street fare, but he decided he had room for one more snack, if for no other reason than to reward the pair for their wonderful performance. A meal and a show, he thought. He could draw up a lot of business if he had something like that back at his inn.

The inn.

Eino scanned the skies in a panic. He'd lost track of time, and might have missed his scheduled pickup for new guests at noon. He patted his pockets, searching for his pocket watch, his hands growing frantic. There were still about twenty minutes until the pickup, so where was the inn? It should have been in the skies outside of town, drifting toward the market square.

"Is that another damn Sinian ship?" asked a woman, shielding her eyes from the suns as she squinted up at the sky.

"No, it's that mushroom. The one that maniac lives on," the woman's friend responded with a sniff.

Eino pulled on his goggles and looked up, letting out a sigh of relief. The inn floated overhead, only slightly ahead of schedule. It had drifted farther than he'd anticipated, but he'd still be in position to make his pickup.

Her friend leaned in, gossiping loud enough to be heard. "They say he was in town yesterday causing havoc. I heard he got into a fight with the Sinians."

A mischievous smile crept across Eino's face as he leaned between the two women. "Didn't just fight them. I beat 'em." Without another word, he strutted past them, letting them see the mushroom hat hanging from his back. Where publicity was concerned, Eino wasn't above telling a small lie, least of all when it was at his friends' expense. He grinned, hoping the rumor would torment Pavan once it reached his ears.

He made his way back to the fountain. The children were too distracted by the snatchbounce game to notice him as he approached. Eino stopped to marvel at the crowd gathered around watching the exotic ballgame. It seemed his plan to drum up business had succeeded. Amongst the children playing and the gawking adults, a woman stood at the edge of the crowd, tall and austere, laden with bags, and looking somewhat lost.

A young girl stood behind her, squinting up at the sky. She was paying more attention to the mushroom overhead than to the game. Eino guessed her to be the woman's daughter, and no older than ten at most. They both wore traditional Cacosshian dresses, long and modest in a pale blue. The lone bit of decoration on their garb was the floral embroidery pattern adorning their square necklines and boxy caps. A plain white undergarment peeked through at their shoulders where their long sleeves were tied on. While the woman wore a thin veil hanging from her hat over her eyes, her daughter had pinned hers out of the way.

It was time to see if the children remembered the most important rule of the game, thought Eino. Taking the aura stone from his necklace, he summoned the basket from the inn.

"Basket!" yelled one young boy, pointing to the sky. "Everybody move!"

The game stopped, and the children cleared the ball court. The basket descended, flanked by the nets with their banners and mushroom toppers. Eino rubbed his chin. Even though it was sporting equipment, it made for a surprisingly professional looking landing zone.

"It is the right place, Mama!" shouted the girl behind the austere woman.

"So it seems." The woman took her bags and stood beside the basket, scanning the market square.

The crowd was dispersing, and it looked as though the only new guests would be the woman and her daughter. Eino adjusted his hat and shuffled over to greet them. "Howdy!"

"Greetings to you." The woman had a thick Cacosshian accent, and even behind her veil, her gaze was piercing.

"Um, Mr. Mushroom Man?" A little boy tugged on Eino's jacket. "Can you move the basket so we can keep playing?"

"This will only take a moment, son." He ruffled the boy's hair. "Then I'll let you get back to it."

"You work for the Driftcap Inn, yes?" The woman stepped forward, her back straight and shoulders tense as she walked. "Kindly bring us to the innkeeper."

"Why, I reckon I can do that." A sly grin crept across his face. He couldn't resist a little mischief, least of all with someone who came across as so very stern. "Can I help you with your bags, miss?"

She bowed her head. "That would be appreciated. Thank you."

He opened the basket door and gestured for them to enter before he retrieved her bags. They were much heavier than he'd expected considering how thin and graceful the woman carrying them was. Judging by how many she had, he guessed that she and her daughter were on a one-way journey.

"Are you two waiting on anyone else?" Cacosshian society was perhaps the most conservative east of the Great Divide, with most of their population adhering to their strict denomination of Deka'arism. Under these tenets, it was very unusual to see a woman unaccompanied by her husband.

"No," said the woman curtly. "I would appreciate it if you can take us to the innkeeper now, please."

Eino checked his pocket watch. She seemed in a hurry, which always compelled Eino to drag his feet. "We'll be up shortly, miss. Just gotta wait for any stragglers."

The woman shifted on her heels. "Very well." Behind her, the little girl leaned over the edge of the basket, tapping her toe.

"Hey there," he said, squatting down. "Would you like to see something amazing?"

The girl looked up at the woman. "May I, Mama?"

The woman nodded, and the girl stepped forward. Eino removed the necklace that held the aurastone from around his neck. He imbued the stone with a dollop of his aura, making it glow a deep blue. "What do you think? Pretty, huh?"

"An aurastone." The girl's eyes sparkled as she stepped forward. "What's it do?"

The woman held out her hand. "Leora, be caref—"

As soon as her hand touched the stone, the basket shot up into the air. The girl squealed, and below the children laughed and cheered, eager to return to their game.

The woman gasped, but remained upright, not even holding on to the edge of the basket to steady herself. She cast a murderous glare at Eino.

The girl giggled as she regained her footing. "That was fun."

Seeing that her daughter was alright, the woman's expression softened, but only slightly. "Some warning would be appreciated next time."

"Beg your pardon. I just couldn't wait to introduce you to the innkeeper." He smiled, doing his best to lay on the charm. With a spin and a flourish, he tipped his hat and bowed. "Eino the Wanderer, at your service."

"Val," replied the woman. Her words came out clipped. "And this is my daughter, Leora."

"Pleased to make your acquaintance, ladies. And it is my great pleasure to welcome you to the Driftcap Inn." As the basket passed through a low cloud, the inn came into view, floating along the aura stream. "Drift on in and stay awhile."

"We will indeed stay awhile," said Val, offering no reaction. "I have ample coin to pay."

Eino slumped. Most guests offered a polite chuckle. Some rolled their eyes. Val, however, seemed to take his cheesy line at face value. Somehow, that felt worse than derision.

As the basket reached the promenade, he opened the basket door for them. "Oh, we can worry about payment later. You folks headed somewhere in particular?"

"Yes. We make for the Sinian capital."

"Muna?" Eino grimaced. "You sure about that?"

"Yes. Is there a problem?" Though the veil obscured her face, he heard the concern in her voice. "It is along your route, is it not?"

"Well, sure, but we'll be taking the long way to get there." He drew the route in the air. "We'll be heading back toward Cacosshia, then down the Stranian coast and around the southern coast of Porocar before we get there. I don't reckon we'll be back near Muna until the middle of summer."

Val paused a long moment, and Eino chewed his lip. By chartering a typical airship, she could be in Muna in a week. A ferry and an overland route would get her there before the end of spring. With as impatient as she was to get to the inn, he was certain she would wish to be brought back down to Nephene.

She broke the silence. "Yes. This will do nicely. Please show us to our quarters."

Eino scratched his head. "I'll uh ... I'll fetch you a key. You can wait in the common room for now."

As he opened the door, Betta stood up from her seat and brushed herself off. "Welcome, friends! You must be our newest guests." For as little as Betta cared for seeing new places, she was always welcoming to new people. Even so, her smile was much brighter than usual.

Eino lifted an eyebrow. "Ladies, meet Betta. She does most of the cooking around here. Betta, this is Val and her daughter Leora. They'll be staying with us for a while."

"Well, we are just as happy as a cacklecaw to have you aboard. Can I get you ladies a cup of tea? I've got a pot of bramble blossom that should be just about ready."

Val bowed her head. "I would be grateful for a cup."

"Do you have sugar?" asked the girl.

"We most certainly do, sweet pea. I'll bring it right out to you folks." Betta sauntered into the kitchen and Eino followed. Beside the doorway was a small end table with a ledger book and a few keys hanging from hooks.

"You're awful chipper today," said Eino, sniffing at the air and taking in the tea's warm aroma. "And just when did you even get your hands on some bramble blossom tea? Don't tell me you've been hiding it since the last time we were in Strania."

"No, I got it in a package this morning. The courier flew in while you were off gallivanting in town," said Betta, pouring the tea. "He brought me some real good news, too."

He looked up from the ledger book. "Don't keep me in suspense."

She handed Eino his cup, a sly grin on her face. "After tea. It ain't no good if you let it get cool." Before Eino could protest, she had already taken the tray of tea out to the common room.

Eino shook his head. Her news was probably some mundane thing, and she was dragging it out to get him back for some prank or tall tale. He finished scrawling in the book and plucked a set of keys from the hook, then followed Betta back out to the common room.

Betta spoke to Val as she poured her cup. "...but, dinner won't be for a few hours, so if you get hungry, you can just come on into the kitchen. I'll whip you something up right quick. And if I ain't in the kitchen, I'll be in my cabin. It's the one with a wool hen on the door."

Val raised an eyebrow. "Wool hen?"

"Ain't you never seen a wool hen before? Well, if you spend any time on the promenade, you'll get your fill of the dang beasts." She snickered and took one last sip of her tea. "Now, if you'll excuse me, I'd better get back to cooking." She gave Eino a bright smile as she went back to the kitchen, humming all the while.

Eino scoffed. She'd eluded him once more. He was starting to suspect that she didn't have any news at all. He put it out of his mind until his work was done. "Here's your key, ma'am. You and your daughter will be staying in the Stormgulper Suite."

Val took a hold of the key, examining the crude carving of the creature adorning its handle. "You seem to encounter some strange creatures in the sky. I do not believe I have ever heard of a stormgulper either."

"Count yourself lucky. They're real nasty creatures that live inside storm clouds. Real big too. Even the babies are the size of a sailing ship. And the adults? Bigger than some small towns!"

Leora's eyes went wide. "We won't run into one of those things, will we?"

"Don't you fret, little lady. We won't be passing anywhere near their hunting grounds. And even if we were, I can handle them. I took on my fair share back when I served in the Sinian Air Legion." Eino rolled his neck and flexed his arms. Of course, he'd never seen a stormgulper in his life. He'd only ever heard accounts from other air legionaries, and based on their wildly varying descriptions, he doubted that the creatures even existed. "I reckon they wouldn't even be able to make it through the aura barrier."

Val pursed her lips. "This barrier. It is powered by a core, is it not?"

"Sure is." Eino pointed to a small door at the far end of the room. There was a warning written on the door in both high and low Aralic script, as well as in Sindhic pictoglyphs, which even the illiterate could understand. The meaning was quite clear. "Do not open." Leora stared at the door, unable to look away.

Val's eyes narrowed as she read the warnings. "That hardly seems like a safe place to store a core."

"Oh, the core is safe as can be. I had the door keyed to my aura, so can't nobody get in without my say so."

"Then I should like to see this core," said Val. "To see if it can maintain the barrier as well as you say."

Eino grimaced. "Now I know it's commonplace for inns on land to show off their cores, but up here it's a matter of safety. It don't offer much by way of amenities, but that there core is what's keeping us in the aurastream with our barrier up. If anything were to happen to it, we'd all be in big trouble."

Val furrowed her brow, pointing to the small door. "A matter of safety? The door is completely out in the op—" She was interrupted by a sudden popping sound followed by Leora shrieking.

Leora had swung the loose door open, and out sprang a three-headed paper serpent and some confetti. The surprise bowled the girl onto her back, but after the initial shock, Leora began laughing.

"Never said the core was behind that door," said Eino, winking at Val. Inside the door was a piece of chalk on a string, as well as several tally marks. Eino retrieved the paper braided serpent and folded it back up, placing it in the door. With a smile, he added another mark to the wall.

Val scowled. "You find this amusing?"

"I ain't the only one." He grinned as he helped a giggling Leora to her feet. "But I can assure you the core is in a very safe place. And it ain't much to look at anyhow. I reckon only an auramancer would find it interesting."

"Your assurances do not inspire confidence." Conflict danced in her eyes, but then the hard set of her jaw softened. "But they will have to do for now." She held up her key, running her thumb over the carving of the stormgulper. "I should like to see my room, if you please."

"Certainly, ma'am." Eino guided them out the door and around the promenade to the rope bridge which held their cabin. The two disappeared inside, leaving Eino to ponder their peculiar appearance at the inn. Not only was Val unaccompanied by her husband, but both she and her daughter seemed particularly willful. Hardly the stereotypical image of a meek and demure Deka'arist woman. He could see why she might want to flee the Tetrarchy. So why then was Val undoing so much of her progress toward Muna by taking the inn back toward the Cacosshian kingdoms?

Eino returned to the kitchen, eager to gossip with Betta about the new guests. As he walked through the doorway, he was greeted by the sound of Betta humming a cheerful tune over a bubbling pot. "Well, them two were an odd sort, don't you think?"

"Oh?" she said, tasting the dark red sauce. "How do you figure?"

"Well, for starters, they didn't give me their full names. No clan name, no honorifics, just their..." Eino trailed off and sniffed the air, and a warm, rich aroma greeted him. "Wait a minute, are you making short ribs on flatbread?" She only whipped that up for special occasions.

"Sure am." Betta giggled. "Ain't had it in a long time, have we?"

"Well shoot, what's the occasion?" He licked his lips and added sarcastically, "The Grand Duke ain't coming for a visit, is he?"

"Now that wouldn't be no reason to celebrate. I told you this was good news!" Betta chuckled. She plucked a letter from her apron and clutched it to her chest. "See that tea the courier delivered came with a letter. And it's from Clofen!"

"Ah, so that's your big news. What's your boy up to, anyhow?"

"He's finished his service term with the guard and he's coming home! Got himself a wife, too. A nice Stranian girl. And he's bringing her with him."

"Home? You mean—"

"Yep! Back to Yel Mor. Once we get to the mountains, I'm gonna meet up with him and we're gonna get the farm back." She giggled like a young girl. "Oh, cast me to the Wynds! I never thought I'd see the day."

Eino froze. "So...you're leaving?" His voice came out quiet. Hurt.

"Oh, don't say it like that. It ain't goodbye forever, you know." She pulled him into a hug.

"No. No, it's alright." Eino squeezed her back, ignoring the tight feeling in his chest. "I'm happy for you."

"I'm gonna miss this place. And I'm gonna miss you, you ol' coastie." She broke the hug, blinking back her watery eyes as she looked up to Eino. "So you'd better come visit us, you hear? You're always gonna be welcome at the farm."

Eino smiled back at her, putting on a brave face. "And you're welcome to visit me again too, but you'll have to pay full fare this time, and Dilgaa knows you can't afford it!"

She laughed and slapped his arm. "Maybe I'll just make you some more short ribs to make up for it." She returned to her bubbling pot. "Or I could show you how to make it."

"Not right now," said Eino, waving as he walked out of the kitchen. "I'm gonna pop back into town to see if there are any more guests who missed the pickup. Who knows? Might even find Joren somewhere down there."

Eino headed back to the basket. His chest didn't ache anymore. Instead, it just felt empty. Maybe he'd head back down and visit a tavern. Or maybe he'd just take a nice stroll through the city. Anything to get his mind off the bad news. Betta had spent more time with him at the inn than anyone else. She was more than just a guest. She was his closest friend. Practically family. He couldn't imagine running the inn without her. But now that she was leaving, his inn felt a little colder and the vast sky a lot lonelier.

9

EINO WANDERED THE FARM fields and palm orchards outside of Nephene's walls. As much as he enjoyed the bustle and excitement of a lively town, there were times when all he wanted to do was take a nice long walk to stretch his legs. Most of the time, he had to settle for walking laps around the inn's promenade. But on days like today when the weather was pleasant and he wasn't running behind schedule, he'd descend to the surface to stroll through the meadows and forests.

In about an hour, the inn would be too far over the forest for him to use the basket, but with Blue so close by, he could take his time to unwind. Perhaps he'd look for pieces of wood to carve, or relax and enjoy the warm air of the beautiful, tropical spring day.

Walks helped him clear his mind, particularly in places full of natural beauty. A cool breeze ran waves through the fields of grain on his left and rustled the palm trees on his right. He ran his hand through the soft grain stalks. How much simpler life must be as a farmer, he thought. To have a real connection to the land. To the people. Maybe that was why Thaena had stayed behind. Why his Sinian lover, and so many lovers before him had stayed too. And it was why Betta was leaving now.

He walked beneath the shade of the palms until he reached the end of the orchard. Dread pooled in his stomach, and no matter how much he tried, he couldn't take his mind off of Betta's departure. She'd come to feel like family in the time he'd known her. Even if every cabin of the Driftcap Inn were occupied, it would still feel empty without her by his side.

Maybe it was time for him to settle down somewhere as well, he thought as he climbed a small hill overlooking the countryside. From there, he saw people dotted across the vast meadows and farmlands. A mother walking with her children into town. A family sharing a meal around a bonfire. Young couples embracing beneath the shade of the trees. At one point or another, each group turned their attention to the sky and pointed. Eino followed their fingers to find his inn drifting overhead.

He smiled. For as lonely as he felt, he couldn't help but feel a sense of pride in what he'd created. The Driftcap Inn was something people looked forward to seeing. He looked forward to it, too. To the sense of freedom he felt in the sky. He shook his head. He couldn't give up on his inn. Just like a driftcap, he too yearned to fly across the sky.

A rutted road led down the hill through a line of wild palm trees. Through the treeline, Eino spied a dark-haired figure by the road, his attention on something in his hands. He shook whatever it was and cursed, then collapsed onto a fallen log, holding his head in his hands. As Eino drew closer, he recognized the cloak the man was wearing, as well as the bright green wrap shirt peeking from beneath it.

Eino waved, happy to see a familiar face, and even happier for a distraction from his woes. "Howdy, Joren!" he yelled as he stumbled out from between the palm trees, tripping over a root in his excitement.

Joren's head snapped up. He glanced up at the inn and then back at Eino. "Th-the basket. It's not working. Why isn't it working?" He shook the large key in his hands. A carving of a crested greatwing decorated the end of the key where a small aurastone was embedded.

"What?" Eino was taken aback, more by Joren's voice than by the basket's failure. It was the most he'd ever heard the man say at one time. "It was working fine earlier. Is something wrong with your aurastone?"

"I-I don't know. I've been trying to get this thing to work for almost twenty minutes. I thought—" His voice trembled, his hand clutching tight to his key. "I thought you were going to leave me behind."

"Now you listen here. The Driftcap Inn has never abandoned a guest and I'm not about to start now." He reached out to pat the man's shoulder, then thought better of it. "So don't you worry. I'll just call the basket down and make sure you get back to your cabin."

Joren slumped down against a tree. A few flecks of mud were splattered on his pants, which he wore tucked into a pair of worn, muddy boots. Plants peeked out of his full satchel, and a lone smoked fish dangled from his sash. A short stubbly beard covered his chin, and the dark bags under his eyes and the smear of dirt on his cheek made Eino think he hadn't slept well since leaving the inn.

Eino reached for his necklace and imbued its stone with some of his aura. "Should only be a minute."

Joren kept glancing up, shielding his eyes against the light of the suns. A long moment passed, but nothing happened. Eino slid his goggles on and looked toward the inn, but he couldn't spy the basket anywhere in the sky. He glanced down at his stone and tried again. It was glowing and thrumming as it should be, but still no basket appeared. "Huh."

"What's wrong? Is it coming? Why isn't it coming?" Joren twitched and shifted. His anxiety was infectious, and unease began to poke at Eino's skin. Had adjusting the core caused this? His mind started ticking through ever more dire possibilities as to what could have happened to the basket. And of what could go wrong next.

He stood straighter, refusing to let himself dwell on an imagined worst-case scenario. Worry would get him nowhere. He needed to take action now, not only for his own sake but for the sake of his nervous guest. Eino plastered on a smile. "I reckon the aurastones are just out of juice. Which means you're in luck."

Joren pinched the bridge of his nose. "How? How is any of this lucky?"

"Because it means you get to hitch a ride back up with me and Blue!" He reached for the whistle dangling from his goggles, pouring his aura into the sound to ensure it reached her. The sound was barely audible to human ears, but as he watched the inn, a familiar shadow descended from her perch and started gliding toward him.

He searched his pockets for a treat to give her, only to come up empty-handed. With how distracted he'd been worrying about Betta, he'd forgotten to get a treat for his greatwing. Looking around in a panic, his gaze landed on the fish hanging from Joren's sash.

Eino rubbed the back of his neck. "Sorry, but the old gal is pretty fussy if she's hungry. I hate to impose, but would you mind if I gave her that there fish?"

"I—" Joren opened his mouth in protest, then closed it and lowered his eyes. With a tired, sad nod, he handed it over. "Yes. That would be fair."

"Oh, don't get the wrong idea. I ain't gonna steal from you. You're bailing me out, so I'll give you a discount off your fare."

Joren gave him another exhausted nod. Eino's curiosity grew as he eyed the man's satchel. What were all the plants for? He wanted to find a reason to ask about them rather than just blurting the questions out. He'd have to be careful if he wanted a straight answer. But maybe the ride up would give him a chance to satisfy his curiosity. And to settle his wager with Betta.

The massive bird landed in front of them, the flapping of her wings nearly blowing them over. Blue clacked her beak, poking at Eino's jacket.

"Aww, here you go, you ol' glutton." He tossed the fish to Blue. She snapped it out of the air, and once she finished gulping down the treat, she lowered herself down. Eino patted her head and climbed onto her back. "There we go. All aboard."

Joren backed up a step, watching Blue warily.

Eino held out a hand. "Need help?"

"Um…" he muttered, tightening his grip on his key. Like a terrified rabbit, he stood frozen, looking ready to run off at any moment. "Are you certain there's no other way up?"

"Afraid there ain't." He pulled down his goggles, and a sly smile crept across his face. "But there ain't a more fun way to see the countryside neither."

Joren hesitated, and Blue nudged him with her beak.

"Better hurry up, or Blue is gonna demand another fish." Eino held his hand out again. "Don't want us to leave you behind, do you?"

"No!" Joren blurted out. He cleared his throat and crept forward, grabbing a hold of Eino's hand and clumsily climbed onto the saddle behind him.

"Hold on," warned Eino. With a tug of her reins, Eino sent Blue up into the air.

Joren let out a gasp. His arms wrapped around Eino's waist as he pressed his face against his back. The man's breath grew faster as they rose until it came in gasps that made Eino fear he'd faint and fall right off Blue.

"Blue's been with me since she was just a lil chick," Eino said to distract him. "Hurt her wing when she was real young and got left behind by her flock. I started leaving food out for her while she recovered. Took a while for her to fly again, but just look at her now."

Joren only squeezed tighter in response, his face still buried in Eino's back. His embrace was warm against the cold wind whipping past them. As they rose higher, Eino spied a clump of scramblers off to their right.

Like driftcaps, bramblepine trees released their fruits into the air, allowing them to drift along the aura streams far beyond the mountains where they grew. These fruits, which the Porocari called scramblers, were a little larger than a fist with long ribbon-like tendrils that twitched in the currents of aura. Some lone scramblers drifted past, looking like bizarre sea creatures on the prowl. Most, however, had clumped together, which combined with their fluffy white outer shells, made them look like clouds.

Joren let out a strangled noise that made Eino turn around. "You alright back there?"

"No! I am not!" His voice was muffled against Eino's back. "Just focus on flying, please."

Eino chuckled. "Oh, don't worry. Blue knows the way back to the inn without my help. Why, I could turn around backwards and upside down and she'd—"

A sudden gust of wind slammed into them, making Blue's left wing hitch. They tilted to the side, and for a moment, Eino felt the tickling sensation of falling in his stomach before Blue was able to right herself. Joren's hold tightened, making it hard for Eino to breathe.

"Sorry about that. She likes to make a liar outta me sometimes."

Joren let out a groan as Blue resumed her ascent. "I'm going to die. I'm riding on an injured greatwing and I'm going to die. Soleivar save me." He reached into his satchel, grabbing a bundle of green leaves and shoving them into his mouth.

Eino glanced back. "Is that dreamleaf?" His heart sank. Betta was going to win their wager after all. "It works better if you smoke it, you know."

"It's briskweed, you dimling," snapped Joren. Terror filled his words more than anger. "Now please just fly us back."

Eino blinked at the sudden outburst. He ignored the insult, distracted by the leaves Joren was chewing. Briskweed was a common remedy for nervousness and a queasy stomach across Itharos. While serving aboard *The Sun Chaser*, the physician often had to administer oil of briskweed to new recruits who got airsick, or more often, those who were scared of flying.

Was Joren afraid of heights? Eino scratched his head, remembering times when he caught a glimpse of the man sipping something from a small vial. Maybe that was briskweed too. Or perhaps something stronger to combat his fear. It would explain his general nervousness and hesitation to ride Blue. It would also explain why he was still squeezing the life out of Eino's waist. But why then would he stay on the inn for so long? It seemed every new answer with Joren only created more questions.

Joren's grip tightened again as Blue dropped down on top of the inn. Even after they landed, his arms remained tightly clasped around Eino. He almost enjoyed the embrace, but after a long pause, he tapped Joren on the hand. "I'll help you down, alright?"

Joren let go and Eino slid down. He offered Joren his hand to help him balance as he climbed off. The man's steps were careful and slow, shuddering as his feet hit the inn. He squeezed Eino's hand tightly, and upon realizing what he'd done, he let go and stepped back, bumping into the garden fence.

"I—" Joren cleared his throat. "P-please forgive my outburst, earlier."

"No need to apologize." Eino waved a dismissive hand. As he turned to guide them both to the hatch into the inn, it occurred to him that Joren had spoken more to him today than he had for the entire rest of his stay combined. He couldn't pass up this opportunity to satisfy his curiosity. He turned back, and with a subtle smirk creeping at the corner of his mouth, he made his guess. "There's lots of folks who aren't comfortable with heights."

Joren grimaced, slumping his shoulders as if he'd been caught in a lie. "It's...something I've been getting over. I thought I was doing well until..." He trailed off, gesturing toward Blue.

Eino laughed. "Yeah, Blue can be a bit of a rough ride. But don't you worry. I'll get the basket fixed up before we reach the next town, so you won't need to ride her again. Not unless you want to, of course." Part of him wanted to ride with Joren again. His embrace had been warm, if perhaps a bit too tight.

"No, I—" Joren shook his head and cleared his throat once more. "I'm sorry, but I will need to ride down once more. This will be my last day here."

"Oh. That's...sudden." Why did his chest ache at that proclamation? He did his best to keep his confusing emotions hidden. "You're really ready to check out, then?"

Joren looked down. "I'll grab my things, then please take me back down."

"Well now, hold on a minute." First Betta, now Joren. Losing everyone all at once was more than his heart could bear. Eino desperately scrambled for a reason, any reason to keep Joren at the inn, even for just a little while longer. "Don't you want to at least wait until the basket's fixed?"

"I-I don't have a choice." He looked down, embarrassment coloring his face. "I'm out of money."

Eino sighed. He was so relieved he couldn't help but smile. "Oh, don't you worry about that!" He put a hand on Joren's shoulder. "It's like I told you. I ain't never abandoned one of my guests before, and it's gonna take more than being short a couple jingles to make me start now."

Joren looked up, hope glimmering in his eyes before he snuffed it out. "No, I couldn't possibly ask you to do that. I don't deserve your charity."

Eino snorted. "This ain't no charity. You're still gonna need to work to earn your keep. But you see, we're coming up on scrambler season and I could use a little help for the harvest. Besides…" Eino turned his head, sizing up Joren once more before making another guess. "I can always find a use for an apothecary."

Joren gripped the strap of his satchel. "And you're certain that would be alright?"

"Wouldn't be the first time I've done it. I reckon it won't be the last, either. Truth is, I'll earn more from an extra pair of hands during scrambler season than I would from you paying for your cabin."

"Then I accept." Joren fought against a smile, bowing his head. "Thank you. Please, do not hesitate to make use of me."

Eino suppressed a childish giggle, reminding himself that wasn't the invitation he wanted it to be. For now, at least. "Don't sound too grateful now. It ain't exactly easy work. You sure you're gonna be able to keep up?"

"Whatever the task, I am up to it. I promise you."

"Well alright. I reckon you can help me with scrambler fishing tomorrow." He strutted over to the hatch leading into his room.

As he opened it, Joren paused, peering at the rows of herbs and vegetables in Eino's garden. "Wait a moment, is that pepperoot?"

"Yes, it's pepperoot. Can't get rid of the stuff no matter how hard I try." Eino shrugged his shoulders and groaned. "Look, I know it looks unkempt, but I'm up here weeding damn near every day. The trouble is everything grows faster in the aurastreams. Even the weeds. Especially the weeds."

"No, no, no, you shouldn't get rid of it. It's a very useful plant. Its oil is effective in treating burns and neutralizing toxins." He pulled a small bronze sickle from the small of his back, preparing to take a bouquet of the leaves before stopping himself, looking to Eino with a sheepish expression. "Oh. Sorry. May I take some?"

Eino scratched his chin. "You say that stuff can treat burns?"

"Not on its own. It must first be mixed into a poultice. The process is very simple, but it does take some time."

"Tell you what. I've got a nasty habit of burning myself whenever Betta tries to teach me to cook. You mix me up some of that there poultice, and you can take as much as you like."

"Then I'll have some ready for you first thing in the morning." Joren smiled as he took a few large handfuls of the leaves.

Eino paused. It was the first time he could remember ever seeing the man smile. It lit up his rugged, unshaven jawline. With the suns glinting off of the loose strands of hair in his face, he couldn't help but stare.

Joren looked up, catching Eino's gaze. "I think I have everything I need." He tucked the sickle back into his sash.

Eino cleared his throat. "Then let's get you back to your cabin. It's just through my room."

Joren wrung his hands. "I'm sorry. I don't mean to invade your privacy."

"Don't apologize. It ain't nobody's fault but mine." Eino scratched the back of his head. "I keep meaning to put in a ladder that goes to the promenade. I'll get around to it one of these days."

He led him through his cramped quarters, chuckling as they bumped into one another. The intimacy of the setting built a warmth in his stomach, but he pushed it down as he opened the door to the loft above the common room. Together, they descended the stairs and stepped out onto the promenade.

Val sat on a chair to their right. She looked up from her book about the history of the Heralian League. It had been a donation from one of his previous guests. Eino had attempted to read it once or twice before. The book covered centuries of intrigue and political maneuvering from the league's inception to its collapse following the Decrian Slave Revolt. And it did so in such a dry and impenetrable manner that Eino had never made it more than a few pages in. What he'd picked up from conversations during his years of travel was informative enough.

Eino opened his arms. "Joren, meet Val and her daughter Leora. Ladies, Joren. He stays in the greatwing cabin."

"A pleasure," said Val. Joren offered her a nod in response.

Leora was too busy leaning over the railing, staring down at the forest below. Val winced. "Leora, please. If you keep leaning over like that, you'll fall."

A sly grin crept across Eino's face. He leaned back against the railing. "Your mother's right. Why, I haven't replaced these railings in—" His arms wheeled as he leaned back over the railing. With the skill of a showman, he leaned forward, and then back again, drawing out the tension of his fall. "Whoa...whoa!"

Val gasped. Joren froze. Leora reached for Eino. He leaned back farther, tumbling right over the railing. He yelled as he flipped in the air, gathering aura around his feet. As he hit the side of the inn's barrier, he slid down and used his momentum to slingshot himself up the other side. Skating back down, he bounced himself back up the side of the barrier and onto the promenade.

"Ta-dah!" He spread his arms wide and took a bow. It was a trick he'd taught himself to do while performing maintenance on *The Sun Chaser*. In his first few weeks on the job, he and Pavan were ordered to pluck scramblers out of the ship's paddle. Pavan finished his section first, then pulled up the rope ladder, trapping Eino at the bottom of the wheel well. Rather than waiting around for him to finish laughing, Eino used the aura from the paddle to help him propel himself back up to the deck. He'd then made sure to deliver a thunderous slap to his future friend's face.

"That was amazing." Leora clapped, a smile lighting up her face. "Do it again!"

"No!" Val slumped in her chair, looking about ready to faint. "Do not!"

Joren had been just as shocked as Val the first time he'd seen Eino's trick, but this time he just shook his head, the faintest smile tugging on his lips. He headed down the bridge to his cabin.

"How did you do that?" Leora asked.

"Can't reveal all my secrets," said Eino with a wink, "but the barrier's been tuned to make sure nobody can fall through, so you can put any fears about falling out of the sky to rest."

"I want to try!" She slapped one hand down on the railing and jumped right over. Val screamed and shot forward off her chair. Leora plummeted, making contact with the barrier and sliding sideways along its edge. Her momentum carried her up the other side, but not high enough to jump over to the promenade. She slid back down, settling at the bottom.

Catching them staring down at her, she gave them an embarrassed smile, followed by a tiny wave.

Eino laughed. "Stay there. I'll get you."

Val leaned her head against the railing. She pressed a hand to her cheek. "This inn will surely be the death of me."

He climbed into the basket. His fingers brushed over the aurastone in his necklace, but the basket refused to move. He imbued the stone with a little more of his aura, but still the basket remained in place. Eino scratched his head, then tried the stone in the basket's control pillar. This time it lowered, shuddering as it descended. He helped Leora inside, and again the basket shuddered as it returned them to the promenade.

Neither Val nor Leora seemed to pay much attention to the basket's slow performance. Eino was relieved that he wouldn't need to think of an excuse to allay their fears. Still, he was determined to resolve the issue, and to do so as quickly and quietly as possible.

He wanted to believe that there was some minor issue with the basket that he'd be able to fix quickly, but with how much faster the inn had been drifting lately, he couldn't help but feel the two issues were somehow related. Maybe there was something wrong with his core.

The inn was still a long way from the auramancer's shop in Sanvileau, so professional help would have to wait a while. For now, he'd just have to check on the core again tonight. Drawing out some of the excess aura seemed to have worked last time, so doing it again might solve these issues. It would have to do, he thought, because he couldn't afford to miss out on the scrambler harvest this year.

Despite the inconvenient situation, the thought of scrambler fishing put Eino in good spirits. Tomorrow, he'd have Joren all to himself as they pulled in nets full of the delicious fruits. A little help made the hard work much easier to handle, especially when his helper had such a handsome face. It'd be a great chance to get to know the man better, and possibly to convince him to stay aboard the inn a while longer. His heart fluttered at the idea.

10

THE NEXT MORNING, EINO helped Betta cook breakfast. He did his best to follow her instructions, learning everything he could about cooking from her before they ran out of time together. But even the simple porridge they were preparing proved a challenge as his distracted mind kept returning to the broken basket.

He'd inspected the core again last night, drawing some more aura out of it to stabilize its rotation. He wasn't sure what was causing the problem, but his quick fix seemed to be working. The basket was now working normally again, and the inn was now traveling at its usual pace. Inspecting and drawing aura out of the core would have to become part of his daily routine.

He grumbled. His chore list was already long, and once Betta left, it would grow even longer. He'd need to hire some help to get everything done. Either that or he'd need to replace his old, underpowered core. Something that could do more than just keep his inn afloat. Whatever he did, it would cost a lot of money. Money he didn't have.

But with scrambler season starting, great clusters of the fruits would soon fill the skies. Demand for scramblers was high, as the Sinian kingdoms and former Heralian League states both considered them a delicacy. They were even gaining popularity as far west as the Ahriqosai Empire. A good scrambler harvest could earn more in days than the Driftcap Inn pulled in for the entire year, and while hauling them in was always a challenge, this time he had help.

Betta squinted, watching the clouds through the window while she stirred the porridge. "Those aren't scramblers, are they? My eyesight ain't what it used to be."

"They sure are. I reckon it'll be a good haul this year."

Betta scoffed. "If them damn Sinian ships don't snatch 'em all up, that is." She shook her head. "We must have flown past three of them things since we got to Brumantis."

Eino waved a dismissive hand before returning to chopping up woodnuts. "If they've got a lick of sense about them, they'll keep them ships far away from the scramblers. It only takes a couple of them to gum up the paddle wheel." Eino remembered the difficulty of cleaning out the aura-collecting paddle wheels of *The Sun Chaser* during one fateful voyage to Porocar during scrambler season. The ship had been moored until mid-spring, so the captain granted the crew an extended shore leave. It was on that very vacation that Eino found the driftcap that would one day become his inn.

"You know, growing up back in Yel Mor, I always wondered why it got so cloudy this time of year." She shook her head and tasted the porridge, and then added a pinch of salt. "It's hard to believe it's been big clumps of scramblers this whole time."

Eino chuckled. "You said the same thing last year. You getting senile, you old goat?"

Betta smiled as she slapped him on the arm with her wooden spoon. "I'm just saying it's hard to believe some of the amazing things I've gotten to see from this place. Even things this close to home."

"You've only been up here a couple years. There's still a lot more to see, you know."

"You sound like Clofen. He always had that sense of adventure in him. I reckon that's why he was so eager to sign up for the Guard. Between you and me, I wish he'd have found himself a driftcap to float around on rather than carting himself all the way off to Heralia." She shot Eino a wink. "Even if it meant he started wearing a big ol' mushroom hat like a coastie."

Eino laughed. "I got bad news for you. If he's been spending time with Heralians, he's gonna be a heck of a lot coastier than me!" He held onto the moment with her. Knowing their days together were winding down made him want to tuck these memories away to keep forever.

She took the porridge off of the burner. "I think you two would get along real nice."

He smirked. "Of course we would. It's my job to get along with people."

"Oh, you know what I mean," she said with a smile. "So you've gotta promise you'll come visit us."

Eino brushed his nails against his coat. He put on a mocking north Porocari accent, annunciating his words and trilling his R's. "Oh, I don't know, my dear. You know how us coasties are. Always too busy for such frivolity."

Betta let out a hearty laugh. "Suit yourself, Mr. Grand Duke. Dilgaa knows this ol' mountain goat is ready to settle down again."

Eino smiled, but he couldn't relate. His family home had been nothing like this. With eight other siblings and dozens of cousins, he felt completely lost in the crowd all too often. His parents called him by one of his brothers' names more often than his own, and at one festival he'd mistaken one of his aunts for his own mother. They always felt more like a chaotic mob than a family, and he was half convinced they never even noticed he left. If he ever returned, would anyone recognize him? Or had they already forgotten about him?

Things were different ever since he'd taken to the skies. He liked to think getting away from the bustle of his old home helped him find his confidence. As a child, he'd been shy and quiet, but aboard *The Sun Chaser* he learned how to use his natural charms for both trade and for his love life. By the time he'd opened The Driftcap Inn, Eino the Wanderer was completely unrecognizable from the meek little boy he used to be.

"Oh, and by the way," Eino said smugly, "you owe me a whole plate of longberry sweet rolls."

"And just how do you figure that?"

He puffed out his chest. "On account of our good friend Mr. Joren telling me his occupation."

"You actually got that boy to talk?" She tossed a hand towel onto her shoulder.

"Sure did. And, like I told you, he is indeed an apothecary. Told me so himself."

Betta smirked. "Well, every good smuggler needs a cover story."

"You're not trying to back out of our little wager now, are you?"

"As I recall, you were the only one doing any wagering." She chuckled as she waved a finger at him. "But I'll tell you what. I'll make up a batch of sweet rolls anyhow, and I'll even show you how to make them."

Eino licked his lips. "My mouth's already watering."

"Alright, but you'd better focus on breakfast first. Porridge is ready." Betta took the pot of porridge off of the stove and shoved it into Eino's hands.

Val and Leora were already in the dining area, both of them looking at a map of Itharos on the wall. Val pointed out places on the map to her daughter.

Leora perked up when she spotted Eino. "Hiya, Mr. Innkeeper!"

"Hey there, little lady." Eino plopped the pot of porridge down on the table. "Whatcha looking at there?"

"Mama was—"

"I was showing her where we are heading," interrupted Val, setting her hand on Leora's shoulder. Her stiff smile did nothing to mask her defensive body language.

"Here. Let me show you something." Eino strutted over to the map, undeterred by Val. He drew a tiny droplet of his aura into his finger and tapped it against the map. At his touch, a route on the map began to glow. "See that? That's the path we're taking."

Leora eyed the glowing route with mild interest. Her lack of enthusiasm surprised Eino. Typically, children were more impressed by auramancy, even for a simple spell like this. He couldn't help but feel a little crestfallen.

She traced the route with her finger. "Will we fly past where you're from?" She put an odd emphasis on the word "you're."

"No, I'm from somewhere I know you ain't never heard of," said Eino, tapping on a village at the western foothills of Porocar. "It's this tiny little village right here. Tetechetech."

"Tetchet...techetet... That is hard to say." Leora tried a few times to pronounce the name before running her finger under the writing on the map, sounding it out as she did so. "Te-te-che-tech."

Eino raised an eyebrow. He'd only recently learned the basics of reading Aralic High Script while trying to court a higher-class clientele. Only a few of his guests were literate, and of those who were, few bothered to learn such an archaic writing system. He'd never seen anyone read the map so effortlessly, let alone a child.

"Come now, Leora. Do not bother our host." Val picked her seat at the round table, sitting with her back ramrod straight. She set her hands on her lap as if expecting a formal dinner service.

"We ain't too fancy with our meals here. Everything is served family-style." Eino spooned out a bowl of porridge for each of them. "Course, that means you can fix it up the way you like. Berries, nuts, mushrooms. Take your pick."

Right on time, Betta entered with the tray of toppings, setting it in the middle of the table.

Val balked at his suggestions. "Mushrooms, you say?"

It was a widespread stereotype that the Porocari people, particularly those from the southern mountains, ate nothing but mushrooms. Eino relished playing into the stereotype with guests to see their reactions. "Oh sure! We'll eat them with just about everything. Soups, salads, desserts. Why, sometimes we'll even mash them up and drink them!"

"Drink them?" Leora scrunched up her nose in disgust, eying her water with suspicion.

He chuckled to himself. "Only on special occasions."

"Eino, quit teasing our guests." Betta shook her head and turned to Val. "I swear you can't trust a word out of this boy's lips."

"So I have noticed," she muttered.

Leora cast a wary eye at the tray of toppings. "Which ones are the mushrooms? I don't think I want those."

"Ain't none of them are, sweet pea," Betta said with a chuckle before pointing out each of the toppings. "We've got longberries, pleniberries, chopped woodnuts, fresh poutamme, and ground spices."

Val stared at all the topping options. She reached for one, then changed her mind. Her hand hovered in the air and she nibbled her bottom lip, uncertainty growing on her veiled face. The choices seemed to overwhelm her. Or perhaps she was simply not accustomed to serving herself, Eino thought.

Noticing her hesitation, Betta sat next to her and scooped herself a bowl. "Personally, I think the best combination is fruit with warm spices, or berries with milk." She topped off her bowl with the poutamme and a generous sprinkle of the spice. Val followed suit, and Leora followed after, mirroring her mother's choices.

"So," said Eino, "You two are heading for Muna, right?"

"We are," said Val flatly.

"Oh, it's a gorgeous city. Real nice." said Eino. He was used to being the one to carry a conversation, but the stern woman gave him little to work with. "King Chandarre's really built the place up recently."

"Yeah! And Mama's gonna be a teacher at the Royal Academy!" said Leora. At her outburst, the girl's mother cast her a stern glance, her gaze piercing even from behind her veil. The girl shrank and resumed poking at her porridge.

"A teacher huh," said Eino, desperate to keep the conversation going. "Do you mind me asking what you teach?"

"I do."

An uncomfortable silence set in as they ate, with the slurping of porridge and the clacking of wooden spoons against bowls the only sounds in the room. The ever-charming Eino found himself at a loss for conversation. He was starting to unravel the mystery of why a Cacosshian mother and daughter were taking such a long journey unaccompanied, but it was clear he wasn't going to get much more information out of Val today.

Perhaps she was a Deka'arist nun who had violated her vows, or a woman exiled for having a child out of wedlock. Maybe she was a refugee from the skirmishes in one of the war-torn northern Cacosshian kingdoms. She could even be a smuggler, using her daughter to help move contraband. His head swam with possibilities, but he couldn't find a good way to broach the topic, or any topic for that matter, in the crushing, oppressive silence.

At last, it was Leora who broke the ice. "Hey, Mr. Innkeeper?"

"No need to be so formal. You can call me Eino, you know."

"Alright, Mr. Eino," she replied. "So, um. Are you gonna slide around the barrier again today?"

"I've got a busy day ahead of me. Not much time for foolin' around." He leaned over and winked at her. "But I just might."

"Then um…" She stirred the toppings around in her porridge. "… could you show me how to do your trick?"

Eino managed to hold on to his smile, but his eyes went wide. "Oh, I don't know if your mother would like that." He grimaced as he turned to face Val.

Leora's question still hung in the air while Val finished chewing her delicate spoonful of porridge. To his surprise, the woman's dour expression had softened. "Your barrier seems adequate to ensure her safety. I would allow her to learn, but only if it does not interfere with your usual activities. Neither I nor my daughter wish to impose upon you."

"Oh, it's no imposition. Cast me, it sounds like a lot of fun!"

Leora wiggled in excitement, barely able to stay seated. "Yes!"

"After breakfast, of course. Please finish your porridge, Leora." Val continued taking dainty spoonfuls of her food, one hand on her lap at all times. Leora, however, maintained no such sense of decorum, grabbing her bowl and shoveling the porridge into her mouth. She had just about finished when Joren stepped into the room.

He lingered in the doorway, watching them. When he glanced back at his cabin as if debating on leaving, Eino ladled another bowl and held it out toward him. "Come get some breakfast. Busy day ahead of us."

"I'm not hungry. Thank you." Despite his words, his eyes lingered on the bowl.

Eino shook his head and smiled. He'd seen Joren top his porridge with spices and woodnuts the last time they'd served it, so he quickly sprinkled some on and pushed the bowl into Joren's hands. "Eat. It'll be tough fishing on an empty stomach."

Joren didn't take the bowl right away. "Fishing. Yes. When do we start?"

"Soon as you're ready, I suppose."

He nodded and wrapped his hands around the bowl. "Then I will get ready at once. Please excuse me." With that, he turned and headed back out the door, the bowl still in his hand.

"Skittish as a city cat," said Eino under his breath, trying to keep his disappointment off his face. Then again, it had taken since the start of winter for him to earn the smallest bit of Joren's trust. He shouldn't have expected the man to dine with two complete strangers yet.

"Can I have another bowl?" asked Leora. She caught her mother's harsh gaze before adding, "Please?"

"Of course you can, sweet pea," Betta said. She looked down the table toward Val. "And how's about I make you ladies a fresh pot of tea after breakfast? I tell you there ain't nothing like having a cup out on the promenade while you wait for the morning to warm up."

"That sounds lovely," Val said.

"Yeah!" Leora made herself a second bowl, this time adding some of everything. "I like seeing the towns below us. All the buildings look so cute. Just like my old dollhouses."

Once again, Eino raised his eyebrow. He'd passed by shops in some of the larger towns and capitals on his journeys. No matter where he went, there was always a toyshop with a dollhouse on display, and it was never cheap.

After they'd all finished, Eino helped Betta carry the dishes into the kitchen. While she put a kettle on to boil, Eino turned from the dish tub and almost knocked right into Joren.

The man stepped back. "Sorry." He held out his bowl, now empty despite him being 'not hungry'.

Eino chuckled to himself and tossed it in with the others. "No worries. You're so quiet I didn't hear you come in."

"Sorry. I don't mean to be quiet." Joren gave him a nervous laugh. He then pulled a small bottle out of his pocket. "Oh, and here's the burn salve you asked for. You only need a small amount. The ingredients I've collected from your inn have a very potent aura."

"Thanks. I'm sure it'll get good use soon." He sat it up on a shelf beside the stove. "But alright. You ready to go fishing?"

Joren rubbed the side of his arm. "I'm not sure. I've never caught anything in the sky before."

"It's like fishing in water. Strak, it's even easier." He turned back to Betta. "You got everything under control in here?"

"Sure do. You boys have fun up there," she said, smirking as her gaze slid to Joren, and then back to Eino. "Not too much fun, though."

"Yes, ma'am." He led Joren out to the common room, pretending not to notice her smirk. As hard as he tried to keep his relationships away from Betta, their time living in close quarters meant she'd caught on to his tastes.

"What did she mean by that?" asked Joren.

"Oh nothing. Just a little joke, I reckon," said Eino, biting his tongue. "See, grabbing scramblers ain't exactly exciting. It's a lot like regular fishing. Lots of waiting around. I'd grab something to pass the time if I were you."

"I thought that might be the case." Joren patted his satchel. "I came prepared."

"Well, alright. Let's go wrangle us up some scramblers."

11

"Here, put these on," Eino said as he handed Joren a pair of old silver goggles that he'd been issued during his service with the Sinian Air Legion. "They ain't much, but they'll keep the worst of the suns' rays out of your eyes."

Joren slid them on. He fumbled with the straps a moment before managing to tighten them. "Is this good?"

Eino pulled his own goggles down. "Perfect! By Dilgaa, you look like an air legionary through and through." Though they obscured his eyes, the goggles highlighted his face, and looked rather dashing against Joren's stubbly beard. Eino was grateful that his own goggles made it harder to see that he was staring.

He led Joren up through his humble quarters to the roof hatch. He savored the intimacy of having him in his room once more, feigning clumsiness and bumping into him again and again in the narrow space. At last, he pushed the door open, and the two stepped out onto the roof.

Blue sat nestled against the garden fence, squawking at the men as they stepped out. Joren jumped, and Eino let out a chuckle, wagging a finger at the greatwing. "Settle down there, missy."

From behind them came a lower, deeper squawk and the sound of beating wings. Another crested greatwing swooped down and positioned itself between the men and Blue.

Joren yelped. "Another one?"

Eino patted him on the shoulder. "Oh, don't mind him. That there's Red. He's Blue's mate," said Eino. He narrowed his eyes at the wad of hay in the creature's beak. "What you got there, big fella?"

Red turned his head sideways, keeping his eye on the men and flashing his bright red crest. Without breaking his gaze, he quickly stuffed the wad of hay beneath Blue, then resumed his defensive stance.

"You building a nest?" Eino asked the greatwing. "Well, good on you for making an honest lady out of Blue here."

Red nestled down beside Blue and the two greatwings watched the men as they made their way toward the longberry tree at the back of the inn. Eino stopped near the edge of the roof.

"Please tell me you're not going to jump off again." Joren took a nervous step back.

Eino laughed. "Nah, it ain't as fun once you know the trick. Besides, we've got work to do." He pointed at the skyline. "See all those clouds of scramblers coming? The wind is in our favor, so we gotta work fast."

"What do we need to do?"

He pointed down at the rolled up netting. "Take an end. It goes quicker if we unroll it together. And keep an eye on the ladies back there." He gestured with his thumb over his shoulder toward the wool hens clustered together beside the chimney. "Ol' Fluffy just loves getting her legs caught in the net."

As they rolled out the net, the aurastones attached to the ends gave off a slight glow, floating and bobbing in the air just ahead of the inn. Fully unfurled, the net stretched wide enough to extend beyond both cabins on opposite ends of the main driftcap, and down far enough to reach just a few handwidths beyond the promenade. Once they finished, Eino surveyed their work. He smiled and took a seat on the spongy mushroom cap. He couldn't remember a time he'd finished so quickly before.

"That's the biggest net I've ever seen," said Joren, taking a seat beside him. "How'd you even find one this size?"

"I cobbled it together from a few different nets. One of my guests was a fisherman, and when he couldn't afford the rest of his stay, he showed me how to splice them together." Eino shifted closer to Joren and pointed to one corner of the net. "See how the ropes are all frayed on that side? That's the end I did."

Joren pulled his goggles to his forehead and rubbed his eyes. "It is most peculiar."

"Hey now, my splicing ain't that bad. She might not look pretty, but she's held together just fine for a couple of years now."

"No, no. Not the net," Joren stammered, holding up his hands. "I was talking about you."

"You're saying I'm peculiar?" Eino leaned back and smiled.

Joren's eyes went wide as realization dawned on his face. "Sorry! No. What I mean to say is—" He squirmed, which only made Eino's mischievous grin wider. Joren paused a moment and collected himself, speaking slowly and carefully. "—is that I'm glad I'm not the first guest of yours who couldn't afford to pay you, and I'm very grateful that you are willing to trade room and board for help around your inn. Not everyone is so generous."

"Generous?" Eino snorted. "I wouldn't exactly say I'm being generous here. That fisherman had to work himself to the bone stitching that whole net together." He gave Joren's arm a playful jab. "And you're gonna have to work just as hard."

"Even so, I am grateful." Joren rubbed his arm and bowed his head.

"Well, what can I say? Good people are worth more than money to me. Folks like you and Betta…" He trailed off, gazing out at the net. The pangs of her upcoming departure still weighed heavily on him.

Joren grimaced. "Yes, but she's different."

"How do you figure? Because she's Porocari?"

"No, no," said Joren, reaching up to scratch the back of his neck. "She's your mother, isn't she?"

Eino sat in shock for a beat, then burst out in a loud, wheezing laugh. "Dilgaa forbid!"

"B-but you two are so close. I always thought that…" He trailed off, wearing a confused expression on his face. As he pondered, his lip curled. "Wait. you two aren't—"

"No! Don't even finish that thought." Eino waved his hands defensively. "She ain't family, and she sure ain't nothing else. She's just my cook."

"I see." Joren chewed his lip. "Sorry. I'm not very good at reading people."

"No need to apologize. We've been up here together so long she does feel a bit like family sometimes. I can see how you might think that way."

"If you don't mind my asking, how'd she come to join you?" Joren adjusted his goggles as he watched Eino.

"Back when I first met her, she was in small Sinian town just west of the border selling Porocari street food. The locals didn't care for it, but damn if those weren't the best fried mushroom fritters I ever had." Eino licked his lips at the memory of the warm, flavorful mushrooms coated in crispy seasoned breading. "Told her she could stay at my inn if she kept making food like that. She's been with me ever since."

As Eino spoke, Joren watched him in a way that made it feel like he was giving each word his full attention. He relished that attention, but he found himself unable to return the courtesy, too distracted by the motion of the man's full lips as he spoke. "I'm glad you have someone like her around to help you."

Eino frowned, heaving a deep sigh. "Don't be too glad. She'll be leaving soon to go live with her son once we get to Porocar. She's been spoiling me with all the work she does around here. It's going to be hard running things without her."

Joren hesitantly patted Eino's shoulder. "I'm sorry. She seems nice." He paused, then withdrew his hand as his fingers started twitching. "I like her cooking." The last statement came out sounding more like a question, as if he wasn't sure what words of comfort to offer.

Eino chuckled. He found Joren's awkwardness charming. "You don't gotta lie. I know you ain't too wild about Porocari cooking."

"No, I mean it! The food is very good!" he said earnestly. His gaze drifted downward. "But the mushrooms...I suppose I haven't developed a taste for them."

"Some folks say they're an acquired taste." Eino leaned in a little closer. "But you stay on this inn long enough, I reckon you'll get a taste for all things Porocari."

Eino's eyes were locked on Joren's as he met his gaze. For once, the shy Sinian didn't flinch away. He finally had a chance to drink in the full richness of his deep brown eyes, the light of the suns making them appear rimmed with gold. They were like two warm cups of cacao flecked with intoxicating spices. Joren shifted closer, their knees touching.

Slowly, Joren's gaze drifted to the side of Eino's head. He pulled his goggles back down and craned his neck to look behind him. "What is that?"

Eino turned around, his jaw clenched in anger at whatever had interrupted his intimate moment. But once his eyes landed on the white hull of an airship peeking out from behind a cloud, he let out a gasp.

Just like the *Ray of Soleivar* back in Nephene, the ship bore an elaborate golden filigree and magenta banners with the heraldry of King Chandarre. Its feathersteel panels, however, had grayed with age, and even though the ship was distant in the sky, a few deep scratches and scars were still visible in its hull. With a silhouette much bigger and bulkier than any of the other ships he'd seen in the skies above Brumantis, there was no mistaking the ship's identity.

"Well, cast me to the Wynds," said Eino, his voice almost reverent. "If it ain't *The Sun Chaser* itself."

"That's a Sinian ship, isn't it?" Joren bit his lip and rolled a strand of hair between his fingers, his full attention on the airship.

"Oh, she ain't just any old Sinian airship. That there was my ship. And she looks just as beautiful as the day I first set eyes on her."

"What's that flashing light?" asked Joren. He stole a quick glance at the hatch down to Eino's quarters.

A bright light flashed from the ship's helm, pulling Eino out of his nostalgic daze. "I think she's trying to communicate with us."

Eino drew a spyglass out of his jacket and watched the flickering pattern of blues, purples, and reds. It was a language which both air and sea vessels used to communicate over long distances, with the color and pattern of each flash corresponding to a different character of Sindhic glyph writing. Eino spelled it out under his breath, "New...boy...looks...cute." He let out a sound halfway between a laugh and a grunt. "Bashann must be on duty."

"Who?"

"Just an old friend," said Eino. He didn't feel it was necessary to tell Joren that it was a former lover flashing the message to him. Instead, he simply stood up and reached into his jacket, producing a small cylinder with an aurastone embedded in one end. With a tug of the handle, it telescoped into a staff slightly taller than himself. He set the end down on the mushroom and flashed out his response, twisting and bumping the staff in a complex pattern that made him look like a bad dancer. "Hands...off."

After a moment, another series of flashes came from *The Sun Chaser* that spelled out "Room...for...one...more?"

Joren looked back and forth between Eino and the airship, a light tremor shaking his voice. "There isn't a problem, is there?"

Eino snorted, grateful that Joren couldn't understand the signals. "Just a little inside joke. Here, let's get out of the sun." With a chuckle, Eino made a rude gesture to his old ship, then guided Joren to the shade of the longberry tree, away from Bashann's prying gaze.

Joren followed behind Eino, his gaze landing on the net. A few scramblers floating ahead of the cloud cluster got caught in the net, their streamers undulating in the wind. "Oh! Looks like we have a few scramblers already. Should we haul them in now?"

"Nope. We'll wait for more of them to get stuck first." Eino remained seated, pulling a small knife and a block of wood from his pockets. "You brought something to do, right?"

Joren nodded, pulling his satchel off of his shoulder and setting it beside Eino. He pulled out a notebook and pen and made his way to the garden.

Eino shook his head. Even when there was nothing to do but wait, Joren never seemed to relax. He was constantly moving around and keeping busy, plucking leaves and roots from the garden and scrawling in his notebook. Probably to distract him from his fear of heights, Eino thought.

As he whittled a new Dilgaa idol from the wood, he couldn't help but notice Joren's open satchel. His curiosity got the better of him, and when he was sure Joren wasn't looking, he tugged on the flap and peeked inside. There he caught the glossy white glint of seashell and recognized the musical instrument inside.

"I don't mean to pry," started Eino, "but that wouldn't happen to be a garanelle in your satchel, would it?"

Joren glanced over his shoulder, startled. He glanced to the side. "Sorry. I didn't realize that was still in there."

"Ain't nothing to be sorry about. I just didn't realize you played."

He chewed his lower lip. "I don't really play. Not anymore."

"Well then, now's as good a time as any to start back up." Eino put his knife and wood block back into his pocket and produced his tarnaaq. "We could play together."

The shyness on Joren's face melted away as the instrument caught his attention. "I've never seen a garanelle like that before."

"It's called a tarnaaq. Got it while I was traveling in Ahriqos." He offered the small black pipe to Joren. "Basically, it's the same thing, just a bit smaller. Not as many notes. Much better for traveling than that thing." Eino pointed to Joren's satchel.

"Maybe you're right, but I just can't bring myself to part with it." Joren pulled out the bulky pipe. It was hewn from a massive seashell with a smaller shell carefully woven into its spiral opening. The horn produced a mellow and resonant sound, and by twisting the shells together, the pitch could be adjusted.

"Well, if it means that much to you, then don't go letting that thing go to waste." He smiled brightly and patted the spot next to him. It had been a long time since he'd played music with someone else on the inn. "It'll take the rest of the scramblers a few minutes to reach us yet. Plenty of time for a song or two. No audience to worry about neither. Just us and the birds."

Joren sat about an arm's length away from Eino, nervously fiddling with his garanelle. "So...how should we start?"

Eino tapped his mouthpiece against his lips and considered all the songs he knew. "Let's do something simple like...*Nadea and Chilbre.*"

Joren nodded. "I'll follow your lead."

Eino gave a sly grin as he started the slow ballad. The song was played in taverns across Sinia, telling the tragic tale of two lovers separated by the sea. Even without lyrics, there was a haunting quality to the sound of the tarnaaq that brought the lovers' longing to life.

A breath later, Joren joined in. At first, his playing came out as a loud, awkward squawk that made Eino wince. Taking a breath and collecting himself, he started again, and this time, he produced a low, gentle bass. Following Eino's lead, he produced a beautiful harmony, turning the ballad's tragic sound into something that sounded hopeful.

Eino watched Joren as he played. He'd always found playing music to be a relaxing activity, both for him and his guests. Joren, however, seemed to be concentrating intently as he played, his gaze fixed on his fingers despite the song's simple melody. Even more curious was how the man hadn't removed his gloves before starting.

As the melody swelled, Joren missed a note. Eino watched him out of the corner of his eye. Once more, Joren reached for the troublesome note, and once again he missed it. He abruptly stopped playing and cursed under his breath.

"Everything alright?" asked Eino.

"Yes. Just a little out of practice." Joren shook his hand and stretched out his fingers. He looked up sheepishly at Eino. "Sorry. I ruined the song."

"The audience don't mind too much," said Eino, chuckling as he gestured to the wool hens. "And there ain't no shame in being a little rusty. Might help if you took off your gloves though—"

"No!" Joren recoiled, then collected himself, squeezing his gloved hands. "Sorry. It's just an old injury."

Eino raised an eyebrow. It was an odd reaction, but he decided not to push further. Instead he offered a smile. "You know, you apologize a lot when you ain't done nothing wrong."

"Sorry," said Joren. Realizing what he'd just said, he looked down and bit his lip.

Eino laughed. "Anyways, if your hand ain't letting you hit that high note, maybe you should try the tarnaaq." He offered Joren his instrument. "Plays just about the same, and it's small enough that you won't need to stretch to hit that note."

Hesitantly, Joren took the tarnaaq, his fingers finding their placement. "This does feel a bit more manageable."

"How about we trade for the next song?" Eino held out his hand for the garanelle. "I'm thinking something more upbeat. Like *My Light*."

"I suppose," said Joren, reluctantly offering his instrument, "but that song isn't quite the same without someone to sing it."

Eino grinned. "Well, I've got just the thing." He reached into his jacket, patting around his pockets before retrieving a small wooden tube.

"What is it?"

"Our accompaniment." Eino drew the tube to his lips and blew into it. Then, with a droplet of his aura, a rune inscribed in the tube began to glow, and even as Eino pulled it from his lips, air continued to flow through the tube. He set it on the mouthpiece of the garanelle, and the instrument let out a constant low droning sound.

Joren laughed. "Is there anything you don't have in that jacket?"

"Ain't no such thing as being too prepared," said Eino with a smirk. With a quick tempo and a bright melody, Eino began. The song was about a man comparing his lover's beauty to the light of the Sinian sun god, Soleivar, and though it was regarded as sappy and saccharine, the song was still a beloved favorite at taverns Eino visited. Crowds loved a dramatic, over-the-top performance, and Eino had never been one to disappoint.

The more they played, the more Joren seemed to relax. Eino stole glances at him, and found him watching back as he played. Even once they'd finished the song, the two just looked into one another's eyes for a long moment.

Eino's breath stuttered. Those warm eyes made him want to drown in Joren's attention. He wanted to kiss him. Badly. He'd sidled closer to him as they played, taking in the sweet aroma of herbs that clung to him. He leaned forward, pulled in by the man's intoxicating fragrance.

Then a scrambler roughly the size of his palm ran into the side of Eino's head. Its long, milky white tendrils flailed around, tangling themselves up in his unruly red hair.

From the side of the mushroom cap with the net came the sound of a girl giggling. "Oops! Sorry Mr. Eino!" Once more, she burst out laughing.

Eino sighed. With some difficulty, he untangled the scrambler from his hair, and tossed it downwind, its flapping tendrils sending the fruit on a wild trajectory. He looked over to see Leora climbing up the net. "And just what are you doing up here, little lady?"

"I heard pretty music, so I came to see where it was coming from. Was that you two playing?"

"Sure was." Eino kept a smile on his face, but inside he cursed the little girl for ruining his moment with Joren.

"Can you play some more?"

Eino glanced at the net. In the brief moment he and Joren had been playing, it had filled up with scramblers of several varieties. "Sorry, kid. We've got a harvest to haul in first."

"Aww..."

"But I reckon we might be able to get back to playing if we had a little help. Ain't that right, Joren?"

"What?" the man looked around in confusion, as if finally remembering where he was. "Oh. Yes."

The little girl giggled in excitement. "What can I do?"

"Just follow my lead." Eino gave a smirk. The girl had cost him a private moment with Joren, but by making her help collect scramblers, he'd have his revenge.

12

Leora squealed, sticking her tongue out in disgust. "Eww!"

"Aww, come on now, don't be shy," said Eino, a bright and mischievous grin on his face as he offered the scrambler to the girl, its thin streamers flapping around wildly. "You gotta take a bite out of the first one of the harvest. It's tradition!"

"I don't care if it's tradition! It's gross!"

"Ain't nothing gross about it. Scramblers are delicious. Especially when they're this fresh." Eino split the pod of the scrambler open, revealing the juicy yellow fruit inside pockmarked with tiny black seeds. He offered one half to Joren and the other to Leora. "Go on and take a bite."

The girl shrieked. "I'm not gonna eat an icky bug!"

"Scramblers ain't bugs, little lady. They're fruits. Or seeds maybe. I ain't really sure. Point is they're tasty."

The girl crossed her arms and shut her eyes tight. "You're lying."

"This time, he's telling the truth." Joren stepped forward. "Scramblers are the fruits of the bramblepine. At the start of spring, they release their pods into the air and they float across the sky until they find a place to land." He took a bite of his half of the fruit, slurping up the juices. "Mmm...I've never had them this fresh. They're so sweet."

Leora opened one eye, swayed by Joren's words. She hesitantly held out her hands to accept the fruit. Its flailing had slowed, but she still held it arms length, recoiling. "It's still squirming."

"Well, yeah. They're called 'scramblers' for a reason." Eino chuckled. "But the streamers settle down once they land."

Slowly, Leora leaned in and took a cautious bite of the scrambler. After a moment, her eyes lit up. "Mmm! It tastes like a star oyster."

Eino quirked an eyebrow. Star oysters were a kind of confection made from dried scrambler fruit. They'd gained popularity in places that were too far away to have easy access to fresh scramblers, but only among those rich enough to pay for such exotic ingredients.

The mystery of Leora and Val was coming together. He'd already guessed that they were from the upper echelons of society, perhaps even nobility. Now he knew that they had to have come from one of the northern Cacosshian kingdoms far from the scrambler harvests. Those closest to the Vinaterians. And to the fighting.

That must be why they were traveling alone, he thought. Leora's father had likely either run away or fallen in battle.

The girl wiped the juices of the scrambler off of her chin. "Can I have another?"

Eino laughed. "Maybe once we finish hauling in what we've caught. Let's get to work." He rolled up part of the net and showed them how to untangle the scramblers.

Joren's movements were stiff as he attempted to pull a scrambler out of the net. His grip slipped, and he jumped. The scrambler's streamers, free of the net, began flailing wildly in response, propelling it high into the air and out of reach. Joren grit his teeth, then looked down apologetically. "I'm so sorry."

"Don't feel bad. You'll always have a few that get away." Eino laughed. "You've just gotta move real slow when you're working with them. If you go too fast..." Eino took a hold of a scrambler and shook it, prompting its streamers to whip around this way and that.

"I'll be more careful," said Joren. "You won't lose any more of your harvest because of me. I promise."

"No need to be so dramatic." Eino waved a dismissive hand as he worked. "Fact is, there ain't hardly any competition up here. See, most ships don't even try to catch scramblers. They all sail too fast, and when these things sense motion, they go and scramble away. But my inn takes things nice and slow. I reckon we'll be able to fill all these here barrels by the end of the day."

Leora peered into the hole cut out of one of the barrels. "Won't they just flop right out of there?"

"Once they're out of the sunlight, they'll calm right down." Eino worked at a deliberate pace, pushing a pair of scramblers into the barrel. "Now come on, you two. Let's get this here net cleared out."

"Last one!" Leora called out as she pulled the final scrambler from the net.

"Nice work. Now let's cast the net again and wait for the next cloud."

Once more they unfurled the net, taking a seat and catching their breath beneath the longberry tree to escape the heat of the afternoon suns. He peered at the horizon, catching glimpses of *The Sun Chaser* through the clouds as it sailed away. A few greatwings and other smaller birds glided across the countryside below. A black wool hen wandered past them. She stopped to peck at the leaves poking through the fence. The gentle breeze went from chilly to pleasant as the heat of the day grew.

He stole glances at Joren, watching as he stared off into the horizon. He still wanted to kiss the man, but the right moment had passed. For now, sitting together while they watched the sky was cozy enough.

Joren looked up at the sky above. "I think another ship may be trying to speak with you."

Eino followed Joren's gaze. Through the low clouds, he saw a bright series of flashes in pink and green. As he tried to decipher it, the clouds parted, and he saw a broad aura stream cutting across the sky. Compared to the narrow aura streams the inn had been drifting along since Sinia, this one was like a mighty river. A few lesser streams branched off of it, shifting with the winds.

"That ain't a ship. That's a confluence." Both major and minor aura streams intersected all across the skies, creating confluences of aura. This one was one of the biggest, with several streams converging at a single point in the sky. Eino furrowed his brow. He hadn't expected to reach the confluence for another day or so. Was the inn speeding up again? Or had it ever really slowed down?

Joren's eyes followed Eino's. "Is that a problem?"

"Shouldn't be," said Eino, "but I might need your help to keep us in the right stream."

"I thought you said there was no way to steer the inn."

"Well, I wouldn't call it 'steering' exactly. It's more like politely suggesting which stream to take." Eino walked over to a glassy black stone embedded in the mushroom's cap. Imbuing his foot with a droplet of his aura, he kicked the stone. It glowed a pale green, then rose out from its hole. The stone was far longer than it first appeared, and as it emerged, a pair of carved wooden wings unfurled at its side, with a long rope running from each wing down into the hole. The stone floated up into the sky, tugging itself toward the aura stream above their heads.

"What is that thing?" asked Leora, her jaw slack.

"That there's my flight kite. Helps keep the inn from drifting too far from the streams. Here, take this." He gestured for Joren to take one of the ropes, then pointed to a thin and winding aura stream to their left. "We're gonna need to get this thing into that there stream."

"How do you know which one to take?" asked the girl.

Eino smirked as he tugged on the rope. "So, you see how that stream is flashing green, then pink?"

Leora squinted up at the sky. "Yeah?"

"But that one over there. It's flashing pink, then green," said Eino. "That's the one we wanna take."

"That doesn't make any sense."

"Sure it does! You just don't have the eye for it like I do." A smile tugged at the corners of his mouth.

Joren pulled at his end of the rope. "I believe he is teasing you, young lady."

"I know," said the girl, giggling. "Miss Betta says Mr. Eino is a big liar!"

"She said that? Well cast me!" Eino laughed. Together with Joren, the two men steered the kite into the correct aura stream. "Why, I ought to go down there and give that old goat a piece of my mind. Maybe I'll have her make me some hot cacao too for besmirching my good name."

Leora quirked her head. "What's a cacao?"

Eino gasped. "It's only the most delicious drink in all of Itharos. You mean to tell me you've never had it?"

The girl narrowed her eyes. "You're teasing me again, aren't you?"

"Some things you just don't joke about." Eino sprang to his feet. "Why don't you come with me and see for yourself?"

"Alright," said the girl, looking around, her eyes lighting on the hatch to Eino's room. "That's the way down, right?"

Eino grinned. "It is, but it ain't the way we're taking." He pointed over the edge of the mushroom.

Realization dawned on the girl's face. "You mean you're gonna show me how to do your trick?" She hopped excitedly, pointing to the barrier.

He nodded, turning to Joren. "You gonna come with?"

Joren's eyes went wide. "No, no. I think I'd much rather stay put, thank you."

"Then how about we bring you some cacao?" Eino sized up Joren, tapping his chin. "I bet you take yours spicy."

"A little spicy, yes." He smiled. "And a little sugar too, if it's not too much trouble."

"No trouble at all." He turned back to Leora. "Alright then, little lady. You ready to go sliding?"

"Yes!" She clenched her fists, bouncing in place. "Teach me, teach me, teach me!"

"Well, now hold on. First thing you've gotta do is hone your aura." Eino slapped his legs. "Now concentrate real hard and try to focus your aura into your feet."

The girl closed her eyes and breathed. A moment later, Eino could sense that her aura had shifted. "Like this?"

Eino blinked. "Uh, yeah. That's perfect." It wasn't a difficult feat of auramancy by any means, but he hadn't expected a child to manage the task so quickly. Even adults could struggle to control that much of their aura at once. Unless, of course, they'd trained.

"I think I get it," said the girl, studying the barrier. "So we just need to focus the aura into our feet to keep our balance, right?"

"That's part of it. But the real tricky part is timing your jump just right so you land where you want to." Eino held out his hand. "Why don't we go together for this first one?"

"Yeah!" The girl excitedly grabbed Eino's hand and followed him to the edge of the mushroom cap.

"Three...two...one...go!" Hand in hand with Leora, Eino took a running start and leapt from the rooftop. Together, they landed on the wispy barrier. Leora's feet slipped out from under her, but she quickly found her footing. She shrieked in excitement as their momentum carried them in a broad arc to the bottom of the barrier.

"Now focus, and push real hard!" said Eino. Tiny flecks of aura flashed at his feet as he glided up to the other side of the inn. To his surprise, the girl only struggled a moment before matching the pace of Eino's slide. He pointed to an open spot on the promenade. "And...jump!"

Concentrating his aura into the soles of his feet, he bent his knees and pushed off of the barrier. In an explosive burst, both he and Leora propelled themselves through the air and onto the promenade, landing with a loud thud.

The girl squealed in delight. "That was the most fun thing I've ever done! Can we do it again?"

"I reckon so," said Eino, leading her around the promenade toward the kitchen. "You know you're a quick learner. Pretty soon you'll be able to do it all by yours—"

As he rounded the corner, Eino met the gaze of Val. She sat on the promenade with an open sketchbook on her lap. Her sketch of the mushroom cabin had a blue streak across it, and the blue pastel stick in her hand had been snapped in two. Her veil did little to hide the wide-eyed, terrified expression on her face. He guessed she'd seen her daughter sliding along the barrier.

Eino clenched his hands sheepishly. "Sorry about that, Miss Val. Didn't mean to give you a scare like that."

Leora, who had been skipping happily beside Eino, stopped and hid behind his legs when she met her mother's gaze. From the woman's stern demeanor, he fully expected to hear some harsh words.

But to his surprise, her expression softened, and she smiled. "No need to apologize. Are you having fun, Leora?"

"Yes, Mama."

"Then that is all that matters." She glanced down at her drawing. "Though I am not certain I will be able to salvage this."

Betta emerged from the kitchen with two cups of tea. She handed one to Val and took a seat beside her. "Are you being a bad influence on that sweet little girl?"

"Not at all," said Eino, gasping in feigned offense, "We were just taking a little break from the harvest to get some cacao. Seems she's never had it before."

"Well then, you are in for a real treat, sweet pea." She looked up at Eino. "The kettle still has lots of hot water."

He smirked down at Betta. "You didn't drink through all our milk, did you?"

"There's plenty left in the ice box." She winked back at him. "Should be enough to make it coastie style like you like."

With a chuckle, he led Leora into the kitchen. She watched with wonder and excitement as Eino took a block of cacao from a jar and grated it into three cups.

"Mr. Eino, what's 'coastie style' mean?"

Eino snickered. "It means mean ol' Betta is teasing me."

"You and Miss Betta like to tease each other a lot. Do you two not like each other or something?"

"Course not. What makes you think that?"

"Then why are you so mean to each other?"

"Oh, we ain't trying to be mean," said Eino. He paused and thought for a moment. "I reckon it's just our little way of saying we care."

"Aww, that's so sweet!"

He waved the grater at her, his voice mockingly threatening. "But you breathe a word of that to her and I'll grate you up and sip you down like a cup of cacao."

The girl giggled. "Would that be 'coastie style?'"

Eino smiled and shook his head. "No, that would be traditional style. With all kinds of awful spices that'll burn your tongue clean off." He grabbed the jar of hot spice powder, offering it to the girl. "Take a whiff of that."

The girl leaned in and sniffed, then began coughing. "You actually drink that stuff?"

"I don't," said Eino. "See, I like my cacao to actually taste good. That's why I add milk and sugar instead. So which one do you want? Traditional? Or my way?"

"Your way for me, please," said Leora. "But Mr. Joren wanted his spicy, right?"

"He sure did. I'll leave out the grated little girl, though." A sly grin crept across his face. "Say, how about we play a little prank on Joren?"

The girl nodded, hiding her smile with her hands. With a villainous laugh, Eino scooped more than triple the usual amount of spice powder into Joren's cup. Part of him wondered if this prank might upset the man. After how close he'd come to him, he didn't want to return to the days of seeing Joren holed up in his cabin again. But then again, maybe a little playful joke would help to bring them closer together. Even if it didn't, part of him wanted to see Joren's face as the intense spice took hold of him. It was worth the risk, he thought. Just to be safe, he'd bring a small creamer full of milk to cool down the spice.

Together, they returned to the rooftop, taking the stairs and ladder back up despite Leora's pleas to slide back up the barrier. Joren was back in the garden, harvesting weeds and making notes in his journal.

Eino handed Joren his cup. "Here you go. Ought to be cool enough to drink now." He winked at Leora, and the girl stifled a giggle, taking a sip of her own cup.

"Thank you very much." Joren bowed his head and took the cup. He leaned down and sipped at it, smacking his lips. Eino waited, but the man offered no reaction to the intense spice. Instead, he took another sip. "This is very good. Absolutely perfect."

Leora looked up in awe, a little brown mustache of cacao on her upper lip. "Is the spicy one really that good?"

"It is," said Joren, offering the cup to the girl. "You can have some if you like."

"Oh, I wouldn't—"

Before he could even finish his warning, Leora had already brought the cup to her lips and slurped. To his surprise, the girl also offered no reaction. "Mmm! This one's even better! You've got to try it, Mr. Eino!" She thrust the cup into his hands.

Eino blinked. Had his spice powder really lost so much of its potency? It must have, if a young girl who'd never tried cacao in her life could handle it. Curiosity got the better of him, and Eino took a sip from the cup. It only took a moment for the spices to explode on his tongue, setting his whole mouth on fire. His face turned red from the heat.

Joren stifled a laugh, taking back his cup. "Are you alright?"

"Just dandy!" he replied, reverse breathing as he fumbled for the creamer. He pointed to Leora. "How'd you do that?"

The girl giggled. "I only pretended to drink it."

As the milk hit his lips, the intense spice subsided. "Well, cast me to the Wynds. You got me good, kid." Outsmarted by a child. He'd have hung his head in shame if he weren't so impressed.

"Just my little way of saying I care!"

"That's it, kid. I'm grating you into powder." He playfully chased the squealing girl all around the mushroom cap.

Joren smiled as he watched them play, sipping at his drink. He then turned his attention to the horizon, squinting at something in the distance. "Looks like another cloud is heading this way."

Eino stopped his chase to follow Joren's gaze. Another fluttering cloud of scramblers was drifting toward them. "It's your lucky day, little lady. Now finish your drink and get ready. We've got another batch of scramblers to haul in."

"Do we have time for another song?" asked Leora.

"A song? You want me to play a song with my lips on fire?"

"Please? Just a quick one."

"Well, I reckon we can do one more quick one," said Eino, tapping his chin. A glint of mischief twinkled in his eye. "Hey, Joren, do you know the tune to *Catch a Twetch*?"

Joren shook his head, giving Eino a stern look. "We can't do that one."

"Why not?" asked Leora. "And what's a twetch?"

Joren coughed, his eyes wide. Eino, on the other hand, let out a snickering laugh. "It's nothing. Just a name for a little bird." Eino did his best to stifle his giggling. A twetch was indeed a small bird with a shrill call native to the mountains of Porocar. It was also a particularly offensive pejorative for a nagging or abrasive woman.

"You can't say that. What if she repeats it to her mother?" Joren elbowed Eino in the ribs, then turned to the little girl. "You really shouldn't say that word. It's a very rude thing to say to a woman. Or a man. Anyone really." Joren rubbed the back of his neck, looking as though he wanted nothing more than to run back to his cabin.

"Oh," said Leora, a devious grin growing on her face. "So it's a bad word, huh?"

"Sure is," said Eino, "so I'll make you an offer. I'll sing it for you, but you've gotta promise not to tell your mom that Joren here has been teaching you bad words. Deal?"

"Me?" exclaimed Joren, his mouth hanging open in shock.

Leora giggled, clapping her hands to her cheeks. "Deal!"

Eino flashed a sly smile to Joren and activated the aura stone on his mouthpiece. He began the song very slowly, annunciating as he sang. "Can you catch and teach a twitchy twetch to etch Tetechetech? I can catch and teach a twitchy twetch to etch Tetechetech!"

Joren shook his head and smiled, joining in the tune. Eino repeated the tongue-twisting lyrics, faster and faster each time. Leora clapped and giggled along until at last Eino could no longer keep up, spouting gibberish and laughing, bringing the song to a stop.

"I want to try now," said Leora, bouncing with excitement. She stammered her way through the tongue twister as a warmup. "Alright, I'm ready!"

"Don't you worry, little lady. You'll get your chance." Eino regained his composure and pointed to the skies behind them. "But the next scrambler cloud's almost ready. Let's get to work."

13

Joren fidgeted as they rode the basket down toward Cachevermal, a small town on the eastern coast of Brumantis. He stood still, hands clinging to the side of the basket with his eyes shut. For anyone else, Eino would have taken this opportunity to tease them by rocking the basket. But for Joren, he just patted him on the shoulder. "Need some briskweed?"

"Brought my own," said Joren, chewing on a mouthful of the green leaves as he spoke. At his feet were a fishing pole and an empty basket.

Eino laughed and slapped him on the back. "Good, because I need you in good shape if you're gonna be catching us dinner."

They landed in a clearing just outside of a town. It was an unremarkable area, with the same farms and palm orchards along its outskirts as any other Brumanti town. Still, it offered some opportunity for trade, and there were a few untamed groves that might offer decent foraging.

Joren opened one eye first, then the other, letting out a heavy sigh as he stepped out of the basket. "I just hope the fish here are biting more than they were in Nephene." He adjusted the straps of his travel pack.

"Well, if you don't catch anything, don't bother comin' back."

Joren gave a look of hurt shock before catching Eino's grin. "Please don't joke like that." He turned his attention to the tree line as he pulled his hair into a messy bun.

"Oh, don't you fret. I'm sure you'll fill up your whole basket. We'll have plenty to eat tonight and a bunch left over to smoke." Having fresh fish to smoke would please Betta.

"I hope you're right. But if I don't?" That anxious look was back. His shoulders hunched against the breeze.

Eino rubbed the man's shoulder. "Then we'll have scramblers for dinner and you can help me catch more."

Joren let out a deep breath. "I'll do my best." He headed into a palm grove, steering clear of a person lounging in the shade of a tree.

Eino smiled as he watched him leave. Ever since they'd fished for scramblers together, he found it hard to take his eyes off of the man. He'd come so tantalizingly close to kissing him that day, and now he latched onto any excuse to be closer to him.

It was a giddy infatuation he hadn't felt in years. Harvesting vegetables and herbs from the garden wasn't a chore as long as Joren was around. Even sharing breakfast with him that morning had been exciting.

Eino climbed out of the basket. Maybe as he was foraging for fruits and mushrooms around the grottoes, he'd bump into Joren at a pond. A nice romantic, scenic pond...

"You there." Eino had been so focused on Joren that he paid no attention to the woman in the shade. He hadn't noticed her standing, stretching, and approaching the basket. She stood head and shoulders above Eino, sunlight glinting off of her ornate golden armor. From the silken magenta mantle she wore to the heavy broach bearing the crest of her order, there could be no mistaking it. She was a Sinian knight.

The orders of Sinian knights were ancient institutions, some of them claiming to trace their foundings back over a thousand years. Their authority was on par with some kingdoms, and as he'd seen in his dealings with the knights while serving aboard *The Sun Chaser*, they made sure that everybody knew it. His crew often mocked them for their pretentious and demanding personalities, but never to the knights' faces.

"You are Eino the Wanderer, are you not?" said the knight, leering over Eino.

No good would come of this, thought Eino. "Nope. Never heard of him."

She gave him a fake laugh. "Amusing. But you're not quite as clever as I was told." She stroked her chin, her head tilting up toward the inn. "It seems the diviners were right. I'd find the one I'm seeking here."

He looked her up and down. "And just who, might I ask, is seeking Eino the Wanderer?"

She stood tall, pounding her chest beneath her broach. "I am Revna of Vilbar, Order of the Golden Sunshrike, loyal knight and servant to his majesty, Chandarre, King of Kings. And by that authority, I demand passage on your inn."

Eino snorted. "You're a long way from Sinia to be making demands like that, missy. Besides, this ain't one of my scheduled stops. Now if you'd like to book a stay at the Driftcap Inn, there will be a pickup in the Cachevermal market square in a few hours—"

"You test my patience, Porocari. This is a matter of Sinian security. You will take me to your inn. Now." She placed her hand on the hilt of the sword she wore on her hip. "Do I make myself clear?"

"Now you listen good." Eino gritted his teeth. He never responded well to demands from authority figures, least of all when they involved his inn. He maintained his composure, but there was no masking the venom in his words. "This here basket is keyed to my aura. So don't nobody get into my inn without my say so. And I ain't the type to scare easy. Do I make myself clear?"

"Your courage is admirable." Revna relaxed the hand on her sword. Her sharp smile looked as threatening as her blade. "Rest assured that the Order will compensate you well for your assistance."

Eino weighed his options. Even if they were within Sinia's borders, he had the right to refuse her service. But for as irritating as the knights were to deal with, they never acted without purpose, and they never stopped pursuing a target. It didn't seem like she was coming for Eino's head today, but she might be tomorrow if he refused her now. For the next few weeks, the inn would be drifting over open water, and he didn't want to miss another opportunity to spend time with Joren on land where he wasn't as anxious.

"Alright then. It's 60 jingles a week. And that's in Kingdom dhareng, not league coin." The fee was more than triple his usual rate, but he could tell she'd be trouble, and if he couldn't scare her away with the price, he'd at least make taking her on worth his while.

"My word on behalf of my order is payment enough." She turned up her nose and stepped into the basket.

"Nuh uh. Nobody gets a free ride. I don't care if you're Chandarre himself." He held out his hand. "Now, are you gonna keep standin' around or what? I thought this was a matter of 'Sinian security.'"

"Indeed, it is." Revna scrunched up her nose and reached into her sash. She produced a few silver bars minted with the face of Chandarre, then dropped them on the basket floor. "Very well. Claim your petty coin, Wanderer."

Eino's blood boiled as he stepped into the basket, but the amount she'd casually dropped was more than he'd received in the past few weeks combined. He'd never had trouble swallowing his pride for the right price, and with Betta leaving and the core still due to be replaced, he'd need every spare coin he could get. With a sigh, he knelt down and picked up the bars. "Then allow me to welcome you to the Driftcap Inn."

They rode up to the inn in bitter silence. Eino caught a glimpse of Revna's smug expression as she eyed the horizon. He counted the bars, refusing to give her any trust.

"So," started Eino. "Dare I ask how long you plan on staying?"

Her eyes remained fixed on the horizon. "I intend to stay as long as I need to."

Eino groaned. "Look, this here is enough to book a three-week stay, but we won't be back in Sinia until the start of summer. If that's where you're heading—"

"It isn't. I'll find the one I'm seeking long before those three weeks are up. The diviners have told me so."

Eino shrugged. "Diviners ain't always right, you know. Not many guests staying here neither. I don't reckon you'll find—"

"My investigation is none of your concern. You will receive your paltry sum, Wanderer, and that is all you need to know on the matter." She turned her back to him.

Eino groaned. Another guest with a secret, but unlike the others, he was less interested in solving her mysteries than he was in getting rid of her. Slapping on his biggest smile, he turned to her. "Why, my dear knight, as you are now my guest, you most certainly are my concern." His words dripped with sarcasm. "I'll need to know whenever you leave the inn to ensure you never get left behind. It's my duty as innkeeper."

Revna crossed her arms, keeping her back to Eino. "I have told you enough. I will not repeat myself."

Eino huffed. Maybe he'd skip checking the core today. If he stopped drawing out the excess aura the next time she descended to the surface, then the inn would speed up and he'd be able to leave her behind.

When they got to the inn, he retrieved the keys and led Revna to her cabin, its door adorned with a carved image of a scrambler. She sniffed, nose in the air, as she took in the room. "It's rather small."

Eino held back a sigh. "What did you expect? This ain't the Grand Royal." The room only had two chairs and a chest, but he'd carved a desk into the wall that could double as a table and a window seat he'd loaded with cushions. Sure, the ladder to the loft was a little uneven, but it was big enough for three and loaded with pillows and blankets. The crooked shelves under the bed added more storage space. Altogether, it was far more room than the quarters aboard even the grandest Sinian airships.

"Indeed, it is not. The Grand Royal would provide adequate space for its guests." She drew her sword, extending her arm to full length as she tapped it against the walls and ceiling. "I cannot perform my martial rites in these conditions."

He shrugged. "All the cabins are about the same size. You'll have to make do."

"Perhaps not." She eyed the main mushroom. "Surely your quarters are more substantial than this. I will take those instead." She produced another silver bar. "The happiness of your guests is your only concern, isn't it, Wanderer?"

Eino gave a mischievous smile. "Well, if it's 'happiness' you're looking for, you're welcome to bunk with me if you like. But the bed's smaller, and there's only room for one kind of 'martial rite' in there." He waggled his eyebrows. While she wasn't unattractive, he found her personality utterly repulsive, and hoped his advance would repulse her just as much. Perhaps then she'd keep her stay brief.

"You're every bit as bold as they say." She smirked and looked him over, as if considering the offer. She leered over him. "But I doubt a man of your stature would be very...stimulating." She tilted her head and tapped the manaque beads on the side of her head. "Besides, the only man for me is my betrothed."

"More's the pity." Eino hadn't noticed before, but the bead showing her marital status was missing. In a typical Sinian marriage proposal, that bead was given as a gift to one's partner. "Who's the lucky fella?"

"No doubt you have heard of Vennick of the Thousand Weapons?" She sheathed her sword and pressed her hands together.

Eino rolled his eyes. "Can't say I have," he said sarcastically. Everyone in the former league states knew who he was. The man's exploits were legendary to the point that Eino doubted he was even a real person.

"Surely you jest," she said, a crazed look in her eye, "The chosen champion of the Grand Duchess. Belaga's Bane. He who daunted the Dauntless Isle, and he who plucked out the eye of the God-Queen herself!"

"The Dauntless Isle?" said Eino with a scoff. "That story's nothing but a steaming boar pile. Ain't no way Vinat floated a whole island clean over the Tetrarchy. And ain't no way one ordinary fella took it down."

"He is far from 'ordinary', Wanderer," said Revna, her words pointed. She stared off into the distance. "And that is why he is the only man for me. The man I will take as my husband. And with his potent seed, I shall bear a child. A child who shall grow into the mightiest hero in Itharos. No, the mightiest and most legendary hero who ever was. Or who shall ever be!"

Eino snickered, "You sure about that? I don't reckon ol' Vennick shares your vision for the future."

She snapped out of her fantasy, scowling at Eino. "Be silent, Wanderer. You know nothing of my beloved."

"Oh, I'm well aware. It's just that there's lots of folks out there claiming to be legendary heroes." He cast her a sly glance. "Are you certain you proposed to the right one?"

"Quite certain." Her eyes narrowed. "And your concern is no longer welcome. You may return to your business now. I have my rites to complete."

"If you need room to swing that thing around, you can do it on the lower dock." Eino strutted out the door. "I'm charging extra if you damage the cabin."

She slammed the door behind him.

Leora sat on the promenade, legs dangling over the side, with a brown wool hen on her lap. "Who's that lady?"

He lowered his voice to a whisper. "A Sinian knight. Real unpleasant one too. I'd stay away from that one if I were you."

"I see." Leora tapped her chin as if in deep thought. "So, she's a twetch?"

Eino tried his best to keep a straight face, but the girl's words drew an ugly snorting laugh out of him, and there was no way to contain it. He steadied himself on the handrail to regain his composure. "Between you and me, that's exactly what she is. But don't go telling that to nobody else, alright? Joren was right about it being rude."

"My lips are sealed." The girl giggled and mimed locking her mouth shut.

When Eino's laughter had subsided, he glanced down at the fat bird on the girl's lap. "I see you've been making friends with the locals."

"Fluffy is my favorite. She's so cuddly!" The girl squeezed the cooing wool hen.

"I'm surprised. The ladies don't usually take too kindly to strangers this quick."

"Really?" The girl's face lit up.

Eino nodded. It was a lie, of course. The hens were friendly to any guest who'd pay them even the slightest amount of attention. But it was a lie he told to everyone to make them feel that much more special. "Keep this up and even Red might warm up to you."

Leora grinned, pulling a chunk of leftover breakfast flatbread from her dress. "Can we pay him a visit now? I was saving this for him. I know he likes treats." She tore off a small hunk and offered it to Fluffy.

Eino chuckled. "You can try to feed him, but he'll probably just give it to Blue."

"Hey, Mr. Eino? Why do you call her Blue, anyway? She's not blue anywhere."

"She used to be back when she was just a little chick. A real pretty blue too, like the sky."

She nodded, though she still wore a confused expression. "So was Red...red when he was a chick?"

Eino laughed. "No, no. I call him that because when he's mad, he'll flash his red crest at you. I had to butter him up for about a year before he stopped flashing it at me."

"But they both do that," she said, her voice growing exasperated.

The two continued to the kitchen. Perhaps later, he'd descend back to the surface to forage for food. He liked a chance to stretch his legs and find fresh greens, tubers, and flowers. Plus, it'd give him a chance to bump into Joren. But for now, he had other guests to take care of. And while Revna had said it to mock him, the happiness of his guests was indeed his biggest concern.

14

EINO INSPECTED THE GARDEN while Leora offered food to Red. There was a new row of herbs growing that he didn't recognize. He'd have to ask Joren what he'd planted. Like his other plants, they grew fast. He brushed past one seedling with long striped strands for leaves, and a strong garlicky scent accosted his nose. He wondered if it would be any good to cook with.

On Leora's third try, Red accepted a large mushroom. He didn't gulp it down, but instead plucked it from her hand with his beak and presented the treat to Blue. She nuzzled his neck before accepting it.

"Aww, that's adorable," Leora crooned.

"He's a real sweetheart," Eino said, the sarcasm heavy in his words. "Trouble is, I can't hang my bedsheets up to dry on the promenade anymore. He keeps trying to steal them for Blue's nest." He glared at Red. "Don't you, you big ol' thief?"

As if sensing Eino's frustration, Red turned his head away, refusing to look at him. He rubbed the side of his beak against Blue's.

"A nest? So they're gonna have a baby?"

He nodded. "I doubt she'll let you see it, but she's sitting on an egg that's bigger than your head. I reckon it'll hatch any day now."

Leora bounded over and perched on the fence. "How'd they meet? Did you have Red since he was a chick, too?"

"Well, not exactly…" It was a rather plain story to tell. Earlier in the year, the inn's path happened to cross the crested greatwings' migration path during mating season. One day, Eino found Blue swooping through the air alongside a male. Ever since then, the male had joined Blue on Eino's rooftop garden, helping her to build her nest and flashing his bright red crest whenever Eino walked by. He'd named him "Red," and while the bird was much more standoffish with guests than Blue, over time, he'd come to tolerate the presence of people without snapping or squawking.

Of course, Eino was not one to tell a plain story. In his embellished version of events, Red fought off a dozen suitors to win Blue's affection, but in his weakened state, he was unable to evade the gaping maws of a passing stormgulper.

"…so that's when Blue picked me up and threw me onto her back, and together we charged the fearsome beast. See, Blue dove straight for Red. Pushed him out of the way of its jaws. That left me to handle the stormgulper, so I leapt off and landed on its back, but— "

"You rode one of those things?" Leora gave him a suspicious gaze.

"Of course I did!" Eino mimed the action. "Threw a rope around his eye stalk and wrangled him away from Red."

Leora's eyes narrowed. "I thought you said the inn didn't go by their hunting grounds."

Eino pursed his lips, giving an approving nod. He hadn't expected to be caught in a lie by a child. She was a clever one, that was for sure. "Well, it was stormy season back then. They came a little farther up north than usual."

"Mama said I shouldn't believe your stories, Mr. Eino." She gave a smug grin. "Stormy season is coming up, so either you lied about us being far from the stormgulpers, or you made that story up."

"Maybe. Maybe not. But even if it weren't true—which it is—it's still a pretty fun story, ain't it?"

"It is fun. Even if you're a big liar." The girl giggled. "Everything here is so much fun. It's fun to feed the birds and catch scramblers and slide around the barrier…" A sourness passed over her features. "A lot more fun than home."

Eino's ears perked up. He couldn't resist a chance to find out more about the mother daughter duo and where they were from. Or more importantly, what they were running from. He'd have to tread carefully. "What's so bad about home?"

"Tutors, lessons, etiquette, aura honing…it's all so boring." She flapped her hands. "Ugh. I hope I never go back."

"Oh, don't say that," said Eino half-heartedly. He couldn't help but relate to the girl. He had no strong desire to return to the place he came from either. Still, he knew he had to choose his words with care. Living without a place to call home could be challenging, and the last thing he wanted to do was paint so rosy a picture of running from home that Leora went off to go find a driftcap house of her own. He feared that might make an enemy of Val. "You miss your friends, don't you?"

She shrugged. "What friends? I don't know any other girls my age. And the only boys I've met are the ones Father wanted me to marry."

He winced. It wasn't the sort of reaction he was expecting. But it did offer him a chance to pry deeper into her and Val's mysterious past. "Your father…" Eino started, drawing a breath. "Where is he now?"

"Gone," she said with no emotion. "And I'm glad."

Eino grimaced. He'd already guessed that her father was dead. Perhaps killed in a battle between Heralia's allies and the Vinaterians. The fighting between the two powers had been going on for ages, with new skirmishes breaking out every time the war seemed like it was finally over. He wanted to offer her words of comfort, but what could he say? She wasn't mourning her father's death. Once more, Eino found himself at a loss, and the pause stretched into a long, uncomfortable silence.

Leora broke the tension. "I wish I was like Blue."

"How do you figure?"

"She gets to fly all over and people bring her food and stuff," said the girl. "But when she needs to, she knows how to jump in and fight. Like against the stormgulper."

Eino smirked. "I thought you didn't believe that story."

"I don't." She smiled back. "But like you said, it's a fun story. And it'd be fun to know how to fight like that. Except I'd need a sword."

"A sword, you say?" Eino scratched his chin. Maybe be could console her after all. "I might have something like that."

"You have a sword?" Leora beamed, but doubt crept across her features. "Or are you teasing me again?"

"Well, it ain't the sword I used to slay the stormgulper but…" Eino patted around his pockets. Once he found the right one, he reached in and produced a small wooden sword. "I could be talked into letting you have this one."

With a flourish, he presented the sword to the girl. It was short and coarsely carved from a stout branch in the shape of a traditional Porocari war machete. He'd carved a small mushroom into the pommel, just as he did with all the other toys he used to bribe village children.

"Whoa." Her face lit up with wonder as she took a hold of the sword. She held it with the reverence of a sacred relic, running her fingers over the burls of the wood and the etched Porocari runes. A sudden jolt of realization shot across her face, and she turned to Eino, crooking her eyebrow. "Did you have this in your pocket this whole time?"

"Don't ask questions, kid. Just take the damn sword."

"Thank you, Mister Eino! I promise I'll train with it every day until I'm the best swordswoman in all of Itharos!"

"Training ain't easy. You sure you're up to it? It's gonna mean more boring lessons and tutors if you wanna learn to use that thing right."

"Yeah, but it's different if they're teaching me how to use this." She beamed as she held the sword aloft. A sudden excited gasp escaped her lips. "Do you think the tall lady would teach me how to sword fight?"

Eino squirmed. Revna was more than just an unpleasant guest. He still didn't know who it was she was looking for as part of her 'investigation,' and with her appearance so soon after Leora and Val's, he couldn't help but feel that this was no mere coincidence.

"Best steer clear of her. But until your mom can find you a real tutor, you can practice swinging that thing around up here as much as you like. I'd avoid swinging too close to the wool hens, though."

"Why's that?"

"Just trust me," he said as he hauled his basket of vegetables down through the hatch into the inn. While he had meant the warning sincerely, he was certain the girl would ignore it. A mischievous grin crept across his face, knowing he'd planted the seed for his own entertainment later on.

He dropped the vegetables off in the kitchen, deciding to put them away later unless Betta got to them first. He leaned over the promenade and peeked at the docking platform. There he saw Revna performing her martial rites. She swung her sword in wide, elegant arcs, twirling it in her hands and bowing toward the suns after each swing.

On the promenade the basket was missing. Joren must have called it down, and soon he'd return. But how long had it been? Had the basket gotten stuck again? Worry nagged at him. If Joren didn't get back soon, he'd have to go looking for him.

Revna stopped her exercises and planted her sword in the deck, resting her hands on it as she peered out to the land below.

"Hey!" Eino yelled down to her, "Watch where you put that thing!"

She raised her head to glare and make a rude gesture at him. Even though she'd already paid much more than her room was worth, he still considered charging her extra for the damage.

She looked away to watch something below. Eino followed her gaze to find the basket creeping back up, carrying a single cloaked figure. It was the slowest Eino had ever seen the basket move. His fingers twitched, wanting to reach for his necklace and speed the thing up. But with how the core had been acting, he was worried he'd somehow make it worse. No need to frighten poor Joren any further.

After what felt like an eternity of waiting, the basket rattled up to the promenade. Eino strutted over to greet him, trying not to look too excited. "Welcome back. Happy fishing?"

In answer, Joren held up a string of fish dangling from his fishing pole and handed it to Eino. Four medium fish and one large one. Plenty for a nice dinner for everyone and then some.

"By Dilgaa, did you leave any fish in the pond?" Eino smiled and slapped Joren's shoulder. "Good job."

"Well, I know we won't be over any freshwater ponds for a while. I tried to make the most of it."

"Ain't a problem. When we're cruising over the sea, you can take the basket to the water's edge and do some deep sea fishing. I have the spears and net for it."

There was a sparkle in Joren's eye as he looked out across the glimmering sea. "Do you suppose I might be able to catch any suncatchers?"

Eino rubbed his chin. "Well, I think it's the right time of year for them, but a suncatcher is an awful big fish. I don't reckon you'd be able to haul one in on your own."

"I must try." Joren licked his lips. "I once had a suncatcher fillet with spicy Mycarade seasoning, and it was perhaps the most delicious thing I've ever eaten."

"It's that good, huh?" Eino chuckled. He'd never seen Joren so excited about food. "Well, if we both go down together, maybe we could—"

The sound of shrieking rang out from atop the rooftop garden. In a flash, Leora appeared, sliding up the barrier near Joren and Eino. She channeled her aura into her feet and launched herself onto the promenade. Her trajectory, however, shot her a little too low, and she clipped her shin on the promenade railing. She tumbled over it and slammed into the wall next to the two men. They both froze in shock.

"Ow," she groaned.

"You alright, little lady?" Eino asked.

"Yeah." The girl put on a brave face, trying to smile as she grit her teeth in pain. She held up her wooden sword. "At least I didn't drop it!"

Eino smiled at the girl. "I'm guessing you went and made Chandarre mad."

Joren gave him a bewildered look. "The King?"

"No, the woolcock." He offered her a hand. "Named him Chandarre II on account of him taking all the ladies for himself."

"He surprised me. That's all." Leora took Eino's hand and pulled herself up. She gripped her right arm where a bright red spot stained her sleeve.

"I heard screaming." Val came running around the corner of the promenade. When she saw Leora, she gasped, letting out a curse Eino didn't recognize. "Ker Dekar! Leora, you are bleeding!"

Leora rolled her eyes. "I'm fine, Mama. It's just a scratch."

"Pardon me," said Joren, clearing his throat. "May I take a look? I'm trained in healing."

Val nodded and Joren lifted the girl's sleeve to reveal a bright red bruise on her arm.

"Looks worse than it is," said Joren, reaching into his satchel. He produced a broad leaf wrapped like a package with twine. "This salve will stop the bleeding. Should help with the pain, too."

"Thank you," said Val, taking the salve. "Now come on, Leora. Let us clean this wound at once."

The girl sighed. "Fine." She limped and winced as she followed her mother back to their cabin.

"An apothecary, I see," said Revna. The two men turned to see the knight staring at them, wearing a look halfway between fury and satisfaction. "How interesting." She rested her hands on her hips. "What is your name, Sinian?"

Joren went wide-eyed. "J-Joren, ma'am."

"Of where?"

"Of … um." Joren swallowed. "K-Koharam," he said, tripping over his tongue.

"Koharam?" She leered over him. "There is no village by that name."

"Sorry! I meant. Koparam!" He gave a nervous chuckle. "Sometimes I confuse it with Kohar, you know?"

"Kohar is quite far from Koparam." She narrowed her eyes at him.

Joren stammered. "I-I move a lot. For my work."

"A Sinian ought to know where he's from." She looked to the side of his head, then held out her hand. "Your manaque. Show them to me."

Joren ran a hand through his hair, his eyes still wide. He patted at the side of his head where his beads should have been hanging.

"Where are your manaque?"

Eino stepped in. "We lost them."

"Lost them?"

"In Poutise. We passed through during Sarbakh." Eino patted down his pockets before producing the spiral bead he'd found in his hair. "Pretty wild festival."

"I will take your words into consideration, Porocari." She turned her intense gaze back to Joren. "But my questions are for this one. This matter does not concern you."

Eino stepped back between them. "Beg your pardon, but it most certainly does concern me. Mr. Joren here is both my guest and employee, so I will not have you harassing him on my inn."

Her nostrils flared. "It is not wise to come between a knight and her quarry, Wanderer. Least of all when her quarry is a dangerous criminal." She puffed out her chest. "The diviners spoke true. You hid yourself well, Joren of Koparam, but no one eludes his majesty's law forever. And I, Revna of Vilbar, Order of the Sun Shrike, will be the one to finally bring you to justice."

Eino struggled to imagine what manner of law Joren could have broken. "There must be some mistake."

"There's no mistake, Wanderer, and there is no doubt. This is the man I have been seeking." She pointed an accusatory finger. "He is the Karaval Kingslayer."

The words hung in the air for a moment. Joren's mouth hung open in shock.

"This is some kinda of joke, ain't it?" said Eino. He snapped his fingers as realization jolted across his face. "Pavan put you up to this, didn't he?"

"I am not the joking type, Wanderer." said Revna. "On the day of the Unification Feast, this man poisoned King Shakaud of Bhaleia. If not for his own incompetence, he would have slain our glorious King Chandarre as well."

"Him?" Eino patted Joren on the shoulder. The man was trembling, one hand behind his back gripping tight to the promenade railing. "Does this really look like a bloodthirsty assassin to you?"

"Looks can be deceiving. But if you require proof, you will have it." Revna snatched Joren's left wrist and wrenched it, forcing a yelp from his lips. "On the day of the assassination, the Kingslayer evaded capture, but he did not escape unharmed. His fingers were cut from his left hand by Vennick of the Thousand Weapons himself. The hand you see before you is a mere prosthetic."

Revna grinned as she tugged the glove from Joren's hand. Her smile faded when she saw all five of his fingers exposed. She tugged each one, twisting and jostling them, but as Joren grunted and winced in discomfort, there was no prosthesis to be found.

"Impossible," stammered Revna. "The diviners...they...no, no, you must be the Kingslayer!" She shook her head in disbelief. "Your other hand. Show it to me!"

Joren leaned away.

"Now hold on a moment." Eino held up his hands. "When did all of this business in Karaval go down?"

"This past year. At the end of the autumn harvest season."

Eino scratched his chin. "Then this can't be your Kingslayer. Joren's been with us here since mid-autumn. Picked him up in Porocar."

"Where in Porocar?" demanded Revna.

Eino tapped his chin as if deep in thought. "I reckon it was Yel Mor. Tiny little backwater you ain't never heard of."

"Impossible!" she repeated. "I demand to see your ledger. I must have proof of this claim."

"Sure thing," said Eino, crooking his eyebrow. "Can you read High Aralic?"

Revna didn't have to admit that she couldn't. The furious scowl on her face told Eino as much. She held her fist to his chin. "If you are deceiving me, Wanderer, I assure you that the whole of my Order will bear down on you. We will find you. We will blow this mushroom out of the sky, and if you survive, I will make you wish you hadn't." She gnashed her teeth.

Eino eyed her fist with smug amusement. Now that she'd lost her composure, he knew he'd already won the battle. But Eino wasn't going to miss an opportunity to rub it in. "What did you say your Order was again? The Golden Twetch?" He squinted his eyes, casting his gaze at Revna's broach.

"The Sun Shrike," corrected Revna, glaring at Eino.

"Oh, my mistake," said Eino. He tapped his chin. "Hey, is Aangvar Swifthand still the grand master of your order?"

Revna spoke slowly, spitting her words. "You will keep his name out of your mouth, mountain mongrel."

"Hey, nothing against the guy. He was one of my favorite guests. Lots of good stories. But he can't play Fool's Gambit for squat." Eino patted Revna on the shoulder. "You tell him if he's gonna blow me out of the sky, he'd better pay me what he owes me first."

For a tense moment, Revna looked as if she were about to explode. She slammed her fist against the wall, then turned and stomped away toward the loading dock. Joren kept his eyes on her as she left. It was only then that Eino realized Joren hadn't been gripping onto the promenade handrail. He'd been gripping his sickle's handle, his knuckles turning white.

"She's gone now." Eino set a hand on Joren's shoulder. The man jumped and turned his head, but relaxed when he realized it was just Eino.

"Thank you." He let out a shaky breath. "But you shouldn't have lied to her."

"Keep your voice down. She doesn't need to know all that." Eino couldn't remember ever having seen Joren wearing his manaque, so it was possible he'd lost them during Sarbakh. Surely there was nothing wrong with a small white lie.

The story about picking him up in Yel Mor, however, was completely false. Joren was actually on the road between two towns near the Sinian border when Eino found him. Incidentally, the area was only about a three-day walk from Karaval.

"If she finds out..." Joren trailed off, his lip trembling, "I don't want you to lose your inn because of me."

"There ain't a damn thing she can take from me. Sure, she'll holler and yell to rattle you. Try to get you to give something up, but she's all talk." Eino waved a dismissive hand. "Besides, she's got the wrong guy. Anyone with half a brain can see you ain't some kind of crazed killer."

"I'm glad you see it that way. I wish she saw it that way, too." Joren shuffled off toward his cabin on shaky legs. Eino grimaced. He'd seen that cold look before. It was the same look he wore before he'd warmed up to Eino and Betta. All of his hard work getting close to the man was about to be lost.

Eino had known Revna would be trouble the moment she set foot in the basket, but after one day, she already had the whole inn in chaos. With all the tension that followed her around, it was going to be a long week of travel over the open seas. He'd need to get rid of her somehow. And fast.

15

AFTER SPENDING THE PAST few days filling his cargo hold with barrels of scramblers, Eino was grateful to have a little downtime. He sat on the promenade, a cup of poutamme switchel in his hand as he watched the shifting colors of the aura stream. He stretched out his legs and let out a contented sigh. Moments like this made all of his hard work worthwhile.

Revna's presence at the inn hadn't disrupted his peaceful days as much as he'd feared. Following their confrontation, he'd only spoken with her once to give her copies of his records. Ever since, she'd locked herself in her cabin, only emerging for meals and to perform her martial rites. The rest of her time was spent poring over the records with only a dull aura crystal to aid in translation.

Eino's record keeping was already sloppy, so it hadn't been difficult to make a few changes that gave Joren an alibi. He was confident that she wouldn't be able to find anything useful for her investigation.

Val and Betta sat nearby, chatting as they sipped on cups of tea. A small sketchpad rested on Val's lap, with a sketch of a wool hen filling the open page. Her model, an orange wool hen named Malan, was perched on the railing, her head bobbing this way and that before taking a break to preen herself. Eino chuckled. He'd named the hen Malan after one of his former flames, and he thought it appropriate that her wool hen counterpart shared in her vanity.

Just outside the barrier, a few creatures flitted about. They were about as long as Eino's arm and their bodies were flat like leaves. Their front ends were honed to long, sharp points, while their rear ends undulated with a mess of thin tentacles.

"Mr. Eino!" Leora called out, sounding equally excited and disgusted. "What are those things?"

"Those would be daggermouths. Real nasty critters." He took a sip of his switchel. "They've got beaks sharp enough to punch clean through feathersteel. Damn things put a few holes in *The Sun Chaser* when their barrier went down."

Val looked up from her sketching. "Should we be concerned? There are quite a few of them."

Eino smacked his lips. "Nah. The barrier will keep them out." As if on cue, Red shot down from above and snatched up a daggermouth, chomping and swallowing before swooping in for another. "Also, greatwings love 'em."

Leora watched with wide-eyed wonder. "Are they tasty? I wanna eat one!"

"No, you don't. Trust me." Eino shuddered, remembering the time that Pavan had dared him to eat a daggermouth. It had a bitter flavor somewhere between rotting fish and metal, and the texture was like eating a leather boot.

"Then are we gonna catch some more scramblers today?"

"No, not today. They'll be pretty sparse all the way to the Tetrarchy, but once we start heading south, I reckon the sky will be full of them again."

Leora swished her sword around. "Star oysters taste so much better fresh. I can't wait to catch some more."

"You'll make a great sky rancher some day, little lady." A board creaked, and he looked over his shoulder as Joren appeared in the doorway. "Ain't that right, Joren?"

The man jumped. "What? Oh. Yes." He took a swig from his own cup of switchel, wiping the sweat from his brow. Ever since his confrontation with Revna, he'd returned to his old, anxious, reclusive self. He was seldom outside of his cabin, leaving only to retrieve his meals and to assist in scrambler fishing. It had been days since he'd even set foot in the herb garden Eino had set aside for him.

"But I don't want to be a sky rancher," said the girl. "Maybe I'll be a great warrior instead." She twirled her sword about in imitation of Revna's martial rites. As she swung her sword about, Revna stepped between the girl and the light of the suns, casting a tall shadow over her.

"You? A great warrior?" Revna snorted. "With your sloppy form?"

Leora shrank under Revna's gaze. She lowered the sword. "I-I just started."

"Cacosshian women are too frail for the battlefield. Do yourself a favor and focus on making yourself a suitable housewife."

"Twetch," mumbled Leora under her breath, glowering at the woman as she walked past.

"And a good morning to you too, Miss Knight," Eino said flatly. "To what do we owe the pleasure?"

"Wanderer." She looked at Eino as if he were a bug she longed to crush beneath her heel. "I would have words with you."

"You can have them here."

"Very well," she grumbled, eying the others with contempt. "There is a ship approaching. It masks its approach with the light of the rising suns. A common tactic among Didinbo pirates."

Eino climbed to his feet and pulled down his goggles, squinting as he stared into the suns. Silhouetted against their light was the pointed bow of an airship flanked by two massive black wings.

"They'll be upon us soon." Revna gripped the hilt of her sword, unable to suppress a grin. "But they'll find I'm not as easy prey as the rest of you."

"Relax, you big ol' bristleboar. They ain't pirates. That's a Gatrai ship."

She sneered, looking down her nose at Eino. "A stolen Gatrai ship, no doubt. I'm not surprised a civilian like you can't tell the difference."

"I was in the Air Legion for years, missy." said Eino with an exasperated sigh. He glanced down at his pocket watch. "Besides, I know the captain. His name's Mebeq and his ship is *The Crosswind*. They're a little early, but I was figuring on running into them sooner or later."

"Then I should like to meet this Captain Mebeq. Perhaps he will be more helpful than you in my investigation." With that, Revna let go of her sword and made her way to the loading dock.

As *The Crosswind* drew closer, it became easier to make out its details with the naked eye. Light glinted off the bright ivory bones embedded in the deep ebony wood of the ship's hull. The broad canvas sails were pointed downward, fluttering in the wind like the wings of a massive beast as the ship righted its course toward the inn.

"Are you sure that's not a pirate ship?" Leora rushed forward and gripped the railing of the promenade, gazing out at the incoming ship with wonder. "It looks like a skeleton."

"That's because it is a skeleton, little lady," said Eino. "Those bones in its hull conduct aura even better than Decrian crystal. That's why Gatrai ships fly so good."

Leora cast an incredulous glance at Eino. "Those aren't real bones. What kind of animal is that big?"

"A stormgulper, of course." Eino smirked. "And those are just the bones from its little finger."

The girl narrowed her eyes. "You're telling stories again. Stormgulpers aren't even real, are they?"

"Well, when you see Mebeq, you can ask him yourself." Eino chuckled. In truth, he also had his doubts about the existence of stormgulpers. He sometimes wondered if the Gatrai made up their sacred beasts to hide the truth behind how their ships flew. But regardless of whether or not the bones were real, the Gatrai had been the first peoples in all of Itharos to harness their power and take to the skies. They still dominated the skies to this day, with the design of their airships barely changing in over a millennium.

The Crosswind blew its horn, announcing its presence with a long blare that sounded almost mournful. The ship tucked in its sails and glided to a stop beside The Driftcap Inn. A young face gaped from the deck at the inn, matching Leora's look of wonder. Eino smiled. It wasn't the first time he'd seen a new crew member's astonishment at seeing his peculiar inn. He bet it wouldn't be the last.

Mebeq stepped out from *The Crosswind*'s helm onto the deck. He was a portly man with skin nearly as dark as the hull of his ship. Like most Gatrai, his long hair was naturally silver, and he had it pulled back away from his face in a high top knot. His hair made him look like a wizened old man despite actually being a few years younger than Eino. The loose, white robe he wore about his waist fluttered around him in the wind as he lifted his ivory goggles and waved.

A crewman slid a gangplank across to the inn's cargo platform. Mebeq strode across the bridge with a bottle in hand. He was greeted not by Eino, however, but by a stern-faced Revna blocking his path.

"Greetings, my friend, and may Solun's blessings be upon you," said Mebeq, bowing his head. "I am Tsekut Mebeq. Please excuse me, but I have business with Eino the Wanderer."

"You have business with me first, Gatrai," she said, pounding a fist against her chest. "I am Revna of Vilbar, Order of the Sun Shrike, and by that authority I demand your compliance with my investigation."

Mebeq snorted. "The Codes do not oblige me to comply with your demand, my friend. However, in the spirit of our new friendship, I will graciously offer my cooperation with your request."

Revna smirked. "Very well. Then stand aside. I will inspect your vessel. The man I am looking for may be aboard." She tried to push past Mebeq, but was stopped by his hand.

"Apologies, but I cannot allow you passage on my vessel."

"May I remind you, Gatrai, that I am a Knight of Sinia, and that your interference in this investig—"

"And may I remind you, Sinian," said Mebeq, his voice calm, yet forceful, "that trespassing on my vessel will be considered an unforgivable insult by both your order and your kingdom against the Tsekut Clan." He leaned in, locking eyes with the knight. "And a Gatrai never forgets a debt. Or an insult."

Revna froze. The Gatrai clans were closely knit, and an insult to one could spread to all. They held a monopoly on airship travel outside of the Sinian spice trade, and while the tribes had no standing army to speak of, a trade embargo from the Gatrai Brotherhood could spell ruin for even the most powerful of empires. Centuries prior, King Pelev II of Herotogast had attempted to force tribute from Gatrai traders in his kingdom. In response, the Gatrai clans declared an embargo that was never lifted, rendering the entire island kingdom a shell of its former glory.

Eino stepped onto the cargo dock, smirking as he watched Revna squirm. "Aww, go easy on her, Mebeq. She's just sore that she can't find the fella she's looking for." He gave Mebeq a look up and down with a playful smirk. "And Dilgaa knows she ain't looking for your sorry ass!"

Mebeq laughed heartily, turning to Revna. "Forgive me, Madam Knight. I forgot that you have had to deal with such an unpleasant dimling of a host." He slapped Eino on the back. "May I offer you a discount on my wares after I have concluded my business with this one?"

Revna cleared her throat, doing her best to maintain some sense of authority. "Yes, that…would be acceptable. Notify me when you have finished." She turned and marched back into the inn, her quick steps giving away her eagerness to escape.

Mebeq watched her leave, turning to Eino. "I see Solun has blessed you with…interesting guests."

He shook his head. "You don't know the half of it."

"Then you must enlighten me." He held up the bottle. "But first, you and I have business."

Eino smiled. "You trying to ply me with cheap Brumanti swill?" He flicked the glass.

"Swill? This is aged raangnectar, my friend. Straight from the hive fields of Scrumbogast." Mebeq dangled the bottle hypnotically. "I had intended to share it, but perhaps you are not in the sharing mood, hmm?"

Eino licked his lips. "Oh, you're playin' dirty. That's gotta be against your codes."

"Not at all. So long as it is shared in friendship, the gods will not frown upon it."

"Then how's about we get started?" He gestured toward the door into his storage pantry. "Send in your crew. I've marked everything for them to take."

"Tsekut!" called Mebeq to three waiting crewmen. "Bring Mr. Eino his deliveries."

"Aye, Tsekut!" replied two of them in unison, disappearing below the decks. The third, the youngest looking of the three, remained in place. Among the Gatrai, it was common to refer to one another using their clan name, though Eino never quite understood how they always seemed to understand when they were being called.

The third crewman stood at attention, though his gaze kept drifting up to the mushroom.

"Eino, my friend, I would like you to meet my young protégé, Tsekut Kannam. This is his first trip with me."

"Family?" Eino guessed.

Mebeq chuckled. "Nothing gets past you. He's my oldest nephew."

The teenager bowed to Eino.

"No need for that." Eino patted the boy's shoulder. "Happy to meet you."

Mebeq pulled a fan from his pocket. "Querrina save me. May she send snow and ice to banish this humidity!" He shook his head. "I shall never get used to this heat."

"Don't you go calling the gods to ruin a beautiful day like today," Eino chided. "You want the cold, you sail on back up to them glaciers."

"Ha! I would sooner face the heat of one hundred desert summers than leave before we have toasted our transaction."

Eino laughed. "Then let's go pour ourselves some cups."

16

"...SO THERE I WAS," said Mebeq, sloshing his goblet of raangnectar as he recounted his tale. "Not a year older than you, Tsekut, sailing alone on a skiff. Back then I did not fear the winds, you see, and I thought I could brave the storm without returning to the ship. But Solun, in his great wisdom, saw fit to teach me humility, and cast my skiff far from my clan brothers."

The three of them sat at the small table in Mebeq's personal quarters. The warm scent of weathered wood clung to the air, a refreshing scent compared to the mustiness that sometimes permeated the Driftcap Inn on days when the air was still. Various treasures from Mebeq's travels across Itharos decorated the walls. Even his hammock, with its intricately woven pattern, looked to be an ornate show piece.

The haggling and negotiations had concluded about a half hour ago, but the young man still listened intently to Mebeq's story like a student at a lecture. "And this is why they call you Mad Mebeq?"

"No, Tsekut. It is because when I finally regained control of my skiff, I was lost. A great fog had rolled in, my guidestone had been blown away, and there was no sign of my clan's ship anywhere." Mebeq laughed at the memory. "Imagine my surprise when out of the fog, there drifts a giant mushroom with a man lounging upon it! I thought for certain that Querrina had reclaimed me to her bosom."

Eino chuckled, recalling the look of terrified wonder on Mebeq's face. The meeting happened during his first year on the mushroom. "You remember what you said to me?"

Mebeq smiled and nodded, holding his face in shame. "I pulled my skiff beside him and bowed my head, saying, 'Forgive your loyal servant, Lord Solun!'"

The three laughed and sipped at their raangnectar.

"Needless to say," continued Mebeq, "there was not a soul alive who believed my tale of a wild Porocari man living on a mushroom in the sky. They all said that the winds had hollowed out my skull!" He held up three fingers. "For three years, they called me Mad Mebeq. That is, until one of my fellow clansmen finally crossed paths with him."

"Hey, I was just happy to have some respectable trading partners," said Eino. "Didn't realize I'd caused such a fuss."

Kannam turned to Eino. "So this is uncommon, yes? For Porocari to live in mushrooms like this one?"

"Sure is, son. My inn is one of a kind." Eino tipped his hat. "Ain't but one place where driftcaps grow big enough to live in, and I'm the only one who knows where it is."

Kannam rubbed his chin. "I would pay a hefty sum to know where this place is."

Eino laughed, enjoying the soft buzz of the sweet liquor. "Well, would you look at that. Mebeq, your boy's already making big deals!"

"The nectar has gone to his head," said Mebeq. He patted Kannam on the shoulder. "And he does not yet know of your penchant for stretching the truth."

Eino rubbed his palms together. "Now you know I wouldn't go around lying about something like that. Especially not with a 'hefty sum' at stake."

He sat back, recalling the spot where his inn's mushrooms had grown. There had been a narrow crack in the mountains, barely wide enough for a pebble toad to squeeze through. When Eino peered through, he saw the crack open up into a massive cave full of mushrooms which had grown far past the point where they ought to have detached from their roots to take flight. Since they had never caught the wind, they simply continued to grow.

With nothing more than a pickaxe, he'd spent weeks expanding the crack until it was wide enough to squeeze inside. From there, he carved out a living space in the largest one and cut it loose. He'd periodically come back to the mountain pass to add more cabins, but with the addition of his smokehouse a few years back, he'd taken the last of the driftcaps from the cave. He doubted any others would ever grow in such an unlikely manner again.

"Even so," said Mebeq, "the only money he has to offer you belongs to me, and I will not be parted with it so easily."

"Sorry, kid. Maybe once you get to be captain of this boat." Eino finished the last drops of raangnectar from his goblet. "Well, do you reckon that's all our business?"

"Not quite, my friend." Mebeq reached into an inside pocket of his long white robe. He produced a rolled-up parchment and handed it over. "I found an old map you may find interesting."

Eino eagerly untied the twine and unfurled the map across the table. He traced his fingers over its intricate details. The script was in an archaic form of High Aralic, but with some difficulty, he could read the text. "Where'd you even find this old thing?"

"Solun only knows how these things end up in my possession," said Mebeq with a chuckle. "But in his great wisdom, he has brought it to me, so that I might present it to you now."

The map was ancient, depicting the old tribal territories of the league states from before there even was a Heralian League. Vinateria's borders remained unchanged, but before the rise of Vinat, the area was still known as the Decrian Theocracy. There were dozens of tribes and city states in the areas where Sinia and Ahriqos stood today. Even Porocar was shown as a never-ending wilderness full of terrifying and fantastical creatures. The only names he still recognized were the Xiphang Dominion in the West and the Gatrai Territories at the north and south poles.

"Palgia? Ain't that kingdom just a myth?" Eino asked, tapping on one of the islands. There had been a rumor that in a furious rage, the God Empress Vinat had sunk the entire island. Many assumed the story was Vinaterian propaganda, with some saying the island had never existed at all.

"Perhaps. Perhaps not. All I know are the legends." Mebeq refilled their drinks. "But it has been said that Palgian silk was the finest in all of Itharos. How I would have liked to have held it in my hands." He rubbed the fingers of his right hand together. "Think of the price it would fetch."

"Either way, this map is incredible. Can't wait to add it to my collection," said Eino, marveling at the map. "How much you want for it?"

"It's all yours. Take it."

Kannam's mouth fell open in surprise, and Eino crooked his eyebrow. "Gatrai don't give nothing away for free."

"What, I can't bring a gift to my good friend?" said Mebeq. "Besides, there aren't many people who would have use for such an old map. And It would be a shame for such craftsmanship to go to waste."

"Can't trick a trickster, Mebeq. I know when I'm being buttered up." Eino leaned back in his chair. "Which means you're about to ask me for a favor."

"It is only a small favor, my friend," said Mebeq, smiling sheepishly.

"I knew it!" Eino slapped the tabletop. "Well, let's hear it then."

"You see, my crew and I are on our way to the East. We have business to attend to in the Stranian capital."

"You're heading all the way to Busani?" asked Eino. "Well, you'd better hurry along then. Won't be long till the scramblers have the skies as thick as mud. They'll gum up your ship so bad you won't even be able to walk from port to starboard."

"That is just the problem, you see. As much as I should like to hurry along, a man and his boy-servant have chartered me to bring them to Apthras in Southern Porocar. We cannot move along to Busani until this charter is complete."

Eino smirked. "You forgot all about the scramblers until now, didn't you?"

"Of course I did not forget! I had everything perfectly scheduled." Mebeq gestured with his hand, clenching a fist in frustration. "My crew, however, is still rather young. Their ambition often outstrips their capability. We have been running behind schedule for weeks now." He shot Kannam a pointed look, and the young man hung his head in guilt.

Eino crossed his arms. "But the codes demand that you bring those two to their destination on time, no matter how many scramblers you've gotta wade through. Ain't that right?"

"Indeed they do, my friend. But with your help, we can still satisfy the contract and deliver them safely to their destination."

"And what makes you so sure I'll help you?" asked Eino smugly.

"Because I will pay you twice your usual fare to accept them." Mebeq chuckled. "And because then I would owe *you* for a change!"

"Well, when you put it like that..." Eino rubbed his chin. "...Ah, cast me. Why not? I've got a spare cabin for them."

"Then let us conclude our business here, my friend." Mebeq refilled their cups, then held his up for a toast. "May Solun's winds be ever at your back."

"And may Querrina's breath return you safely to your home." Eino clinked his cup with Mebeq and Kannam.

When they had finished, Mebeq called to the young crewman at the door. "Tsekut! Send word to Mr. Vennick and his boy. Tell them that they will be given new accommodations." He smiled at Eino. "Better accommodations, no doubt."

"Aye, Tsekut!" replied the crewman before dashing off.

Eino gaped at Mebeq. "Did you say Vennick? As in Vennick of the Thousand Weapons? That Vennick?"

"You will forgive me if I did not learn all of his titles." Mebeq waved a dismissive hand. "But yes, that sounds about right."

Eino leaned back. "He's gotta be a fake, right? Ain't no way you've got the real one."

Mebeq's face wore a genuine confusion. "Why are you so convinced he is a fake?"

"Well because the real Vennick of the Thousand Weapons is only the most legendary hero in all of Itharos. The man's a Heralian war hero. At least if you believe the stories, that is." He quirked an eyebrow. "How have you never heard of him?"

"Bah. I have little interests in wars and their heroes. They are usually bad for business." Mebeq finished his drink. "But what difference does it make who he is?"

A jolt of realization shot through Eino, and a wicked grin crept across his face. "The difference is you won't have to wait long to do me that favor."

"Sounds like you have a plan. Come. Let me take you to him." Mebeq smiled and led Eino out onto the main deck. After a moment, a young teenage boy emerged from below deck, clad in a simple red tunic. The boy's dark complexion contrasted sharply with his severe green eyes. He wore his hair tucked into a yellow Heralian headscarf.

Eino craned his neck as the boy made his way toward the gangplank, trying to catch a glimpse of the legendary Vennick of the Thousand Weapons. The man following behind the boy was tall, but otherwise unremarkable. He looked to be in his forties, with a well-groomed beard and mustache that contrasted with his long, messy blond hair. He wore a simple lamellar cuirass more suitable for a footsoldier than for Heralia's greatest champion. His orange headscarf hung loosely over his shoulders rather than wrapped around his head, and he had a broad leather satchel at his waist.

Eino blinked. The man didn't wear a sword at his belt. He didn't carry a spear or a shield. Even the boy wore a knife at his sash, but this man, who had supposedly mastered a thousand different weapons, did not have a single weapon on his person.

Likely an imposter, thought Eino. It wouldn't have been the first fake Vennick he'd ever met. But even the fakes carried at least one weapon to help sell their stories. No matter, he thought. All that mattered was whether or not Revna thought he was real.

The teenager kept his attention affixed on Eino as he approached, while the man seemed distracted by the towering mushroom cap, holding up a hand to shield his eyes as he stared at the inn.

"Mr. Vennick, my friend, please meet Eino the Wanderer." He clapped a hand on Eino's shoulder. "He will see you the rest of the way to your destination."

The teenager stepped up. He bent forward in a slight bow. "Greetings, Mr. Eino. My name is Fulko, son of Lokar." He gestured to the older man. "I trust my master requires no introduction."

The man continued gawking up at the inn, seemingly oblivious to the conversation until Fulko nudged him in the side. Catching everyone watching him, he gave them a sheepish smile. "Right. Sorry." He offered his hand. "Pleased to meet you, Mr...."

Fulko leaned over, irritation in his voice as he whispered through gritted teeth, "Eino. Eino the Wanderer."

Eino smiled, giving Vennick's hand a shake. "Pleasure's all mine. It ain't every day I get to meet Vennick of the Thousand Weapons himself."

"Please. Just Vennick is fine." He held up a hand, and once again his gaze drifted to the inn. "Sorry, I just...I mean...it's really a mushroom, huh?"

"Sure is! That there is the Driftcap Inn, and you can think of it as your home away from home till we get to Apthras." Eino led them to the gangplank. "Let me show you to your cabin."

As they reached the bow of the ship, a sudden shriek cut through the air. "Vennick!" Everyone's eyes darted to the source on the promenade, and there they found a giddy, bouncing knight clad in glimmering armor. She flung herself over the edge of the promenade, landing with a somersault on the loading dock below and clearing the gangplank in a single bound. She pushed Eino and Fulko out of the way in her dash to Vennick, taking hold of his hands. "I can't believe it's really you!"

Eino grinned. She seemed convinced that this was the real Vennick. The man, however, blinked at her in response, no recognition showing in his eyes. "I can hardly believe it myself."

"Isn't it romantic? The two of us meeting in the sky like this?" Her wide grin and the predatory glint in her eyes unsettled Eino. "I can't imagine a better place for you to finally accept my offer."

"Oh yes. Your offer." He rubbed the back of his neck, looking lost. "It's a very good offer, I think—"

"I beg your pardon, noble knight," interrupted Fulko, stepping between them. "Master Vennick is on a mission of utmost importance. You must not distract him with such an...enticing offer." The boy tried and failed to suppress his grimace as he spoke.

Revna stared daggers at the boy. "Beloved? Who is this dimling who presumes to speak for you?"

Fulko bowed his head. "Again I beg your pardon, but Master has been so focused on his training that he has entrusted me, his loyal servant, to attend to all other matters until his mission is complete."

There was a bewildered look in Vennick's eyes. "Yep. It's all true."

"I see." Her smile fell briefly before an excited jolt shot through her features. "Then I will accompany you on your mission! Surely, there is no foe who can stand against our combined might."

Eino stepped closer. "Oh, that's gonna be a problem. See, I ain't got enough cabins for everybody. But you don't mind giving yours up for Vennick here, do you?" Eino put on his most sincere smile, hoping Revna wouldn't realize that one of the cabins was still available.

"Oh, it's no trouble. We'll share a cabin," said Revna, her hands resting behind Vennick's neck as she stared into his eyes. Vennick attempted to lean away from her, but she held on tight. "That will give us plenty of time to catch up."

Eino cast a panicked look to Fulko. The boy matched his expression, quickly turning and tapping Revna on the shoulder. "Noble knight, Master Vennick needs you to protect this merchant vessel in his absence. It is under constant threat, and it needs someone of your skill to defend it."

"It does?" Vennick shot the boy a confused look until Fulko kicked him in the shin. His eyes widened. "It does! Very much so."

Fulko nodded along. "Master Vennick needs your help. Will you see these Gatrai along to their destination?"

She stepped back, closing her eyes and drawing a deep breath. "For my beloved, I would do anything." She drew her key from behind her breastplate and tenderly placed it in Vennick's palm, closing his hand around it and placing a kiss on his fingers. "Until next we meet, my love."

"Uh, thanks."

Revna turned to Mebeq, her expression returning to its usual severity. "Captain. I would like to see my quarters now."

"Yes, of course, my friend." Mebeq shot Eino a desperate look before turning to his crewman. "Show our guest to her quarters, Tsekut."

"Aye Tsekut." The crewman led Revna below deck.

Eino craned his head to make sure she was out of earshot, then patted Mebeq on the shoulder. "I reckon we're square on that little favor you owe me."

"Somehow, I think I have made a poor deal," said Mebeq, smiling and shaking his head. "Until Solun sees fit to guide us back together, my friend."

"May his winds be swift and in your favor." With that, he led his new guests across the gangplank. "By the way, kid, thanks for your help back there. That was some quick thinking."

Fulko nodded. "It was nothing. We've dealt with her in the past."

"We have?" asked Vennick. "Who was that?"

"Revna of Vilbar," Fulko answered. "She asked you to marry her after that incident in Karaval."

"Karaval?" Eino quirked an eyebrow. "You talkin' about the Kingslayer?"

"The same," nodded Fulko. "But Master Vennick put an end to her terror. The Kingslayer was slain before she could poison anyone else. Thousands might have lost their lives if not for his quick action."

"Huh. I heard a rumor she got away," said Eino. He chuckled at the thought that Revna was chasing after a criminal who was already dead. But why did her story differ so far from this one? In the end, it didn't matter, he thought. "I'm just glad that criminal was brought to justice."

"Wait, Revna..." Vennick furrowed his brow, seemingly unaware of their conversation. "Was she the one who kept going on about my 'potent seed?'"

Fulko grimaced. "That's the one, Master."

Vennick shuddered. "Innkeeper, please tell me I don't have to stay in the same cabin she was in."

"Oh, don't worry about that," said Eino. "That was only a bluff about needing her room. I'll switch you room keys and get you into a clean cabin. But first, how about I give you the tour? Then you can sit down to some drinks and rolls."

Eino waved to *The Crosswind's* crewmen as they pulled back the gangplank and the ship sailed away.

17

Eino carried dinner into the dining room, cutting off the light chatter among his guests. Fulko looked up from the carved triangular puzzle full of pegs he'd grabbed from the common room.

Today's meal was grilled stuffed sea gourds. With generous helpings of meat, the dish had its roots in the more refined cuisine of the northern Porocari coast. It was also Betta's favorite meal, despite Eino's teasing remarks calling it "coastie chow." She justified her love of the dish by preparing it in a suitably rustic southern style, using the sea gourds' charred outer skins as the serving dish.

"Now I wouldn't eat the skin," Eino warned as he served the gourds. "Won't kill you, but it's tougher than bristleboar hide, and about half as tasty. But everything else is damn near perfection. And we've got plenty more in the kitchen, so dig in."

Satisfaction slithered through his chest. The dinner table hadn't been this full in a long time. It felt good to serve his guests a nice hot meal, and the food always tasted better when he could share it with others.

"This looks wonderful," said Vennick, sliding his gourd closer and rubbing his hands together. "I admit I've been looking forward to enjoying some south Porocari barbeque on this trip."

"Barbeque don't get no better than this, hun," Betta added, puffing out her chest. "Plucked and grilled them sea gourds this morning. They're stuffed with fresh spring driftcaps and aged ibex bacon, all smoked with mountain brothwood by yours truly."

He tried a forkful of the gourd filling. His eyes fluttered shut as he let out a small groan of delight. "That's delicious. The sauce is fantastic."

While the others started eating, Fulko bowed his head and clasped his hands together, mumbling a quiet prayer. Leora peeked over at the boy, setting down her sword and imitating the motions of his prayer. At last, the boy opened his eyes and turned to Eino. "Thank you for the meal, innkeeper."

"You're welcome, but no need to be so formal here." Eino uncorked a bottle of poutamme wine. "Besides, today's supposed to be a celebration."

Vennick rubbed the back of his head. "Oh no, please. That's not necessary."

"Oh, this ain't about you." Eino poured himself some wine and went around offering a goblet to each of the adults at the table. "We're celebrating getting rid of Revna!"

Everyone at the table laughed, with even the stern faced Val covering her mouth to hide her smile. "I'll drink to that," said Vennick, raising his goblet.

"But we can't be forgetting our new guests, neither," said Betta after everyone had drank. She held her goblet in a salute to the man. "It ain't every day you get to dine with Vennick of the Thousand Weapons himself."

He scratched at the side of his chin, his gaze tilting down. "I'm just a soldier on a mission, ma'am."

"A mission?" Leora's eyes beamed. "Who are you gonna go fight?"

"Leora. Manners," Val reminded her. "It is impolite to ask such things."

"It's alright," said Vennick. "The Grand Duke of Porocar requested aid with an issue in the southern mountains. Apparently, some plants have been terrorizing the locals. I'm not needed on the Vinaterian front anymore, so they're sending me to take care of it."

Eino snorted. "You're the most legendary fighter in Itharos. And you're telling me they have you dealing with some weeds?"

"Master Vennick's humility is one of his few shortcomings," said Fulko. "These are no mere 'weeds'. These are strangleweeds, and they are monstrously deadly. They can grow as tall as a man, with vines that strike as fast as whips with a poisonous touch that can paralyze its victims." He lowered his voice and wiggled his fingers. "But most terrifying of all is the speed at which they spread, creeping through the undergrowth."

Leora let out a gasp. "Those things can't reach us up here, can they?"

"Now, now. No need to frighten everyone." Vennick shook his fork at the boy. "In my experience, people tend to exaggerate the dangers they think they're facing. I'm certain this won't be much trouble at all."

Betta snorted. "Well, at least the Grand Duke got off his backside to do something for us mountain folk." She sipped at her wine. "And with a handsome young man like you on the job, I reckon this will all be wrapped up by the time I get back home."

Eino listened to the conversation, but he couldn't help but keep glancing at the door, each time hoping that Joren would be there. He'd thought that getting rid of Revna would put things back to normal. The whole reason he brought out the wine was because he'd been looking forward to sharing it with Joren. So why was the man still hiding in his cabin? Unease crawled across his skin, making the fine hairs on his arms stand on end.

Then again, if Joren didn't show up, that gave him the perfect excuse to pay a visit to his cabin with a tray of food. That meant more alone time with him. The thought bolstered his mood.

"And what about you lovely ladies?" asked Vennick, flashing Val a charming smile. "May I ask where you're coming from?"

Val cleared her throat. "Of course. We hail from Gathia."

Eino raised an eyebrow as he ate his sea gourd. He finally had an answer for where in the Tetrarchy Val and Leora were from, though based on her accent, he'd already guessed as much. As the former capital of the Heralian League, Gathia had been a bustling metropolis and a hub of commerce in the region for centuries. Eino had met many Gathians in his travels, so he was very familiar with their distinctive way of speaking. Those he'd met, however, were much more casual than the extremely formal Val.

Vennick frowned. "That's a pity. I take it you'll be getting off when we reach the capital?"

"Not at all. My daughter and I are on our way to Muna."

"Is that so?" Vennick smiled. "Then it seems we'll be seeing more of one another. I'm happy to have such enchanting travel companions."

Leora giggled while Val politely covered her smile. Fulko rolled his eyes as he poked at his gourd. "If you are going to Sinia, then I assume the Sinian man is your husband?"

Val tilted her head. "I beg your pardon?"

"The nervous one I saw carrying a bag of plants into his cabin. If he's your husband, he ought to be at your side. Even at dinner. It's his duty."

"You mean Joren?" She shook her head. "He is not my husband. I hardly know the man."

"Then who is your escort?" Fulko's brow wrinkled, his eyes narrowing.

Val looked around uneasily. "We do not have one."

Fulko's steely gaze bored into Val. "Then you violate the Deka'ara."

"That's enough, Fulko," chided Vennick. "Not everyone is bound by the laws of your religion."

"Quite right, master." Fulko's accusatory glare was unrelenting. "So why do you think she's wearing the veil of a Deka'arist supplicant?"

Vennick's voice was stern. "I said that's enou—"

"No." Val held up a hand. "The boy is right. And he has every right to be upset with me." She stared into her goblet and drew a deep breath. "I pray that God will forgive me, but my time was short, and I had no one to ask to escort us." She hesitated. "The war. It...it claimed my husband's life."

A heavy silence fell upon the table. Eino pushed the contents of his sea gourd around, the squelching sound now deafening.

After a long moment of silence, a look of determination crossed Vennick's face. "Then it's settled. I'll be your escort."

Fulko finally broke his glare. "Master, you can't!"

"Sure I can. The Deka'ara is all about looking out for one another, isn't it? And you're always telling me I should be more religious." He gave Val a soft smile. "As long as we're heading in the same direction, I'll gladly act as your escort. If you'll have me, of course."

She bowed her head. "That would be a tremendous honor and I thank you, but I cannot ask you to make such a commitment on my behalf. A man like you has far more important matters to attend to."

Vennick put down his fork. "Listen. When I die, and the Thresher claims my soul, I'll need to stand before your God and face the Long Night of Judgment, right? Being your escort for this brief trip is the least I can do to make up for all the times I've gone against the Deka'ara." Vennick gave a sly smile. "Unless Vinat really is God. Then I'm gonna be in real trouble."

Val covered her hand with her mouth to hide a smile. "If she truly were the incarnation of God, I believe we would all be in a great deal of trouble."

Fulko sniffed and stabbed his fork into his gourd. "Don't even joke about that false prophet. Her heresy has poisoned enough minds already. The Thresher can't claim her wretched soul soon enough."

"It's alright, Fulko. You can relax." Vennick patted Fulko on the arm. "The Vinaterian front is far, far away."

The boy grumbled and ate his gourd. "Not far enough."

For a brief moment, everyone ate in silence. Then Leora reached over and tugged on Vennick's sleeve. "Mister Vennick, will you teach me how to use a sword?"

Vennick lost some of the food balanced on his fork from the sudden motion. It plopped back onto his gourd. "Oh, I don't know about that, little one. Teaching takes a lot of time."

"But you have to teach me," the girl pleaded. "Because when you leave, Mama's still gonna need an escort. But if I knew how to use a sword, then I could do it."

Fulko let out an exasperated breath. "That doesn't—"

"That doesn't sound like a bad idea at all," said Vennick, tousling Leora's hair. "I'd be happy to train you, and I know Fulko here is eager to have a sparring partner."

Fulko dropped his fork in shock. "Master!"

"What? You said you wanted to practice your swordplay. And I'll just bet that you might learn a thing or two sparring with this girl." He turned to Val. "With my supervision, of course. And only if that's alright with her mother."

Leora looked to her mother expectantly, pressing her hands together. "Can I, Mama? Can I please?"

"You know I do not much care for that sword of yours, Leora." Val shot Eino a pointed look. She then sighed, swirling her goblet. "But I suppose if you are going to be swinging it around anyway, you may as well learn how to use it properly. You will cause less damage that way."

"Yes!" Leora pumped a fist in the air. She reached for her sword.

"Ahem. After dinner." She cast a glance across the table to Vennick, a subtle smile on her lips. "That goes for you too, hero."

Vennick chuckled. "Yes, ma'am."

After they had finished eating, Leora led the charge into the common room, sword in hand. "I'm done eating, Mr. Vennick! Can me and Fulko fight now?"

Vennick groaned and patted his stomach. "Give me a moment, kid. I'm not as young as I once was. I'm gonna need a moment to digest that fantastic meal."

"What, you didn't save room for dessert?" Eino chuckled, clearing away table scraps before joining Betta in the kitchen. While she put on the kettle for tea, he finished slicing up the fruit, arranging it on a serving tray with three bowls of dipping sauces.

When he brought the tray out to the rest of the guests, he found Vennick's attention drawn to the "Do Not Open" sign along the wall.

"What's in there, do you think?" He tilted his head toward the sign.

"It doesn't matter," Fulko said as he claimed an armchair for himself.

"I saw in there once when we first came on board," Leora said. "I couldn't believe what was in there."

Vennick's eyebrows rose. "What is it?"

Leora dropped her voice. "I can't tell you. You've gotta see for yourself."

He waved toward the sign. "I shouldn't."

"Why not?" teased the girl. "You scared?"

Vennick's lips pursed in offense. He set his jaw and reached for the little door.

Fulko held out a hand. "Master, don't—"

Just as when Leora had peered inside, the door flew open with a loud popping and a burst of confetti. This time, however, there followed a bright flash and three loud *thunks*. A long, thin throwing knife pierced each of the paper serpent's three heads, pinning it to the wall. Vennick held a ready stance, his hand at his satchel, before realization dawned on his face.

Fulko groaned. "Master, you must be more careful." Fulko pulled the knives from the wall, dropping them and the paper serpent into Vennick's hands.

"Well, it ain't every day I get to pull one over on a legendary hero," said Eino with a laugh. He set the tray down on a low tea table, then added a tally to the inside of the door. "But since Leora helped you, I'll only count it as half."

Val let out a laugh that seemed to dazzle Vennick. It was the happiest Eino had ever seen her. "My apologies. It seems my daughter has become a bad influence on you."

Vennick smiled sheepishly at Val, then turned to Eino and cleared his throat. He slipped the knives into his satchel, offering the paper serpent back to him. "Sorry. I didn't mean to break it."

"Don't be sorry. It's just some cheap papercraft I got while traveling in the Xiphang Dominion." He took a hold of the serpent and inspected it. Surprisingly, the knives had pierced the serpent so cleanly and precisely that he was able to fold it back up, setting the trap up again. "Good as new."

"Now, don't you boys go raising the Grymwynd in here," said Betta, carrying a tea set to the table. "Come get some tea. That ought to settle you down."

"That smells like burnbush tea," said Val.

"Sure is," said Betta. "Eino and I like to bust it out when we've got something to celebrate."

Vennick sniffed at the air. "Whatever that is, it smells fantastic."

"Then allow me to pour you a cup," said Val, smiling behind her veil. "It is the least I can do for my new escort."

Vennick graciously accepted the cup. He sipped at his tea, his nose scrunching at the taste.

Val smiled, lifting a hand to her mouth to hide her amusement. "You need not finish it. Burnbush is something of an acquired taste."

"No, no, it's uh…" He trailed off and took another sip, staying stone faced as he gulped it down. "The flavor is very…complex."

Fulko's gaze flickered between Vennick and Val, but said nothing as he grabbed himself a bowl of fruit.

Eino bit his bottom lip to hold in his laugh as he dished out a small bowl of fruit for Joren. He couldn't stand to wait any longer to check in on him. He added the fruit to the dinner tray and headed out to Joren's cabin.

A few stray scramblers floated around the inn. He batted them away to keep them out of the food. One clung to his sleeve, and he shook it off as he reached the cabin's landing, careful to not spill anything.

He took a deep breath before knocking on the cabin door. Silence answered him. Another knock, but still no response. His mind raced, jumping to conclusions about Joren's whereabouts, each more awful than the last. Had he gone down in the basket without telling Eino? Was he lost somewhere on the surface? Had another Sinian knight come to find him? Maybe he'd gathered some poisonous herbs by mistake. Or maybe—

The door opened a crack, snapping Eino out of his panic. Joren peered out, his body blocking the view of his cabin. He looked just as anxious and standoffish as he had the day he first arrived at the inn. Even so, Eino found the aroma of fresh herbs to be welcoming. He couldn't look away from the man's entrancing, warm cacao-colored eyes.

"Yes?" said Joren when Eino didn't speak up.

"Oh. hey." Eino felt his ears turn red. "I brought you some dinner."

Joren glanced down, then craned his neck to peek around Eino. "Oh. Thank you." He made no effort to grab the tray.

"Also brought some wine. And dessert. We were having a little celebration. Didn't want you to miss out." Eino cleared his throat, gesturing with his chin at the two goblets and two plates of fruit. "And it ain't as much fun to celebrate on your own."

"Oh!" A jolt of realization shot over Joren's face. He glanced back into his cabin and grimaced. "I'm sorry. It's a bit of a mess in here."

"No problem," said Eino. He set the tray on the small deck and sat down, dangling his legs over the edge. "Right here's fine."

Joren rubbed the back of his neck. "Just a moment." He closed the door. From inside came the sounds of the frantic shuffling of papers and the clanging of glass and ceramics. He heard a loud thud followed by a muffled curse. After some more shuffling, Joren finally opened the door and stepped out.

His red wrap shirt was sloppily tied around his back with a loose knot. Combined with his patchy stubble, he looked like a mad vagrant. At least his thick, dark hair still looked well groomed, pulled back into a loose ponytail and tied off with a red ribbon. It made his hair look soft, and Eino couldn't help but imagine tugging that ribbon loose and running his hands through the man's silky locks.

Joren nervously sat on the deck beside Eino, leaning back against the cabin wall. With an awkward smile, he took hold of his sea gourd. "Thank you. You really didn't need to do this."

"Sure I did," said Eino, taking a sip of his goblet. "You've holed yourself up in your cabin ever since that twetch came aboard. I reckon you'd want to celebrate now that she's gone."

Joren silently nodded as he chewed, offering only silence.

"None of us believed her, by the way. We know you ain't a killer, Joren."

He stopped chewing. "Why?"

"What?"

"Why would you trust me?" asked Joren, shifting his weight. "You trust so easily, but you barely even know me."

Eino sat back and snorted, taking a sip of wine. "You're right. I don't know you all that well. I reckon it's possible you could be some sort of dangerous criminal. Maybe you are the Kingslayer like she says. Strak, you could even be the Butcher Bishop for all I know." He set a hand on Joren's shoulder. "But you ain't."

"How can you know for certain?"

"Easy! I can't!" Eino smiled. "See, I'm used to being around folks I don't know. Eating and falling asleep alone in the skies with complete strangers. It don't leave much time to trust your brain. So you gotta just trust your gut. And my gut says you're a good person, Joren."

Joren cracked a sad smile. "I'm glad you think that way, but my gut doesn't seem to agree with you."

"Oh, cast it. Who cares what your dumb old gut thinks?" Eino slapped himself on the belly. "It ain't got the years of experience mine does."

Joren chuckled. It was the first time Eino had seen him laugh since Revna came aboard. He loved seeing him smile. It made his head go fuzzy as his gaze locked onto Joren's lips. He imagined how those soft lips must taste. Like fresh aromatic herbs. Or maybe something even spicier.

He shook his mind loose of the distraction. "Look, I don't know what she said that got under your skin, and you ain't gotta tell me. It ain't none of my business. But if there was something I could do to help, I wish you'd tell me."

"It's nothing. It's just..." he paused, gazing back at his door. "I'm grateful. Truly. It's just that I have a lot of work to do. And I should probably get back to it."

Eino put a hand on Joren's shoulder. "Whatever you're working on in there...it can wait a moment, can't it?" Eino's gaze lifted toward the lights dancing on the aura stream above them. On clear nights like tonight, the aura graced the inn with more vibrant flashes of color and brighter coronas than usual.

Joren sat in silence, watching the sky. "I suppose it can." He took a bite, then another, taking his time with that same deliberate precision of his he used in his music and picking scramblers out of the net. "I think it's growing on me."

"What is?"

"Your Porocari cuisine. I found it rather plain at first, but this dish is very good."

Eino grinned. "Glad you like it. I made it myself."

"Really?" Joren quirked an eyebrow. "You're not trying to trick me, are you?"

"No trick this time." Eino smiled and sipped at his wine. "I promise."

"Well," Joren looked away, a smile playing on his lips. "I'd say it's probably the best thing I've eaten since coming here."

Giddiness swept over Eino as Joren returned to his meal, his gaze glancing up now and then to enjoy the light show. It felt romantic having a meal under the aura stream's flickering lights. He hoped to spend more wonderful nights like this with Joren. A lot more.

"I've been wondering," Joren said, pausing as he took another bite. "You're Porocari. So how did you serve in the Sinian military?"

"Easy," said Eino. "By lying."

Joren snorted, nearly spitting out his wine.

"See, I was traveling around the kingdoms at the time, taking odd jobs wherever I could find them. I ended up in Makal after it joined the Unified Kingdom, and I came across some soldiers trying to get recruits for the Air Legion. The Legion was brand new back then, and nobody thought ships made of feathersteel would fly. I reckon that's why they didn't ask too many questions about where I was from."

"You weren't afraid?"

Eino shrugged. "Not really. It seemed like a good way to see the world. Maybe make a few jingles along the way. And I figured they probably weren't gonna execute me or anything if they found out the truth."

Joren coughed, slapping his chest as he reached for a drink. "Probably?"

"Like I said. I went with my gut." Eino patted his stomach.

"You're mad." Joren stared at him. "I don't think I could ever do something like that. Not without knowing all the facts."

"Then you'd have lost your chance." Eino scooped up some fruit. "You don't always get all the facts. Sometimes you just gotta jump."

Joren considered that as he ate. "You make it seem so easy."

"It wasn't. Believe me." Eino laughed. "I was shaking in my boots the first time I went on *The Sun Chaser*. But the more you put yourself out there, the easier it gets."

Joren rubbed at the stubble on the side of his jaw. "I guess that's something I need to get better at." He glanced up at the light show.

Eino smiled. "Well, I don't reckon there's anywhere better in all of Itharos to practice."

They sat in comfortable silence while Joren finished his meal. He glanced at Eino and then to the side, rubbing the back of his neck. "I understand if you need to get back, but do you have time to play a song or two?"

"Sure do."

Joren smiled, and the sight made Eino melt. He'd play a song or two. He'd play music all night, just as long as it made Joren keep smiling like that.

18

To avoid having everyone come through his quarters to get to the rooftop garden, Eino had draped a section of his scrambler net over the edge down to the promenade as a ladder. It was a much shorter route, but the swinging rope net proved a more challenging climb than he'd anticipated. At the top, he found Fulko and Leora sparring with wooden swords under Vennick's watchful gaze. His arms burned from the climb, but everyone was too focused on Leora's string of wild thrusts to notice his discomfort.

"You're still overextending on the thrust," said Fulko, parrying Leora's strikes. "You need to keep your feet underneath you at all times. Otherwise…" He sidestepped her attack and struck her on the back of the knee. She yelped and fell forward, dropping her sword and wincing.

"Fulko, please. Don't hurt the girl." Vennick leaned against the garden fence, puffing on a thin ceramic stickpipe. "It's only her first lesson. Go easy on her."

"It's not supposed to be easy." Fulko turned his attention to Leora, making no offer to help the girl up. "In a real fight, your enemies won't go easy on you. If that's too much for you to handle, you should just give up."

She grabbed her sword and used it to push herself to her feet. "It's alright. I can handle it. And I won't give up."

"I'm glad to hear it." Vennick gave an approving nod. "But he's right. You do need to work on your stance and your footwork. I want those to be perfect before we move on."

"Right." Leora gripped her sword, but when she caught sight of Eino, she craned her neck around Fulko and waved. "Hi, Mr. Eino!"

"Hey there, little lady!" said Eino, rolling his shoulders. "Has ol' Vennick here turned you into a master swordsman yet?"

"Not yet, but look!" The girl gestured to Blue roosting on her nest. As if in response, a small, fuzzy blue head popped out from beneath his greatwing. Blue craned her neck down and nuzzled the hatchling before tucking it back beneath herself.

"Well, cast me to the Wynds!" Eino exclaimed as he slapped his thigh. "Her first baby. Can't believe I'm already a grandpa."

Fulko loudly clacked his sword against Leora's. "Focus. We're not finished here."

"Sorry." Eino held up a hand and stepped into his garden. "I'll let you get back to your training."

Vennick gave a nod of acknowledgement to Eino before turning back to the children. "Fulko, I want you to attack while advancing. Leora, try to parry his strikes like I showed you. Remember to focus on maintaining your stance." He gave Fulko a pointed look. "Don't swing too hard."

The boy advanced, swinging his sword in slow, controlled strikes. Leora parried each blow, each time more confident than the last, but the boy's advance was relentless. She almost toppled over as she backpedaled all the way to the edge of the mushroom cap.

"Stop." Vennick held up a hand. "That's far enough. Come back before you two fall off the edge."

Fulko relented. "You should be more aware of your surroundings."

The girl grinned. "I am." She leapt backwards over the edge of the mushroom cap.

Both Fulko and Vennick gasped and froze. Eino watched, amused. Fulko's face reddened, his chest heaving as he clutched his sword. He looked around wildly before meeting Eino's calm gaze. "Mr. Eino! There's been a—"

"Relax," said Eino, returning his attention to digging up cobbleroots. "She knows what she's doing."

Fulko wore a look of furious bewilderment. "How can you be so calm? She just—"

A loud wooden clack interrupted the boy as Leora glided back up along the barrier and delivered a leaping slash with her sword. The force of the strike bowled Fulko over, knocking the sword from his hand.

"You should be more aware of your surroundings," she said, grinning as she stood over her sparring partner. She offered her hand to help him up.

Fulko rejected her hand, grumbling as he stood. "Dirty tricks like that are no replacement for skill and discipline." He picked up his sword and assumed his guard. "Again."

Eino paused from gathering the vegetables to watch the action. He leaned over the fence next to Vennick as far as the netting allowed. "Pretty intense kid, ain't he?"

"Life is intense where he's from," said Vennick, blowing out a puff of smoke. "I know it doesn't excuse him, but has a lot of scars he's learning to live with. He sometimes forgets that life isn't always battlefield."

"He's Cacosshian, ain't he?" Eino quirked an eyebrow. "I'm guessing he's from the north?"

Vennick nodded. "There's a small island called Coceps at the mouth of the Northmaw. Right in the middle of all the fighting." He took a deep breath as Fulko and Leora set up for another spar. "Disease claimed his mother at a young age. And his father..." He took a long drag of his stick pipe. "...he fell in battle at the Dauntless Isle."

Eino tried to suppress his groan. Whenever he met someone claiming to be Vennick of the Thousand Weapons, they'd tell tales of their glorious victory over the God-Queen Vinat on the floating Dauntless Isle. Normally, he enjoyed picking apart their stories until their lies collapsed in on themselves. But this man seemed much more somber than the other Vennicks he'd met, so he'd take a more diplomatic approach. "You're telling me the Dauntless Isle was real?"

"Of course it was real. I was there." Vennick stiffened. "A lot of good men and women died there. A lot."

"Beg your pardon. In my line of work, you hear a lot of stories. It ain't easy telling apart from all the rumors and tall tales." He turned his head and offered a sly smile. "Strak, this ain't even my first time meeting 'Vennick of the Thousand Weapons.'"

"Oh. Sorry." Vennick blanched. "I hadn't realized we'd met before. You'll have to forgive me. I'm terrible at remembering faces."

"No, you ain't met me before," said Eino with a laugh. "But I have met a few fellas in taverns claiming to be you."

Vennick let out a huff and a spiral of smoke whirled out of his mouth. "Everyone wants to be a hero. People like that Sinian knight...what's-her-name..." His expression darkened. "Fame. Prestige. It all sounds pretty good. Right up until it's time to make the hard choices."

Under Fulko's onslaught, Leora backed up against the longberry tree. She clambered up onto a thick branch, ducking behind it to avoid his attacks.

"Quit hiding and take this seriously!" growled Fulko.

She giggled. "I'm using the environment just like Venny said."

"Do not call him 'Venny!'" Fulko climbed up after her and pushed her to the branch's end.

Leora leapt from the branch, once more plunging over the edge of the mushroom cap.

"That trick won't work twice." Fulko let out a snarl as he dropped from the tree and held his sword up to defend himself. He glanced around, keeping a wary eye out for where she would appear next. But she didn't pop back up as she had before. "Come back here! We're not done."

From below came Leora's voice. "Help!"

"I'm not falling for that," Fulko grumbled.

Vennick jogged to the edge of the mushroom cap and peered over. "Leora? I can't see you. Where are you?"

"I'm at the bottom of the barrier." The girl's voice was calm, more annoyed than afraid. "I'm alright. I just bumped into one of the cabins. Can you get Mr. Eino to send me the basket?"

"Sit tight. I'll be there in a minute." Eino scratched his neck as he headed for the garden gate. The barrier extended well beyond where the cabins floated. How could she have struck one? As he made his way to the rope ladder, there was a loud creaking sound from the other side of the inn. He glanced over the edge and gasped. "Oh, Strak—"

The vacant cabin that Revna had been staying in was floating far below the others. It tugged at its tethers, smacking against the aura barrier. Small fissures emanated across the barrier from the point of impact like cracks on a glass, but ever shifting and crackling like a fire. The whole inn began listing toward that side, making Eino stumble.

Vennick steadied his footing, holding onto Fulko to keep the boy upright. "What's going on?"

"I-I don't know. Something's wrong with one of the cabins. We need to get Leora. Now."

"Leave her to me," said Fulko, dashing for the edge of the mushroom cap. The boy pulled a rope from his satchel and leapt down to the promenade below.

Eino threw open the hatch down into his quarters. "This way!" With Vennick, he sprinted through his room and down the stairs, out to the falling cabin's rope bridge. Desperate to stop it, he grabbed the bridge and yanked at it, leaning backward as he tried to pull the cabin away from the barrier.

Vennick joined in, grunting as he pulled. Even with their combined efforts, the cabin continued to slump against the barrier, its chimney punching through with a loud glassy crunch.

"Something's draining the aura!" Eino crouched down and grabbed the chain below the bridge that tethered the cabin to the main mushroom. He let his aura flow through the chain into the cabin, but he was no auramancer. Even with his untrained senses, he felt how slowly the aura was building back up. "Come on! Help me pump aura back into this thing."

Vennick gritted his teeth. "It's no use. We need to cut this bridge before it pulls us all down with it."

"No. We can still save it! It just needs more aura," said Eino, trying to convince himself as much as Vennick.

He glanced around, looking for any source of aura he could use. Instead, his eyes caught sight of Leora, standing on shaky legs at the glassy bottom of the barrier. To their left, Fulko had finished tying off his rope to the promenade's handrail and was rappelling down to her. "Take my hand," he yelled as he reached down to her.

The girl wrapped her arms around Fulko's waist as he tried to pull them both back up. But his trembling arms struggled to climb the rope. Leora took a hold of the rope to alleviate the burden, but with a sudden crack, the handrail that anchored the rope above snapped. The children yelped as they fell to the bottom of the barrier, the rope falling on top of them in a heap.

"Fulko!" called Vennick, dropping his end of the bridge. He grit his teeth and reached into his satchel, producing an impossibly large blade. It resembled a giant meat cleaver with a coarse, jagged edge. Despite its massive size, Vennick wielded it as easily as a wooden training sword. "Stand back. I'm cutting the bridge loose."

"Wait!" Eino stepped in front of him. "If this thing falls, it'll tear a hole clean through the barrier and those cracks will spread. We need to get the kids out first."

Joren rounded the promenade, skidding to a halt from his mad dash. "I heard screaming. What's happening?"

"Joren!" a flash or relief shot through Eino as he looked up to see him. He pointed down to Leora and Fulko. "Get to the basket. You've gotta grab the kids before the broken cabin smashes through the barrier."

Without a word, Joren sprinted off. Eino grabbed a hold of the bridge once more and tugged, pouring as much of his aura into it as he could muster. He turned to Vennick. "We need to buy him some time."

With a frustrated grunt, Vennick planted the tip of his cleaver into the deck, then reached into his satchel once again. This time he pulled out an oddly shaped hooked blade attached to a long chain. In a flash, he swung the chain around and hurled it at the cabin, embedding it in the mushroom's cap. Aura flowed from Vennick into the chain, and with a forceful tug, he managed to pull the cabin closer, bringing the chimney back inside the barrier.

With his heart in his throat, Eino glanced up. He wished he hadn't. There was still a massive scar in the barrier where the chimney had punched through, and the cracks were spreading, nearly reaching the bottom. Leora screamed as she clung to Fulko. He stepped backward, keeping them as far away as possible from the approaching cracks.

Joren made it to the basket and started his descent, but the basket moved at a snail's pace. Eino grabbed his necklace, trying to speed the basket up. It shuddered, only making it a little over halfway down before stopping.

"Damnit! Not now!" Eino's pulse raced, the roaring of it in his ears joining the crackling and pops of the spreading cracks. Even with Vennick helping, the aura was draining from the cabin as quickly as they pumped it in. It was like trying to fill a dry lake bed with a pair of buckets.

Vennick stumbled backwards. His chain blade pulled loose a chunk of the mushroom cap, its flesh blackened with rot. The chunk fell, crashing against the bridge and plunging through the barrier below, leaving a new crackling scar in the aura.

There was now little more than a thin shard of the barrier supporting the children. Suddenly, the edges of the barrier started glowing with a fiery, pale blue aura. Fulko pulled Leora backward until they could go no further. He grabbed the rope and quickly tied a safety line around both of their waists, fashioning the other end into a lasso. The boy looked up to Joren, swinging the rope around and tossing it toward the basket.

Joren reached out to grab the rope, but as he did, the cabin slammed into the barrier once again, making the whole inn shake and tilt. The basket plummeted and suddenly stopped, sending the man to his knees and making him miss Fulko's lasso.

Joren climbed back onto his feet and leaned over the basket's edge. He was floating slightly below the children, but there was still a large crack in the barrier between them that was too big to jump over. "Come on," yelled Joren. "Throw me the rope."

Fulko didn't hesitate. He tossed the rope, but it fell short. He tried again, and this time it slipped through Joren's fingertips. On the third try, the man grabbed the lasso and wrapped it around one arm, keeping a tight hold.

The shard of aura beneath the children crackled with blue fire, expanding and re-forming itself. There was now just enough barrier to walk on to reach the basket. "Go! Jump!" yelled Fulko, pushing Leora toward the basket.

With tears streaming down her face, Leora stood up and ran across the barrier, screaming as she leapt into the basket. Joren caught her, then turned his attention to Fulko, beckoning the boy to follow.

Fulko stood and stepped back, giving himself more space to get a running start to his jump. Just as he was about to leap, the aura cracked and gave way beneath his feet. The boy hollered as he fell, but both Joren and Leora acted quickly, grabbing hold of the rope and holding tight.

When he saw Fulko dangling from the basket, Eino released the chain and stood back. "Now, Vennick!"

Vennick grabbed his blade and with a single swing, he slashed through the bridge, chain and all. Unfettered, the cabin punched the rest of the way through the barrier, the loud glassy crunch making the whole inn shudder.

With a shaking hand, Eino reached for the aura stone at his neck and tapped it. The basket shot up, wobbling as it made its way to the promenade. The massive hole in the barrier remained, continuing to pop and fizzle. Slowly, the cracks retreated, and the holes began knitting themselves back together in flashes of pale blue fire.

When the basket reached the promenade, Joren and Leora were still trying to pull Fulko in. Vennick reached down and pulled the boy onto the deck. He flopped onto the promenade face first like a fish. Leora knelt down beside him, sobbing.

Fulko caught his breath and sat up. He spotted Vennick's blade and his eyes widened. "The Man Splitter? Master—"

"I know." Vennick's expression soured when he looked at the blade. He shoved it back into his satchel. "I'm sorry, but it had to be done. All that matters now is that you're safe."

Eino glanced down over the edge. He couldn't see where the cabin had fallen. Only clouds and the endless sea below. "Let's all get inside. If we leave the barrier alone, it'll fix itself right up."

Fulko pried himself off the deck and helped Leora to her feet. Vennick held the door open for them, but Joren walked past them back toward his cabin.

"Whoa, where are you going?" asked Eino. "You're not going back to your cabin, are you?"

He froze. "I need to get back to my work."

Eino leaned in, whispering, "You can't do that. What if your cabin falls next?"

He glanced at the horizon and shuddered. "I...I'll be fine. I just...I need to get back to work." He bowed his head and continued on his way.

"Joren, wait—" But the man was already gone. Eino wanted to chase after him, but he felt himself being pulled in two directions. All he could do was shake his head and follow the others inside. Val had already crouched down and wrapped Leora in a tight hug. Her hands were pale, and even behind her veil, she looked to be on the verge of tears. "My sweet little girl! I was so worried."

"I'm fine, Mama, b-but..." The girl broke the hug and turned to face Eino, wailing. "I'm sorry, Mr. Eino, I'm so sorry! I didn't mean to destroy your inn." She wiped at her eyes, sobbing in great, heaving breaths interrupted by hiccups.

Eino crouched down, patting her on the shoulder. "Aw, hush now. Don't you cry, little lady. This ain't your fault."

"Then whose fault is it?" asked Fulko, his words pointed as he steadied his heavy breathing.

All eyes turned to Eino. His thoughts whirled. None would settle into a reasonable explanation. "I don't know."

"You don't know?" Vennick's voice came out strained, his expression twisted with fury. "So you're saying this could happen again? Without warning?"

"No, No. That ain't it. It's just..." Eino trailed off. There was no time to figure out the truth. Panic was the enemy now, and keeping his guests calm was his top priority. He snapped his fingers. "Revna. That was Revna's cabin."

Vennick took a seat on the divan. He rolled his right shoulder and stretched his arm. "You think she's involved somehow?"

Eino scratched his chin. "She always said the cabin was too small for her martial rites. She must have damaged it swinging her sword around in there." The lie tasted sour, but it would buy him some time to figure out the real problem.

"You don't sound very certain," said Fulko, his words full of suspicion. "Until we know for certain, we should head down to the surface."

"We can't do that." Eino grimaced. "We're still over the open sea. It'll probably be a week or so before we're close enough to land to send the basket down."

"A week?" Fulko demanded, his voice breaking.

"That's right. Ain't nothing we can do about that. For now, you all should stay put here in the common room. I'll double check each of your cabins myself and make sure they're safe."

Betta peered over the loft railing. "What's going on down there?"

Eino took a step back to get a better view of her. "Where the Strak have you been?"

"You watch your language." She yawned and stretched. "I've been working all damn morning. Ain't I allowed to take a little nap?"

Eino slapped a hand against his forehead. "A stormgulper could chew and swallow this whole damned inn and you'd sleep clean through it." She'd always been a heavy sleeper.

Betta walked down the stairs, concern on her face as she took in the scene before her. "You folks look like you've been through the Grymwynd. What did I miss?"

"I'll explain later." He fiddled with his goggles. "For now, just get everyone something to drink. I need to go check on things."

19

Eino flopped onto his bed and stared at the ceiling. He'd spent all day looking each of the cabins over, not entirely sure of what it was he was looking for. None of them were floating too low, and nothing he saw seemed out of the ordinary. There was clearly a problem with how aura was flowing through the inn, but he was no auramancer. He wasn't sensitive enough to identify if anything was wrong, and even if he was, he wasn't powerful enough to fix whatever the problem might be.

As he thought the predicament over, he kept coming back to the same uncomfortable conclusion. Something must be wrong with his core, and it was only going to get worse. But what could he do about it? They wouldn't reach his auramancer in Sanvileau until the middle of summer. There might be towns with other auramancers along the way, but he couldn't be certain that they'd have the skills needed to repair his core. Or that he could afford their services if they did.

He reached under his bed and pulled out a small wooden chest. With a drop of his aura, the stone lock glowed and popped open, revealing Eino's personal treasury. Inside were stacks of coins from all over Itharos, as well as a few strips of silver bullion and some pieces of jewelry he'd won from gambling. The chest held a fair amount of money, but he doubted there would be enough for a new core. He shrugged. Maybe he had been giving away too many free rides on his inn.

There was a knock at the door. Eino shot up to his feet. "Coming," he called, slamming the chest closed and sliding it back under his bed. He ran a hand over his head, failing to tame the mess of his hair. Who could be visiting him now? Hope kindled in his heart that it was Joren, coming to comfort him. But with how his luck had been lately, he knew better than to expect something so pleasant. More likely, it was Val. The whole day, he'd been expecting to get an earful from her after the danger Leora had gone through.

He took a deep breath and threw open the door. To his surprise, it was neither Val nor Joren waiting for him, but Fulko. He stood with his hands clasped, shoulders stiff. "I would like to speak with you, Mr. Eino. May I come in?"

"Uh, sure." He opened the door. "Take a seat wherever."

"I'll stand," said Fulko as he walked in, closing the door behind him. His gaze wandered about the room in a way that made Eino uncomfortable. His gut told him the kid was looking for anything suspicious to use against him.

"So." Eino stepped back and sat on his bed. "What's on your mind, kid?"

He picked up one of Eino's wooden idols from his desk and inspected it. "This is a carving of Dilgaa, isn't it."

"Sure is. Carved it myself." He resisted the urge to yank it out of the boy's hands.

Fulko nodded as though Eino had just confirmed something for him.

"In my understanding of Porocari myth, Dilgaa sends the souls of the unworthy to be blown across Itharos by the Grymwynd, never to find their rest."

"You know your stuff, kid," said Eino, giving a mischievous smile. "You thinking of becoming an acolyte of the Mountain King?"

"Hardly. I simply find it rather...peculiar."

Eino snorted. "I've been getting called that a lot lately."

"Porocari culture views wind as something to fear," Fulko continued, "yet here you dwell on those very winds, in direct opposition to Dilgaa's strength and stability, existing among the very Grymwynd you purport to fear."

"What can I say? I don't frighten too easy."

"I also heard you offer prayers to the Gatrai wind gods when we left *The Crosswind*," said the boy. "How do you reconcile these differences?"

"I ain't too picky about who I'll pray to. It doesn't hurt to make an offering here and there to the local shrines and mystics. As you've seen it can be dangerous up here, so it ain't exactly the place to be making enemies of the gods."

"There's only one God, Mr. Eino." He set the idol back down on the table. "And so long as you accept these false idols, you stand in opposition to his will."

Eino smirked. "I'm guessing you didn't come here just to convince me to become a Deka'arist supplicant."

"Indeed I did not. So let's get down to it." Fulko crossed his arms with a grim expression. "You and I both know that Revna had nothing to do with the cabin falling."

Eino squirmed. He was more than twice as old as the boy, but Fulko's intensity made him feel like a child facing down a strict teacher. "How do you figure?"

"Please. You don't need to play dumb." Fulko held up his hand and shook his head. "I understand why you lied. It was the right decision to avoid causing panic." He leaned in conspiratorially. "But this was clearly no accident."

"Alright," said Eino. "Let's say you're right. Suppose it weren't an accident. So what was it then?"

"Well, I'm assuming your driftcaps don't usually drop out of the sky like this, do they?"

He shook his head. "First time it's ever happened. Cast me, I didn't even think it was possible, what with how a driftcap soaks up aura like a sponge."

"Then I doubt it's just a coincidence that barely a day after Master Vennick's arrival, your inn starts to fall apart." Fulko pointed to Eino. "Which means someone sabotaged that cabin."

"You don't think I—"

"No, not you," he said, rolling his eyes. He started pacing the room, hands resting behind his back. "You're smarter than you let on, and I doubt you'd be so incompetent that you'd make a move this obvious and still drop the wrong cabin at the wrong time. Besides, you were on the roof with us. It would have been hard for you to act unnoticed." He bumped into the side of Eino's desk, rattling the carved knick knacks on it.

Eino smirked. "Thanks for the vote of confidence, kid."

Fulko rubbed his chin. "Master has plenty of enemies, the Vinaterians in particular. And the empress has a long reach. She has pawns all over Itharos." The boy rubbed his chin as though he had a thick beard. "It's not hard to believe that one of them is staying at your inn."

Eino's eyes darted around. "Who, Val? You don't seriously think she's some kind of Vinaterian spy, do you?"

"I'm not certain. But I know I don't trust her. She's definitely not from Gathia. Her accent and her mannerisms are off, and I find it hard to believe she'd lose her husband to war that far from the front lines." He paused his pacing. "She's hiding something. You must have noticed how suspicious she is."

"She's mysterious, alright. But that don't mean she's trying to kill Vennick. Strak, everyone at this inn is a little mysterious."

"You're right," said Fulko, leaning in closer. "Especially the Sinian. I find him more suspicious than anyone else."

"Wha— You mean Joren?" Outrage tinged his voice. "Kid, he saved your life!"

"He did. But I won't let that cloud my judgment of him." He stared at Eino. "You shouldn't let how you feel about him cloud your judgment, either."

Eino stood and glared back. "And just what is that supposed to mean?"

"You know exactly what it means," came Fulko's retort. "I see the way you look at him."

Eino shook his head. "I don't care what you say. Joren's not a killer. And neither is Val. They're good, kindhearted people."

The boy snorted. "The rivermink looks kind too. Right until it bares its venomous fangs."

Eino narrowed his eyes. "You really think everyone's out to get you, huh?"

"Everyone *is* out to get him. Spies. Mercenaries. Didinbo pirates. There's no danger that Master hasn't had to face."

"Then maybe you can tell me why he was riding on a second-rate Gatrai ship with just a young pup like you for a bodyguard."

"Despite what you may have heard, Master Vennick prefers to live by humble means."

Eino stood up, leering over the boy. "Fakes live by humble means too."

"Believe whatever you want. Master Vennick has proven himself time and again. He doesn't need to prove anything to you. Just know that I won't sit idly by and allow anyone to harm him."

"Fine. But keep your hunches to yourself for now, kid. No matter how mysterious everyone may be, we ain't got no reason to think anyone here is out to get us. So I ain't gonna have any violence at my inn. "

"If the culprit doesn't give themselves up, you may not have a choice." Fulko stomped out of the room.

Eino rubbed the back of his neck with a sigh. Everything Fulko said reeked of paranoia. And yet, Eino couldn't help but think that it all made sense. Maybe there was more going on than a simple failing core. Every one of his guests seemed to be hiding something. Under normal circumstance, Eino wouldn't have gotten involved in the business of others. But there was more at stake here than just his inn. A lot more. He'd have to make their lives his business.

He'd have to keep a closer eye on his core and his guests. All their lives depended on it now.

20

Eino gathered his basket for the morning mushroom harvest. An unpleasant sight greeted him, however. Most of the clusters on the inn's main stem hung limp, covered in slimy brown rot. He cursed as he climbed each rung of his haphazard wooden boards, plucking one or two tiny mushrooms still fit to be consumed from each rotting cluster. The rest he cleared away, tossing them down to the barrier below for the birds.

He shivered. The cracks in the barrier had stitched themselves back together, but a thin, almost imperceptible scar remained suspended in the aura along the side where Revna's cabin had been. He swore there was a chilly draft sweeping through the barrier now. Maybe that was why his mushrooms were rotting. Fortunately, none of the rot seemed to have spread to the main driftcap body.

When he'd finished, he looked down into his basket, cursing at his meager harvest. He'd expected to at least fill the basket, but what he gathered barely covered the bottom. He was glad that Blue hadn't swooped by to beg while he picked. She must have been too busy watching her new hatchling to beg for scraps. For as small as his harvest had been, he was grateful to hold on to it. When he climbed down and looked up at his inn, his stomach knotted up with all his worries.

He left the basket of mushrooms in the kitchen. If there was anyone who'd be able to turn a few small mushrooms into a wonderful meal, it was Betta. There was enough dried food in the pantry to get them through Strania. After that, he'd have to add food shortage to his ever-growing list of problems.

Someone cleared their throat. He turned and found Val standing in the doorway, her right hand clenched around the threshold. She looked shaky and distraught, glancing this way and that. The dark bags under her eyes stuck out beneath her thin veil. "I would like to speak with you."

"Of course." Eino took a deep breath and steeled himself for the harsh words he expected her to unleash on him. He closed the kitchen doors, intent on keeping this talk private. He didn't need the whole inn hearing him getting berated. "So, about yesterday—"

"You must listen to me." She raised a hand, leaning in to whisper. "There is something wrong with the aura in this inn."

Eino grimaced. "I know. And when the inn gets to Sanvileau, I'm gonna get it all sorted out."

"We cannot wait that long." She drew a shaky breath, pointing to the cellar pantry. "Bring me to the core. I know it is somewhere in there."

Eino furrowed his brow. "Now I already told you I can't do that. It's a matter of safety."

"Safety?" Val struggled to keep her voice low. "This whole inn could fall out of the sky, and you would speak of safety?"

He shook his head. "I know, I know. But ain't neither one of us is an aura-mancer. We'd only end up doing more harm than good."

"Well, suppose..." She drew a deep breath and steadied herself. "Suppose I was."

"Was what?"

She held out her hand. In her palm, there danced a pale blue flame. "An auramancer."

"That flame," said Eino, his mouth agape. It was the same blue flame he'd seen supporting the barrier when the cabin was falling. Even though the flame was small, Eino felt the power emanating from it. It utterly dwarfed his own ability to manipulate aura. "That was you?"

She nodded. "I would have preferred to have kept my abilities hidden, but if I had done nothing, the barrier would have shattered. And Leora..." She trailed off, her lip quivering. She shook her head and steadied herself. "You must take me to the core now. The barrier is weakening every moment. Even you must be able to sense that."

Hope danced behind Eino's eyes. Maybe she could figure out what was wrong with the core. Maybe even fix it. Or maybe...

A sudden cold wind whistled through the barrier, and Fulko's warning echoed in his mind. If he was here, he'd tell Eino this was all some elaborate ruse, and that she was the one causing these problems. His gut knotted from indecision. "I...I can't..."

"Please," she said. "For Leora's sake. Undertaking this journey has been hard enough on her. I cannot allow anything else to happen to her." She twisted the edges of her veil through her fingers.

Even through her veil, Val's blue eyes were piercing. Eino drew a deep breath, the weight of Fulko's words still hanging heavily on his mind. With a heavy sigh, he pressed his hand against the door to the pantry, his aura flowing in and unlocking it. "Follow me."

"Thank you." Val followed close behind.

As they wound their way down the spiral staircase, Eino began piecing together more of the mystery of Val's background in his mind. To become that proficient in auramancy, she must have studied for years, perhaps decades. Only the wealthy could afford to dedicate that much time to poring over tomes and honing their aura to manifest their will. A woman with that level of wealth and power would have been able to make a comfortable life for herself in Gathia, even as a widow. So why was she running away to be a teacher in Sinia? Or was there something she was running from?

He shook his head. Whatever her motivations, he knew for certain that her first priority was to protect Leora. As long as she had her daughter, Eino trusted her to not do anything to damage the inn or its core. At least not intentionally.

Eino broke the tense silence. "So...auramancy, huh?"

"My powers have their limits," snapped Val, "and I am not your personal wishgiver."

"Hey, take it easy." Eino held up his hands. "I've met auramancers. I get how it works. At least sort of."

Val let out a shallow breath. "My apologies. In my experience, not many share in your understanding."

"No need to apologize. I ain't surprised you wanted to keep it a secret." That kind of power tended to draw a lot of attention, either from those begging for favors or those who sought to control it. He dared to pry a little further. "But I'm guessing that's what you were gonna teach at the Royal Academy."

"That is my hope, yes."

"Your hope?"

She sighed. "I had heard rumors that King Chandarre of the Unified Kingdom is seeking experts from across Itharos to teach at his academy in Muna." She let a small blue flame dance between her fingers. "It is unbecoming to boast, but it would not be wrong to call me an expert. I trust this will be enough to secure me a position in the academy."

Eino chuckled, feeling his way down the dark staircase. "You mean you came charging across the world over a rumor?"

"You are hardly someone to be giving a lecture about taking risks." Val glowered. "Enough delays. Where is this core of yours?"

"Should be right behind here." They arrived at the small door at the bottom of the staircase. He turned to face her. "You got any experience working with cores?"

"Not specifically." She looked to the side, her confidence faltering. "But I am familiar with the principles at work. If I can see the core, I can find out what is causing this imbalance. I may even be able to repair it."

"Let's hope so." With a drop of his aura, he pressed his hand against the sigil at the back of the shelf and dropped the false back, revealing the core.

A thick green band of glowing aura surrounded the core, with blinding pink auroras shooting off all around it. Val held a hand up to shield her eyes. "Is it always this bright?"

"No," said Eino, squinting at the core. "But this don't make no sense. If there's this much aura, how is it so off balance?"

She closed her eyes and held out her hands. "I can sense something diverting the aura away from the inn. If I can just..." She drew the aura into herself, slowing the whirling green field enveloping the core into a gentle purple band. Her veil and dress fluttered as if in a gentle breeze, and a subtle blue glow seemed to emanate from beneath her underdress. As she drew her hands closer, nearly touching the core, the stable band of purple aura started wobbling. "Is...is that a seed?"

"Looks like one, don't it?" said Eino, puffing out his chest proudly. "Carved it myself from a chunk of Tetebarech ivory pine."

"A wooden core? Are you mad?"

"Hey now. Ivory pine is tougher than most rocks. It's done the job this long, just as well as any cheap old aura stone would."

She slowed the spinning of the core to a near standstill. The whole inn seemed to rumble for a moment. "The wood may be tough, but your core has cracked. Look."

Eino had to squint to see it. A thin crack along the side of the core following the grain of the wood. It was roughly the same shape and position as the crack in the barrier. He grimaced, wondering how long it had been there. "Can you fix it?"

She traced her finger, wreathed in blue flame, over the crack. "I should be able to—" Suddenly Val recoiled, letting out a gasp.

"What's wrong?"

There was a long pause before Val finally spoke. "It...it's nothing." She cleared her throat, then steadied her hands and passed her finger over the core. The blue flame of her aura reached into the crack and knit it back together. She withdrew her hands, and the glow beneath her dress subsided.

Eino looked up expectantly. "Is it done? Did you fix it?"

"Hardly," she said, rubbing her hands. "The seal that I have placed will keep the barrier from getting any worse, but the core needs to be replaced as soon as possible."

Eino nodded. "As long as it can get us to Sanvileau." Inside, his stomach twisted. He still wasn't certain he'd have enough money to get the core replaced. He'd likely need to go into debt, but for the sake of his inn and his guests, he'd do it.

Val shuddered. "I am not certain that it will." She tapped her chin. "Tell me, will the inn pass near Levenham in Strania?"

"Sure will," he scratched his head. "I reckon we're two or three weeks away. Maybe sooner with how fast the inn's been going lately."

She drew a deep breath. "There is an auramancer there. An old friend who owes me a favor. She will be able to enchant a crystal and replace your core."

"Crystal?" said Eino, wide eyed. "Let's not go crazy. Maybe I can get a halfway decent aura stone, but there just ain't no way I can afford a Decrian crystal core."

Val held up a hand. "Do not concern yourself with the cost. I will take care of that."

Eino shook his head, stammering. "That's too much. I can't possibly accept something that generous." He'd feel indebted to her rather than the core maker. With how much Decrian crystal cost, it was hard to imagine anyone offering to pay for it without demanding something in return.

"The decision is out of your hands. The sooner the core is replaced, the sooner I will be able to put my heart at ease." She gave a subtle smile and squeezed her hands together. "Besides. Leora is rather fond of this place. I will see to it that she does not lose it."

She hurried up the stairs, giving him no time to ask any questions.

Eino stood stunned for a long moment before sealing the door. With a core made of genuine Decrian crystal, he'd never need to worry about core maintenance for the rest of his life. Chores like washing linens or harvesting mushrooms or even cooking could all be done by the core. He wouldn't need to worry about replacing Betta, and he might even gain greater control of where his inn drifted.

Still, he couldn't help but read into Val's expression before she left. Something had startled her while inspecting the core, and he couldn't shake the feeling that she was still hiding something from him.

Eino tempered his expectations, but for now, he'd play along. He'd act as though he were getting a life-changing core in a few short weeks. And that meant celebrating.

21

JOREN GRUNTED, A SMALL barrel over his shoulder as he trudged his way up from the pantry. "Is all of this truly necessary?"

"Nope. Not in the least," said Eino, hoisting a barrel onto the table in the kitchen. "But this here is a celebration. Necessity's got nothing to do with it."

Joren set his barrels down beside Eino's, one full of poutamme wine, the other filled with a stout Sinian ale. "There's enough alcohol here to drown a tavern. There's no way we're going to drink it all."

"Maybe. Maybe not. All I know is that it's tough to make merry without a little variety in the beverages."

"Doesn't look like much variety for the children."

Without looking, Eino pointed to a trio of pots bubbling away on the stove. "Which is why I'm boiling down a pot of longberries and two different flavors of scrambler juice. They'll have plenty of syrups to make some kid-friendly cocktails." He chuckled as he slapped a barrel of Brumanti grain liquor. "Might use some myself. A little sweetener might just turn this swill into something worth drinking."

Joren eyed the barrel with apprehension. "If you say so. I certainly hope you enjoy it."

"Oh, I won't. This here's mostly for Betta. That lady has an iron stomach, let me tell you." Eino chuckled and shook his head. "And what about you? What's your drink?"

"I'm not much of a drinker." Joren rubbed his arm shyly.

"That's alright. We'll have good food and games and music—" Eino snapped his fingers. "You should bring my tarnaaq!" The two had swapped instruments after their most recent session, and while it barely fit in his jacket, Joren's garanelle had become one of Eino's most prized possessions.

"I still have a lot of work..." said Joren, his voice sounding sorrowful as he trailed off.

"Oh, don't tell me you're gonna sit this party out too," said Eino, exasperated. "Just what are you doing in there anyhow?"

Joren grimaced, a stammering groan as his only response.

"I know, I know. It's none of my business and I shouldn't ask." Eino held up his hands and let out a sigh. "I just don't like the idea of you sitting in there all alone while we're out here having fun."

"Thank you. That means a lot to me." Joren looked down. "But this is something I have to do. I...I have a lot to make up for."

"You're not still worried about not being able to pay for your room, are you?"

"No, it's..." Joren stammered once again, as if searching for just the right words to say. "It's more than that."

Eino flashed a sly smile. "Well, if you did want to pay me back, I reckon I'll be hungover tomorrow morning. You got any sort of concoction to fix that?"

Joren chuckled. "I'll put together a tea blend just for you. It should help a little."

"I'll take as much as you can put together."

"I said it would only help a little." Joren snorted. "So please try not to overdo it."

"Oh alright. But don't you overdo it neither," said Eino. "It's alright to take a break every now and again. Whatever you're doing in there, it won't be no good to nobody if you work yourself to death."

Joren tilted his head, considering Eino's word. "I suppose that is true."

"Of course it's true! And I can't have you dying before the scrambler harvest is over. Ain't no way I can do it all by myself." Eino patted Joren on the shoulder and dared to add, "Plus I'd miss you."

Joren gave a bashful smile.

"So we'll see you tonight, alright?"

Joren offered no response, but simply nodded, a smile still on his face. As he walked out to the promenade, Eino couldn't help but grin. The vain hope that he might actually come to the party made him feel a warmth deep in his chest. It almost made him forget about the mysterious project he was carrying out in his cabin.

Fulko's warning clawed at the back of his mind, but he refused to give it a second thought. Whatever Joren was doing in there, it had nothing to do with either the falling cabin or his cracked core. He was certain of it. Before his mind could keep prying at the topic, Eino descended back down into the pantry. There was a lot left to do to prepare for tonight. Plenty to keep his mind busy until the party.

That evening, Eino insisted on serving up a lavish dinner of dry aged ibex brisket. He'd spent all day smoking the meat, and served it atop mashed cobbleroots with a mushroom cream sauce that Betta had taught him to make. It was a feast fit for the Grand Duke, and everyone gorged themselves on it. Everyone, of course, except Joren. As usual, he was still in his cabin, and even though Eino had come to expect his absence, he couldn't help but feel disappointed. But even Joren's absence couldn't spoil his mood tonight. There was plenty to celebrate.

After dinner, everyone retired to the common room. Vennick slumped onto the divan, groaning as he rubbed his stomach. "That was incredible. I couldn't eat another bite."

"Well, don't get used to it," said Betta. "If Eino keeps burning through all our food like this, it's gonna be nothing but porridge for supper till we get back to Porocar."

"Oh, come on now, Betta. After yesterday, you can't blame me for wanting to celebrate, can you?"

Fulko cast a suspicious glance at him. "You're celebrating the loss of a cabin?"

"I'm celebrating the safety and well-being of all my guests." A crack appeared in Eino's usual confidence. "And...I'd also like to apologize for putting you in danger. Keeping you safe is my job, but I'm ashamed to admit that I couldn't have done it without help from all of you. I have standards here at The Driftcap Inn. And if I can't live up to them, then I can sure as Strak make up for them. Which is why tonight, all drinks are on the house." With his usual showmanship, he presented the tapped barrels of alcohol, as well as three jars filled with brightly colored juice over ice.

Vennick, who just a moment prior looked ready to fall asleep, sprang to his feet. "It's hard to say no to hospitality like that."

Val smiled, bowing her head. "Shall I get you something to drink, my escort?"

"Ale for me," he turned to Fulko. "And what about you? You're old enough to have a little drink now."

"No thank you, Master. I'd rather keep my wits about me." He turned his head. "At least one of us ought to." Vennick seemed too lost in Val to hear his remark.

Leora bounded over to her mother. "What about me, Mama? Can I have some?"

"Absolutely not," said Val, pouring a flagon of ale and another of wine for herself. "Why not try some of these lovely juices Mr. Eino has made for you?"

"Ugh...fine." The girl skulked over and ladled herself a glass of green scrambler juice.

"Don't you fret, sweet pea. The booze ain't all it's cracked up to be." Betta patted the girl on the head as she poured herself some of the grain liquor. "Besides, there's something even more fun you can do at a party like this. More grown-up too!"

The girl perked up as she sipped at her juice. "What's that?"

With a gleam in her eye, Betta strode over to a side table, lifting its top and revealing a deep bowl filled with several sets of dice. "Gamble!"

Eino chuckled. "Now don't go teaching the girl how to play fool's gambit. At least wait till her mother's out of the room."

"Oh hush. It ain't like we're playing for money." She turned and gave Val a wink. "It'll just be for fun."

"I suppose that would be alright." Val sipped at her wine. "I must say, I have seen people playing, but I could never make much sense of the game from watching. I confess I am curious about the rules."

"What kind of rock have you been living under that you don't know fool's gambit?" Betta snickered, but explained the rules for both Val and Leora. It was a simple game that involved throwing dice into a bowl or box, with dice landing closest to the middle scoring their shown value. Variants of the game were played all over Itharos, but all versions required some degree of skill along with a great deal of luck.

"What? That's not how you play," said Vennick, joining in at the table. "You've got to throw your dice one at a time, not all at once."

Betta shook her head. "We ain't playing by Urunta rules. Drags the game out too long. It'll be sunrise before we finish a single round."

"Well, of course it drags it out. That's what makes each throw so exciting! It's no fun to be done in one go."

"If we were betting on it, you'd be right, but this here's just for fun, remember?"

A sly smile crept across Vennick's face. "There are other things we can wager besides money while still keeping things fun." He held up his flagon and swirled it.

Eino patted Vennick on the shoulder. "Easy there. You may have faced down whole armies, but I reckon this is a fight you can't win."

"Too late," said Betta, a wicked smile on her face. She turned to Eino. "Would you be a darling and bring me a drink? Mama's got a legendary hero to wallop."

Despite their initial arguments, they finally settled on a set of rules and played a few rounds, laughing and cheering after each victory and defeat. While Betta ended up winning most of the time, it wasn't long before everyone, even Leora, had won a round.

Eino sipped away at his tall flagon of grain liquor with each loss. The longberry syrup helped to make the drink palatable, but no amount of sweetness could tame its burn.

A sound at the door caused everyone to look up. There in the doorway stood Joren, sheepishly poking his head in.

"Oh." He looked around, hiding behind the door. "I can come back later..."

"Joren!" said Eino, his voice full of excitement. He stood up and held out his arms. "Get them cute lil buns in here!" He stumbled forward, his head now feeling warm and floaty. He held out a hand to support himself against the wall, pausing briefly to suppress a belch and to find his bearings. Funny. He'd felt perfectly fine when he was sitting down just a moment prior. Maybe Betta's challenge was becoming a bit too much for him.

The others returned their attention to the game, but Joren remained awkwardly in place like a skittish forest horse. The wide-eyed terror on his face softened as Eino approached him, pulling him into an embrace. "I'm so glad you could make it."

"I'm just taking a break. Like you suggested."

"Well, you're just in time." Eino gestured to the table. "How about you join us for a couple of rounds?"

Joren rubbed his elbow. "I'm not much of a gambler."

"Well, if you ain't here to drink and you ain't here to gamble, then there's only one thing left to do." With a bright smile, Eino took him by the hand and led him to a bench beside the fireplace. "Did you bring the tarnaaq?"

Joren, practically forced into the seat, looked up at Eino with a worried expression. "Y-yes, but—"

"Great!" Eino clapped and turned to the rest of the room. "Who's ready for some music?"

"I am!" Leora bounded over, abandoning the game mid-round. "Can you sing your one song again? The one that's really hard to say?"

"Let's warm up with something a little easier." Eino wasn't drunk enough to try singing *Catch a Twetch* in front of Leora with her mother present. Instead, he opted for something much simpler. Something that might break Joren out of his shell. He patted the man on his shoulder. "You know *The Jolly Sailor Man*, right?"

Joren grimaced. "Everyone knows that, but I don't think I—"

"Perfect! I'll start. You just jump in whenever." Clapping his hands to keep time, Eino began singing the song. It was a simple, lively tune common across former league state taverns. Vennick and Betta stomped their feet in time, swinging their drinks and joining the chorus. Even Fulko joined in, a rare smile appearing on his face. It wasn't long before the sound of the tarnaaq joined in the melody. Eino took Leora by the hand and danced arm in arm with the giggling girl.

When the song had ended, both he and Leora took a bow for the other cheering guests. Even Joren, while he didn't look completely at ease, was smiling and laughing along with everyone else. Eino couldn't help but feel pride swell up within him. These were the moments he lived for. The moments that made all the struggles of running The Driftcap Inn worthwhile. Basking now in the room's joyful atmosphere, it was easy to forget the perils of the previous day.

Eino refreshed his drink and joined Joren on the bench, laughing as he wrapped an arm around the man's shoulders. He pulled the garanelle from his coat pocket, and though his head was swimming from the alcohol, he was still more than capable of playing a few songs. His arms and legs playfully brushed against Joren's as they harmonized.

During a slow ballad, Vennick took Val by the hand and they danced. Fulko declined Leora's invitation to join them, but Betta graciously accepted, the two of them laughing as they dramatically dipped and spun one another.

After a few more songs and a few more drinks, Fulko tapped Vennick on the shoulder. "Master, may I have my lyre?"

"Of course." He fumbled with his satchel, pulling out a shield and a stout short sword before finally producing the lyre and handing it to the boy. "I take it you're going to play your song for us?"

"It's not my song, Master. It's yours." He walked over to Joren and Eino. "Do you know the tune to *The Dauntless Isle*?"

"I've heard it a few times." Joren nodded, turning to Eino.

Eino put a hand to his stomach, slurring his words as he spoke. "Sorry, kid. I'd better sit this one out." The last few drinks had caught up to him, and the longberry syrup that had made them go down so easily just a moment ago now felt sickly sweet in his mouth. He set down the garanelle and stood up, nearly falling over. The room was hot as it spun around him. He stumbled to the promenade to get some fresh air.

Unfazed, Fulko held up his lyre, drawing his aura into his fingertips and plucking at the strings. Despite the instrument's small size, its vibrant sound filled the room. Joren joined in a moment later with a beautifully layered harmony.

Fulko then began singing, reciting in verse the tale of the Dauntless Isle. He told of how Vinat plucked the island from out of the Miasmic Ocean. She had a fortress full of soldiers built on the island, and then raised it high into the sky, casting it like a massive, unstoppable warship toward Heralia. He sang of Vinat's champion Belaga, whose connection to the God-Queen made him nearly invincible in battle, and of the chaos and ruin he wrought to anyone, Cacosshian or Heralian, who stood in his way.

As he sang the chorus, the dire tone of the song shifted, and the boy wore an almost reverent look on his face as he sang.

"Hail Vennick! O, Vennick of the Thousand Weapons!

He found himself pushed to the brink,

He stood eye to eye,

With the wicked Vinat,

And a man made a God-Queen blink!"

Eino leaned against the doorway and joined in for one chorus, but opening his mouth was a mistake. He quickly turned and retched over the promenade railing.

A voice chuckled to Eino's left. "I hope that makes it through the barrier."

"You and me both." Eino coughed, looking up to see Vennick. "What are you doing out here? Ain't you gonna listen to your song?"

"I've heard it." He said flatly, sliding a paper-thin roll of sparkbark into his stick pipe. He pulled a bladeless handle from his satchel, and in a flash of aura, a blade of pure flame emerged from the handle. Vennick held the dagger of flame to the end of his pipe and puffed until it caught alight.

Eino wiped his mouth and leaned against the inn, still holding his mostly full flagon and trying his best to look nonchalant. "Aww, come on now. If they made songs about all my glorious battles and such, I don't reckon I'd ever get sick of hearing them."

He took a long drag of his pipe. "You were in the Air Legion. Did you ever see combat?"

"Nope. Nothing deadlier than a few bar fights." He took a sip of his flagon to rinse the foul taste from his mouth. He swished and spit the liquor over the railing, then took another sip. "We were more like spice merchants than soldiers."

"Then trust me. It's not as glorious as you might think." He gazed out into the darkness of the night. "That song doesn't tell the whole story."

"Then why don't you tell me the whole story?" said Eino. "I've got time."

He shook his head. "I shouldn't."

"Don't you go all shy on me. I can tell you've got something on your mind, so it's best to just let it out," said Eino. He took another swig of his drink. The burn felt less intense than usual. "Besides, I'm so drunk I'll probably forget anyhow."

Vennick cracked a smile. "Then I guess there's no harm in it." He took another drag of his pipe.

"It all started when the scouts first reported back about the Dauntless Isle. At first, we didn't believe it. But as more reports came in, we started to realize what was coming for us. Thousands of us joined the Guard. We were green, but we had numbers. The generals told us we could handle the few hundred Vinaterians garrisoned at the fortress, and when we rode up our sky chariots and no one shot at us, we believed them. But none of us could have anticipated Belaga…"

Eino held his fist to his mouth as if deep in thought, trying to look serious as he suppressed a belch.

"He was waiting for us when we landed on the island. He was alone. Unarmored. All he had was this." Vennick drew the massive blade he'd used to cut Revna's cabin loose. "The Mansplitter."

Eino whistled, taking time to appreciate the weapon's finer details. The ornate engravings on the blade glowed with aura, and a small carving of a ram's skull dangled from a chain on its hilt. "That's some knife you've got there."

"You've seen what this 'knife' can do." Vennick snorted, his face grim. "But in Belaga's hands, our armor was like paper. He cut us down like sheafgrass. We panicked, and we would have all surely fallen if it wasn't for Lokar."

"Who's Lokar?" asked Eino. In his drunken haze, he was certain he'd heard the name before, but he couldn't recall where.

"Fulko's father. He was a brave man. A real hero. He rallied us between a few stone outcrops to make our stand. Then he alone charged out to meet Belaga, taunted him, and baited him into our trap. Once we had him surrounded, we struck. Our spears pierced him from all sides. But it was no use."

Eino leaned over, enraptured by the story.

"Belaga just laughed, and in a bright flash of aura, he sent us all reeling. A dozen spears and swords in his body didn't slow him down at all." Vennick stared off into the distance, his fingers trembling as he took another puff of his stickpipe. "He got Lokar."

Eino's head swam. He wanted to reach out and comfort the man. To offer some words of consolation. "Damn," was all he could muster.

Vennick shook himself loose from his daze. "Somehow, I escaped his blade, but I was pinned beneath my fallen comrades. I couldn't run or hide. All I could do was watch. That's when I saw it. From beneath his tattered tunic, I saw a massive crystal embedded in his chest. I figured that must be the source of his power."

"So that's when you got up and struck him down, right?" He held onto the railing to keep himself from swaying.

"Hardly." He sighed. "Belaga saw I was still breathing, so he marched over to me and picked me up. He laughed in my face. Taunted me. It took all the strength I had left, but I struck the crystal with the butt of my knife. It shattered, and in another flash of aura, he fell over, dead."

Eino blinked. Everyone in every tavern he visited knew the tale of Vennick of the Thousand Weapons, and it was nothing like this.

With another puff of smoke, Vennick continued. "When the others saw Belaga's body, pierced by what looked like a thousand weapons, and they saw me standing over him, they acted like I did it all myself. I wanted to tell them how ridiculous that was, but I put the mission first. That's what Lokar would have done." He shuddered. "Together with the others, we routed the Vinaterians, drove them out of the fortress, and found the giant crystal that kept the island afloat. 'The Eye of Vinat,' they called it. We destroyed it, and the island came crashing down just off the coast of Coceps."

"Well, cast me!" said Eino, his speech slurring. He took another drink from his goblet. "So, you took the best Vinat had to throw at you and beat it! I reckon you could've pushed right on in to Atrenem and gave her the business."

He shook his head. "I'll always be loyal to Heralia, and I'll always fight to keep her safe. But I refuse to take part in an invasion of Vinateria. I'm tired of fighting. Tired of killing. We should be trying to make peace, not getting more soldiers killed in an endless war."

Eino snorted. "You mean to tell me the man who's mastered a thousand weapons is sick of fighting?"

"I should confess something," Vennick said with a sad smile. "Even if you counted all my throwing knives separately, I only have about twenty weapons in here."

Eino chuckled. "Well, I ain't never been one to trust rumors."

"But whether I like it or not, the generals made me into a symbol of hope against Vinat. I've been doing my best to live up to that idea of a hero ever since. Hunting down criminals. Wiping out killer plants. And yes, mastering new weapons. I owe that much to all those who fell on the Isle." He glanced over his shoulder as Fulko played. "I owe that much to him."

"Well, I might be drunk," said Eino, "but he looks like he's doing alright to me."

"That's not good enough." Vennick batted a stray scrambler away from his pipe. "I promised Lokar that if anything happened to him, I'd take care of his son. But all I've shown Fulko is a life of fighting. He deserves better than that. He deserves to become his own man."

"Hey. Listen." Eino patted Vennick's shoulder. "That kid? He's damn lucky he's had someone like you to look after him. And He's a bright kid. Real bright. He'll find his way."

Vennick let out a puff of smoke. "I hope you're right."

Eino finished the last of his goblet. A cool wind swept across the promenade, making him shiver. "I'm heading back in. Do you want another drink?"

"Thanks, but I think I'll stay out here a little while longer."

Fulko and Joren concluded their performance, and while Val applauded politely, both Betta and Leora whooped and cheered. Eino joined in the applause as he stumbled his way back inside, making his way to the barrels. He held his flagon beneath the tap for ale, but missed and poured it all over the floor. "Oops," he said, trying to blink away his double vision. After a moment, he closed one eye and managed to line everything up..

Joren appeared behind him and tapped him on the shoulder. "Don't you think you've had enough?"

"What? No....no..." Eino's words came out slow and slurred. "Just one more. That'll be fine."

Joren chuckled. "I think you've already had one too many."

"Are you alright?" Val asked as she got herself a cup of juice.

Eino grinned. "Val! You're just the person I wanna see!"

"What?" She blinked at him.

"No, no. Not me. Vennick." Eino jerked a thumb toward the door. "He's outside and could use some company."

"Oh. I'll take him some juice then."

As she walked off, Eino turned to Joren. "Here, here, here." Eino patted Joren excitedly on the back as he leaned into him. "Let's uh…let's walk for a minute."

Joren pulled the drink from Eino's hand and set it down. "Alright," he said, sounding uncertain, "and where are we walking to?"

"My room! I'm gonna go sleep before I pass out on the promenade." He made his way to the promenade with Joren in tow. He dropped his voice to a whisper. "Don't tell anyone, but I think I got a little carried away with the booze."

"This is the wrong wa—"

"Shhh." Eino clumsily pressed a finger to Joren's lips and giggled. "We're just taking the scenic route."

"We should get you ba—"

"No! I don't wanna go yet." Eino wrapped his arms around Joren and buried his face in the man's shoulder. "You smell nice. Like dirt."

"What?"

"No, no. Not like that. Like…uh…good dirt." He took a long, loud whiff of the herbal scent clinging to him. His thoughts felt as thick as honey as he tried to get them out. "You know, like a garden."

Joren patted Eino's back. "Let's get you into bed." He guided Eino back inside and up to his room, catching him as he stumbled on the stairs. Joren kept a hand on Eino's back as he headed toward the bed.

"Cast that boy. I don't care what he says." Eino mumbled as he flopped onto the bed, feet dangling off the side.

"What boy?" Joren yanked Eino's shoes off. "Fulko?"

"Yeah him!" Eino's voice slurred more and more. "I don't care what he says about you. You're a great guy."

Joren paused, making a strange noise in the back of his throat that sounded halfway between a snort and a laugh. He pulled Eino's goggles off and set them on his bedside stand. "You need to sleep. You've had too much to drink."

"And you've got a…good face…nice arms…" Eino muttered, his eyes were already closing of their own accord. Exhaustion settled over him like a heavy blanket. All his worrying had thoroughly worn him down. "…a tight butt."

Joren snorted. "Good night." He moved away, his scent lingering like a warm blanket.

22

Morning greeted Eino with a pounding headache. He tried to pull the sheet over his head to block the sunlight, but found he couldn't move his arms. The quilt had been wrapped around him, trapping his arms at his sides. Not the oddest situation he'd ever found himself in after a night of drinking and revelry, Eino thought. It wasn't even the first time he'd ever found himself trapped in his own bed. But after a night like that, he wasn't used to waking up alone. With a groan, he managed to wiggle his way out of his quilt cocoon.

His memory of the previous night became hazy midway through his conversation with Vennick on the promenade. He racked his mind to fill the gaps in his memory, but only got dreamlike flashes of events, unsure if they had really happened. He recalled talking to Joren on the promenade, but not what he'd said. All that stood out was getting sick over the railing. He grimaced, hoping that it had only been a dream, but the foul taste in his mouth made him certain it had been all too real.

"Ugh," he groaned, hanging his head in his hands and rubbing at his sleepy eyes. He'd hoped a night of fun and games would be good for everyone. That it might help them relax and let go of their fears. He hadn't realized how badly he was trying to drown his own anxieties until now.

"Damn that Betta," he muttered to himself. Her unnaturally strong stomach and her uncanny luck in games of chance had bested him once again. He should have known better than to go up against her at fool's gambit. She had to be cheating somehow, but he couldn't for the life of him figure out how. His only consolation was the thought that she'd probably beaten Vennick as well.

He sat for a minute, begging his headache to go away. When he looked up, he spotted a cup of tea sitting on the table beside his bed. It was still lukewarm when he picked it up, the scent of citrus and herbs drifting off the cup as he brought it to his lips. His face scrunched at the flavor. The citrus cut through the bitterness of the herbs, but it wasn't enough to save the concoction's awful taste. He coughed. At least it took the edge off of his headache.

He squinted at the window, the bright light feeling like a hammer against his already aching head. As his eyes adjusted, he saw that the skies were clear, or at least they were on this side of the inn. That made him feel slightly better. If this weather held, the inn might make it to Levenham before it encountered a storm. Val's repair to the core had been hasty, and he didn't want to put it to the test.

Glimpsing up at the height of the suns in the sky, he guessed it had to be almost lunchtime. Why hadn't anyone tried waking him? Not that it would have done much good. His stomach gurgled, but not from hunger. The thought of eating anything at all made him queasy. Still, he pushed himself to his feet, got dressed, and made his way to the common room.

For Eino, meal times were sacred. A well-fed guest was a happy guest, and even the sourest of attitudes and worst of tempers could be softened with good food. He wasn't sure if he'd caused any new problems among his guests last night, but if he had, then a nice meal would be his first steps toward setting things right..

As he plodded down the stairs from his loft, he found Fulko on the divan, scrawling away in his notebook. Leora stood behind him, looking over his shoulder. She caught sight of Eino and flashed a bright smile.

"Hi, Mr. Eino!" said the girl, bouncing on her heels, a purple blanket slung over her shoulders. "Are you feeling better today?"

"Better?" asked Eino, still fighting the urge to climb back into bed.

"Yeah, you were sick over the edge of the promenade a few times and you kept talking funny. Mama said you probably had a fever."

"I sure did, but I feel a lot better now," said Eino, trying to hide his embarrassment. "What are you two up to?"

"Fulko's showing me his drawings. He's really good!"

Fulko sighed, a slight annoyance in his voice. "They're not just drawings. This is my journal. It's a record of Master Vennick's and my travels around Itharos."

"Well, it's a really pretty journal." The girl tapped her chin. "I should make a journal like this for all the places Mama and I visit."

"Where is your mother, anyway?"

"She's with Mr. Vennick. Mama said she had to tuck him into bed."

Eino and Fulko exchanged a glance. The boy cleared his throat. "Leora and I have been camping out here in the common room since last night. I hope you don't mind."

Leora bounced on her heels. "They've been sleeping a while now. Should we go wake them up?"

"Oh, I wouldn't," said Eino. "It ain't easy to uh…'tuck in' a fella like Vennick. I reckon your mama needs her rest."

He suppressed a chuckle, but with his current lack of a love life, he couldn't help but feel the slightest pang of jealousy. In a matter of days, Vennick had already surpassed the progress it took Eino weeks to make with Joren. Being a legendary hero certainly had its perks.

He stumbled his way into the kitchen and found Betta humming cheerfully while she tended to a sizzling skillet. "Mornin', Sunshine! Sleep well?"

"It ain't fair," grumbled Eino. "You damn near finished off that whole barrel yourself, but you can still wake up grinning like a cacklecaw in spring."

"It's just the way us mountain folk are built." She turned and flashed a mischievous smirk. "You coastie types can't keep up."

"Ha ha," said Eino flatly. "Anyhow, what's for breakfast?"

"Lunch," corrected Betta. "And since I cleaned you all out at the dice, I figured I'd make some hens' nests to make up for it."

"Sounds like breakfast to me." The 'nests' were made from long thin slices of vegetables mixed with egg and molded into round fritters. The dish was common Porocari fare, but after a morning of harvesting eggs, Eino had been inspired to shape a well in the fritters and fill it with fried egg. To the best of his knowledge, hens' nests were a dish completely unique to his inn.

She shrugged. "Well, it might as well be breakfast. Wasn't hardly anyone awake this morning. Just me and your Sinian. We had porridge. He even thanked me for it! I'll never get used to hearing him speak."

"I'm guessing he's the one who made me this." He held up his cup.

"Sure was. Couldn't have been more than an hour ago he brought it up to you." Betta's smile softened the chiding tone in her voice. "But you had us all a little worried, what with how deep in your cups you were. He told me he tucked you in tight last night so you wouldn't go rolling around and wandering off."

Eino grimaced, his embarrassment making him want to hide in his room. "Where is he now?"

"Back in his cabin, I reckon. Said he had to 'get back to work.'"

"I suppose I ought to bring him his breakf—I mean lunch." Eino rubbed the bridge of his nose, then loaded a plate with a couple of nests. "It's the least I can do after making an ass of myself."

Eino took a deep breath before grabbing it and marching off to Joren's cabin. As he walked, he searched his mind, trying to piece together the hazy memories of the previous night. What had he said to him? Had he made a drunken advance on the man? Dread carved a pit in his stomach. What if he had made some sappy confession of love? And what if he had been rejected?

Eino's hands trembled at the imagined rejection. What was it about that man that made him feel all twisted up inside? Maybe it was because Joren was someone like him. Someone who wasn't rooted to the land below. Someone who could join him in drifting around the skies of Itharos, sharing in his adventures. Together they could spend peaceful days tending the garden, fishing, and playing music. And at night, they'd have one another. When Eino imagined running his fingers through Joren's soft, silky hair...

His steps slowed as he reached the bridge. Joren's door hung wide open. Odd. Eino squinted at the door, trying to see inside. As his eyes adjusted, he saw what looked like a thick vine laying across the threshold. Then he caught a glimpse of something flailing inside, followed by the sound of broken glass. He dropped the plate and dashed across the bridge, barreling through the door.

A twisting, writhing mass of vines covered the far window, climbing across the ceiling and floor of the cabin. For a moment, Eino stood dumbstruck at the sight. Then he spotted Joren, pinned against the wall in a tangle of thrashing vines. One thick stalk wrapped around his left arm, another around his right leg. His free hand clawed at a vine tangling around his neck.

"Joren!" Eino drew his knife and charged forward, slicing at the thin flailing vines. He grabbed the one around Joren's neck and stabbed through it. The vine went limp, and Joren coughed.

"Careful..." gasped out Joren, his voice hoarse and wheezing. "Poison...don't...touch..."

"I don't care about poison! I ain't leaving you." Eino started chopping at the vine binding Joren's arm. It was thick, seeming to grow thicker by the second. It took three heavy strikes before he chopped through the squirming vine. Finally, it fell limp and released his arm. Eino grabbed Joren's hand and tugged him away from the wall. "Come on."

Joren reached behind his back and drew his sickle, slashing at the vine holding his leg fast. He grit his teeth and pulled his leg loose, but as he did so, he fell and dropped his sickle. He cast a wide eyed look at Eino, his voice desperate. "Going numb." He sucked in a wheezing breath. "Run!" A few more vines wrapped around his limbs. They were thin, but Joren seemed unable to resist them.

Eino snatched up Joren's sickle, slashing with both hands at the spreading vines, but he was making little progress. They only grew faster and faster, and as if sensing the danger he posed, a few vines shot toward him. He ducked out of the way, slicing them as he backpedaled, but the uneven vines sprawling out across the floor tripped him up. He fell over backwards, falling out the door.

"Vennick! Help!" cried out Eino, as loud as he could. He looked right and left as he tumbled out the door. Again and again he sliced through the thin vines winding themselves around his boots. "Vennick!"

A pair of arms hooked under Eino's and dragged him back out of reach of the vines. Eino looked up to see Fulko pulling him back to the bridge. The boy was surprisingly strong despite his skinny build.

"Where's Vennick?"

"He's coming. Now get to safety."

Eino climbed to his feet. "Joren's still in there! I ain't leaving him."

"We won't either." Fulko drew a dagger from his sash and stepped forward, slashing at the vines with a wild, youthful vigor. "Now go! You'll only get in our way."

The sound of heavy footsteps raced around the promenade. Relief poured through Eino as he glanced back to see Vennick, shirtless, and rounding the corner.

"Fulko! Support!" called out Vennick. He reached into his bag and produced an odd-looking bladed gauntlet, then threw it in the air toward the boy.

"Yes, Master!" In one fluid motion, the boy caught the gauntlet, slipped it onto his left hand, then unfolded the blades to form a short bow. He drew the bow back, and his aura coalesced into a glimmering arrow between the blades. "The Sinian is still inside."

Once more, Vennick reached into his satchel, this time producing a thick double-bladed axe. He tapped an aura stone on the handle and a blazing fire roared to life on the axe head. Eino barely had time to get out of the man's way as he came barreling across the bridge and into Joren's cabin. Fulko followed, standing guard in the doorway and loosing bolts of aura.

Eino glanced down at the knife and sickle in his hands. They felt like children's toys compared to Vennick's arsenal. Frustration gripped him as he stood there. He wanted to charge in and save Joren, but in the cramped quarters, he knew he'd just slow down the real hero. Reluctantly, he stepped back across the bridge, his eyes never leaving the cabin.

Val rounded the corner of the promenade. Unlike Vennick, she wasn't missing any clothes. "Leora said Vennick needed to come quick. What's happening?"

"There's a plant," said Eino, panting. "Vines. Poison. Joren's trapped in there."

From inside the cabin came the sound of chopping and the flashes of aura illuminating the darkness.

"Ker Dekar…" She pressed her fingers against her cheeks. "Are they using aura weapons?"

"I think so." He looked up at her. "Can you help them?"

She shook her head. "I can't. Aura is only going to make that thing bigger."

"What? How do you know that?"

"I can feel it sucking up the aura like a sponge. Oh God, please. You need to tell them. They need to stop now." She chewed her lip, her hand picking at a loose thread on her sleeve. "It has to be you. They don't know that I'm a—"

The sound of glass shattering rang out as the plant punched its way out of the cabin's windows. Flailing vines fell limp and tumbled out of the cabin as Vennick chopped them, only to be replaced with more vines.

"Hurry!" said Val, gripping the railing of the promenade.

Eino grumbled and charged back across the bridge. In front of him, Fulko worked like a machine, loosing arrows wreathed in flaming aura all over the cabin. Some found their mark, but many struck the walls behind the flailing vines. "The fire isn't working, Master!"

Illuminated by the aura of his axe, Eino saw Vennick slashing furiously at the massive tangle of vines, which was nearly as thick as a tree now. "Keep shooting, damnit! We need to find this thing's roots."

"The aura!" called out Eino. "It's making the plant bigger. You've gotta stop."

"Let us handle this," snapped Fulko. "Fire kills these plants."

Vennick held up his hand. "Hold, Fulko." He watched the vines. "He's right. This is only getting worse." He stepped back and doused the flame on his axe, putting up his guard. "We need a new plan."

The boy tapped his finger on his chin, his eyes darting about. "The dragon gourd?"

"Right!" Vennick slammed the axe into a wall, then reached into his satchel. With one hand, he drew the flaming dagger he'd used to light his stick pipe. With the other, a wide squat gourd etched with a rune Eino didn't recognize. With his teeth, Vennick pulled the cork from the gourd, then held it to his lips. He took a swig, then set his dagger alight. In a bright, dramatic flash, he spat the liquid out across the burning dagger, spewing white-hot flames all over the tangle of vines. They writhed and recoiled as if in pain.

"Come on," said Fulko, glancing back at Eino, "let's grab the Sinian."

Together they tore through the limp vines burying Joren and pulled him out of the room.

"The pot." Joren let out a body shaking cough. "Roots..."

Eino scanned the room and found a ceramic pot on Joren's desk. It was cracked at the bottom, with thick woody vines that had rooted into the wall of the cabin. "There! That's where the roots are."

Vennick followed Eino's finger to the pot, and taking one last swig of the gourd, he bathed the pot in fire. The thick woody roots shriveled, while the rest of the vines spasmed violently until at last they fell limp and stilled.

In the stillness, Eino took in the cabin. Handwritten notes and diagrams were strewn about the room, with a few stray flames licking at the corners of some of the books and loose papers. Broken glass vials full of herbs lay scattered across the floor. The mortar and pestle had been toppled, spilling a thick paste onto the floor.

"What the Strak was that thing?"

"Strangleweed, most likely," said Fulko, anger making his words sharp. "Which means your friend has been poisoned. Badly, from the looks of things."

Eino looked down at Joren. His clothing had been torn in a few places, revealing thin lacerations across his neck, arms, and waist. "There's gotta be an antidote somewhere." Eino's searched through the mess of broken vials and jars on the shelves.

Joren wheezed, his trembling fingers reaching into his sash. He fumbled a moment, but managed to pull out a small leather pouch. "Here...your arm...it's cut." He strained out, pointing his hand to Eino.

"Me? You need this a lot more than I do." He grabbed the pouch and opened it, finding a glob of light green salve. He slathered up his finger and traced it over the man's wounds. How ironic, thought Eino. He finally had the chance to lay his hands on Joren's body, but instead of savoring the moment, he was praying to Dilgaa that he'd survive the night. He might have laughed at the absurdity of it all if not for the pit in his stomach.

"Don't use it all up on him," warned Fulko. "He may be harboring more strangleweeds, and who knows when we'll be able to get more of the antidote."

Eino nodded. He checked himself, finding only one small cut on the back of his forearm. He smeared a small bit of the salve on the wound. Though it barely broke the skin, the cut was already tingling. He looked up at Fulko and Vennick. "Either of you hit?"

They checked themselves. "We're alright," said Vennick, "But we have bigger problems." He pointed back to the inn. Eino glanced back and startled. The cabin had sunk well below the main mushroom, the bridge back to the prom-enade now angled up like a ramp.

"For our own safety, we'll need to cut the cabin loose," said Vennick. "And for the safety of everyone below, we'll need to set it on fire. Burn it up and make sure nothing in there survives."

"Wait!" Joren let out a hacking cough. He wheezed as he struggled to catch his breath. "My...research."

"Your research?" said Fulko, rounding on him. "You've put all our lives in danger. You're lucky we don't let you burn up with the rest of the cabin."

Eino found his voice, forcing the words through his aching throat. "We need him. It's like you said. We might not get any more antidote for a while, and he's the only one of us who knows how to make more."

"You can't be serious," said Fulko. "What makes you think he won't turn on us? He had that thing in a pot. Who knows how many more he's smuggled aboard!"

Vennick retrieved his axe from the wall and placed his armaments back into his satchel. He turned to Eino. "It's your inn. Your decision."

Eino hung his head, shoulders hunching against the wind. Joren was in no shape to collect his own things. There was nothing to be done to save the cabin. "Please. Gather whatever you can from in there. Then do what you need to do."

"Right, then." Vennick patted Fulko's shoulder. "Come on. Let's grab every-thing we can. We'll figure out what's useful later."

Fulko grumbled, but tucked the blades of his bow back into his gauntlet. "Yes, Master." He knelt down and began gathering up loose pages.

Eino turned his attention back to Joren, helping him to his feet. "Let's get you to the common room. Can you walk?"

Joren nodded. He took a step forward and stumbled on his injured ankle. He sucked in a hissing breath.

"Stop. Let me." Eino tossed one of Joren's arms around his shoulders and helped him up the bridge.

Joren grunted as he hobbled forward. "Should've just...let me die."

Eino grunted. "Don't say that. Ain't nobody dying on my inn."

Val was waiting on the promenade. "Here, let me help," she said, slipping her shoulder under Joren's other arm. A faint blue glow emanated from her palm, and Joren seemed to relax.

Together they lay him down on the divan in the common room. His eyes were closed, but his breath was steady. Eino eyed up the deep cuts all over Joren's body. His fingers itched to clean and bandage them, but he hesitated. Would cleaning the antidote off kill him? It felt awful not knowing what to do, but he resolved to wait until Joren woke to ask.

He pulled an armchair closer and sat to keep watch over him. The tingling on his own arm had subsided. He ran a hand through his hair with a long sigh. At least now he knew that Joren's secret project had something to do with strangleweeds. But what was he doing with them? And why did it feel like he knew even less about him now? Who was this man?

23

"Master, this is pointless." Fulko groaned as he looked over the notebooks and loose papers scattered across the dining table. He slammed a fist down, shaking the vials and jars they'd gathered from Joren's cabin. "Everything is out of order, and most of these notes are illegible."

"Keep at it, Fulko. The recipe for the antidote might be in there somewhere." Vennick patted the boy on the shoulder. "If anything happens to him, we'll need you to find out how to make more."

Eino paced the common room, unable to take his eyes off of Joren. The man lay across the divan, his breathing haggard, but steady. It had been about an hour since Vennick cut Joren's cabin loose. Fulko had riddled the mushroom with flaming arrows as it floated away into the setting suns, and all Eino could do was watch as it burned to ashes.

He knew it had to be done, but that didn't stop his throat from tightening, or his hands from balling into angry fists. This inn was the only place in his life that had ever truly been his, and now it was falling apart around him, piece by piece. Pretty soon, there wouldn't be anything left to save. He hated how helpless it left him feeling.

What would he do without his inn? Go back to the Air Legion? No, he wanted a home. His home. He still had a lot left to fight for. And once Joren woke up, maybe he could start getting some answers.

Betta emerged from the kitchen with a tray full of cups and a steaming teapot. "He ain't awake yet, is he?"

Eino shook his head, not trusting himself to speak.

Fulko looked up from the papers. "Why are you serving tea to that criminal?"

"Now I don't know if he's a criminal. But after fighting off poison, his throat's probably parched. No one is going to go thirsty while I'm around."

"He *is* a criminal. There's no doubt about that." The boy slammed his fist into the table. "Our lives may all be in jeopardy because of him, and you want to make him more comfortable?"

"I'm gonna let you in on a little secret, son. If you bait a trap with vinegar, all you'll catch is hog gnats." She poured a cup of tea. "If you want some answers, then a little hospitality goes a long way."

Fulko snorted and returned to studying the notes. She set the tray on the tea table beside the divan and poured cups for everyone. As she did, Leora leaned over the backrest, her eyes full of concern. "Is Mr. Joren going to be alright?"

"Ain't nothing you need to worry about, sweet pea," said Betta, taking the girl by the hand. "Come on now. I could use some help in the kitchen."

Eino reached down to take a cup. As he did, Joren let out a groan. With limp hands, he rubbed his eyes, slowly sitting up and squinting around the room.

"Hey," Eino knelt down beside him. "How are you feeling?"

"Head hurts." Joren rubbed his forehead. When he looked up and met Eino's gaze, his face showed the hint of a relieved smile. "But I'll be alright."

"Good," said Vennick, his voice authoritative and booming. "Then you can answer a few questions. Starting with why you had a potted strangleweed growing in your cabin."

Joren's voice hitched as he stared wide-eyed at the man towering over him. He opened his mouth, but only a choked sound came out.

Eino set his hand on the man's shoulder and handed him a cup of tea. "We ain't gonna hurt you. Just tell us the truth."

Joren took the cup and sipped at it. He drew a deep breath and let it out in a long, painful shudder. "I...I was studying it."

"Why?" Vennick's voice sounded more like a command than a question. "Why were you studying something that dangerous?"

"T-to stop it!" stammered Joren, holding up his hands defensively. "The plant. Strangleweed. I was studying how to cure its poison. And how to stop it from spreading."

Eino let out a relieved sigh. "So that's what you were always working on every time I stopped by."

Vennick pressed further. "Then why be so secretive about it?"

"I didn't..." Joren avoided eye contact, his voice small. "I-I didn't want to frighten anyone..."

"There's more to it than that. Much more." Fulko stood up and joined the others in the common room. "You've heard of the Karaval Kingslayer, haven't you?"

Joren blanched. "I-I've...yes. Yes, I have."

"I'm not surprised. At this point it's a well-known story. The Kingdom of Bhaleia was set to join the Unified Kingdom of Sinia, but on the day of the celebration, the Kingslayer poisoned the Bhaleian king." Fulko paced back and forth as he spoke, his tone like that of a prosecutor at trial. "What most people don't know is that the Kingslayer didn't directly poison King Shakaud." Fulko's stare turned intense. "Of course, you already knew that, didn't you?"

Joren gulped.

"Yes. Those who were in the crowd that day saw what happened. Master Vennick and I were there, you know. We saw Shakaud present a bouquet to King Chandarre. And we saw the strangleweed that lashed out and wrapped itself around his neck. The guards acted quickly, but it was too late." Fulko paused his pacing to stare Joren down.

"What's your point?" snapped Eino. There was a growing terror on Joren's face. Part of Eino knew that should have been cause for suspicion, but in that moment, all he wanted to do was defend him.

"This brings me to why the Grand Duke specifically requested Master Vennick to investigate the strangleweeds in the southern mountains of Porocar." Fulko steepled his fingers together. "You see, most people consider the Kingslayer as nothing more than an isolated act of terror. Just the actions of a lone madwoman." Fulko waved a folded letter in the air. "The Grand Duke of Porocar, however, does not. He believes there may be another kingslayer on the loose, and that he is his next target."

"And you think it's him?" Eino scoffed. "We've been over this with Revna. Joren ain't a killer."

"Maybe not. But he knows a lot about strangleweed." He turned his intense gaze back to Eino. "Mr. Eino, are you aware of where these plants came from?"

"Kid, I ain't never heard of a strangleweed before you two showed up."

"I'm not surprised. But even among those who do know of them, there is some debate as to their origin. Some believe them to have come from Strania, others say they come from the Tetrarchy near Corsana Bay. Still others—"

"Get to the point, kid."

Fulko cleared his throat. "Still others, like Master Vennick and myself, have reason to believe these plants come from Vinateria."

"Why would a Vinaterian plant be in Porocar?"

"For the same reason that it was on your inn. Someone brought it with them. Someone with extensive knowledge of plants." The boy's gaze narrowed on Joren. "Perhaps someone who, at the time of these deadly plants' first appearance, was in Yel Mor."

Joren gave a confused look, but the blood rushed from Eino's face. "Yel Mor ain't nothing but a tiny little village in the mountains. What's it got to do with anything?"

"It may be small, but it's very close to all of the areas known to have had strangleweed attacks." Fulko turned. "And according to your ledger, Mr. Eino, Yel Mor is where you first picked up Mr. Joren here."

Eino bit his lip. The alterations he'd made to the ledger to convince Revna that Joren wasn't the Kingslayer were now painting him in a guilty light.

"So if we consider the facts, we have an apothecary capable of handling these deadly Vinaterian plants, fleeing from the epicenter of their attacks in southern Porocar, bringing one such plant along with him to the northern coast.

This leads us to our conclusion." The boy sipped his tea. "Mr. Joren here is a Vinaterian spy."

Eino's jaw hung slack. "Dilgaa's sakes, that's the most ridiculous thing I've ever heard!" He looked to Vennick. "You can't possibly agree with him."

Vennick shook his head. "Fulko has my full confidence. He has a sharp mind for these things." He peered over at Joren. "But so far, Mr. Eino, you've said much more in defense of this man than he's said himself. Perhaps the accused can offer a better explanation?"

Joren trembled in silence. He looked down, unable to meet their gazes.

Fulko smirked. "Don't bother defending yourself, Vinaterian. Your guilt speaks for itself." The boy dusted his hands. "And once we get to Apthras, you'll be thrown into the Grand Duke's prison to rot for your crimes."

"Stop it."

All eyes turned to see Val standing at the threshold to the promenade, her knuckles white from gripping the doorway.

"Val, please," said Vennick. "Let us handle this."

"I said stop it. That man is innocent."

"Ah yes," said Fulko, his smirk growing. "I was wondering when you'd make your move, auramancer."

Her eyes narrowed. "What did you say?"

"I'd long suspected it was you who produced the blue aura that mended the barrier when Leora and I fell. Why else would you have stayed out of sight when she was in such danger?" He turned his back. "I'm grateful for what you've done, but the Deka'ara is quite clear. The only women who should wield such powerful auramancy are the Esshedrel warrior-nuns. Still, you did save my life, and out of gratitude, I will not report this to the arbiters."

Her hands fisted. "How dare you—"

"How dare I? You masquerade as Cacosshian, strutting around in mockery of our faith as if no one would notice." Fulko glowered. "I do not know who you are or where you're really from 'Val of Gathia,' but you are neither warrior-nun nor an arbiter of justice. Your mastery of aura is impressive, but that alone does not give you any insight into the mind of a Vinaterian spy."

Val grit her teeth. "I tell you, this man is no Vinaterian spy. If he were, his target would not be someone as insignificant as the Grand Duke of Porocar. He would..." She drew a deep breath. "...he would be planting those things in farmlands. Using them to devastate farmers and their crops. That is what they were designed for."

Fulko paused, confused anger stirring behind his eyes. "How could you know that?"

"Because I was there when the plan was first devised," she shuddered, "by my husband. Mastam koa Ha'aldi."

"The Butcher Bishop of Atrenem?" Fulko's eyes went wide, "Then that means—"

"Yes," said Val, removing her veiled cap. Her steel blonde hair was pulled back into a tight and elaborate braid, exposing the tattoos on her pale forehead. She removed her sleeves, and the elaborate tattoos along the length of her arms started glowing with a pale blue aura. "My real name is Chelival koa Ha'aldi. Lady of the Noble House of Ha'aldi in Atrenem."

For a moment, everyone stood in stunned silence. It was as if the air had been sucked from the room. Time stood still. Then at last, a sound came. The shuddering breath of Fulko.

"You...a Vinaterian...all this time..." his mouth hung agape in disbelief. In a swift motion, he drew back the blades of his gauntlet bow, aiming an aura arrow at Val. "The Thresher take you, Vinaterian witch!"

Before anyone could react, Vennick had already grabbed Fulko's arm and pulled the bow away from its mark. "Fulko, stop!" The arrow struck the wall beside Val as he wrested the gauntlet from Fulko's hand.

"Master, let go! She's the spy." The boy tugged and clawed desperately at his gauntlet, but Vennick's grip held fast. "She's one of Vinat's pawns. She said it herself!"

"I do not belong to Vinat!" Val's voice boomed, far louder than seemed natural. For a moment, her tattoos flashed, but then subsided as she collected herself. "I despise the so-called God-Queen. She is the very reason Leora and I left our home."

"You lie!" the boy yelled. "She's the one who drew the aura from the cabins, Master! And she'll plunge this whole inn to the ground if you don't stop her."

Eino stepped forward. "Calm down, kid. It was the strangleweed that took down the cabin, not her. She ain't got nothing to do with it."

"Then how does she know so much about them, huh? How does she know how they were designed?"

Vennick and Eino turned to meet Val's gaze, but she looked down in response. "My...husband told me about the Council's plans after I—" Her eyes went wide and she paused, biting her bottom lip.

"...after you what?"

"After I—" she exhaled. "—helped to create them."

"You...you created those things?" Vennick stared at her.

"Not on purpose. I swear it to you!" She held up her hands. "But sadly, it is true."

Confusion and hurt was painted across Vennick's expression. "Why?" Why would you do something like this?"

Val sighed. "Before we left home, the war with Heralia consumed all aspects of life. Even the noble houses of Atrenem were expected to contribute to the war effort, and as I was an auramancer, mine was to be a mighty contribution."

"What did you do?" Vennick asked.

"The soil of Vinateria is poor and our harvests are fickle, so I applied myself to the study of plant life. By honing the aura of our crops, I was able to triple their output. But my meddling had an unexpected consequence." Val shuddered. "To control pests, the farmers plant a weed around their fields called verminsbane. It is harmless to humans, only a threat to small rodents and insects. Yet by honing the crops, I inadvertently honed the aura of the verminsbane as well."

Vennick stroked his chin. "Creating strangleweed."

"Yes. When I told the Council of Bishops what had happened, they cared little for the crops. Only the verminsbane held any interest for them, and my husband ... he pushed to have the plant deployed as a weapon."

"The Butcher Bishop...your husband..." Vennick shook his head. "I thought you said he died."

"I said I lost him. And I did." She looked out the window, her eyes vacant and sad. "I lost him a long time ago. I just had not realized it until then."

"So you just created a mess and ran away without cleaning it up?" Fulko spat the words at her.

"I tried to fix it, but there was no way I could stand against the whole Council of Bishops. They wanted to reward me, and the only reward they thought to offer was a high-ranking husband for Leora. I couldn't force this life on her. So I ran away. I hoped that perhaps I could outrun my problems. Now I see that is impossible. But perhaps I have a chance for redemption." She locked eyes with Joren. "I would like to assist you in your research. Together, I believe we can find a way to defeat the strangleweeds, and get rid of them altogether."

Fulko crossed his arms with a scowl. "Do you all expect these two to save us? The Sinian's bumbling nearly brought the whole inn down." He glared at Val. "And the only language a Vinaterian speaks is death. She and her daughter—"

"Be silent, child." Val's voice boomed, her eyes glowing with aura. "I will hear no ill spoken of my daughter. She is innocent in all this."

Fulko stepped forward, his expression hard. "I've faced death before, witch. Your threats don't frighten me."

Val met the boy face to face. Her words were slow and calculating. "If I truly sought your death, boy, I would have already had it."

Vennick stepped between them, a firm hand on each of their shoulders. "That's enough, Val."

"Mama?" Leora stood in the kitchen doorway, a tray of cookies in her hands. "What's wrong?"

Val straightened her back and adjusted her collar. "Nothing is wrong, dear. Nothing at all."

Leora set her tray down on the table. "Um...Mama your..." She adjusted her own hat.

"It's alright, Leora. They know now." She set her veiled cap back on her head and made for the door. "Those cookies look lovely. Why don't we have some out on the promenade?"

Leora hesitated. "Oh, um... alright, Mama." The girl looked to Fulko and Vennick, a confused look on her face. She then gathered up some cookies and followed her mother outside.

"Well?" Fulko cast an accusatory glance at Vennick. "Aren't you going to do anything?"

"And what would you have me do, hmm?" he replied. "Strike her down like a beast in front of her daughter?"

"I would have hoped you'd remember who your enemies are," said the boy, bitterness dripping from his words. "But I see now. One night of passion was all it took for you to forget." With that, he stormed out onto the promenade.

"Fulko, wait," said Vennick, reaching after the boy. With a heavy sigh, he followed after him.

"Hope you've all worked up an appetite!" Came Betta's voice from the kitchen. She emerged with another tray of cookies. She met Eino's gaze, then cast a confused look around the room. "Well, cast me to the Wynds. Was it something I said?"

"My head..." Joren's eyes fluttered, and he slumped back limply across the divan. He grabbed Eino's arm, his fingers squeezing hard. A sheen of sweat clung to his forehead. "May I please...rest here?"

"Nonsense. You'll rest a lot better in a proper bed." He helped Joren to his feet. Joren leaned his full weight against Eino, causing him to stumble. "Come on. Let's get you to my quarters."

It was slow going, but after some difficulty, he managed to help Joren to stagger up the stairs and into the captain's quarters. To think that just last night, Joren had been helping Eino to his bed. He didn't know whether to laugh or cry at how ridiculous the whole situation had become.

Joren reached down, straining to pull off his boot.

"Here. Let me." Eino knelt down and helped him pull it off. He inspected his left ankle. It was swollen and red from where the vines had squeezed.

"No wonder you can't hardly walk on it," muttered Eino. He reached for his pocket. "Let me get you more salve."

"No, no." Joren held up a hand. "I'll be alright. The only thing that can help me now is rest."

"Ain't there anything else I can get you? Tea? A blanket? Some of them cookies?"

"You've already done so much for me. So much more than I deserve..."

"What are you talking about? You don't deserve all that." Eino was incensed. "First that damned knight, and now you've got that little brat going around saying you're a killer. How long are you just gonna keep letting folks spout all these false accusations?"

He hung his head in his hands. "They're not entirely false."

Eino paused, then let out a nervous chuckle. "That poison's doing a real number on you, huh?"

"No, Eino...they were right," said Joren, his voice strained. "I'm the Kingslayer."

24

For a long moment, Eino stood in stunned silence. "No, that...that's impossible." He refused to believe it.

"But it's true." Joren laid back down, rolling onto his side. "I'm the Kingslayer."

"No, you ain't!" shouted Eino. He gestured wildly, stammering as he struggled to find the right words. "You ain't a killer, Joren. I know you ain't." Had he really spent these past weeks sighing over the Kingslayer of all people? Had his ability to read others failed him that badly? Or had his loneliness and Joren's good looks gotten the better of him?

"You don't know me that well." Joren rolled over, hiding his face against a pillow. "You've been kind to me. Kinder than I deserve. But you wouldn't do it if you knew all the terrible things I've done."

Eino's mouth hung agape. "But the Kingslayer is dead. Vennick killed her. He said so himself."

"She was...she—" Joren's voice hitched. "It's a long story."

"I've got time." Eino sat on the bed beside him. He lifted his hand to touch Joren's back, then changed his mind and rested in on the bed. "Tell me the truth, Joren. I deserve that much with how much I've stuck my neck out for you."

"I suppose you do." His words came out muffled. Joren sat up and drew a deep breath before continuing. "Her name was Fryssa. She was an apothecary, and I was her apprentice. She was also the closest thing to a family I ever had."

The words hung heavy on Eino's chest. Nothing happy ever followed a statement like that. "What happened to your parents?"

Joren shrugged. "Don't know. I never knew my father, and my mother...." He trailed off. "When I was ten, she dropped me off with Fryssa. She told me I was her apprentice now, and I had to work for her. After that, I never saw my mother again."

Eino's hand balled into a fist. Hearing the bitterness in Joren's voice made him want to do something to fix it. But there was nothing he could do about Joren's parents. All he could do was relax his fist and set his hand gently on Joren's leg. "I'm so sorry."

"Don't be," he said, a rueful smile pulling at the corners of his mouth. "Fryssa always made sure I was well fed, and she taught me everything she knew about being an apothecary and a healer. We traveled across Bhaleia, collecting ingredients by hand and treating the wounded and sick. It was a good life." His voice hitched again, and he cleared his throat. "I never worried about her abandoning me. She loved me. Like a real mother should. And I loved her too."

Eino ran a frustrated hand through his hair. "Well, beg your pardon, but that don't exactly sound like the life of a killer. You said it yourself. You treated the wounded and healed the sick. Why the heck are you beating yourself up about it?"

"Because of those...things." Joren gestured in the direction of where his cabin used to float. "One day a few years ago, the strangleweeds showed up on the outskirts of the kingdom. The poison was pretty mild at first. People would come to us with a rash or a headache, and we'd treat them and send them on their way. But as we went from village to village, the plant's poison just got worse and worse. Eventually, someone came to us, and we couldn't save her." He took a deep breath, burying his face in his hands. "I can't believe I was so stupid."

"Stop that." Eino grabbed his wrists. "You did all you could to help. But you can't save everyone all the time. Don't blame yourself for what the plants did."

"Don't you get it? The plants weren't spreading on their own. Fryssa spread the spores across Bhaleia so she could study the strangleweeds!" He drew a shuddering breath. "And she used me to help her do it."

"Joren, you didn't know."

"It doesn't matter! Those people are still dead because of me." His lip quivered. "I'm the one who figured out which oils could put the strangleweeds into a state of temporary hibernation. I thought it would make it easier to retrieve plants to study. But she used my discovery to move plants from village to village. All over Bhaleia."

"But why? Why was she doing this?"

"She was practicing. Getting ready to kill the king. Of course, she kept me in the dark. When we made it to the capital in Karaval. I thought we were just there to protest Bhaleia joining Chandarre's Unified Kingdom. I should have seen there was more to it than that."

Eino's nose scrunched in disgust. "She was ready to kill the king just because he was going to join the rest of Sinia?"

"King Shakaud wasn't her target. She was trying to kill Chandarre." He crossed his arms, hugging himself. "Lots of people were upset over unification. Some feared that the smaller kingdoms would be swallowed up and forgotten. Others were upset at Chandarre for marrying Bhaleia's beloved Princess Shavenne, adding her to his harem." He shook his head. "I never knew exactly why Fryssa hated Chandarre. All I knew was that I didn't want to disappoint her, so I hated him too." Tears welled in his eyes. "That's why I did it."

Eino's blood ran cold. "You didn't."

"No one was supposed to be killed," he said, his voice straining, barely above a whisper. He shuddered and collected himself. "On the day of the Unification Feast, Chandarre was to be given a bouquet of local flowers. Fryssa told me we were going to replace it with a bundle of javelin thistles, because the flower was the symbol of Bhaleia, and because they had sharp thorns that would give Chandarre a nasty rash for weeks. It wouldn't be the first time one of the kingdoms struck out at him. She told me I had to swap out the bouquets when I went inside the palace to treat a few ill servants. So I did. The flowers seemed like such a small thing at the time. But I never noticed the strangleweed wrapped around the bottom of the bouquet."

Eino chewed his lower lip. "And when the king gave Chandarre the bouquet..."

Joren nodded. "After the strangleweed wrapped around Shakaud's throat, I didn't stop to watch what happened. Once the screaming started, I just ran." He stared off into the distance. "I didn't know the plants could do that. I planned to hide away in the Great Cistern. People were always coming in and out to fetch water, so it would be easy to blend in. Maybe I'd even find Fryssa again."

"But she never showed up," said Eino, "did she?"

"She did. But she wasn't looking for me." He looked down. "She'd collected a whole flask of concentrated strangleweed poison with her." He rubbed his eyes. "I told her we should just run away. We could grab our things and start over somewhere new. But she just yelled at me. She said it was my fault Shakaud was dead. My fault that Chandarre survived. And she said she was going to fix my mistake. Even if it meant poisoning half the city."

Eino's eyes widened in horror. "But you stopped her."

He shook his head. "I tried. I pleaded with her not to do it, but she struck at me with her sickle." He tugged on his right glove, pulling it off and revealing the stump where his ring finger had been severed. "That knight was right. I was missing a finger. She just got the wrong hand."

"By Dilgaa." Eino sucked in a breath. Revna had been only seconds away from discovering the truth, and Eino had been none the wiser.

"I realized then there'd be only one way of stopping her, but I couldn't do it. I didn't have it in me. Even though she was about to kill all those people, I just...she was my only family. She taught me how to save lives, not take them." He hung his head. "But I didn't need to. He did it for me."

"Vennick?"

He nodded. "Before I even knew what was happening, he'd drawn his sword and cut her down. I don't know if he saw me. Maybe someone did. I don't know. I just ran. And I've been running ever since."

Eino's eyes darkened. "You must hate him."

"At first, I did. For a while, I blamed him. Hated him for taking her away from me. But now I see that the woman I thought I knew was gone for a long time before we even came to that city." Joren rubbed his eyes. "No, I don't hate Vennick. Not anymore. I wish I could be brave like him. Strong. Fearless. The only thing I ever do is run."

"You don't need to run anymore. Fryssa is the one who caused all this. Not you."

"Do you think anyone's gonna care?" snapped Joren. "I killed a king. I created a deadly poison and spread it across Sinia. And now—" Tears began streaming down his face. "Now I'm destroying your inn. After you've been so kind to...to..." He hiccuped.

"Listen to me. I care," said Eino, grabbing the sides of Joren's face to force him to look Eino in the eye. "You trusted your mother, and she took advantage of that. That doesn't make you a monster."

"Yes it does!" he cried out. "I was too old to be so naive. I wanted her to be proud of me. To see me as her real son. In the end, I lost her anyway. I should have pulled my sickle on her rather than let a stranger strike her down, but I'm a coward. The world would be better off without me."

"Don't you dare say that." He pulled Joren into a tight embrace, letting the man cry on his shoulder. "Now, maybe you've made a mistake or two. Anyone in your situation would. But you've been working all this time cleaning up a mess you didn't even make. And if there's anyone who's gonna find a way to beat those damn plants, it's you."

"I don't...I can't..." He squeezed his eyes shut as he hiccuped again.

"Shh. Get some rest for now. Tomorrow you'll get right back to it. And this time, you won't be alone. I'll go get you another drink."

He laid Joren down and pulled a blanket over his shoulders. For a moment he watched the man's chest rise and fall as he drifted off to sleep, but the whole time, Eino's head spun. He wanted to believe Joren. He did. But could he? He bit his bottom lip as he mulled over that question.

There was a creak outside the door. In a flash, Eino rose to his feet, drew his knife, and threw the door open. He locked eyes with a startled Fulko holding his journal. "It ain't polite to eavesdrop, kid."

The boy tried to hide the journal behind his back. "I was just checking—"

"Don't you give me that," said Eino. "How much did you hear?"

Fulko drew a deep breath. "Enough."

Eino tightened his grip on his knife, his nerves taut. He slowly drew the blade up, before folding it and placing it back in his pocket. "Alright. So what are you gonna do about it? Gonna tell your precious Master everything you heard?"

Fulko quirked an eyebrow. "Why would I do that?"

"Don't play with me, you little—"

"Listen." Fulko held up his hands. "The Karaval Kingslayer is dead. She's gone now. As far as I and Master Vennick are concerned, the issue is resolved." He cast a shy, sad look past Eino toward Joren. "The only thing left to do is to take care of her victims."

Eino narrowed his eyes. "It ain't like you to be so trusting." Not after how he'd handled Val.

"You're right. That's why I was checking everything he said against Master Vennick's account of the Karaval incident." He pulled the journal from behind his back, holding open a page of his notes. "Parts of this account were never made public. Only Sinian royal guards ever knew that the kingslayer attempted to poison the cistern. If Joren knows that detail, then either he's a royal guard...or he was there."

Eino glanced down at the boy's notes, and his expression softened. "So...you believe him?" There was desperation in his voice. Desperation to believe that Joren truly was an innocent victim in all of this.

"I see no reason to doubt his story." He stared off into the distance. "Family is...very important. I can't condone his actions. But I understand them." He cleared his throat. "That said, keep a close eye on him. He doesn't fit the profile of someone trying to harm the Grand Duke, but he might accidentally hurt us if we're not careful."

Eino smiled, looking back at him. The man was fast asleep, no doubt exhausted from the poison and from his tearful confession. "Don't worry, kid. I'll make sure he doesn't get into any more trouble."

"Good," said Fulko, "the Vinaterian, on the other hand—"

"Oh, don't you start on her now," said Eino. "She's a victim in this too."

"She's a war criminal," said Fulko, his gaze intense, "by her own admission."

"Kid, you just got done saying how important family is. Ain't it clear to you that everything she's done, she did for her daughter?"

"That doesn't—" the boy paused. Something stirred behind his eyes, but then he buried it. "She's Vinaterian. That makes her a threat."

Eino sighed. "Like it or not, kid, you're stuck with her till we reach land. Till then, you're gonna have to figure out how to deal with that."

"The moment we make landfall, I'm going to report her location to the Heralian Guard."

"Fine," said Eino. "But it's gonna be a few days yet, so I suggest you get some rest."

"Very well." The boy tucked his journal under his arm. "Good night, Mr. Eino."

Eino closed the door and turned to Joren. Despite everything, the man was sleeping peacefully. He so wanted to join him in that bed. To hold him close. To let him know everything would be alright.

He shook his head. It wouldn't be right, he thought. Instead, he dragged the chair from his desk up against the wall, watching Joren sleep. Eino leaned back and nestled his head against the spongy mushroom wall. It wasn't comfortable, but it was far from the worst place he'd ever fallen asleep. A wistful smile crept over his face as he remembered his time in the Sinian Air Legion, and eventually, he drifted off to sleep.

25

Morning greeted Eino harshly. His eyelids were too heavy to open, especially against the bright morning light pouring in through the window. With some effort, he leaned forward, resting his chin on one hand, and rubbing his stiff neck with the other. Despite his uncomfortable pose, he still found himself nodding back to sleep. He nearly fell out of the chair before he finally opened his eyes.

He expected to find Joren still recovering in bed, but the man was nowhere to be found. Guilt crept up Eino's back. He'd meant to keep better watch over him as he slept. To make sure he was still breathing. His chest rising and falling. His hair cascading over his pillow in the morning light...

Eino shook his head. He shouldn't be thinking like that now. He'd thought he was making progress getting to know Joren, but last night had been a cruel reminder that he barely knew the man. Joren had almost died, and if he had, Eino never would have learned that Joren had technically killed a king, or that he had a brush with the most legendary hero in Itharos. That made him wonder what else he didn't know.

Eino groaned as he forced himself to his feet. A thin, drafty wind whistled past his window. He shivered against the chill in the air. Even in his half-awake state, he understood what that meant. There was another crack in the barrier, but this time, the cold was sharper. The air whipped by faster, and it carried with it the distinctive smell of a coming storm.

He cursed under his breath. Val's previous repair to the core was already failing, and it would still be another week or so until they reached Levenham. Maybe she could try patching the barrier once more. But even if she did, how long would it be until he lost another cabin? He held his head in his hands. It seemed like all of his troubles had been solved just a couple of days ago. Now, his inn was falling apart, and his life felt like it wasn't too far behind.

He stood up and stretched. Moping wouldn't get him anywhere. His guests needed breakfast, and so did he. He opened the door to the loft and crept down the stairs to the common room. There he saw Leora, still fast asleep, and splayed out across the divan. Below her on the floor was Vennick, lying on his back and snoring peacefully.

As he rounded the corner, he heard voices coming from the dining room. Joren stood over the table, looking surprisingly well considering his near-fatal poisoning yesterday. His dark stubble had grown into a short beard that suited him. He and Val stood side by side, surveying a mess of books and notes spread over the table. Across from them sat Fulko, his suspicious gaze following their every move.

Val pointed at a page with a messy drawing of a flower. Her veil was nowhere to be seen. "I do not understand. This is an entirely different plant."

"No, no. This flower is the gamete form of the strangleweed." Joren gestured toward the drawing's stem.

"It is?" Val held up the page and squinted at the drawing. "It looks more like a sunhood tulip."

"Sorry. The petals aren't meant to be that big." Joren rubbed his injured hand. He cleared his throat. "The point is, the flowering form is harmless."

"That still does not help us. It will just produce a deadly vine in the next generation." Val chewed her lip. Then realization dawned on her face. "Unless..."

While Val talked out the specifics with Joren, Eino sidled up next to Fulko and whispered. "You following any of this?"

"I'm starting to," he replied. "The details are hard to follow, but from what I gather, neither auramancy nor herbology is enough to solve this puzzle."

Eino dropped his voice to a whisper. "So, does this mean you trust Val now?"

"Of course not." The boy snorted. "Why do you think I'm keeping an eye on her?"

"...but could that really keep the plant in its harmless flowering form permanently?" asked Val.

"That's what I've been hoping I could do," said Joren, "but I can't determine which environmental pressure prevents the weed from growing into deadly vines. I've tried heat, cold, sunlight, every kind of plant oil—"

"But I assume you have never tried honing the plant's aura." The tattoos on the back of Val's hand glowed a pale blue.

Joren nodded. "I've never had much control of my aura, so I never even considered the option."

"With your knowledge of herbology, perhaps we can determine which part of the plant's aura to manipulate."

Joren shook his head. "The only sample I had was the one that went berserk in my cabin. If we're going to be doing experiments, we'll need a new sample from the surface."

"You can't be serious." Fulko stood up. "You're suggesting we bring another one of those things up here?"

"You need not worry," said Val. Holding out her hands, she formed a barrier of blue aura around her teacup and set it to float around her. "It is trivial for me to isolate the sample. No aura will get in, and no growth will escape."

Fulko narrowed his eyes. "So you say."

"It don't much matter anyhow," said Eino. "We won't be anywhere near land till we get to Levenham."

Val glanced at the map on the wall. "How far away exactly?"

"I reckon we've got a couple more days yet." With all of the chaos at the inn lately, there hadn't been much time to check his location. "But we might be close enough to see the Great Lighthouse. I'll go take a look and see if I can't spy it on the horizon." He ran a hand through his messy hair as he made his way to the kitchen. "After breakfast, of course."

"Ms. Betta made some pottage earlier. There should be some left in the kitchen." Fulko sat down on Joren's free side. He grabbed Joren's notebook and started writing.

"What are you doing?" Joren reached for the notebook.

Fulko stopped him. "I'm rewriting your notes. Your handwriting is even worse than Master's, and if we're going to find a solution, we'll need good documentation. I can't have you making a mistake because of your messiness."

Joren's mouth opened in surprise, but he let him keep the notebook. He watched Fulko work for a moment, brow knitted. "Can you redraw the plant diagram, too?"

Eino chuckled to himself as he ladled himself a bowl of Betta's breakfast pottage. It was still warm, with a rich and comforting flavor despite the simplicity of its ingredients. He closed his eyes and savored its taste. But when he opened his eyes, the sky outside the window gave him pause. The suns shone brightly, but dark storm clouds loomed on the horizon.

By the time he'd finished his breakfast and climbed to the top of the mushroom cap, a dense fog had enveloped the inn. The suns were little more than dull white circles in the gloomy sky. He could barely make out the shapes of daggermouths as they flitted out from the fog beyond the barrier. He might not have noticed them at all if not for the bright white flashes of Red and Blue swooping down and gobbling them up.

It was a bit early in the season for storm clouds this intense to reach so far up the Stranian coast, and the shoals of daggermouths seemed to be unusually large considering how far north of the Miasmic Ocean they were. Of course, he'd seen plenty of freak storms before, both as an innkeeper and as a legionary. Still, with everything that had gone wrong lately, he couldn't help but feel that the worst was yet to come. Tension wove through his shoulders, making them stiff.

He shook his head. There was no sense worrying about it, he thought. Instead, he'd try to get some work done while he waited for the storm to clear. He took a basket and started gathering up longberries from the tree, snacking on a few of them as he did so. The tree was still free of whatever rot had taken the mushrooms, so there'd be no reason to worry about his guests going hungry. He held onto that bright spot in his sea of gloom.

Voices came from the makeshift rope ladder to the roof. A moment later, Leora appeared with Vennick in tow.

"That's the real reason I wanted to learn to fight," said Leora, her voice apologetic. She gripped her wooden sword close. "I wanted to tell you, but Mama made me promise not to say where we're from." She paused to pet the wool hen pecking at her dress.

Vennick grunted as he crested the net. "Your mother was smart to keep that a secret. But it doesn't matter if you're fighting Vinaterians or not. The rules are still the same. You remember the rules, don't you?"

"'Never start a fight, and don't fight if you can run,'" recited the girl, sounding bored as she rubbed the hen's head.

"Don't forget the most important rule." Vennick smirked, creeping up behind Leora's back and drawing a training sword from his satchel. "If you're cornered, and you've got no other choice…"

With a whoop, Vennick lifted his sword and swung at the girl. He was only moving at about half speed, but it still made Eino wince. To his surprise, however, the girl whipped around and parried Vennick's strike. And the next. Again and again he struck at her, but she parried every strike. There was a fire in her eyes as she reversed her teacher's momentum, releasing her own flurry of full speed strikes.

"Never. Give. Up!" Her sword clacked loud against Vennick's as he blocked her attacks. She reached up and grabbed the man's sword. He backpedaled, and she slipped past his guard to strike him in the shin.

"Ow! I yield, I yield!" said Vennick, chuckling as he dropped his sword and held up his hands. He knelt down and rubbed his shin. "That was excellent, Leora, but don't forget we're just training."

"That's not what Fulko says." She scrunched up her face as she did a mocking impression of the boy. "He says, 'You must train as if you are fighting for your life. Myeh.'"

Vennick let out a hearty laugh. Eino strolled over, clicking his tongue. "It ain't enough that you're beating up on poor ol' Vennick here. Now you're making fun of Fulko too?"

"Why not? He makes fun of me all the time." The girl widened her shoulders and puffed out her chest, tucking her chin to her neck as she continued her impression. "'You must never laugh, Leora. Even when having fun. Poor fundamentals and such. Myeh, myeh, myeh.'"

"Sheesh, Vennick. What have you and Fulko been teaching her?" said Eino with a chuckle. He glanced over to the net ladder. "Where is he anyhow? Ain't he training with you?"

Vennick shook his head. "He's downstairs with the others, still trying to figure out the strangleweed. I can barely follow what they're talking about." He patted Leora on the shoulder. "So, I figured we could at least get in a little practice."

Leora flourished with her sword. "Wanna play with us, Mr. Eino?"

"Sorry, little lady. I've gotta keep my eyes peeled for the Great Lighthouse of Levenham." He pointed to the horizon behind the girl. "Might be tough to see through the fog, but let me know if you see a light flashing bright yellow out there."

Leora squinted and pointed behind Eino. "Like that?"

Eino scoffed, chuckling and shaking his head as he turned around. "No, not that way—"

He froze. It was dim through the fog, but there was a point of golden light on the horizon, flashing at regular intervals. It was unmistakable. Only the Great Lighthouse could generate a light that powerful. So why was the inn moving away from it?

Eino's blood ran cold. The inn was running fast again, and this time it was moving far faster than it ever had before. He hadn't expected to have made it to Levenham for another day or two at the earliest, but based on the size of the light, the inn must have passed by the lighthouse sometime last night.

"Why, just like that. Good eye, little lady!" He painted a bright smile on his face. There was no need to frighten the girl, he thought. "Well, I'll let you two get back to training. I've still got some work to do…"

He trailed off and made his way to the far end of the mushroom cap. With a trembling hand, he reached into his pocket and pulled out his signal staff. He signaled a distress message in bright flashes over and over again. His heart pounded in his chest, his muddled thoughts making it too hard to think of any other plan.

"What are you doing, Mr. Eino?" Leora asked, oblivious to the message.

"Well, uh…" Eino stammered. "The lighthouse is waving at us. I'm…waving back!"

Vennick chewed his lip. "Leora? Work on your forms for a moment." He walked over to Eino and tapped him on the shoulder.

Eino jumped. "Oh! Hey the—"

Vennick drew close, his voice low. "Don't lie. I know that's a distress signal. Now tell me what the Strak is going on."

Eino knew he'd been caught. But lies were what got Val and Joren in trouble. Besides, who could he trust if not the hero? He took a deep breath. "The inn is out of control. We're already way past Levenham."

Vennick's eyes went wide. "Who are you signaling?"

"Everyone. Anyone. We're gonna need help if there's gonna be any hope of getting everyone off this inn alive."

Eino knew it was a desperate ploy. With the skies still thick with scrambler clouds, any Sinian airships in the area would have docked for the season already. He held onto hope that some Gatrai who were bold enough to brave the skies might still be in the area. Maybe even a ship on the waters below would notice and send a greatwing courier up to the inn. But with the fog rolling in and only growing thicker, his desperate hope waned.

Vennick looked down, his puckered expression showing his displeasure. Then he extended his hand. "Give me the staff. I'll keep calling for help. You go tell the others."

Eino tried to remain calm as he opened the hatch down to his room, but once he was out of Leora's sight, he made a mad dash down to the dining room. Val, Fulko, and Joren were all still poring over the pages scattered across the table.

Joren looked up. "Did you see the Great Lighthouse?"

"Sure did." Eino grimaced. "Which is a problem. Seeing as how it's a ways behind us."

Fulko's head snapped around. "You said we were a couple of days away! How could we possibly have already passed it?"

"I don't know!" Eino held up his hands. "The core must be making us run fast again. I reckon the strangleweeds are messing with the aura. I've lost control of the core."

"But if we're already past Levenham…" Val chewed her lip, trailing off. "Where are we now?"

"We must be halfway across the channel. At this rate, we'll be in Apthras by tomorrow night. Maybe sooner."

Joren gave a shy smile. "Well, that's some good news. It shouldn't be hard to gather samples in the Porocari countryside." Joren's eyes went wide with embarrassment for a brief moment. "With Val's help, of course. We can make sure there won't be any more loose strangleweeds at the inn."

"Oh, I can guarantee there won't be any more," said Eino, "because once we're over land, every last one of you is getting on the basket and checking out."

Joren's face wore a look of betrayal. "You're kicking us off?"

"Don't get me wrong. Everybody's getting a complete refund down to the last jingle." Eino brushed his hair back, holding the back of his head. "Fact is, it's only by the grace of the gods that all of us are still alive. I ain't gonna keep tempting them by keeping you in the skies."

Val's expression hardened. "I am not leaving."

"The Strak you ain't!" said Eino, "I know you must feel just awful that your research was used to make these things, but this inn ain't safe. You've got to think about that little girl of yours."

"You do not understand." Val clenched her fist. "If we leave now, no place in Itharos will be safe."

"She's right," said Joren. "The plant in my cabin might have released its spores, meaning the whole inn could be infected." He rubbed the back of his neck, wearing worry on his face. "And if we just abandon it, the inn will drift all over Itharos, spreading more and more of those...things."

Eino's heart sank. It had always filled him with pride to see the excitement on people's faces whenever the Driftcap Inn came to town. He'd made friends and lovers across his travels, and even complete strangers always greeted him with a smile. But if his inn was hurting them, there was really only one option. It was too terrible to think about, but what choice did he have? He shuddered.

"You two probably know more about these damn plants than anyone, and if anything happened to you..." He'd seen Joren grapple with death once already. He didn't think he could bear to see it again. "I'd sooner see my inn destroyed than see any of you get hurt."

"Do not say that." Val stood up. "We will find a solution, and we will save this inn."

"How?" asked Joren. "Without a sample—"

"There is one, though I had hoped we would not need to use it." Val cleared her throat. "It is sealed safely in my cabin."

"And just how long did you plan on keeping that a secret?" Fulko slapped the table. "Don't you realize how dangerous that is? This is exactly how we lost Joren's cabin!"

"So long as it is sealed, the plant is completely harmless." She took a breath. "But I am not certain of what will happen when I break the seal. I feared it might damage the inn, so I will not unseal it without your permission, Mr. Eino."

Eino sat and chewed his lip. For a long moment he was silent. "If I let you do this, can you save my inn?"

She shook her head. "I cannot say. But there is a chance."

He drew a deep breath and slowly let it out. "Then do it."

26

"You need not follow me like a troupe of lap hounds," said Val, grabbing the railing of the promenade in front of her cabin. "I am quite capable of doing this on my own."

"Beg your pardon, ma'am but, I can't let you go this alone," said Eino, flanked by Joren and Fulko. A cold wind blew in through the crack in the barrier, carrying with it the scent of the coming storm. "It's risky. Something might happen to you."

"And if something were to happen, what then would you do?" asked Val. "Cut me loose?"

"If we have to." Fulko patted his gauntlet.

Eino shot Fulko a look before turning back to Val. "Please. Just tell me what you're looking for and I'll run over and grab what you want."

"It would be too much trouble to explain," she said, waving a dismissive hand. "This will only take a moment."

With that, she turned and strode across the rope bridge and disappeared into her cabin. A minute passed. Eino bounced on the balls of his feet. He searched the door, but no sign of Val emerged from her cabin. He might have thought that time was standing still but for the flashes of the signal staff's light reflecting off of the cabin's windows.

Joren shifted uncomfortably. "I should go get Vennick." He started toward the net ladder to the roof.

"There's no need to trouble Master," said Fulko, drawing back the bow of his gauntlet. An arrow of flaming aura coalesced on the bowstring. "If the Vinaterian causes any problems, I'll handle her."

"Damnit, kid. Put that thing away," said Eino.

"It's merely a precaution," said the boy, "But don't expect me to wait for your approval to keep us all safe."

"This is my inn. I call the shots. So put the weapon away."

Fulko huffed. He slowly lowered his arm, but the waiting arrow remained.

At last, Val appeared in the doorway, putting an end to the argument. Her right palm was extended, and floating above it was a glowing pale blue orb. It looked like a crystalline bubble, and there in the center was a tiny green sprout emerging from a seed.

"Finally!" exclaimed Eino. "What took you so long?"

She bowed her head. "My apologies. It was not my intention to trouble you. I merely took a moment to gather some personal effects." She had a purple blanket slung over her other arm with a small golden trinket in her hand.

Joren's eyes lit up. "A seedling? This is perfect! Where did you find it?"

Val paused, casting her eyes down a moment before looking back up. "All that matters is that we have it now. Come. Let us test your theory." She led the way back to the dining room.

Joren didn't seem to care, but his unanswered question still hung in the air for both Eino and Fulko. The boy cast Val a suspicious look as she walked away, but said nothing. For once, Eino shared in his concern, but desperation made him ignore the feeling. There was hope to beat the strangleweeds. Hope to save his inn. His home. And so long as there was even the faintest glimmer of hope, he'd cling to it.

Small raindrops pitter-pattered against the dining room window. Betta poked her head out of the kitchen, a cup of tea in her hand. "If anybody else wants a cup of smoked pine, there's plenty left in the pot."

"Quiet," said Fulko in a hushed whisper. He kept his gaze fixed on the table where Joren and Val were working, and on the seedling in the crystalline barrier between Val's hands.

Betta scoffed, sidling up beside Eino. "Can you believe the mouth on that boy?" she asked, craning her neck to watch Val and Joren work.

"Yeah, the kid's a real bristleboar," said Eino. His eyes followed Joren's fingers as they danced over vials of powders and tinctures. "But I'd take a cup if you're offering."

She chuckled. "You can get it your own damn self. I ain't missing this."

"Almost ready," said Joren. With methodical precision, he mixed a few vials into a mortar, mashing them into a paste. He slid it over to Val. "There. Those are all of the extracts from the dormant flowering form. Will this be enough?"

Val's eyes remained closed as she dipped a finger into the paste. "Yes. The aura is faint, but docile. I think I understand now."

"So can you, um..." Joren stammered, searching for the right words. "...infuse them? Those oils, I mean. Into the seedling?"

"Not exactly," she said with a slight smile, "but if I use these extracts as a guide, I may be able to hone the plant's aura into its dormant form."

Eino scratched his head. "Does that mean it won't try to kill us?"

"In not so many words, yes." Val opened her eyes and met Joren's gaze. "Though I must caution you that if this test should fail, we will not be able to reuse the sample."

Joren looked down, chewing on his thumbnail for a long moment. Eino could read the doubt written across the man's features. He strode over and set a hand on his shoulder. "It's your call. I trust you, Joren."

He looked up, putting a hand on Eino's. At his touch, a shy smile replaced the doubtful expression he'd been wearing. "Sometimes you just need to jump, right?" Joren cleared his throat. "Go ahead, Val."

She closed her eyes once more and drew a deep breath, smearing the paste on her palms. Her tattoos glowed, and when she opened her eyes, they too seemed to be alight with a pale blue flame. She pressed her fingers through the small aura barrier, its surface rippling like water as she reached inside. She held her hands on either side of the seedling, and after a moment, the paste appeared to dissolve from her palms. At last, she withdrew her hands and closed her eyes. "It is done."

Eino squinted at the seedling. It looked as though nothing had changed. "So what now?"

"Now, I will lower the barrier, and the seedling will grow." She opened her eyes and turned to Eino. "If I have honed its aura correctly, it will sprout flowers, and it will be completely harmless. Otherwise..."

"Otherwise this," said Joren, sliding over a small leather pouch. "Black kindlewood sap. We'll burn it to a crisp before it can hurt anyone."

Eino blanched. "Dilgaa's sake, Joren. You light that up and we won't be able to put it out! Are you trying to burn down the whole damned inn?"

"Fear not," said Val. "I will not allow the flame to consume anything but the plant."

Eino stepped back and steadied his breath. "Well, alright then. Don't keep us all in suspense."

Val nodded, then held her hand over the barrier. She drew the aura into her palm, and the seedling fell to the table beside the pouch of sap. She held out a finger wreathed in fire only a handbreadth away from the pouch, ready to set it alight at a moment's notice. For a few tense moments, nothing happened. Everyone in the room held their breath.

The seedling twitched. It slowly began to grow. Thin green tendrils no bigger than a hair sprouted forth from its stem, writhing across the table. Eino sucked in a breath. They moved the same way as the tendrils which had ensnared Joren in his cabin. "Val—"

"Wait," she said. "Look."

Eino's eyebrows shot up. A tiny bulb formed at the tip of each tendril. He couldn't keep himself from letting out an excited laugh as the bulbs unfurled into delicate white flowers.

He slapped Joren on the back. "You did it! You really did it!"

Joren jumped up and pulled Eino into a tight hug. Val sat and smiled, tears welling in her eyes.

"I don't believe it," said Fulko, his eyes wide. Even his sour, skeptical expression gave way to giddy excitement. "Does this mean we can wipe out the strangleweeds in Apthras?"

Joren collected himself. "Well, sort of. The strangleweeds that have already taken root will need to be destroyed, but if my theory is correct, it might be possible to prevent any more from planting themselves."

Val dried her eyes and nodded. "From up here, I can hone the aura of any spores we come in contact with. It will propagate to the entire continent."

Fulko sprang to his feet. "I have to tell Master Vennick at once! He'll be—"

The sudden sound of shattering glass cut short the celebrations. Eino shielded his eyes from the spray of shards, and when he looked out the window to find the source of the noise, he let out a yelp of terror. There outside the broken window was Val's cabin, mashed against the promenade. Even more terrifying was the writhing mass of tendrils stretching out from the cabin and across the promenade, each vine as thick as a stout tree branch.

"Get back!" yelled Eino, grabbing Joren and pulling him to the other side of the table. The inn listed toward the window, making the table and everything on it slide into the mass of tendrils. Betta and Eino held on to the doorway for support.

Val was quick to react. Holding out her palms, she formed a wall of shimmering blue aura against the tendrils. She grimaced and strained as her wall pushed the vines back out the window, but the thicker vines hammered against the wall, bending its surface like fabric. Her voice was strained as she yelled, "Leora! Where is Leora?"

"She's with Master Vennick!" yelled Fulko, springing into action. He drew back his bow gauntlet. "Now stand back!" He let loose a flurry of flaming arrows at the tendrils reaching around the edges of Val's wall. Several arrows missed their mark, embedding themselves in the walls of the common room. The arrows' flames licked at the walls before the vines reached up and snuffed them out.

"Stop! It is draining the aura!" yelled Val, groaning as she strained to hold up the barrier. "You must run. I cannot hold it back for long!"

"Don't gotta tell me twice," said Betta, clawing her way into the kitchen. Eino turned to follow her, but a tug on his arm stopped him.

"Wait!" said Joren. "The kindlewood sap. There's enough to burn it up."

"That much will burn the whole damn inn down." He tried to pull Joren into the kitchen. "Ain't nothing we can do. Leave this to the pros."

A thick vine pushed through Val's barrier, cracking it like stone. Her wall dissolved, and she fell to one knee.

Fulko gritted his teeth. "I won't run," said the boy, jumping in front of Val. He riddled the vine with arrows, but the strangleweed was unrelenting. It sloughed off the arrows that found their mark, and it snuffed the arrows' flames as quickly as they struck. The vine undulated across the floor, creeping closer and closer.

Suddenly, the thick vine and all of its offshoots fell limp. There were bright flashes of light outside the window and the sounds of fierce chopping.

"Master!" said the boy, his voice full of hope and reverence.

Vennick moved like lightning, a sword in each hand as he plunged into the fray. He leapt and dashed across the promenade, slicing through the thick vines as if they were made of paper. The plant's tendrils flailed at him, but with an effortless grace, he dodged them and cut them down. With each sliced vine, the strangleweed lost its grip on the bridge and the cabin lurched back. The inn wobbled before righting itself.

Val struggled to her feet, supporting herself on the overturned table. Her breathing was heavy from exertion. "I need...to find Leora."

"Mama!" came a voice from the loft. Leora charged down the stairs in the common room and stood at her mother's side, a steel shortsword clenched in her hands. "I'll protect you, Mama!"

"Oh, my sweet girl," said Val, wrapping her arms around Leora. "Thanks be to God."

"No, Mama, not now," said Leora, annoyance in her voice as she shrugged off her mother's embrace and took up a guard stance. "Mr. Vennick said to stay with you and chop up any vines that make it past him, so that's what I'm gonna do."

"Right. Of course." Val stepped back and smiled through teary eyes. "Thank you, Leora. Be brave."

As Vennick drove back the strangleweed, Fulko followed behind and drew back a large flaming arrow. "Fire is ready at your signal, Master!"

"Hold!" yelled Vennick as he sliced through a vine. With one more cut, the strangleweed lost its grip on the inn and the cabin flew backwards, crashing against the inn's barrier. Vennick turned. "Now!"

Fulko loosed the arrow, and it found its mark at the base of the cabin's mushroom. Yet the cabin did not catch alight. Again Fulko drew an arrow and shot, this one burying itself in a thick vine growing out of the window, but the flame fizzled out.

"It's the rain, Master. The cabin is too wet to burn. We have to cut it loose."

Vennick shook his head. "We can't do that. A strangleweed that large could destroy a whole village." He furrowed his brow, his eyes dark and his jaw hard set. "I need to burn it from the inside."

"You can't go in there! The plant is too big. Look at how thick those vines are." The boy shuddered. "If you get caught, we won't be able to pull you out."

"Then I'd better not get caught," said Vennick with a confident smile. He reached into his satchel and produced the dragon gourd. "I hope this thing has enough juice."

"Wait!" said Joren. He dashed to the overturned table and retrieved the pouch of kindlewood sap. "Take this. Once it's lit, water won't quench it, and there's more than enough here to torch the whole cabin."

"Perfect." Vennick returned the gourd to his satchel, instead pulling out the dagger he'd used to light his stick pipe and tucking it into his belt along with the pouch. He turned to Fulko. "I have one more important task for you. You can refuse if you wish, but once you say yes, you must follow through with it. Do you understand?"

"I don't understand what you mean." Fulko wore a determined expression. "But whatever it is, I'll do it."

Vennick took a deep breath and let it out. He pulled out the massive blade he'd used to cut loose the other cabins, the Mansplitter. He held it up and grimaced, then slowly offered it to Fulko. "If anything should happen to me—"

"No," said Fulko, shaking his head. "I won't. I won't cut you loose."

"I know this is hard, Fulko, but you're brave. And you're ready." He crouched down to look the boy in the eye, setting a hand on his shoulder. "I'll be fine. This is just a backup in case I—"

"No!" Fulko pushed Vennick's arm away. "No, I'm not gonna lose you too. Don't ask me to do that." His voice shook. Tears welled in the corners of his eyes.

"We ain't got time for this," said Eino, stepping forward. He pointed to the cabin. "How's about I hold on to your fancy sword while you go do what you need to do?"

Vennick hesitated, but turned and held the blade out for Eino. As he reached for it, Fulko held out his hand. "Stop," said the boy, his voice quavering, "I'll do it."

"Thank you, Fulko." He turned his attention to the cabin, taking a breath before charging in."

"Wait." Val shambled forward, holding her arm. "Just one more—"

She stumbled over her own feet and tripped forward. Vennick leapt forward and caught her, flashing a smile. "Careful. I still need to escort you to Muna, remember?"

"I do. So please...return to me." She pulled him into a kiss. As their lips touched, a pale blue flame spread across Vennick's body, wreathing him in a glowing aura. "A barrier. It will keep you safe."

Betta yelled from the kitchen, "Finish up later, lovebirds!" She pointed to the cabin, which was already starting to sink below the promenade. Tendrils from the strangleweed snaked their way up the bridge.

"Right." With one last kiss, Vennick steadied Val and drew his twin swords, charging across the bridge. He sliced through the thin flailing vines, each slash looking as though it cut through the rain itself. The cabin door had already burst from its hinges, and the doorway was blocked with a mass that looked more like a stout tree trunk than vines. Vennick circled to a window and smashed it, diving inside.

The others gathered at the promenade, gripping the railing as they watched. For a tense few moments, all they could hear was the sound of steel against vine through the background of rain. The pale blue of Val's barrier shone through the windows dimly. Then, there came an orange glow from inside the cabin. Wisps of smoke peeked out from cracks in the door and windows. The smoke billowed out in thick black clouds.

"He did it," said Eino, his voice full of awe, yet no one celebrated. All eyes remained silently transfixed on the cabin, darting between the doors and windows. The cabin sank lower, but Vennick did not appear.

"Where is he? Where is he?" muttered Fulko. He leaned over the railing, his eyes desperately searching.

Val closed her eyes, her hand held toward the cabin. "I can feel him. He just—"

The cabin crunched against the inn's barrier with crackling flames of aura licking at its edges. It twisted to its side and slid down the barrier, straining the rope bridge as it tugged at the inn. Everyone steadied themselves as the inn listed forward once more.

Suddenly, the woody mass of vines blocking the door was smashed apart, and a pale blue glow emerged from the threshold.

"Master!" yelled Fulko, tightening his grip on the Mansplitter. The others bounced in excitement.

Vennick huffed as he started across the bridge, which had now become a steep ramp. Behind him, the flames inside the cabin rose. Its windows shattered, and long vines wreathed in flame emerged and flailed about. With a sound like scraping metal, the cabin made a sudden shift down the barrier, coming to a rest at the bottom. Vennick stumbled as the bridge twisted further, now vertical like a ladder, but he found his footing and began his climb.

The burning vines swatted in all directions. Vennick drew a broad-bladed chopper from his satchel, cutting through the vines before they could strike him. But above him, a thin tendril wrapped around the rope of the bridge. Fire clung to the sticky black sap on the plant, and though the rain had picked up, the water only seemed to make the flame grow.

"Hurry!" Fulko watched Vennick, eyes wide.

Vennick reached into his satchel and drew another weapon, a long chain with a hooked blade at the end. "Stand back!" he yelled as he swung the chain and tossed it up to the promenade. The blade hooked over the railing.

"That railing's gonna snap!" Eino yelled, grabbing the chain and pulling. Joren joined, and then Fulko. Even Leora and Betta grabbed on and pulled. Only Val stayed back, holding out her hand, her breathing heavy as she maintained his aura barrier.

Slowly, they pulled Vennick up. He was halfway up the bridge when a thick vine reached up and wrapped around his ankle. Then another. As he reached down to slash at them, there came a shrill screeching sound from below. With a crunch, the barrier below shattered, and the cabin dropped. The left side of the bridge dipped down. Another crack, and the second rope gave way. The bridge fell, the end of it whacking against the inn's stem. Fulko, Joren, and Eino stumbled forward as the cabin pulled on the vines and the chain.

Vennick grit his teeth, slashing at the vine around his ankle. But then there came another. And another. Stretched between the cabin and the chain, he couldn't cut cleanly through any of the vines, and each laceration he opened up on the plant just produced a new writhing mass of tendrils, slowly climbing up his leg.

He looked up, his eyes meeting Fulko's. He held his chopper to his heart, then closed his eyes and let go.

"Master!" The boy reached out to grab at air, but both Vennick and the cabin had already been swallowed up by the dense fog below. "No!"

Val collapsed, her breathing haggard. "Too...far...can't..."

Eino looked down in shock at the gaping hole in the barrier, then followed the growing cracks in the glassy aura that stretched to the very top. There was a crashing sound as the barrier shattered into tiny shards that dissolved in the air. Wind howled across the promenade. "Get inside!" he yelled, ushering everyone into the common room.

When he slammed the door shut, no one spoke. Leora wrapped her arms around her sobbing mother. Fulko ripped his headscarf from his head, letting his shaggy brown hair fall to his shoulders. He buried his face in the headscarf, muffling the sounds of his sobbing.

Betta and Joren looked to Eino as if hoping for guidance. But with Vennick gone, his barrier destroyed, and a storm rolling in, he was all out of ideas.

27

"Alright," said Eino at last, "everybody's getting off."

"What?" said Joren.

"I said everybody's getting off the inn. I want you all to grab whatever you can and head for the basket. We're all heading down to the surface before things get worse."

"W-we can't just abandon this place," Joren stammered. "We could still be spreading strangleweeds!"

"You think I haven't realized that?" He shook his head. "Look, I know you want to solve this, but there just ain't anything else we can do from up here. So let's live to fight another day. Once we're back on land, you and Val can figure out some way of stopping those things."

"But what about your inn?" asked Joren.

"We ain't too far from Sinia. I'll get word to the Air Legion. I reckon they can haul it out over the ocean until we get this all figured out." Eino took a deep breath. There was only a slim chance that the Legion would actually listen to him. Even if they did, they were much more likely to blow his inn out of the sky than bother trying to save it. But as long as he held onto that faint hope, he could stomach the idea of leaving his home.

"Well, that's one plan," said Betta, "but we're still over the channel, ain't we?"

"We've gotta be close to the Porocari coast. If we drop down now, we'll wash up just outside of Apthras. Might be a rough trip over the water in stormy season, but I'd rather take my chances down there than up here."

Betta grimaced and looked out the window. The fierce winds howled outside. "We're going awful fast. You sure the basket—"

"Enough," snapped Eino. He clapped his hands once. "Now I ain't trying to be rude, but I'm gonna have to ask you fine people to please leave my inn. I suggest you gather what you can and head to the promenade now. We're getting off of this inn and that's final."

Eino stormed up the stairs to his quarters and slammed the door behind him. He sucked in a deep breath, but his pulse wouldn't calm. He gazed at his messy quarters. The thought of never seeing them again felt like a knife to his gut. His eyes skittered over everything he'd collected. As much as he hated to lose the mementos of his travels, he didn't have space for them. He settled for pulling down his new map from Mebeq and rolling it up to cram into a pocket.

Eino choked back his tears and steadied his breathing. For the sake of his guests, he had to put on a brave face. Collecting himself, he marched back down the stairs. Betta and Leora were gone, and Fulko hadn't moved at all. Joren and Val gathered up notes and vials from the overturned table.

"But it doesn't make any sense. How could the vines have overtaken the entire cabin that quickly?" asked Joren, gathering up the last of his notes from the table. "It couldn't have been spores from my sample. Not with how quickly it had grown. And your sample was contained by that barrier, wasn't it?"

"It was. The barrier was perfect." Val looked down. "But while I had it up, I interrupted the flow of the inn's aura. Once I dropped it during our experiment, aura came rushing back in, not just to the sample, but to all the seedlings in the inn. That sudden wave must have pushed them into growing."

Joren blanched. "'All the seedlings?' You mean you knew there were others this whole time?"

"Of course she did." muttered Fulko. He hadn't moved from his position, hugging his knees and facing the wall. "She's a puppet of Vinat. Who do you think put them there?"

"I am no puppet of Vinat!" said Val, sniffling. "But my husband...he must have deployed the spores. They could be all over Itharos already with spores riding the aura streams."

"And did he package that seedling up for you as well?" asked Fulko, rising to his feet and turning to face her with teary eyes.

"No. That..." Tears welled in her eyes.

Eino stepped forward. "Where did you get the seedling, Val?"

She took a deep breath. "The seedling...I pulled it from the inn's core."

Eino's eyes narrowed. "You what?"

She collected herself, drying her eyes and standing with as much of her poise as she managed to muster. "The crack in your core. It was not caused by age, but by the seedling burrowing into it. I feared the plant may be verminsbane, so I plucked it out without informing you of the danger. I thought I could contain it before it spread." Her voice hitched as she held back a sob. "I was mistaken. I should have told you the truth."

"You...let her touch the core?" Fulko turned to Eino, rage in his eyes. "You let her touch the core! You absolute dimling! I warned you, you empty-headed mud weasel, and you still let her do it?"

"Relax, kid. She's the only reason we even made it this far."

"And you're still too blind to see that she's doomed us all!" Fulko drew his bow and aimed it at Val.

Eino stood between them. "What are you doing?"

"Get out of the way. She'll face justice before the end."

"This ain't the end, kid," Eino pleaded, trying to keep his voice calm and steady. "We can still make it out of this, and when we do, Val here is one of the only people who can make sure the strangleweeds never hurt anyone ever again."

"I don't care about anyone else!" yelled Fulko. "Master is gone because of her!"

"And what would he say if he could see you now, huh?" asked Eino. "Is this what he'd want?"

"It doesn't matter what he wants. He's gone. He..." Fulko's arms trembled. "He's dead."

"Now you listen to me," said Eino. "You've been with Vennick for years now. Had adventures all over Itharos. Can you honestly say this is the most danger he's ever been in?"

Fulko made a choking noise in response, keeping his bow trained on Val.

"We've all heard the songs. Vinaterian assassins. Didinbo pirates. Monsters in the Forlorn Sea. He's faced them all, and he came through without so much as a scratch on him. So you can't tell me you seriously think a couple of plants were enough to take him down."

"But he...I saw—"

"Now I don't know what you saw, but I saw him fall and grab a hold of that driftcap. And an old driftcap can stay afloat for weeks on the water. So I reckon he's making his way down the channel now."

The boy's arms trembled. "How can you say that? You don't know that for certain!"

"I don't," said Eino, "But I trust my gut. And my gut tells me that Vennick ain't the type to just roll over and give up."

"That's right," said a small voice behind them. Eino turned to see Leora peeking her head around a bag much too tall for her. "That's Mister Vennick's most important rule. To never give up."

Fulko snorted, lowering his bow before Leora could see.

Betta rounded the corner, laden with bags and satchels. She looked everyone else up and down. "Is that all you folks are bringing with you?" She shook her head. "You all sure travel real light."

A sudden gust of wind blew through the smashed window. It shook the whole inn. Everyone held out their hands to steady themselves.

"What's going on?"

"Without the barrier, there ain't nothing to keep the wind from batting us around." Eino beckoned his guests to follow him. "All the more reason to get off this thing while we can."

He led everyone out onto the promenade and peered over the railing. The fog was still thick around the inn, but through the low clouds, he caught glimpses of the water below. The inn looked to be moving fast, but as he squinted through the clouds, something caught his eye that made him gasp.

"I don't believe it," said Eino, a growing smile on his face. "Land! We made it to the coast. Finally, some good news."

"The coast of where?" asked Joren. "Apthras?"

"Who cares! It's dry land." Eino tapped at the aura stone in his necklace. A moment later, the basket pulled up beside the promenade. "Alright. Everybody in. Quickly now."

"Wait," said Val, holding up a hand. "This basket...its connection to the core is faint."

Eino grit his teeth. "What's that mean? Can we still ride it down?"

"Yes, but it may not hold all of us at once," she said. "Only one, perhaps two at a time."

"Right, then," said Eino. "Leora, Fulko, you're up."

"No! I'm not leaving Mama." Leora scooted closer to her mother.

"I'm not leaving either," said Fulko, still glaring at Val. "Not until everyone else is safe."

Eino groaned. "Fine. Val, take Leora down."

Val shook her head. "I will be better able to support the connection from here." She held out her palms toward the basket.

Eino threw up his arms. "Well, somebody's gotta get on! We can't all stay behind."

"Dilgaa's sake..." said Betta. She hoisted her bags into the basket. "Out of the way. I'll go."

"Are you sure you want to go first?" Sending her down alone didn't seem right. What if she needed help when she landed? Bettta was no spring wool hen, but he knew she wouldn't appreciate being reminded of that fact.

"Like you said, someone's got to do it." Her steely determination gave no one room for argument.

"I know, I just..." Eino pulled her into a tight embrace. "I ain't ready to say goodbye yet."

"Oh, you hush now. This ain't goodbye," said Betta, patting Eino on the cheek. "Tell you what. We're somewhere in Porocar, which means we ain't too far from a tavern. How about we all meet up at the closest one, and then we'll make our way down to Yel Mor. You're all invited to stay with me."

"Alright," said Eino, stepping back. He bit down on his quivering lip. "But you send that basket up the moment you hit the ground, you hear?"

"I ain't some old fool, you know," said Betta with a smirk. She closed the basket door and gave them all a cheerful wave. "See you soon." She pressed her key to the control pillar, and the basket shot down. Eino pulled out his spyglass and watched until she disappeared into the clouds of mist.

Then there was nothing to do but wait. The thunder grew closer. The misty rain thicker. Joren slid closer until his shoulders and arms pressed against Eino's. As another minute ticked by, Eino's heart hammered in his chest. No one spoke. Everyone watched the foggy clouds below, looking for any sign of the basket.

Eino chewed his lip. "Val, did she land safely?"

"I cannot say," said Val, her eyes closed, "But the basket maintains its connection to the core."

"Well, what the Strak does that mean?" Eino tightened his grip on the railing.

Joren held his arm. "Don't worry. She'll be alright."

Another minute and Eino reached for his key. "I should check—"

A gust of wind howled across the promenade, shaking the inn. Everyone clung tight to the railing, struggling to maintain their footing as the floor tilted below them.

Fulko grunted as the inn righted itself. "Don't you have any other way off besides this damned basket?"

"What about Blue?" offered Joren. "We could ride her down."

Eino shook his head. "No good. Her wing's injured, so she can't carry us all in one go, and there ain't no way she'd be quick enough to make two trips. Not with how fast the inn's going.

Fulko scoffed. "So you expect us to just sit here and do nothing?"

Eino chewed his lip. "I might be able to stabilize the inn. Val, you stay here and keep feeling for that basket. Joren, you come with me. I'll need your help with the flight kite."

He led him around the promenade to the rope ladder. As they rounded the corner, he caught sight of the massive wall of black clouds swirling in the distance. The inn was charging headlong into a storm.

Something else caught his eye. Something large shifting and shimmering in the dying light of the setting suns. He squinted and rubbed his eyes. It wasn't lightning, and it was too low in the sky to be an aurora from the aura stream. And it seemed to be getting bigger as it twisted through the clouds. Then his eyes went wide as he recognized what it was he was seeing. He tugged on Joren's shoulder. "Get everyone inside. Now!"

"Why? What is it?"

As if in response to his question, something slammed into the wall beside the door. Its pointed, leaf-shaped body, roughly the length of his arm, had plunged deep into the wall, and its tentacles flailed wildly as it struggled to pry itself loose. The creature opened its mouth, revealing rows of sharp teeth, and let out a hideous shriek.

"Daggermouths," said Eino, "a whole damn flock of them."

28

EINO SLAMMED THE DOOR shut behind them, grabbing an end of the divan as he barked out orders. "Block the windows!"

The others sprang into action, tipping over the divan and tea table to reinforce the windows. No sooner had they finished then came the sound of breaking glass and a loud thud as another daggermouth plunged its beak into the overturned table. Then came another. And another, each one letting out a shrill cry as it withdrew.

Joren ducked, covering his ears against the creatures' shrieking. "What do these things want?"

"Dilgaa only knows," said Eino, "but they're here, and they ain't going away on their own."

Fulko ground his teeth. "So, what's the plan now?"

"It's the same plan. I get the kite into the stream and stabilize the inn," said Eino. He turned to the boy. "The only difference is now I need your help to keep the daggermouths off our backs."

Fulko drew his bow. "You can count on me."

"I will join you as well," said Val, the flames of her aura enveloping her fist.

"No," said Eino, his expression hardening. "You stay right where you are and try to bring that basket back up here. You're the only one who can."

"Then let me come with you." Leora brandished the blade Vennick had given her. "I can help."

"I know you can, Leora. That's why you have a very important job." Eino squatted down and patted the girl on the shoulder. "Now you listen to me. The minute that basket comes back up, you make sure both you and your mom ride it all the way down the surface. Once you get down there, you keep her safe. Don't wait for any of the rest of us, you hear?"

The girl slowly nodded. "Alright. I'll do it."

"Atta girl." He patted her head. "Alright, fellas. Let's get moving."

Eino charged up the stairs, leading Fulko and Joren through his quarters, pausing at the hatch to the outside.

"Just one sec," said Eino. He reached into his coat, fumbling a moment before pulling out a length of rope and offering one end to Joren. "Here. Tie this around your waist."

"You really do have everything in that coat, don't you?" Joren said with an amused smile. "What's this for, anyway?"

"Oh, it ain't nothing. Just a precaution," said Eino, chewing his lip.

"To keep us from blowing off the inn, right?" asked Fulko, nodding. "Smart plan."

Joren blanched. "I'm sorry, to keep us from what?"

"Great job, kid," said Eino sarcastically.

"What? That's what it's for, isn't it?"

"Well, yeah, but don't say it like that," said Eino, throwing his arms up in frustration. He gestured to Joren. "He's scared of heights."

"Really?" Fulko cast an incredulous eye to Joren. "Then what are you doing on a flying inn?"

Joren offered no response. He simply stared off into a corner of the room, stuffing his mouth with briskweed leaves from his satchel.

"Now ain't the time to talk," said Eino, finishing the knot around his waist. He grabbed Joren by the shoulders and shook him. "Listen. Just stay close to me and you'll be alright. We're gonna release the kite and guide it into the stream like we did last time. Easy, right?"

"Yeah. Easy." Joren steadied his breath. "And the daggermouths?"

"I'll handle them," said Fulko, patting his bow.

Eino grimaced. "Daggermouths can move pretty quick, kid. Are you gonna be able to hit them with that thing?"

The boy smirked. "Trust me. I'll handle them."

"Before you do, run over to the garden and tie off the other end of that there rope to a fencepost. We ain't leaving anything to chance."

"Understood." Fulko leaned forward into a fighting stance. "Ready at your mark."

Eino steadied his breathing and drew his pocket knife, then grabbed a hold of the latch. "How about you, Joren? You ready?"

Joren drew his sickle. "No."

"Close enough." Eino flung the hatch open and peered out. Dozens of daggermouths filled the sky, a few of them flitting across the roof. Blue was perched on her nest, gobbling up any that dared to fly too close. Overhead, Red swooped down through the cluster and snatched the creatures up by the mouthful. His movements seemed slower than usual, thought Eino. As though he were struggling to keep pace with the inn.

Eino kept a wary eye for any lull in the creatures' onslaught, and once the last few daggermouths in the cluster zipped past, he sprang into action. "Now's our chance. Let's go!" He dashed forward and made for the flight kite embedded in the mushroom, glancing back to check on the others. To his surprise, Joren was close behind, a determined look in his eyes.

When Eino reached the aura stone embedded in the mushroom cap, a sudden gust of wind buffeted his face. He lost his footing, and with nothing to brace himself against, he fell to one knee. He called back to the others, "Stay low!"

When he looked back, Joren was already lying flat against the ground. He had plunged his sickle into the mushroom cap and was holding on. Fulko was clinging to a fencepost around Eino's garden. He finished securing the end of the rope to the post, then tugged at the knot a few times to test it. Satisfied, he gave Eino a nod, then drew his bow and watched the skies.

Eino tapped Joren on the shoulder. "We're secured. Let's go." With that, he imbued the kite's stone with a droplet of his aura. As before, the stone glowed and rose out of the cap, unfurling its carved wooden wings. He took hold of one of the kite's guiding ropes and motioned for Joren to take the other.

Joren held tightly, looking up at the aura stream above. "Is it working?"

"It'll work. Just keep her steady till she's in the stream," said Eino. A low, distant rumble echoed across the sky. Looking up, he saw a cluster of daggermouths moving toward the kite, and gently tugged on his rope to guide it out of the way.

"They're coming. Look!" Joren pointed to the cluster. He pulled hard on his rope, snapping the kite this way and that.

"Whoa! Easy, easy. Give her some slack. She'll be fine."

"Right. Sorry." Joren steadied himself and loosened his grip. The kite righted itself and continued its ascent.

"That's it. Just keep her steady." A pair of daggermouths emerged from the clouds, much too close for the kite to avoid. Eino quickly looked back at Fulko and gestured. "Now!"

In a bright flash, the boy loosed an arrow of glowing golden aura. As it flew through the air, it expanded into a broad net and struck one of the creatures, knocking it out of the sky. His second shot missed its mark, as did his third, but the fourth shot caught the other daggermouth before it connected with the kite.

"That's some fancy auramancy, kid," said Eino, giving an approving whistle. "Cutting it a little close, though."

Fulko huffed. "It's not as easy as it looks."

Eino chuckled. "Well, it must be damn near impossible then, because it sure don't look easy."

The kite had nearly reached the aura stream when a sudden gust of wind battered the inn, making it twist in the air and tilt to one side. Behind them, Blue let out a cry. Eino reacted quickly, crouching down and slamming his knife into the roof to stabilize himself. Fulko was just as fast, wrapping an arm around one of the garden fence posts.

But Joren was not so quick. With a yelp, he lost his footing and let go of the kite's rope. Sliding to the edge of the roof, he quickly dug his sickle into the cap.

He dragged a deep gouge into the mushroom, only barely coming to a stop with his legs dangling off the edge of the roof. A gust of wind drowned out his cry for help.

"Hold on! I've got you!" shouted Eino. He held tight to one of the bolts that secured the kite's guiding ropes to the mushroom, then inched his way closer to the edge of the roof. He held his hand out. "Grab on."

Joren shook his head. "I c-can't. I'll fall."

"You ain't gonna fall." Eino tugged on the rope around his waist that connected them. "I won't let you."

Joren grabbed Eino's hand. He started to slip through his fingers, but Eino grabbed on with both hands and pulled hard. Joren hung on, his sweating palm making it hard for Eino to keep his grip. He didn't stop until Joren was on his knees on the roof. Joren lunged at him, wrapping his arms around him.

Red flew past them, landing next to Blue to offer her a daggermouth.

"Don't let go. Please don't let go." Joren shook, his grip tightening on Eino.

"I'll never let go," said Eino. "That's a promise."

Above their heads, the kite finally dipped into the aura stream. The inn righted itself. Even with the roof now level, Joren did not break his tight embrace, clinging tightly to Eino even as he was lying on top of him.

Eino smiled, patting Joren on the back, and daring to run his fingers through the man's soft hair. "As much as I'm enjoying this, we still got some work to do."

"Right." Joren pushed himself up with his shaking arms.

"Look out behind you!" warned Fulko. He loosed an arrow over their heads toward a massive cluster of daggermouths bearing down on the two men. The net cast by his arrow was broad, wrapping around several of the shrieking creatures and sending them hurtling below. But even with a second and third hit from his net arrows, the cluster was still too large to stop.

Eino pushed Joren to his back and rolled on top of him. He held up his coat and closed his eyes, bracing himself for impact. It wasn't much protection, but maybe his body would be enough to save Joren from the worst of it.

Behind him came a series of loud thuds, like the sound of a whole bushel of poutammes striking a window. The shrieking ceased, and when Eino peeked out from under his coat, he saw the daggermouths slamming into a glassy barrier. A barrier of pale blue aura.

He turned his head to see Val standing in front of the hatch to his quarters, her tattoos glowing with aura. At her side was Leora, calling out over the howling winds, "We can help with the kite now, Mr. Eino!"

"Ain't nothing left to do, kid. The kite's already in place," called out Eino, waving them back. "Now get back inside. It ain't safe out here."

"It's over?" said Joren, forcing himself to stand on shaky legs.

"For now." Eino looked out toward the storm. They'd made it through the worst of the daggermouths, with only a few little black dots flitting about in the distance. He turned to Fulko and gave his waist rope a tug. "We're done out here. Unhitch us."

"Not yet," said the boy, drawing back his bow. "Two more."

Far above their heads, two little black dots darted toward the kite. The boy loosed his arrow nearly straight up into the air. He did not wait for the first to make contact before shooting a second and third arrow, each expanding into a net of glimmering aura. The creatures darted around the first shot, with the second catching the leading daggermouth, and sending it plummeting. But the third shot missed its mark by little more than a hand's breadth, and as the creature swerved around it, it plunged headlong into one of the kite's wings.

Rather than slicing cleanly through, the creature got stuck, pinning the wing to the side of the aura stone. It flopped and writhed as it worked to free itself. With its wing pulled down, the flight kite began to twist and turn, dipping in and out of the aura stream.

The winds had only grown more fierce as they drifted closer to the coming storm, and each time the kite fell out of the stream, it jostled the entire inn. Eino and Joren bounced up into the air, held fast only by their waist ropes. Val held on tightly to Leora, gritting her teeth as she braced herself against the threshold. A moment later, the kite passed back into the stream and the inn stabilized.

"Damnit!" yelled Eino, untying the rope at his waist. "I've got to get that daggermouth free." He whistled for Blue.

Joren's eyes went wide. He reached out and grabbed a tight hold of Eino's arm. "What are you doing? Have you gone mad?"

Eino smirked. "No more than usual." He patted Joren on the shoulder and pulled himself loose. The greatwing rose up and trotted over to him. The hatchling was exposed for only a moment before Red swooped down and took a turn tending the nest.

One of the daggermouths felled by Fulko had fallen on the mushroom cap, its mouth agape and its tentacles twitching. "Mind if I borrow this?" asked Eino, stooping down to grab the creature and tossing it to Blue. She snapped the morsel up in a single gulp, then lowered herself for Eino to climb on.

"Wait!" Joren climbed onto his feet. "What can we do?"

"You can get inside. Don't you worry. I've got this."

Joren nodded. "Alright. Be careful."

Eino chuckled. "Ain't I always?" With that, Blue spread her wings and Eino took to the air.

She spiraled up slowly, riding the storm's gusts of wind. As they rose, Eino glanced back and saw that the inn seemed to be moving away from them. And fast. He grit his teeth. "Come on, girl. Let's get a move on." With a crack of the reins, the greatwing picked up her pace, flapping hard to reach the kite.

The rain grew heavier, with tiny pieces of hail now pinging off of Eino's head. Little coronas sprang forth from the aura stream as Blue drew closer to the kite. He was now close enough to reach the daggermouth lifelessly wedged in the wing. He grabbed at the creature, but with the buffeting winds and the flapping of Blue's wings, he struggled to grab hold of anything but the creature's slimy tentacles.

"Let me try!" came a tiny voice behind him.

Eino startled, wheeling to find Leora clinging to Blue behind him. He shook his head. "What the Strak are you doing here?"

"I wanted to help," said the girl. She held up the short sword that Vennick had given her. "And I brought this."

"You can't just—" Eino sighed and rubbed the bridge of his nose. There was no time to argue. "Alright. I'll hold on to you. You see if you can't pry that thing loose."

The girl beamed, brandishing her blade. "Yes sir, Mr. Eino!"

Eino shook his head. "When this is all done, I ain't gonna be the one to explain all this to your mother later."

Leora stood up, and with Eino holding onto the back of her dress, she reached for the kite. She grabbed hold of the rope, then dug her sword into the kite's pinned wing, using it to pry out the daggermouth.

"Ugh...gross..." The girl grunted and strained, but after a moment, the dead creature came loose. "Got it!"

Without warning, a gust of wind slammed against them. Blue let out a squawk, and her injured wing hitched. The greatwing dropped suddenly, and Eino lost his grip on Leora's dress. She screamed, holding on to the kite for dear life. Blue quickly righted herself, but Eino had now fallen much too far below Leora to reach her.

"Just hold on, kid!" Eino yelled, his voice desperate as he goaded Blue to fly faster. But the greatwing could only groan, favoring her injured wing as she struggled to maintain her current altitude. There'd be no way he could fly up to reach her. Eino's mind raced for a solution.

"Leora, listen," called Eino over the whipping winds. "Hug the rope and slide down. Got it?"

The girl nodded. With her short sword tightly in hand, she wrapped her arms and legs around the rope and began her descent. Eino hoped that as the girl got closer, he'd be able to pull her back onto Blue, but her slide down was inconsistent. She stopped her fall and started again without warning, screaming all the while. As Eino spiraled back down, he couldn't reach her before she was nearly at the bottom.

Then her grip slipped, and she let out a shriek as she fell. With a rope around his waist, Fulko charged out from the hatch to Eino's quarters and dived for the girl, but he overshot his mark and missed her.

"Leora! No!" shouted Val. Straining, she held out her palm and formed a chute from her aura. Leora slid over the pale blue chute, her own aura dancing at her feet until she reached the bottom and slid through the hatch to Eino's quarters.

Fulko was still clawing his way back up the mushroom cap when a sudden wind picked up. Red flapped hard to keep his balance, but as he lifted himself from the nest, the hatchling tumbled out. Both birds squawked, drawing Fulko's attention. He leaned over and caught the tumbling hatchling, the effort making him fall to one knee. The heavy winds blew them both off of the inn, but the rope held them fast. "Pull us in!" the boy yelled. Both Joren and Val tugged them into the hatch.

Eino practically fell off of Blue when she finally landed, charging headlong into his quarters and closing the door shut behind him. "Is everyone alright?"

He looked from Joren to Val to Fulko. The hatchling shuddered and twitched atop Fulko's chest. Everyone was panting heavily, but seemed to be uninjured.

A desperate tapping came from the hatch. In a panic, Eino threw the door open, unsure of who he'd left outside. To his surprise, the one behind the door was Blue. The greatwing squawked and craned her neck around before her eyes lighted on the hatchling. In a flash, she plucked the baby up with her beak and plodded back to her nest. Eino blinked. A cold wind blew through the door, bringing him back to his senses. He closed the hatch.

He glanced down at Leora. A dark brown line marked where the rope had dug into the front of her dress, and a red rope burn marred her hand and cheek. The girl held back her sobbing. "I didn't give up."

"You sure didn't," said Eino, squatting down to tousle her hair. "You're a real brave kid, you know that?"

She smiled through her tears.

Joren reached into his satchel and applied some salve to her wounds. "This will help with the pain."

Eino stood back up and grimaced as he caught Val's gaze. "I'm sorry I put her in danger."

"Do not apologize. The fault is with me," said Val, her voice somber. "She slipped out of my grasp when I tried to place my barrier."

"Don't be too harsh on her. She fixed the kite," said Eino. "I'd say that earns you two the next trip down on the basket. Is it back yet?"

"That is...that is why I came up." Val bit her thumbnail. "I cannot sense the basket's aura anymore."

Eino blanched. "What's that mean?"

"It means that the basket will not come back up."

A cold panic gripped Eino's chest. "What about Betta? Is she alright? Did she make it down safe?"

Val grimaced. "I do not know. I am sorry."

"What do you mean you don't know? How can you not know?" He grabbed her by the shoulders and shook her. "It's your job to know."

Joren grabbed him and pulled him loose. "Eino, stop."

"Without that basket, we're all trapped up here!" Eino's breath came faster. "And Betta...Dilgaa's sakes, Betta..."

Fulko stomped forward, and in one swift motion, struck Eino in the stomach. "Get a hold of yourself. She's fine."

Eino doubled over and gripped his stomach, his voice strained. "But how can—"

"How can I be so sure?" asked Fulko, a smirk on his face. "I'm not. But apparently I'm supposed to just trust my gut. And my gut is telling me that the old crone is much too stubborn to die."

Eino gave a pained chuckle. "Gotta hand it to you, kid. You're a quick study."

Val cleared her throat. "I believe I have a way down. It may be possible for me to drain the core and bring the entire inn down to the surface."

"If we can get it in the middle of the channel, we'll be able to burn everything up before the strangleweeds can spread their spores," added Fulko.

Eino cleared his throat and straightened his back, trying to ignore the pain from Fulko's strike. "It ain't like you to go along with a Vinaterian's plan."

"If you've got a better idea, I'm sure we'd all love to hear it."

"It's a good plan, but we won't wanna set down just yet. Not till this storm passes," said Eino. "Southern storms can bring all sorts of nasty critters up from the Miasmic Ocean. Much worse than daggermouths."

"That's what I can't understand," said Fulko. "I've read that daggermouths love storms. They use them as hunting cover. So why are they running from this one?"

Eino turned to face the storm, searching the clouds. "I reckon it ain't the storm they're running from."

From deep within the storm, flashes of lightning illuminated the clouds. With each flash, something in the storm took shape. The shadow of something truly titanic. Something big enough to dwarf a small village.

"Cast me..." said Eino, his mouth agape. "It's a stormgulper."

29

STARING OUT THE WINDOW of his quarters, mouth agape, Eino could only look on in terror as his inn charged headlong into the storm. The skies were dark, illuminated only by flashes of lightning in the distance. Each flash cast the shadow of the stormgulper against the clouds, offering a brief glimpse at the creature's movements. It was flat like a broad rug, with a long, whip-like tail that undulated with each flap of its enormous wings. Eino's eyes glazed over, hypnotized by the sight of it.

"Eino? Eino!" came Joren's voice. It seemed muffled. Distant. He turned to find the man was right next to him, shaking him by the shoulders.

"Huh?" asked Eino. He felt numb. Joren must have been shaking him for some time, but Eino hadn't heard him over the roaring of his pulse in his ears.

"Snap out if it!" Joren stepped in front of him, forcing Eino to look at him. Sweat dotted his brow. The hands clinging to Eino's shoulders trembled.

Seeing the man's face stirred Eino from his daze. "Right. Uh...right."

"Come on. Focus." Despite the desperation in his voice, there was something Eino found comforting about the sincerity with which he spoke. "You've dealt with those things in the past, right?"

"Uh..." Eino closed his eyes tight and opened them. Until now, he hadn't even been sure that the creatures existed, but now hardly seemed like the time to divulge that fact. "Yeah. Once or twice."

"Then how do we deal with them?"

"Well, the uh…the barrier should…" Eino trailed off, chewing his lip and shaking his head. He let out a rueful laugh. "But we ain't got a barrier, do we?"

"Perhaps I can repair the barrier long enough to protect us," said Val. "Please. You must bring me to the core at once."

"Mama, wait," said a teary-eyed Leora. She held out her hands, still marred with rope burns. "I'm coming too."

Val bent down. "No. Stay here and let Mr. Joren treat your wounds."

"But, Mama," pleaded the girl, "Mr. Vennick said I needed to protect—"

"Hush. You have already done so much for me, my sweet girl." Val pulled her daughter into a tight embrace. "But right now, I need my protector to heal herself. She needs to be ready for whatever comes next."

The girl offered a smile. "Alright, Mama."

"I'll take care of her," offered Joren, producing a few vials from his satchel.

"Thank you," said Val. She turned to Eino. "Now let us proceed."

Val led the way out of Eino's quarters and down the stairs from the loft. She moved with surprising speed. Eino struggled to keep up. "That's a real tough little girl you got there."

"Indeed," said Val, her stride not once breaking as she led the way into the kitchen. "Ironic, is it not?"

Eino chewed his lip. "How do you figure?"

"The reason I left Atrenem was to keep my daughter safe. To ensure that she would never need to be 'tough.'" She sighed as she flung open the door to the storage cellar. "I had hoped that Sinia would be far enough away from my husband and his lust for conquest. I had thought your inn, with its meandering path, would hide us from him and from anyone he would send after us. But despite my efforts, Leora has faced more danger these past few days than I had ever imagined."

"I'm so sorry, Val. I never—"

She held up a hand, cutting him off. "And yet, she has blossomed. She does not run and hide from danger, as I once did. I am proud of her, and I have you to thank for instilling such confidence in her."

Eino scratched the back of his neck. "I reckon that was mostly Vennick's doing."

"Your humility is most admirable, Mr. Eino. I am fortunate to have met both of you on this trip. It is comforting to know there are still good men in this world."

Eino shook his head. "I ain't a good man, ma'am. I'm a liar and a cheat."

"Perhaps. But I am certain that you will see us all safely to the surface." She smiled. "As you have said, one must trust one's gut."

When they reached the shelf that held the core, Eino paused on the landing. Green tendrils cascaded down from the core door. "That ain't good, is it?"

Val glanced around his shoulder and gasped. "Oh, God."

Carefully, Eino pressed his hand against the sigil, lowering the shelf's false back and revealing the core. It glowed far brighter than he had ever seen it before, shining gold like the suns, and its spinning had stopped. The core was now suspended on all ends by a web of spindly roots that emerged from the walls.

"Well, alright then," said Eino, his voice shaky. "Go ahead and do your thing."

Val shook her head, her eyes wide. "I cannot expand the barrier now. I dare not even touch it."

"What? Why not?"

Val pointed to the core, her finger hovering just above its surface. "Look. The barrier was not destroyed. It merely shrank. Even now, it keeps the verminsbane roots at bay. But only barely." She stepped back. "If I were to expand the barrier, I could not keep the roots from the core, and all of the aura stored within would become fuel for the weeds. Such rapid growth would be catastrophic. It would tear this very inn asunder."

Eino groaned. "Fine then. Drain the core. Setting down in the mouth of the Miasmic ain't ideal, but it's a damn sight better than facing a stormgulper with no barrier."

Again, she shook her head. "I cannot drain the core without removing the barrier, and the moment I do so, the plants will take root."

"Damn it all!" Eino cursed, slamming his fist against the far wall. "So what the Strak do we do?"

"I do not know." Val chewed her thumbnail. "Perhaps it would be best to destroy the core."

"Lady, are you crazy? Without the core to pump aura through its gills, we'll fall out of the sky and be at the mercy of the storm. The winds will knock us around like a child's toy."

"It is merely a suggestion."

"Well, we'd better come up with a better plan. And fast."

A deep, low rumbling growl shook the entire inn. No amount of wishful thinking could make him believe it was the wind.

Val braced herself against the wall.

"Upstairs. We've got bigger problems," said Eino, gesturing at Val to head back up the spiral staircase. He dashed past a few barrels and stopped. "Hold on. I have a plan."

Val glanced at the barrels. "Is your plan to get drunk again?"

"No. Nothing that fun." Eino hoisted a barrel onto his shoulder. "Do you reckon you can carry one of these?"

With a flash of her hand, three of the barrels were wrapped in her pale blue aura and began floating behind her in an orderly line.

Eino snorted. "Show off." Together, they dashed back up to the captain's quarters, where the others were huddled together in the cramped space. Leora's tears had dried up and Joren had bandaged her palms.

"What's in the barrels?" asked Joren, his voice hopeful. "Some sort of weapon?"

"Nope. Scramblers."

Val turned, confusion written on her face. "Your 'plan' was to drag the scramblers up here?"

"Well, there ain't much written down about gulpers. Some folks don't think they exist, so all I've got to go on is hearsay. But I've heard that for as big as they are, they only eat real tiny things. Scramblers and driftcaps and the like. I reckon if we part with all the scramblers we gathered, then that big ol' fella will leave us alone."

"Or you'll create a trail that leads right to us!" Fulko protested.

"Which is why I need your help. See, Val here is gonna give each barrel a good throw way up high into the air with her fancy auramancy, and then you're gonna shoot 'em open."

Val cleared her throat. "My auramancy has its limits. I cannot cast such a heavy object very far. But I may have a solution. With young Mr. Fulko's assistance, of course."

"Of course." The boy rolled his eyes. "What do you need?"

"Your bow," she said, opening the hatch. "Draw an arrow and aim into the sky."

Fulko hesitated, but then shook his head and complied. The golden aura of his arrow crackled as he drew it to its full length.

Val drew up behind him, floating a barrel in front of his arrow. She poured her aura over his arrow, wreathing it in a pale blue flame. The arrow grew, crackling with more energy until it reached the size of a spear. "Now, loose."

The tremendous arrow pierced the barrel and sent it soaring high into the clouds above. It burst in a brilliant flash of blue and gold, scattering the scramblers to the storm's winds.

"Perfect shot!" Eino laughed in disbelief. With the speed of the inn, they had already drifted far from the burst of scramblers. "That ought to throw that big ol' fella off."

The sky behind them darkened. Against the clouds, a shadow undulated up and down, drawing closer and closer to the burst of scramblers.

"That's it. Take the bait."

The mass of the beast nearly covered the horizon with its wide, flat silhouette. But it didn't fly up to meet the burst of scramblers. Its shadow only grew larger and larger as it drew closer.

"Oh." Eino blanched. He slammed the hatch shut.

"Did it work? Is it gone?"

Eino gulped. "No."

The entire inn rattled and shook. Outside one window, the smokehouse bobbed about, a plume of smoke still rising from its chimney. In a flash, a massive dark gray mass filled the view, and the smokehouse vanished. The inn lurched, throwing everyone to the floor.

"What's happening?" Joren called out, unable to stand on the inn's shaking floor.

Eino grit his teeth as he peered out the window. "That thing swallowed the damn smokehouse. It's dragging us along."

A moment later, the shaking of the inn stopped, and it was once again cast adrift. Eino looked out the window. The only sign of the creature was its long tail disappearing into the clouds. At the end of its bridge, the smokehouse drifted into view, or rather what was left of it. Smoke poured out from its insides, with little flames licking at the exposed wooden floor. The mushroom's cap was mangled beyond recognition, with pieces hanging limp and falling off. It sagged in the air, tugging on its bridge and making the inn list to one side.

"Damnit all. Gonna have to cut the smokehouse loose." He turned to Fulko. "Hey kid, where's that big fancy blade Vennick gave you?"

"The Mansplitter?" The boy's voice came out hoarse. He paused, then cleared his throat. "I think...I think it's in the common room."

"You think? I figured you'd keep a closer eye on something like that." Eino scoffed. He stood up and made for the door. "But it's alright. I've gotta go cut that smokehouse loose before it drags us all down. Back in a sec."

"No!" Fulko pushed himself to his feet. "I...I'll do it."

Eino squinted. Not once since he'd met Fulko had the boy ever come across as scared to jump into something. But now he seemed timid. As if he, too, was trying to hide something. But there was no time to figure out his secret now. "Fine. You come and do it then."

Together, they descended into the chaotic scene of the common room. Books and broken glass were strewn across the floor, making it hard to find the blade despite its massive size. As Eino squatted near the fireplace, he spied the weapon's ornate handle buried beneath a pile of firewood. "Found it!" He grabbed the handle and tugged at it, but the blade was impossibly heavy, refusing to even budge.

"Don't touch it," snapped Fulko, pushing past Eino. With a drop of his aura, he took hold of the blade, and its engravings glowed once more. The weapon was now brimming with aura and the boy easily hefted it up onto his shoulder.

Eino pushed aside the divan that was still propped up against the door, and led Fulko out onto the promenade. Clinging tight to the railing, the two made their way to the smokehouse bridge.

"Alright. Do it." He pointed at the rope.

Fulko hesitated. "Right," he said at last, taking hold of the blade.

Eino scanned the skies nervously. "You mind picking up the pace there, kid? That thing could be back here any minute."

"I know that," he snapped. "Just...give me a moment."

"Son, we ain't got a moment." Eino reached for the blade. "Here, let me—"

"No! I said don't touch it. I need to do this!"

"Then do it quick because..." Eino trailed off. The horizon darkened, and the broad flat shadow came into view once more. But this time, its silhouette expanded in the center, slowly growing taller and taller until its height dwarfed the inn. The blood rushed from Eino's face as he realized what he was seeing. The creature was opening its gigantic maw. "Now, damnit. Cut it now!"

"I-I...I can't..." Fulko mumbled.

Eino grabbed Fulko's wrists and used them to wield the Mansplitter, swinging down in a wide arc at the bridge. He couldn't help but be taken aback by how light the weapon felt and by how effortlessly it passed through both rope and wood. The smokehouse, still smoldering, fell into the clouds below, and the inn, now free of its burden, rocked back into an upright position.

The shadow drew closer, clouds curling around its form as it emerged from the storm. Its mouth came into view first, gigantic and pale, lined with deep dark ridges. With a flap of its wings, wispy clouds passed over its steely dark gray flesh. Eino and Fulko backed against the wall of the inn to brace themselves.

The stormgulper's jaws were large enough to swallow the entire inn whole. But as the beast drew closer, it adjusted its angle and dove for the falling smokehouse. It disappeared into the clouds beneath the inn, sending up a massive draft that almost bowled the two over.

Fulko sank to his knees, a strangled breath escaping him. Eino dared to peer over the promenade railing, unable to see the creature in the dark, stormy clouds below. Then he too collapsed, stunned, but grateful to be alive. For now.

30

FOR A LONG MOMENT, they both sat in quiet shock. Once Eino had steadied his breathing, he wobbled over to Fulko and knelt beside him. "Look kid. I know it has to be hard on you losing Vennick and all. We all miss him, and I can't even imagine how tough this is for you—"

Fulko's eyes were dark, his lip quivering as he spoke. "That's not the problem."

"Well, whatever the problem is, you'd better get over it quick," snapped Eino, "because that thing out there doesn't give a damn."

"This blade..." The boy took a deep breath and held up the Mansplitter. "This was the weapon that killed my father."

Eino grimaced, the boy's words hitting him like a punch to the chest. Ever since hearing Vennick's tale of the Dauntless Isle, he'd assumed that Fulko never knew the Mansplitter's full history. Why else would Vennick have waved such a grim momento in the boy's face? "He should have gotten rid of that thing a long time ago."

"He wanted to, but I wouldn't let him. I made him promise to give the blade to me when I was ready to be a hero." Fulko hung his head. "But I'm not ready to have this. I'm no hero."

"Fulko, you've got to be the bravest kid I know. And believe me, I've been around, so that's saying something."

"Bravery doesn't matter if I can't save anyone," said Fulko, his eyes dark. "Twice I tried to save that girl, and twice I've failed. Then again with that woman. And once more with Master. And then just now..." His voice hitched. "All I am is a disappointment."

Eino scratched the back of his neck. "Kid, how old are you?"

"I've seen fourteen winters. Why?"

"Listen. When I was fourteen, I was a dumb kid playing pretend with my cousins. We used to run through the woods picking up sticks to sword fight with each other. The closest I ever came to doing anything heroic was helping gather in the mushroom harvest every year. There were so damn many of us that I barely made a difference."

Fulko stared off into the storm, avoiding eye contact. "Why are you telling me this?"

"Because you're pushing yourself too damn hard. Kids your age aren't supposed to be legendary heroes. They're supposed to be...well...kids."

"I have to push myself. For Vennick's sake," said Fulko. "He never had a son of his own, you know. That's why he's been training me in all forms of combat and strategy. So that one day, I could be his successor."

Eino scoffed. "Son, that's not what he wanted for you."

"And I suppose you would know better than me?" Fulko gave him an incredulous look.

"He told me himself. That night we sang songs and played fool's gambit together."

Fulko narrowed his eyes. "You mean the night you got slobbering drunk?"

"Hey now. I got slobbering drunk *after* he told me," said Eino, his cheeks flushing with embarrassment. "And he wanted better for you than just roaming around fighting all the time. He wanted you to become your own man. To figure out what you want out of life and to live for that."

"I appreciate what you're trying to do, Mr. Eino, but it won't work," said Fulko. "I know you're only lying to spare my feelings."

"Look, you don't have to believe me. If you want to keep trying to be the next Vennick of the Thousand Weapons, you go right ahead. But is that really how you want to spend your life? Trying to be someone else?"

"It's not like I have a choice in the matter. Master showed me that there's too much trouble in the world. I don't have the luxury of being able to 'become my own man.'" He tightened his grip on the Mansplitter. "I have to fight. And if I'm not strong enough, then I just have to fight harder."

"You sound like an old man, kid." Eino smirked. With how often the boy scowled, there were times when he nearly looked like an old man as well. He wondered what kind of kid Fulko would have been if he hadn't had to grow up in the midst of a war. "You're way too young to be putting the whole world's problems on your shoulders."

"And what if that's who I want to be? If Master really wanted me to be myself, then he should have known that I can't just drift around the skies doing odd jobs for the Grand Duchess. I want to be someone who makes a difference."

"Fighting ain't the only way to make a difference, kid. If you really want to make the world a better place, why not do it your way? Why not do the things you love doing, or the things you're already good at?"

"The only thing I've ever been good at was taking care of Master Vennick." He snorted. "That, and solving puzzles."

"Puzzle solving, huh..." Eino rubbed his chin. "You do have a pretty sharp mind. I reckon you'd make a pretty good diviner if you put your mind to it."

The boy wore a bewildered expression. "How? I can't see the future!"

"Most diviners can't either," said Eino with a chuckle. "But you don't need strong auramancy to do what they do. Folks come to them looking for answers, and I reckon they don't care how you get them. You're clever. Clever enough that you could do it without needing any aura at all."

Fulko shook his head. "You overestimate me. I can't even figure out what motivates the stormgulper. Its actions make no sense."

"How do you figure?"

"Well, the gulper completely ignored the scramblers and instead tried to eat the smokehouse. And even though it spat it out, it swooped by to come gobble the smokehouse up again."

"Maybe the smoke drew its attention?"

"I doubt it. It's unlikely it can differentiate smoke from storm clouds." The boy tapped his chin. "In fact, it didn't look like the gulper had eyes at all. Or at least not eyes like ours."

Eino raised an eyebrow. "You could tell?" He'd been too distracted by the monster's horrifying gaping maw to look for eyes.

"But it was able to find the smokehouse twice, which means it can somehow see without using its eyes..." He snapped his fingers. "I've got it!"

"Got what?"

"I think I know how it's finding us," he said with a smile, "and I know how to get away from it."

"Oh, come on," said Fulko, aiming a fiery arrow at Betta's cabin. "It's just a cabin."

"Just a cabin?" Eino stepped in front of him, his hand clenching as he debated ripping the bow gauntlet off of the boy's hand. "It's the last cabin! I ain't letting you burn it up to see what happens."

"It's not to 'see what happens.' It's to see if the stormgulper tracks its prey by heat. If I'm right about this, we'll know exactly how to avoid it."

"And if you're wrong, then we burned up our last cabin for nothing!"

"What does it matter? It's most likely contaminated with strangleweed spores. We'll need to burn it up eventually."

"I don't care. Find something else to burn." He wasn't willing to give up on what remained of his inn yet. What remained of Betta. Eino glanced around, his eyes settling on the netting hanging down over the promenade. "There. That net. Use that instead."

Disappointment flashed across Fulko's face for a moment. "I...suppose that will work as well."

Working with his dagger, it took Fulko a moment to cut loose a corner of the scrambler net and a few of its floating aura stones. Eino gathered some older, dustier tomes that had been knocked off of their shelves in the common room. The two laid the books out on the net and bundled them together, and with the skills Eino had learned from the fisherman guest years ago, he spliced the ropes of the net into a tight bundle.

"Perfect," said Fulko, drawing his bow and making for the promenade. "Let's send it out there."

A gust of wind shook the common room. Eino wheeled his arms to keep his balance. "We'll do it from my room. The windows are smaller. Less risk of being blown clean out the window."

Fulko sighed. "Very well."

They joined the others in Eino's quarters, and Joren gave them a bewildered look. "What were you two doing down there?"

Fulko gave a smug smile. "Outsmarting that creature out there." He opened the window and pushed the bundle out. Once it was a fair distance away from the inn, he shot it with an arrow of flaming aura. He only hit a corner of the bundle, but the flame was enough to get a book to catch.

The others crowded around the window to watch. Even in the wind and rain, the stack of books continued to smoke and smolder, glowing a pale orange that was visible from far away in the dark. Eino squinted, watching as flaming bits of paper and rope gave way and fell from the bundle.

"Damn. Looks like our trap fell apart," said Eino. "I reckon we can try putting together another one."

"Wait," said Fulko. "That monster was able to find the smokehouse even with its cool fires. If I'm right, the aura stones will be more than warm enough for it to find. Let's watch."

A tense moment passed, but then over the howl of the wind and the pattering of the rainfall, the dull rumbling of the stormgulper rattled the room. In an instant, the glowing orange embers still clinging to the aura stones were gobbled up by a shadow in the distant darkness. The others shuddered at the sight, but Fulko clapped his hands.

"I knew it!" he shouted and pumped a fist in the air. "We're saved."

"How?"

"Easy. This proves that the beast tracks its prey by heat. So if we avoid lighting a fire until we're out of the storm, it won't be able to find us."

"Tonight will be chilly," warned Joren. "We'll have to huddle together for warmth."

Eino's heart fluttered at the thought, but he shook himself back to his senses. "Now hold on. We'll probably be the warmest things in the sky till sunrise. Won't it find us, anyway?"

"Not if we give it something else to chase after," said Fulko, pointing out the window, "like that cabin."

"No way, kid." Eino crossed his arms. "I already told you I'm not letting you torch the cabin."

"Why not? A large fire is exactly what we need to distract that creature while we slip away." Fulko narrowed his eyes. "Are you really going to get sentimental about a mushroom when our lives are at stake?"

"It ain't about being sentimental. If we cut it loose, it'll still be riding the same aura stream as us. Ain't no way we'd get far enough away. If anything, we'd just be giving that thing a snack before it has us for the main course."

"Well, we have to try something. It's already come for us twice. Would you rather sit here and wait for it to finish us off?"

Leora slowly looked up. "Why don't you ride it?"

Eino quirked an eyebrow. "Do what?"

"The stormgulper. Why don't you just ride it and steer it away? You said you rode one before, didn't you?"

Eino chewed his lip. The cold tingling of embarrassment welled up in his gut. "I thought you didn't believe that story."

"I don't," said the girl, "but it would work, wouldn't it?"

Fulko scoffed. "Don't be ridiculous. Of course it wouldn't work. That thing is way too big to fit any sort of reins around."

"Well, now hold on a minute," said Eino, scratching his chin as he stared out the window. "Maybe the idea ain't so ridiculous after all."

Fulko squinted in confusion. "You're kidding, right?"

"It's like you said. We have to try something. And I have a plan." Eino looked around the room, stroking his stubble before his eyes lighted on a pair of fishing poles leaning against a corner of the room. "Yeah. Those will work."

"Work for what?" Fulko asked, his voice rising in alarm. "What are you planning?"

"It's like Leora says. I'm gonna take Blue out and land on the gulper, then I'll steer it away." Eino turned to Joren. "You still got any of that kindlewood sap?"

He blanched. "Wha... Have you lost your mind?"

"Ain't too sure I ever had one to begin with." Eino snatched up the fishing poles and a small log from the pile beside his fireplace. "Now, do you have the sap or not?"

"I-I do, but what do you—"

"Great! Now take these." Eino thrust the poles into Joren's arms. "I need you to lash these together into one long pole."

Joren opened his mouth to protest, but Eino had already turned his attention to Fulko.

"Good news, kid. We're gonna torch that cabin after all, and I'll need your help to do it."

31

As Eino built a fire in the hearth of Betta's cabin, the room distracted him. It had been a long time since he'd set foot inside. Little needlepoint tapestries dotted the walls, and the distinctive smell of woodsmoke clung to the air. It was the same scent that clung to Betta.

Striking his flint, he ignited the wood shavings at the bottom of the fire, breathing life into them and pushing them under the kindling. For a long moment, he squatted there, making sure the wood pile caught fire. At least that's what he told himself.

Bunched up at the bottom of her bed was a blue and brown quilt with a pattern that made Eino think of Porocar's mountains. She'd spent months making it while she sat on the promenade. He grabbed it, bundling it up in his arms. Maybe it hadn't mattered enough for her to take with her, but Eino wasn't going to just let it burn.

With one last look back, he closed the door and locked it, smiling at himself halfway through the act. It was so silly, he thought. So pointless. But if Betta were here, she'd have yelled at him for leaving her door unlocked. "Just because you own the place don't mean you can barge in and do whatever you damn well please," she'd say. He could almost hear her voice in his head. Somehow, it made her absence just a bit easier to bear.

Fulko was waiting at the end of the bridge, hefting the Mansplitter over his shoulder. "Is the cabin ready?"

"Yeah," said Eino. "What about you? Are you ready to use that thing?"

"No." Fulko grimaced, examining the blade. "But if I sat back and waited until I was ready, I'd be waiting forever."

Eino smiled, patting the boy on the shoulder. "I'll be counting on you, kid. As soon as you see me in the air, cut her loose."

The boy nodded. "I won't let you down."

Eino climbed the stairs and pushed open the door to his quarters. Val sat on the bed, holding Leora tightly in her arms. Joren stood and handed Eino the poles, lashed together to double their length. A small log hung from a length of fishing line at one end. "Here. It's as you requested."

Leora looked up with a smile. "I helped too!"

Joren offered him a small leather pouch of kindlewood sap. "I still don't quite understand what this is all for."

"Ain't nothing you need to worry about," said Eino. He took the pouch and pole, then pulled the quilt from his shoulder and offered it to the man. "Hold on to this for me till I get back, alright?"

Joren's mouth hung open, but before he could protest, Eino had already thrown open the hatch. He climbed out onto the roof and calmly stepped over to Blue.

Neither Red nor the hatchling were anywhere to be found. Perhaps they'd recognized the danger and flown away from the inn. Eino couldn't blame them. At least Blue was still in her nest, as reliable as ever.

"I'm going to need your help," he said, sidling up behind her and setting a saddle on her back. He didn't usually bother to strap her saddle on, but with these winds, he didn't want to take any chances.

She shook her head, flashing the red of her crest. She let out several quick pulses of aura that made the hairs on his arms stand on end.

"Easy, girl. Easy," Eino rubbed her neck, "I know you're scared. I'm scared too."

A timid voice spoke up behind him. "She's not scared. It's her wing. These winds have to be aggravating it."

Eino turned to face Joren.

He offered a small ceramic jar. "Here. Use this poultice. It should numb the pain."

Eino dipped his fingers into the jar. The cold paste made his fingertips tingle. After calming Blue down, he shuffled to her side, finding the joint where her wing had been injured so many years ago. He rubbed the paste into her wing, and though she flinched at first, she settled into Eino's hands. When he had finished, she flapped her wings, letting out a low pleased squawk before lowering herself down.

"Thanks, Joren. I really owe you one." Eino climbed up onto Blue's back.

When he turned to glance down at Joren, he found the man struggling to climb up onto the mount behind him. "Wait. I'm coming too."

"What? No you ain't," said Eino, "Get back inside. This is gonna be danger-ous!"

"I know," he said. "Which is why I'm coming along. You might need some help out there."

"Joren, I'm serious. If something bad happened to you..."

"I'd feel the same way if anything happened to you." He patted Eino on the shoulder, speaking in that quiet way of his. "So let's do this together."

Seeing Joren so calm made Eino's pounding heart slow. Even over the rumbling thunder and the pitter patter of rain, the soothing sound of his voice seemed like it was the only thing he could hear.

Eino smiled. "You sure you're up for this? It's gonna be a bumpy ride."

"I'm becoming accustomed to bumpy rides." Joren stuffed a briskweed leaf into his mouth.

With a flap of Blue's wings, they were off. Eino circled Betta's cabin. The fire he'd lit in her wood pile had spread, and smoke was now pouring out of the windows. He waved to Fulko, and the boy nodded, hefting the Mansplitter. For a long moment, he held the blade aloft, staring at its glowing runes. Eino grimaced, mumbling under his breath. "Come on, kid. You can do this."

The boy closed his eyes, and in one sudden swing, he sliced through the rope bridge to Betta's cabin.

Eino pumped his fist and cheered. "Attaboy, Fulko!"

"What did he do?" Joren asked, his eyes shut and his breath shaky against Eino's neck.

"Oh, it's nothing. The kid just overcame one of his fears."

"Lucky him." Joren wrapped his arms around Eino's waist and squeezed him tightly.

A warm feeling rose through Eino's chest. He relished that feeling just as he had the first time they'd flown together. For a moment, however briefly, he wasn't worried about the inn or the stormgulper. All that mattered was Joren's warm embrace.

Eino guided Blue to remain above the cabin as it drifted away from the inn. Out of habit, he didn't push her very hard, but the greatwing flew with surprising grace and power, unbothered by the old injury to her wing. She soared high above the cabin, circling its growing plume of smoke.

"I ain't never seen Blue this spry before," he called back to Joren. "What was that stuff you gave her?"

Joren spoke curtly through clenched teeth. "Mostly pepperoot."

As much as Eino was enjoying the close embrace of a terrified Joren, he thought it might help to take his mind off of his current predicament. "So you're telling me that stuff can treat burns and injured greatwings? How'd you figure that one out?"

"A little research," said Joren, "And a little guesswork."

"Guesswork?" Eino laughed. "Since when do you trust your life to guesswork?"

"What can I say? You've been a bad influence on me." He offered the bravest smile he could muster.

Lightning crackled across the sky, striking at the aura stream and illuminating the massive form of the stormgulper. Its flat body had tilted, swooping toward the cabin with a low, ominous rumble.

"About time you showed up, big fella." Eino pulled Blue into a dive, matching the gulper's speed. The creature emerged from the storm clouds, its massive mouth wide open. In an instant, the smoking cabin disappeared into the gulper's mouth. Both Eino and Joren held their breath as they drew closer, taking in the full scale of the creature. Only Blue seemed unfazed by the titanic beast, slowing her descent and landing gracefully on the middle of its back.

"I can't believe it," said Eino with a laugh. "We're riding it. We're actually riding a stormgulper!"

Joren tightened his grip. "Yes, it's very impressive. Now, will you please hurry up and do what you need to do?" He shivered.

Eino glanced back and smirked. "Maybe once you let me go."

Joren reluctantly peeled his fingers back and released his grip. Eino dismounted, taking a moment to enjoy the surreal feeling of standing on a monster the size of a small village. Its flesh was slick and sparsely covered in rows of fine, stiff hairs. He bounced up and down on its spongy, undulating body, the feeling somewhat similar to stepping in stiff mud.

A sudden shuddering interrupted the moment. The beast made a groaning noise, and a moment later coughed up the smoking cabin. They were far enough away from the cabin to avoid disaster as it came tumbling across the stormgulper's back. Still, not even Blue could keep from flinching at the sight of the tumbling, giant flaming mushroom.

Joren reached out a hand and grabbed Eino's wrist. "Please. Be safe."

"Don't gotta tell me twice," said Eino, his voice bereft of his usual bravado. He gathered up the fishing pole contraption and a leather pouch from Blue's satchel. "Just sit tight. I'll be quick."

Too aware of Joren watching him, Eino kept his body low as he dashed across the gulper's slippery back. He crouched down near the creature's head, or rather the vague area where its head should be. It had no neck, and contrary to one of the stories he'd heard, the beast did not have eye stalks. In fact, it was too dark to see if it had eyes at all.

No matter, thought Eino, reaching into the leather pouch and smearing kindlewood sap on the log dangling from the fishing rod. Somehow this creature could sense heat, and while he might not understand how, he'd find wherever its "eyes" were. With a strike of his flint, he set the log alight, then held the fishing pole over the edge of the creature's head. He plodded along the edge of the monster's head until at last the stormgulper let out a rumble and started listing toward the log.

"Whoa there," said Eino, quickly withdrawing the log. The beast righted itself. "There. Found your eye."

Eino knelt down and patted the gulper like a dog. The gulper let out a low rumble that vibrated through Eino's feet. "Aw, did you like that?" He patted it again. The rumbling came a little louder this time. "You ain't so bad, you know? Maybe I'll build my next inn on your back. Dilgaa knows I'd have a lot more room."

Eino used his coat sleeve to wipe the rain away from a patch of the gulper's slick skin. He slathered the handle of the fishing rod in a sticky sap, then pressed the rod against its skin, stamping down some of its fine hairs to hold it in place.

"Sorry to trick you, big fella," said Eino. Once more, he dangled the log over the edge of the beast's head, and once more, the creature began turning toward it. At the rate the log was burning, it should keep the stormgulper soaring in circles for an hour or so. More than enough time for the inn time to drift out of the storm and to escape drawing the creature's attention again.

He turned to flag down Joren, but the slippery gulper's back banked farther and farther to the side as the creature followed the log. His arms wheeled as he struggled to keep his balance. Then the gulper opened its mouth, its head rising up and sending Eino skittering across its back.

His hands grasped for purchase, but the slick back of the gulper gave him nothing to hold on to. He dug his feet in, slowing his slide. Flailing wildly, he managed to grab a handful of the monster's thin hairs, holding on to keep from sliding down the ramp of the creature's slick back.

"Eino!" yelled Joren. Without hesitation, he sprang forward and dug his heels into Blue's sides, urging her forward. The greatwing complied, and with a squawk, she swooped forward.

Joren held out his hand and Eino grabbed it, swinging himself onto Blue's back. "Let's go!"

With a whoop, Joren goaded Blue away from the gulper.

"Ha! I guess someone else overcame his fears today too, huh?"

"Not by a long shot. I'm positively terrified." Joren panted, letting out a victorious laugh. "I'm just glad it's over."

"Don't go celebrating just yet. We still gotta get back to the inn."

"Right." Joren looked to the left and right. "Which way do we go?"

A cold jolt ran up Eino's spine. He scanned the skies, but his inn was nowhere to be found among the dark storm clouds.

Keep calm, he thought. Joren's nerves were already at their limit. The last thing Eino needed to do was make the man panic. With a deep breath, he looked upwards, hoping to use the aura stream to orient himself. Except the stream wasn't there. He looked all over in a panic before seeing that the stream was below them. Far below them.

"There," said Eino, pointing down. "Just follow the stream and we'll run into them for sure."

"Got it." Joren took Blue down, his breathing steadying. Eino's lie had worked, but it still left a bitter taste in his mouth. He hoped he was right. He hoped they could find the inn and reach the others, but without the flight kite to anchor the inn to the stream, they could be anywhere in the vast night sky.

Eino chewed his lip. His inn might already be lost. His business. His home. And most importantly, his new friends. A numb sensation swept over him as he realized they might not find the inn.

An icy, dark thought wormed its way into his mind. Maybe it was hopeless to try and find the others. Maybe they were already lost. So what if he and Joren just glided down to the land below and started over? They could make a new life for themselves. Just the two of them...

Eino shook his head. He could find a way to live without the Driftcap Inn, but he couldn't live with himself if he gave up on his guests. If he behaved that callously, then how could someone as kind-hearted as Joren ever love him?

No, he thought. Fulko, Val, and Leora were all still counting on him. And he wouldn't let them down.

As they passed below the aura stream, Joren craned his head and squinted. "What's that?"

Below them, there was a flash of light. It didn't look like lightning or an aurora burst from the stream. It was a bright and constant pulse, glowing a distinctive pale blue.

"Val! It's Val!" said Eino, laughing and excitedly tapping Joren's shoulder. "We found them!"

As they glided back toward the inn, Eino wasn't thinking about how high and fast the inn was moving, or how much Blue had to flap her wings to catch up. He wasn't thinking about the strangleweed in the core or how he was going to get everyone safely down to the surface. The only thing on his mind was Joren.

He looked up. The storm clouds looked like they were thinning, and the skies above already looked lighter. It wouldn't be long until sunrise. If only there was time to watch it with Joren.

32

EINO CLUNG TO JOREN's back, his warmth pleasant against the cold stormy winds. He listened to Joren's shaky breaths as he guided Blue toward Val's glowing beacon, but as he squeezed tighter, he thought he felt Joren's breathing steadying.

As they glided, the inn kept moving away from them. Eino grimaced. They'd need to move faster or risk being left behind. He rubbed Blue's back, speaking into Joren's ear. "Don't be afraid to push her a little. The ol' girl can take it."

"Got it." Joren tugged on Blue's reins, guiding her into the aura stream. The edges of her feathers glowed with aura as she used the stream to give herself a boost. Even so, it took longer than Eino would have liked to catch up to the inn.

By the time they reached the inn several minutes later, the worst of the storm clouds had cleared. Joren climbed off Blue, took three steps, and then collapsed to his knees. Val ceased flashing her beacon, and together with Fulko, she dashed over and helped the two men back into Eino's quarters.

"Is it done?" asked Val.

Eino nodded. "We sent the gulper chasing its own tail in the opposite direction. We should be in the clear." He smiled and slapped Joren on the back. "Not sure he'll ever recover, though."

Joren gasped, sucking in a deep breath. "I'm fine. I might not be when we hit the surface, but for now I'm hanging in there."

Eino smiled. "Well, I reckon we're through the worst of it. Let's worry about getting you back down on solid ground."

He glanced out the window. The rain lightened to a gentle patter, and sunlight streaked through the storm clouds. Hazy mist continued to obscure whatever lay below, but the inn was still following the course of the aura stream. He breathed a sigh of relief. It wasn't enough for him to get his bearings yet, but at least the gulper hadn't pulled them too far off course.

He guessed they were somewhere along the South Porocari coast, and with the storm clearing, the skies might be clear enough for him to signal down an airship for help. It was his best hope of getting everyone to safety. He might even be able to save the Driftcap Inn, or rather, what was left of it. Even a small Gatrai vessel could easily tow his inn out to sea until he found a way to destroy the strangleweeds. Eino strained to listen through the storm, but he didn't hear any blaring horns.

He patted his coat pockets, searching for his signal staff. Unable to find it, he cursed under his breath. "Hey, Val, you reckon you could put up another one of them beacons?"

She nodded. "Most certainly. It will be easier once the storm passes."

"Good, because we—" Eino's mouth hung open. As the inn spun in the air, the view from the window turned to reveal something massive towering over the horizon. "Well cast me..."

Fulko's eyes showed concern. "What is it? What's wrong?"

There was no doubt now about where they were. They'd drifted deep into the heart of Porocar, and were now staring down the peak of the tallest mountain in Itharos. "It's Mount Chilbrin."

"That's good news, isn't it? It should be easy to flag down help now."

"There's a reason I don't normally let the inn come this way." He'd been on this particular aura stream only once during his time aboard *The Sun Chaser*, and even with the airship in full working order, they'd barely managed to navigate the dense and craggy Tetebarech mountain range. With his inn so broken that not even his flight kite still worked, there was no chance they'd make it through in one piece. "We can't wait for rescue. We need another way down. And fast."

"There is no other way down."

"There's one," said Eino, glancing toward the roof hatch. "We'll take Blue."

Joren blanched. "Are you mad? We barely made it back to the inn from the gulper. If she takes one trip to the surface, she'll never be able to catch back up to the inn."

"She won't need to. We'll all ride down together in one go."

Joren gaped. "You said she couldn't hold us all."

"Your little salve worked wonders, Joren. I ain't never seen her looking so nimble. I reckon she'll be strong enough to carry us if we just glide down real easy." Eino rubbed his chin. "It might be a rough landing, but if we touch down on a mountain peak with some nice soft snow, we'll all make it just fine."

"But what about the strangleweeds?" asked Val. "If the inn were to crash in the mountains, the winds could carry spores all across Porocar. Perhaps even further."

Eino grit his teeth. Those damned strangleweeds. They might as well be assassins waiting in the shadows, and even if he escaped, they'd still just strike out at someone else. He closed his eyes. Eino didn't want to face the grim truth he'd been grappling with ever since his inn first started falling apart. He didn't feel ready to face losing his inn. But what other choice did he have?

"Alright then," said Eino. He drew a deep breath. "Then before we disembark, we'll torch the place."

Joren placed a hand on Eino's shoulder. "Wait. Maybe...maybe we can still—"

"I've made up my mind." Eino pressed his hand against the wall of his room, feeling the stiff woody texture. "I've been drifting around up here in my inn for over half a decade, but if the old girl is rotten to the core, then it's up to me to put her down."

Joren's shoulders slumped. "I'm sorry. I wish I'd figured out how to beat stranglers earlier. Then I could have prevented all of this."

"Don't go blaming yourself. This ain't your fault." He put a hand on Joren's shoulder, grazing his neck. "But if you want to make it up to me, then you can give me some more of that kindlewood sap."

Joren grimaced. "I used up all I had on the stormgulper."

"You what?" Eino blinked. "You had so damn much of that stuff."

"I'm sorry. I didn't think we'd need to save any. It takes a lot to keep it alight in the rain."

"It's fine," said Fulko, stepping between them. "We have everything we need to make something even stronger."

Joren looked bewildered. "We do?"

He nodded, rubbing his bleary eyes. "There's still plenty of pepperroot on the roof. I read in your notes that its oil extract is highly flammable."

Joren shook his head. "It would take a week to process enough of the extract to burn down this inn."

"Using conventional methods, yes," said Fulko, turning to Val, "But you can hone the plants' aura to increase their yield, can't you?"

Val rubbed her arm nervously. "I suppose I can try, though I will require some guidance to best apply my skills."

"It still won't be enough." Joren tapped his chin, looking to Val. "But with your help, we might be able to infuse the aura from sapgrass directly into the extract as a catalyst..."

The three of them began delving into the methods and technical details of creating the flammable extract. Eino scratched his head, unable to keep up with the conversation. At least Joren seemed to have recovered from his harrowing flight. He was now fully engaged in the conversation, seemingly too distracted by the problem at hand to remember his fear of heights. Fulko also seemed to be in better spirits, his eyes bright as he offered up suggestions and alternatives.

Leora leaned around as they spoke. "Um...can I help?"

"Yes," said Joren, pulling her into the conversation. "We need you to gather up all the pepperroot you can find, along with some sapgrass, and the stamens, not the pistils, from the longberry blossoms."

The girl crooked her head. "The what?"

"Come on," said Fulko, patting her on the shoulder. "I'll show you what to grab."

Val followed close behind, her tattoos glowing. "And I will ensure that neither of you falls."

"Very good. I'll set up my equipment on the dining room table. Meet me down there once they've gathered everything." With that, Joren dashed out to the common room.

Eino looked around, now alone in his quarters. "I'll just uh…I reckon I'll keep an eye on things right here." As he sat on his bed, the back of his heel kicked something heavy beneath it. He glanced down and saw his treasure box. This was no time to relax, he thought to himself. There was still plenty of work to be done.

While the others prepared the pepperroot extract, Eino grabbed what remained of his net and cut it loose, dragging it into the common room. There, he piled a few of his heavier belongings, like Blue's saddle and his treasure box, along with the rest of his guests' belongings.

Leora's feet came pounding down the stairs as she returned with a basket of plants. Fulko followed close behind her, stopping when he spotted Eino. "What are you doing?"

"Blue ain't gonna be able to carry all of us and all our stuff too. But I reckon we can pile all our stuff into this here net, then toss it overboard before we take off. With a couple of aurastones to mark it, we should be able to find wherever it lands." Eino looked up. "So anything you wanna bring, you come toss it in the pile."

Fulko nodded. "I don't have anything I need to bring along."

"What about your big ol' chopper?" Eino patted the net. "I know you wanna keep that thing to yourself, but for Blue's sake, it's gotta go in the net."

"I think…" Fulko hesitated, touching his chin. "I think I'll be leaving the Mansplitter here."

Eino's eyes widened in surprise. "Kid, there's no way that thing is gonna survive the fire. Even if the blade don't melt, the enchantment on the aura stones will get burned away. I reckon there won't be nothing left of it but a chunk of steel."

"I'm aware," said the boy. "But it has caused enough destruction. This seems like as good a place as any to lay it to rest."

Eino stood up, offering Fulko a sympathetic look. "Kid, I know how much you'd been looking forward to getting your hands on that blade. You sure you're ready to let it go?"

"I'm certain. I've let it define me for long enough." He turned his head toward Joren, who was laying his instruments out across the table. "It's time I stopped trying to fill Master's shoes."

He joined Leora at the table, helping Joren to organize the plants and instruments. The girl started washing ingredients and equipment while Joren walked Fulko through the recipe. Eino raised an eyebrow, surprised to see Joren working without his gloves on. It brought a smile to his face to see the man no longer trying to hide himself.

Eino finished tying up the net and dragged it out to the promenade. Glancing through the broken window, he saw Joren guiding Fulko through the steps in processing the ingredients. "Yes, very good. Mix it very gently. Just like that," said Joren, his voice soft, but with the authority of an expert.

"Understood." The boy nodded, a faint smile on his face. "So, this is what apothecary work is like?"

"A little," Joren gave him a small smile. "Though things typically aren't this stressful."

The trio appeared to have everything under control. Eino was certain that if he joined in now, he'd only get in the way. With nothing to do but wait, he walked the promenade to burn off the restless energy coursing through his veins.

After a few loops, he noticed the empty kitchen. He rubbed his chin. If Betta were here, she'd get some drinks or cook up some snacks. Something to make everyone feel a little more comfortable, even with the inn falling apart around them.

She might not be here now, thought Eino, but there was a whole jar of cacao that would end up going to waste if nobody drank it, and that was something he absolutely could not accept. He pushed open the door to the kitchen and started warming a big pot of water.

Val poked her head in from the dining area. "May I be of assistance?"

"Don't you gotta do something with the plants and their aura and whatnot?" asked Eino, grating the cacao into a bowl.

She shook her head. "My part will come later. It seems there's still a great deal of processing to be done."

"Well, I could use another pair of hands." Eino handed her the grater and the block of cacao. "Here. Keep grating this into the pot till it turns silky. I'm gonna prepare the spice for everyone."

Val bowed her head. "No spice for me, thank you."

Eino smiled, setting out five cups on the counter and putting a spoonful of sugar in each. He made careful mental notes of which was which, putting a gentle sprinkling of spice powder into Fulko's and Leora's cups, and piling a Joren's with a few heaping scoops.

"Alright," said Eino, turning around, "Let's get these cups pour—"

Val was manipulating the cacao with her aura, grating it far more quickly than Eino anticipated. She'd nearly grated the entire block into the pot, turning it into a thick brown sludge. The concoction bubbled like a swamp, releasing wisps of black smoke.

"Whoa!" he yelled, dashing over to pull the put from the fire. "Lady, are you trying to kill us?"

"Have I done something wrong?" said Val, wringing her hands. "My apologies. I am...not accustomed to cooking."

He looked up at Val and chuckled. "Aww, don't fret. It's nothing a little milk can't save."

The gentle swaying of the inn made pouring the thick sludge into the cups difficult, but with some difficulty and a little bit of spillage, Eino managed to fill them all.

With Val's help, he carried out the cups and served the others. The cacao was thick and burnt, with the sugar so poorly mixed in that it couldn't cut through the drink's bitterness. Even so, it was the best cup of cacao any of them had ever had.

Val and Eino sat at the corner of the table. "It is simple. You need only set the oil alight, and I will contain the explosion," Val explained, sitting across the table from Eino. "Once sealed, we can place it atop the core, and when we are a safe distance away, I will drop the barrier, unleashing the explosion."

"Right." Eino picked up the matches. Joren had already cleaned up his equipment, leaving only the small wooden bowl full of flammable extract in the middle of the table.

"I'll go get Blue," Joren offered. He ushered Fulko and Leora out.

"I am ready," said Val. Her tattoos glowed as she waited for him.

His hand shook as he struck the match. A tiny flame lit up the tip.

She watched, waiting, but his grip on the match tightened as the flame burned. "Mr. Eino?"

"Right. Yeah. I'm dropping it." He sucked in a breath. "Right now." He took another few quick breaths. "Alright. Here we go." With a trembling hand, he finally let go of the match and squeezed his eyes shut.

A tense moment passed before he opened them. Val sat confidently with her hands on either side of a glassy aura barrier. Within its crystalline shell, the flaming explosion silently roared, like a raging fire seen through rippling water. She grabbed a hold of the orb and handed it to Eino. "Do not be afraid. The explosion is contained."

"Right." Eino gingerly took hold of the barrier, holding it at arm's length. "And you're sure this thing won't blow up in my face?"

"I am quite certain." Val covered her smile with her hand. "Even if you were to drop it, the barrier would not shatter."

Eino grimaced, unconvinced. "I'll take your word for it." With that, he made his way for the storage pantry. The roots dangling toward the core had grown thicker and longer since he last checked on them. He set the crystalline barrier down beside the core. Thin tendrils slowly shot out of the roots and opened slightly, wrapping themselves around the glassy orb as if accepting an offering.

Satisfied with the placement of the explosion, Eino darted back up the stairs. He detoured to the promenade to push the net off, watching as it gently drifted down. Then he headed back inside to climb onto the roof.

Atop the inn, he looked to the side where Mount Chilbrin waited on the horizon. The mountain dominated the skyline.

"Time to go."

Fulko was the first to mount Blue, taking the front. Eino helped Leora on next, then Val.

Eino gestured for Joren to climb on. "Your turn."

"Please," Joren said, "You go first."

"Nope. The captain is always the last one to leave the ship. Them's the rules."

The man raised an eyebrow. "This isn't a ship. It's a mushroom."

"My mushroom, my rules," said Eino, forcing a smile.

Joren gave a sad smile as he climbed onto Blue. Everyone else scooted forward, making space for Joren at the back. Leora wrapped her arms around Fulko, burying her face in the boy's back. There wasn't any space left for Eino at Blue's back, and without her saddle, he'd have to cling tightly to Joren.

"So if this is to be the last day that the Driftcap Inn sails the skies, then I'm gonna send the ol' girl off with a bang!" Eino tried his best to put on a confident face for the sake of everyone else, but he couldn't keep his lip from quivering or keep the tears from welling up in the corners of his eyes. He cleared his throat and took a hold of Blue's reins.

Fulko scoffed. "Then quit stalling and hop on."

"Not yet. Not till I'm certain those damned plants are dead. I ain't leaving till I see those flames catch." Eino guided Blue to the edge of the mushroom cap. "Val, if you would be so kind."

Val closed her eyes, and the glow of her tattoos subsided. "The explosion has been unleashed."

Everyone held still and listened, not daring to make a sound. Even Blue seemed more alert than usual. For a long moment, it was difficult to hear anything but the whistling wind blowing past their faces. Then there came a dull pop from somewhere below the inn. There was another long pause before anyone spoke.

"Was that it?" Asked Leora, sounding almost disappointed.

Val opened her eyes. "It must have been. I sensed the fires roaring out from the barrier."

"We used so much extract," said Fulko. "I'd have thought the explosion would be louder."

There was another long pause while everyone looked around, desperate for any sign that the strangleweeds had been destroyed.

Eino finally broke the silence. "I'm going back in there."

"Eino, wait," said Joren, taking a hold of his jacket.

"Don't worry. Ain't nothing bad's gonna happen." Eino set his hand on Joren's. Without his gloves on, his hands felt wonderfully soft. He drew a deep breath. "But if anything does happen before I get back...if you so much as see a little green root wiggling around, you fly everybody down without me. You hear?"

Joren tightened his grip. "But—"

"I'll be fine. I promise." He squeezed Joren's hand, savoring the feeling of it.

Joren sighed and released the jacket. "Fine. But please—" He reached for his belt and took hold of his sickle, handing it to Eino. "—take this."

He smiled, taking hold of it. "I'm sure I won't need it."

"Then you can bring it back to me." Joren hesitantly took hold of Blue's reins, then nodded.

Eino threw open the hatch to his quarters, but as he did, he felt a sudden, violent rumbling from below. He held on tight to the hatch handle to keep his footing as the inn listed to its side. Blue squawked and flapped her wings, clawing at the mushroom's flesh to maintain her perch, but it wasn't enough to keep her from sliding off. She spread her wings and drifted down, clearly struggling with the extra load of everyone on her back.

"Eino!" yelled Joren. But he was already too far down. Even if he jumped, Eino wouldn't be able to land on his greatwing's back. He was all alone now, with no way down.

Then something burst through the roof, snapping the ropes that held the flight kite fast. Eino dashed forward, grabbing at the air, but he was much too far away to keep the device from flying off into the sky. When he looked back down, and his stomach plummeted. There before him was a thick green vine wreathed in flame, writhing and flailing in the air.

33

THE INN SHUDDERED AGAIN. The driftcap righted itself for the most part, but there was still a slight tilt to it. Bile rose in his throat and he swallowed it down. He glanced at the horizon again, and then at the mountains that seemed to shrink the longer he watched. Horror dawned on his face as he realized that the inn was rising higher and higher.

He hoisted himself through the hatch and into his quarters. The strangle-weed had already burst through the floor and was sprouting little tendrils, flames licking at the writhing mass of vines. The plants were burning, but were not consumed before spreading fire everywhere they touched. One flaming tendril smacked against the wall, setting alight his painting of Mount Chilbrin.

"No, no, no!" shouted Eino, desperately running over to smother the flames. Scorch marks marred the edges of the painting. He ripped it from the wall, looking for a safe place to set it down. Then he paused, the smoke stinging his eyes and making them water.

"What am I doing?" he asked himself, letting the situation sink in. The smoke. The flames. The writhing vines. He barked out a laugh. Once he started, he couldn't stop. The laughs grew more and more crazed as tears flooded down his cheeks.

There'd be no saving himself. Much less his inn or his trinkets and maps. At once, it all seemed so pointless. His entire life's legacy was quite literally going up in flames. All there was to do now was delay the inevitable.

Out of the corner of his eye, he saw a tendril swing at him. On instinct, he leaned back to dodge, but it still caught him on the cheek, leaving a shallow cut. He drew Joren's sickle and sliced through the vine. The severed vine wriggled about on the floor. He stomped on it until it stopped moving.

He looked down at the sickle. No, this wasn't pointless. The Driftcap Inn was ruined, but the flames hadn't slowed the strangleweed down at all. If he gave up now, this thing would spread more of its spores across Itharos. Countless innocent people would get hurt. People like Val, and Leora, and Fulko. People like Joren.

Eino tightened his grip on the sickle and grabbed a few more of his rolled up maps, stuffing them into one of his coat's pockets. He wouldn't let that happen. But to stop this strangleweed he'd need to make the flames even bigger. Much bigger

The wall bulged, and several small tendrils popped out of it, slithering across the floor and ceiling. Eino recoiled, but he wasn't quick enough to avoid a few small sprouts that lashed at his neck. He rubbed at his wounds, feeling a drop of blood smearing across his fingertips.

The room tilted farther. Eino held onto the rafters to maintain his balance as books and trinkets fell off of the shelves and went crashing against the far wall. A vine as thick as a tree trunk blocked the door down to the main room. That left the window as his only escape option.

Eino let go of the rafters and slid across to the window. He kicked out the glass and clambered through. The whole inn was practically sideways now, with vines sprouting all around, most of which seemed untouched by the flame. A gust of wind battered at him, and his left foot slipped. He grabbed onto the windowsill, making the mistake of looking down. The inn was above the aura stream now. Vertigo assailed him as he tried to make sense of the landscape below. He clutched at the windowsill, steadying himself.

Now wasn't the time to be afraid, he reminded himself. He'd already ridden a hungry stormgulper. He could do this too. Eino steeled his nerves and made for the edge of the mushroom. A tendril whipped at him. He dodged, stumbling as he struggled to navigate the slanted inn. Small tendrils took advantage of his mistake, whipping at his arms, leaving shallow lacerations behind.

One grabbed his ankle, dragging him to his knees. Another wrapped around his knee, and another his throat. Swinging furiously, Eino sliced off the three tendrils restraining him, then stood at the edge of the mushroom. Taking a deep breath, he leapt for the promenade.

He struck the floor and grabbed a hold of the railing. The inn bobbed from the impact, sending the mushroom into a slow flip. A few woody vines waved in the wind. He grabbed them and swung himself into the kitchen as the inn finally settled. He pushed through the broken door into the pantry.

The mushroom was nearly inverted now, and the staircase down to the cellar had become an arduous climb covered in dying vines. Luckily, the closer Eino got to the core, the thicker and stiffer the vines got. They were no longer swinging wildly, but gently pulsing and writhing. A few were still burning, while others smoldered like coals. Eino carefully grabbed at the unburnt vines for leverage as he ascended the stairs. A bottle of raangnectar from Mebeq's visit rolled down the stairs, miraculously unbroken. Eino chuckled as he pocketed the bottle. If he made it through this alive, he'd drink the whole bottle himself in celebration.

For as short as it was to the core, the climb seemed to take far too long. He let out a breath of relief when he finally reached the core's shelf, the false back blown completely apart. He'd expected to find the core burnt to a crisp, but instead found it glowing as bright as the suns. It seemed that the explosion had not destroyed the wooden core, but had set it ablaze, wreathing it in an intense fire of pure aura. The thin roots reached into the burning core, growing as fast as the fire was consuming them. They must have been leaching off the core's aura to feed the vines all throughout the inn.

There was no way the core could maintain this level of power for long. The wood would burn up soon, but Eino had waited long enough.

"Ain't never had to kick someone off before," said Eino, using both hands to grip the sickle. "But Mr. Strangleweed, you've done overstayed your welcome."

With that, Eino swung the sickle with all his might, striking the white hot core. Again and again he struck, until at last the core cracked in half. A thunderous boom and an incredible blast of heat knocked Eino from his feet.

When he opened his eyes, the core was nowhere to be found. In only a moment, the roots had turned to ashy white cinders, and the writhing of the vines slowed. Fire blazed around him. Embers caught the collar of his jacket alight. He quickly patted the flames out, then hoisted himself to his feet, tucking the sickle into his sash. His left leg had gone numb, slowing him down as he limped his way down the staircase.

He clambered out of the kitchen's inverted door. All around him, the fire had spread, and great billows of smoke poured out from the mushroom's gills. The writhing tendrils slowed, then ceased. He'd done it. It had cost him his inn, and it would cost him his life, but he'd finally bested the strangleweed.

The smoke drifting off the fire made it hard to see. He coughed as he reached for the spare apron hanging beside him to dab at his watering eyes. Then he stuffed it into his lowest pocket on his right. A nervous laugh escaped him. Another followed until he was bent over with tears blurring his vision. Anger and misery mixed with disbelief over his predicament, yet all he could do was laugh.

His feet rose from the ground. Wind howled past the doorway. In his stomach, he felt the unmistakable sensation of falling. The inn had lost its core, and without the core there was nothing to keep the mushroom in the sky.

Weightless, Eino drifted out of the doorway. He should have been afraid, he thought. He should be screaming in terror. And yet, as he glanced out, he looked on in silence at the beautiful vista before him.

The Tetebarech mountain range stretched out below him with steep, snow-capped peaks, with Mount Chilbrin standing tall above the others. It was a sacred place for devotees of Dilgaa, and only the boldest Porocari dared to climb it. How jealous they would be if they could see it from up here, he thought. How lucky he was to see the morning suns peek out from behind the mountains, and bathe him in their golden light.

As he plummeted, the aura streams got closer, and he watched in awe as bright, beautiful auroras sprang forth from wherever the sunlight touched. His hand had gone numb, but still he held it out and smiled as the inn plunged through the stream, feeling the tingle of aura dancing across his skin.

Tears welled in his eyes. It wasn't regret that plagued him. He'd lived his life just the way he wanted. Rather, he was grateful to have been able to return to Porocar and to have witnessed perhaps the most beautiful view in all of Itharos on his last day. His heart pounded with the smallest pang of sorrow that he didn't have anyone to share the beautiful view with.

The howling of the wind got quieter, and the feeling in his stomach subsided. As he'd fallen, he had drifted above the inverted promenade, and while his body still felt weightless, gravity firmly planted his feet on its underside. The ground no longer rushed toward him. The inn was slowing its descent.

Eino looked up at the aura stream. The mushroom must have collected a little bit of energy when it passed through. Enough to stop him from falling to his death. He drew a deep breath and gave a cheer so loud and so long that he went light-headed. If he kept descending so gracefully, he would land on the side of the mountain. It would be a cold and miserable few days of camping in the mountains, but someone would come back for him.

Yet the inn didn't descend gracefully. It simply bobbed in midair, drifting about in the cold winds. It was still far too high up for Eino to survive a jump. He glanced around at the empty skies. Airships didn't typically come this close to the mountain range, but he held on to a spark of hope that one might pass by. But how would they find him? He glanced down, supposing that they could follow the massive smoke signal.

The fire. The plunge had only fanned the flames, and now the inn was completely ablaze. His heart sank. He'd been saved from plummeting to his doom, only to be burned alive with his inn. He grumbled as he wondered which god he'd angered to receive such a cruel fate.

Eino reached into his pocket for the bottle of aged raangnectar. He'd been saving the spirit for a special occasion. There was no reason it should go to waste. His hands were still so numb he could barely hold the bottle, much less uncork it. He dropped it on the floor, but when he bent over to pick it up, he suddenly felt dizzy. Too dizzy to stay on his feet. He slumped forward, landing on his knees and then his face.

He rolled onto his back and looked at his hand. Through his blurry vision he spotted the blood smeared cuts and scrapes all over his arms. Poison. Of course. With as many tendrils as had broken his skin, he'd be taken by the poison long before the flames got to him. It seemed the strangleweed would have its vengeance. Eino let out a bitter laugh.

Defeated, he laid there for a long moment. He rubbed his eyes, but his vision was still blurry. His lungs burned from the smoke. With nothing else to be done, he let his regrets seep in. He regretted not getting one last taste of the raangnectar. He regretted not making more offerings to Dilgaa, or Solun, or Querrina, or Soleivar, or even the nameless God of the Deka'arists. Most of all, he regretted not getting to see Joren one last time.

Joren. Eino patted at his sash. With a little effort, he drew the sickle and held it close to his chest, gripping it tightly. He turned his bleary eyes up to the clear blue skies overhead. Wisps of smoke at the edges of his vision smudged the view of the auroras dancing on the aura streams.

"Ain't it pretty, Joren?"

He went numb to the cold of the mountain air and the heat of the fires around him. All he felt was the warm, comfortable haze of sleep as the poison trickled through him. He closed his eyes and basked in the sunlight. The wind whistled gently, and the fires crackled and popped. A little cloud darted in front of the suns, but it couldn't upset Eino now. Everything was so peaceful.

"Joren..." whispered Eino. As he did, he thought he could almost hear him whispering back.

"...Eino..."

Eino smiled. His mind was fading. It had to be if he was hearing Joren's voice so clearly. There was no way Blue could have carried everyone down to the surface, then climbed high enough in the air to bring Joren to him. He gripped the sickle with all the strength left in his hands. There was no hope of seeing him again, but it was comforting to think that even now Joren cared to come back for him. He let his mind accept the fantasy.

Once more the cloud blocked out the suns. "Eino! Where are you?"

Eino raised an eyebrow. That sounded like more than just a hallucination. He opened his eyes, scanning the skies for the source of the distant calling. Again, a little black cloud blocked out the sun for a moment. But as he held his hand to his forehead and squinted, Eino could see that the cloud appeared to be flapping its wings.

"Blue?" His voice was a hoarse whisper. The sight was impossible. A trick of the light. A hallucination. Yet the flapping wings drew closer, and Joren's voice grew louder. A gust of wind washed over him as Blue landed on the promenade, letting out a squawk.

"Eino! By Soleivar, you're alive!" Joren leapt from Blue's back and knelt beside Eino to inspect his wounds.

Eino rubbed his eyes. "But...how?" His voice scratched at his dry throat.

"You've been poisoned," said Joren, hurriedly digging through his bag. He pulled out a small jar of poultice and slathered it all over Eino's arms and neck. "We need to get you out of here. Can you move?"

With a great deal of effort, Eino reached up and grabbed Joren's hand. It felt so warm compared to the numbing cold of his own hand. Joren pulled him to his feet, practically carrying him as he limped over and onto Blue's back. Joren sat behind him, guiding the greatwing back into the sky.

Eino smiled and leaned back. Even with the cold mountain air whipping at his face, he felt warm and safe in Joren's arms. "You came back," he murmured before drifting off.

34

Eino squinted into the gloom. He turned his head from side to side, searching through the dull haze for any sign of where he was. It was dark, but he could just make out the craggy rocks that made up the walls and ceiling. His eyes shot open. It was a cave, and it stretched back in all directions as far as he could see. He rubbed his chin. He always hated exploring caves when he was younger. Why would he be in one now? He could have sworn he was somewhere else a moment ago. None of this made sense. Unless...

Unless he was dead.

That had to be it. He must have died, and this must be the afterlife.

It wasn't fear he felt. Not dread. All Eino felt was a sort of calm resignation. And perhaps a hint of relief. It could be worse, he thought. His life had been far from virtuous, so he would have had a hard time facing the Dread Thresher on the Long Night of Judgment. An even harder time if he'd had to face Vinat. But if the nameless Deka'arist God hadn't laid claim to his soul, then who had?

The cavern wasn't cold, so he hadn't been returned to the cool embrace of Querrina's bosom, and this certainly wasn't the icy depths of Nerca. But the cave wasn't too hot either, so he knew he hadn't been cast into the fiery bowels of Strak.

A faint light appeared through the haze, illuminating a narrow, rocky corridor. At the end of its twisting path, it opened to an impossibly large chamber.

A ray of sunlight illuminated a small pond in the middle of the chamber. A waterfall flowed from a tall stone in the middle of the pond, and on top of the stone sat an old man. His long white beard hung well over the edge of the stone, dipping right into the waterfall.

"I bid thee welcome, Wanderer," said the man. His voice was loud, seeming to come from every direction within the massive chamber, yet somehow the sound was oddly soothing. "I knew thou wouldst return, O wayward soul."

Fish swam up the waterfall, jumping into the man's beard. Distracted by the sight, Eino looked closer, and noticed that the old man's beard didn't just dip into the waterfall. It was the waterfall. "D-Dilgaa?"

The old man's eyes darkened, storm clouds swirling behind his head. "Thou darest address thy god in so irreverent a manner?"

Eino fell to his knees. "Uh...sorry, sir. Forgiveth thou...me." He gulped. "Please."

Dilgaa let out a bellowing laugh. "Naw, I'm just messin' with ya, son!" He slapped his knee, the sound like thunder. "On your feet now. Ain't no need to put on airs like a damned coastie."

Eino let out a nervous laugh, pushing himself to his feet. Relief washed over him, but a twinge of wistful regret teased at the back of his mind. "Wait. So I...I'm really dead, huh?"

The god gave a sad nod. "Afraid so, son. Damn shame too. I really thought you were gonna pull through there in the end." In an instant, Dilgaa disappeared from the rock, reappearing beside Eino and setting a hand on his shoulder. "But my oh my, what a life you lived."

"Was it a good life?"

"Ha! You tell me, son. That ain't for me to decide." Dilgaa plucked a small driftcap growing out of his shoulder, letting it float away. "But let me tell ya, you sure kept things entertaining. I mean, a fella braving the Wynds, livin' on a mushroom in the sky? I don't gotta tell you I've been around a real long time, but I ain't never seen nothin' like that."

Eino scratched the back of his head. "I was always a little worried that you might be mad about that. What with me leaving Porocar to go live in the sky and all."

"Well..." Dilgaa's grip tightened on his shoulder. He seemed to grow larger, leering over Eino with a stern look on his face. "I'll tell ya, I weren't too happy when I seen you were making offerings to the other gods. I mean, when's the last time you offered up so much as a cheap cup of beer at one of my totems?"

Eino made a choked sound. In his travels, he'd stopped to pray at Dilgaa's totems a few times, but he hadn't made an offering since he first left Tetechetech.

Dilgaa cracked a smile. "But I can't be too mad. I mean, just look at all these things!" Dilgaa held out his hand. In it were dozens of small wooden idols.

Eino recognized the distinctive nicks and notches on each carving. "That's every single idol I've ever made."

"Sure is! See, you spread the good word of ol' Dilgaa all across Itharos, and ain't no other Porocari in history's ever done that." He waved his hand toward the stone in the pond. It rose out of the water, revealing a doorway. "So how could I look at you, my greatest prophet and missionary, and deny you entrance to my mountain hall?"

The doors in the stone swung open, revealing a light even brighter than the suns. Tears pricked at the corners of Eino's eyes. "I can come in? Really?"

"Son, you ask too many damn questions. I oughta just send you to Querrina's bosom. Then her and Solun can yap at you for all eternity! I tell ya, that's how them two made the winds. Can't neither one of em stop talkin'!" He slapped his thigh, pleased at his own joke.

"Sorry...it's just...one more question, sir." Eino shielded his eyes against the door's light. "Is...is Joren in there?"

"Joren? That Sinian boy?" Dilgaa shook his head. "Afraid not. See, he survived your little ordeal, but when it's his time, I reckon Soleivar will take him for judgment."

Eino stepped back and shook his head. "Then I'm sorry, but I can't come in."

"He's just one boy, you know." Dilgaa pointed his thumb at the doorway. "We've got all sorts of handsome fellas in there. Beautiful ladies too. And can't none of them wait till you come on through that door."

"I'm grateful, sir. Real grateful." Eino swallowed hard. "But it don't matter who else is in there. I won't be happy if he ain't there."

Dilgaa clicked his tongue. With a snap of his fingers, the door slammed shut, and the stone sunk back into the pond. "Damn shame." In a sudden motion, the god grabbed Eino by his jacket and leapt high into the air, soaring up the impossibly tall chamber. They emerged from a small opening at the very top. The skies opened up around him, and Eino saw they were now atop a mountain surrounded by swirling storm clouds.

"W-what are you doing?" yelled Eino.

"You made your choice, son." Dilgaa's voice was no longer soothing, but roared like thunder. "If you ain't gonna enter my hall, then the Grymwynd can have you!"

Dilgaa wound up and tossed Eino from the mountaintop. A wind wrapped around him and ripped him high into the air, dragging him screaming into the black clouds.

Eino shot up, still screaming. The wool hen resting on his chest squawked and flapped away, leaving behind an egg and sending the hammock swinging from the sudden movement. The egg rolled into the crook of his arm. Bewildered drowsiness took hold of him, and unable to open his eyes, he collapsed back down.

Half conscious, he spent what felt like ages clawing his way through waves of pain that drowned him in darkness. It felt as though his body was burning him from the inside out, and the pounding in his head was worse than any hangover he'd ever had. He wished the darkness would swallow him up completely and free him from the agony. But it never did, and as time ticked on, the pain eventually receded. His body was left feeling heavy, with dull aches that refused to let go of him.

When he finally managed to open his heavy eyelids after several failed tries, the first thing he saw was a rickety-looking wooden roof. Then the hooks for his hammock. He glanced down at his body. It was all in one piece, and even though his arms felt as flimsy as scrambler strands, his hand remained wrapped in a tight grip around Joren's sickle. He let go and stretched his creaky fingers, working the stiffness out of them.

With great effort and a long groan, he forced himself to his feet to explore the strange room he was in. He wobbled on his shaking legs and leaned against the wall to keep upright. The clean scent of wood filled the room, a more enticing smell compared to the smoke and fire from his inn, and something about it felt oddly familiar.

Despite the weathered look of the wooden flooring planks, the room was well appointed with paintings and intricate tapestries that livened up the small space. A set of fine golden goblets sat on an old well crafted desk, as well as a stack of maps and navigator's tools. From somewhere outside, Eino could hear the bellowing of a familiar voice barking out orders.

He stumbled to the door and pushed it open, bracing himself against the threshold. He immediately got a face full of scramblers. One made it past him into the room while two more tangled themselves up in his hair. He batted them away, then squinted against the brightness of the setting suns. As his eyes adjusted from the dark, he realized he was standing on the deck of a ship.

It was *The Crosswind*. And silhouetted against the sunset was its captain, standing at the helm.

"Mebeq?" asked Eino, his voice hoarse. The sound of rushing wind muffled his words, but the creaking of the planks beneath his feet drew the captain's attention.

Mebeq turned, doing a double take before flashing a bright smile. "My friend! You are awake! Praise his winds." He offered the helm to one of his crewmen and moved toward Eino, batting aside the clumps of scramblers that drifted over the deck. "I hope the accommodations were to your liking."

Eino laughed and stumbled forward as the muscle in his left calf twitched, wrapping his arms around Mebeq in a tight embrace. He'd never been happier to see his old friend.

Memories flooded his aching head. He grimaced. Then panic shot through him. He pulled away as terror slithered its way back through his guts. "The others. We have to go back—"

Mebeq grabbed him by the shoulders. "Easy, my friend. Your guests are safely below deck. We didn't think you'd awaken until tomorrow."

"You mean they're here?" Eino looked around wildly. "But how? This ol' boat ain't quick enough to get from Busani to the mountains that fast."

He gave an overly dramatic sigh. "Sadly, I never made it to Busani. It seems that Solun, in his great wisdom, had other plans for me."

Eino chuckled. "Don't tell me you called off your business trip just to keep an eye on little old me?"

"Not for you, no." He gave a hearty laugh and took Eino under his arm, walking him to the railing overlooking the deck. He pointed to a figure on the deck illuminated by the golden light of the setting suns. "But a Gatrai must always aid a traveler in need."

The figure looked out over the side of the deck and took a drag from his stickpipe, the winds carrying the smoke away. His blond hair blew in the wind, as did the ends of the ornate Heralian headscarf draped over his shoulders.

"Mr. Vennick!" called Mebeq, waving. He gestured to Eino. "Look who is finally awake!"

When Vennick's eyes met Eino's, he snuffed out his stickpipe and thrust it into his satchel before running over to join them. "Eino! It's good to see you again." He reached out and enthusiastically shook Eino's hand.

Mebeq patted Vennick on the shoulder. "We found him floating in the middle of the Stranach Channel, clinging to the charred husk of one of your mushroom cabins. He told us everything that happened, so we came looking for you."

Vennick smiled sheepishly. "It's actually because of you that I was able to flag them down." He reached into his satchel and produced Eino's missing signal staff. A wool hen flew over from the railing to perch on it.

"So that's where that thing ran off to."

"I must have stuffed it into my satchel before I fought the strangleweed. This thing saved my life." He looked down, wearing the same haunting look of guilt he'd worn the night they'd played fool's gambit. "Still, I'm sorry I took it away from you when you needed it most."

"Don't apologize. It's because of you we're all still alive." Off to the side he spotted a cloud of scramblers too large and thick to see through. Eino leaned against the railing.

"Hey, all I did was wave a stick around." Vennick flicked a scrambler away from his arm.

"You did a damn sight more than that," said Eino, patting Mebeq on the shoulder. "You even convinced this ol' sky hound to come wading through all these here scramblers to come hunt for us in the mountains. That ain't no small feat."

Mebeq scoffed. "You make it sound like such a terrible struggle. *The Crosswind* is not some fragile Sinian vessel. It will take more than a few errant seeds to make me turn my back on the Codes of the Brotherhood."

Eino laughed. "You'd better hope the Air Legion's ships stay so finicky. Once they build one that can survive scrambler season, you're gonna have some stiff competition in these here skies."

"I welcome the competition." Mebeq puffed out his chest. "How else can I prove myself the superior trader?"

"You sure? Them Sinians don't give up easy. You might have to work through your vacation to keep up."

"Solun forbid," said Mebeq. "If there comes a time when I am unable to enjoy my vacations, then I will surely retire!"

"Well, you're safe for now." Eino looked over the horizon, taking in the rolling Porocari hills and distant mountain ranges. "But the clouds ain't too bad. I reckon you could get these two back to Apthras and still make for Busani without losing too much time."

"Oh, we're not going to Apthras. Not much point in investigating the cause of the strangleweeds now." Vennick held up his hand. "No, everybody's heading to Muna."

"Everybody, huh?" Eino narrowed his eyes, looking around in a sudden panic. "Oh Strak, Revna ain't here, is she?"

"No, no, my friend." Mebeq laughed. "Your Sinian knight disembarked in Levenham a few days ago. She said something about seeking diviners and continuing an investigation, but I confess I paid her little mind."

Eino gave Mebeq a wily smirk. "Ah, so that's the real reason you came back this way." A small part of him was now glad the inn had left Levenham behind.

"I do not set my own path, my friend. I merely follow the winds that Solun lays out for me." He gave a knowing smile. "It is not my fault he chooses to bless me so."

Eino looked around, propping himself up with the signal staff like a walking stick. The wool hen clucked in annoyance before flapping away and waddling off. "Well, if she ain't here, I think I'm ready to see the others."

"They're all down in the mess hall. Follow me." Vennick led Eino below deck and through the threshold into a raucous scene.

Inside, Fulko strummed on his lyre, leading *The Crosswind's* crew in song as they drank and celebrated. The hatchling flew in circles above his head, and Leora laughed as she danced on one of the tables.

Val turned and smiled at Vennick, stepping forward to take his hand. "Back so soon?"

"And I brought company." He slapped his open palm against the threshold of the door a few times to get everyone's attention. "Announcing... Eino the Wanderer!"

Leora gasped. "Mr. Eino!" She leapt from the table and wrapped her arms around his waist.

"Hey there, little lady," he groaned as the girl squeezed him. "Oof, you've gotten strong! Must be all that sword training."

"You think so?" The girl beamed. "Well, Mr. Vennick's gonna keep training me once I'm in the Royal Academy, so I'm gonna get even stronger!"

"The Royal Academy, huh?" Eino turned back to Vennick, giving him a playful punch in the arm. "I guess you ain't just Val's escort anymore."

"I suggested he become a teacher." Val set a hand on Vennick's shoulder, offering him a goblet of ale. "I confess I was not entirely certain that my own skills would be enough for the position, but they would be positively foolish to let Vennick of the Thousand Weapons slip through their fingers."

"Don't be so modest." Vennick smiled, brushing his nose against hers. "Your skills are more than enough."

Leora giggled, covering her mouth with her hands. Eino politely turned away, watching Fulko as he finished his song. The boy took a bow, and as he did, the hatchling lighted on his lyre. The boy scowled at the bird, but made no effort to shake it loose.

Eino chuckled. "I see you've made a new friend."

Fulko sighed. "It's been following me ever since we landed on this ship. I keep trying to give it back to Blue, but she keeps letting her loose."

"Oh, a greatwing is the most loyal bird in the sky. That little guy ain't leaving you anytime soon." Eino rubbed his chin. "So I reckon he'll be joining you at the Academy then, huh?"

"Not exactly." The boy rubbed the back of his head. "I've been speaking with Joren, and I think I'd like to study under him. Maybe become his apprentice."

Eino's eyebrows shot up in surprise. "You really liked apothecary work that much?"

"Well, it wasn't exactly the most ideal of circumstances," said the boy, giving a shy smile, "but being an apothecary was a lot like solving a puzzle. If not for all the danger, it might even have been fun."

"Fun?" Vennick laughed. "You don't think anything's fun!"

Fulko pouted. "That's not true, Master."

"No need to call me Master anymore, Fulko." He patted the boy on the shoulder. "Mr. Joren will be the one to see to your training now."

"Not just yet. I still have a lot to learn, so I'd like to come with you to Muna and study at the Great Library first." The boy shifted on his feet. "If that would be alright."

"If it helps you find your way, Fulko, then I'll be happy to have you at my side once more. But have you discussed this with your new master?"

Eino looked around the room. "Where is he anyway?" the anticipation was killing him.

"I believe he's still in his cabin. Follow me." Fulko guided Eino toward the rear of the galley down a narrow hallway flanked by cabins. Dim candlelight shone from one of the open doors.

Eino silently nodded, patting the boy on the shoulder. With a deep breath, he stepped forward and knocked on the open doorway. Peering inside the cramped cabin, he saw Joren sitting on the narrow bed, his long silken locks pouring down his back as he studied his notes. At the creak of the door, the man looked back, his eyes wide. In an instant, he jumped up and pulled Eino into a tight embrace.

For a long moment, no words were said. At last Joren broke the embrace, and his expression turned from relief to concern. "What are you doing up? You really should be in bed. There was so much poison..."

"I couldn't sleep. I was having some pretty strange dreams." Eino reached up and patted Joren's hand. "Besides, I just...I had to see you. I had to know you were alright."

"Of course I'm alright. I had Blue." Joren weaved his fingers through Eino's, then guided him to sit on the bed. "She found the ship before I did. Once everyone else stepped off, she didn't even beg for a treat. It's like she knew you were in trouble."

Eino smiled. "Then remind me to give her extra treats later." He let Joren tug him down to sit on the bed, his gaze stuck on their entwined hands.

"Oh! Here." Joren reached under the bed and pulled out Eino's treasure box with Betta's quilt folded neatly on top. "I know it's not much, but we found where the net fell. I thought maybe you'd like to have these back."

Eino ran his fingers over the quilt, and as he did so, a bizarre, hollow feeling overwhelmed him. He'd been so relieved to see the others that the weight of losing his inn hadn't quite set in yet. "So. This is it, huh?" His vision went blurry as tears began streaming down his cheeks. All his years aboard that inn. All his hard work. All his memories. It had all gone up in flames, and now these few possessions were all he had left of it.

"I'm...I'm sorry," said Joren, "Maybe if I'd been faster—"

"No, no. Don't you go apologizing. This ain't your fault." Eino sniffed and dried his tears, grabbing Joren's shoulder and squeezing. "And I'm grateful. Really. Thank you. This is gonna keep me going till I'm back on my feet." He looked around the cramped cabin. The sight made his stomach churn and his hands clench. "I should get used to airships again. I reckon I'll have to sign back on with the Air Legion."

"You're going to re-enlist? But why?" Joren's eyes went wide. "Aren't you going to try to rebuild your inn?"

Eino shook his head. "There ain't but one place in Itharos where the driftcaps grow big enough. And I used up the very last one. On a smokehouse." He ran a hand through his hair and sighed. "Am I a dimling or what?"

"That's not true," said Joren.

"It is true. I'm a dimling. I took something so precious and squandered it."

"No, I meant about the driftcaps. You didn't use the last one."

"What do you mean?" Eino looked around in confusion. "Ain't no way you could've found more."

"Well, no." Joren collected his thoughts. His gaze strayed to the notebook beside him. "But we can grow more."

Eino squinted. "You what?"

"Val and I have been talking, and she showed me the parts of the mushroom where the aura would need to be honed. With enough time, you don't even need to be an auramancer to do it."

"You...you can..." Eino gasped, drawing in short, excited breaths. "You can give me back my inn?" He thrust the treasure box into Joren's arms. "Take it! Take it all!

"Wha—" Joren held his hands up. "I can't accept this!"

"Sure you can. Look, I know you're short on money. But me? Strak, I don't care if I make another jingle again. If it gets me my inn back, you can have everything I own."

"Th-that's an appealing offer." Joren cleared his throat. "There is one thing I'd like to request. I-if it's not too much trouble, that is."

"Anything. You name it."

"I was hoping maybe I could possibly...keep staying on your inn. Your new one, I mean. I'll only need a small cabin. And I'll keep helping out around the inn, of course. I'll fish and cook and help harvest scramblers. Anything you need, I'll do it."

"You wanna come back into the skies with me?" Eino grinned. A new inn and Joren? He couldn't imagine anything better. "You sure? It's pretty high up."

Joren glanced toward the window. His eyes went wide as if he just now remembered how high in the air he currently was. "I'm still not used to that part yet. But if it was with you..." Joren swallowed and slowly turned back. "I think I could handle it."

Eino locked eyes with Joren. He couldn't help but bite his lip in excitement. "I could kiss you right now."

"Y-you could?" Joren stammered. His eyes met Eino's, but he didn't look away. "I suppose—"

Eino didn't give him time to finish his sentiment. He reached up and ran his fingers through the man's hair, pulling him into a long, slow kiss. His hair was every bit as soft and silky as he'd hoped, and the aroma of herbs that clung to him was positively intoxicating.

Joren froze in surprise, but a second later recovered. He returned the kiss, his own fingers running through Eino's hair. When they finally broke the kiss, Joren took a moment to catch his breath, a broad smile on his face. "Sometimes you just have to jump, right?"

"I've been trying to do that for weeks! Guess I should've taken my own advice." Eino chuckled. "But to answer your question, no. I ain't gonna give you a cabin."

Joren's eyes went wide. Shock faded to disappointment on his face as he steadied his breathing. "Oh. I understand," he said, voice quiet.

"Because my new quarters are gonna be big enough for both of us. It'll be the best room on the inn." He grinned. "Now, how's that sound?"

"That sounds wonderful." Joren gave him a shy smile. "The less bridges I have to cross the better."

With a mischievous smile, Eino leaned in and planted another kiss on Joren's lips. "Now what was that you were telling me...I should be in bed, right?" He reached his foot back across the cramped cabin and kicked the cabin door closed.

Epilogue

"...It's true!" said Eino, "Aangvar was this close to betting his gold broach at the table. I damn near had to drag him away from those dice!"

Clofen laughed, cradling his newborn daughter in his arms. "And they called this guy 'Swifthand?'"

"Oh, he was real good with a sword, but your ol' Ma damn near cleaned him out at fool's gambit. If I hadn't stepped in, she would've ended up as head of a whole order of Sinian Knights!"

The two men laughed as they sat on the porch of Clofen's cottage, sipping at cups of strong, malty Porocari tea. Behind the towering mountain range in the distance, dawn lit up the cool, late autumn sky in an array of pinks and golden oranges.

It had been about a half-year since Eino first arrived in Yel Mor, and every day since had left him feeling a bizarre mix of emotions. Harvesting mushrooms with Clofen gave him a wistful sense of nostalgia, and it was nice to have a real connection to the land again. But as beautiful as the mountain views were, he couldn't help but feel they were boxing him in. The skies kept calling him toward that endless horizon, and he knew he couldn't suppress his wanderlust forever.

Clofen chuckled. "I swear you've got a new story about my Ma every time I talk to you."

"And you ain't even heard half of them," said Eino. "Don't tell me you're getting sick of them?"

"Not on your life," said Clofen, casting his eyes to the glimmering aurastream above them. "Growing up here, she was always such a homebody. I just can't imagine her drifting around the skies like that. Strak, I couldn't imagine her even leaving the farm."

"Oh, she always complained the whole time. 'Ain't nothing out here worth leaving home for,' she used to say. But I think she liked seeing Itharos a lot more than she let on." He took a sip of the strong brew, a wistful smile on his lips. "I'm really gonna miss that ol' mountain goat."

A voice piped up behind them. "Now I know my hearing's going, but you boys know I ain't deaf yet, right?"

Eino wore a playful grin as he pretended to ignore her. "Sometimes, it's like I can still hear her voice on the wind."

"Now you cut that out." Betta smacked him on the arm with a wooden spoon. "Elsewise, I ain't gonna let you have none of these spiced mushroom dumplings for your little trip."

"Aww come on now, Betta," pleaded Eino, feigning concern. "You wouldn't deprive poor Joren of your tasty treats, now would you?"

"That sweet boy already got his. I gave him a whole pouch full." She waved her spoon at Eino and Clofen. "You two troublemakers could learn a thing or two from him."

Eino looked up, then checked his pocket watch. "You mean he's up already?"

"I reckon he's still round the back loading up the birds." Betta pointed her thumb over her shoulder.

"Aw, cast me," said Eino, drinking down the rest of his tea and jumping to his feet. "I told him I'd be done packing before he was up!"

He dashed back through the cottage, offering a polite curtsy to Clofen's wife as he passed her in the kitchen. He collected himself and strolled out the back door, trying his best to look nonchalant. There he saw Joren tending to the greatwings, loading a few packs onto Red's saddle.

"Hey! Didn't see you there," said Eino. "Grabbing a few extra things?"

"Just a few non-essentials," said Joren, giving a knowing smile, "like your signal staff, your treasure box, the navigation stone..."

"Alright, I get it," Eino held up his hands. "I may have gotten a little distracted." That happened a lot when him and Clofen started gabbing.

"Eino, it's alright. I understand. If you wanted to stay a little longer—"

"No, no." Eino shook his head. "Being here's been real nice and all, but this ain't where I belong." He turned back to Joren, a hint of concern on his face. "What about you? Having second thoughts about leaving?"

Joren scoffed. "After all of our hard work on the inn? Not a chance." It was the first time he'd ever seen Joren look offended. "Besides, we still have someone to meet in town, remember?"

"I didn't forget," said Eino, his voice playfully chiding. He patted Blue on the beak and turned back toward the cottage. "But if you're ready, then let's get going."

Joren looked back, lifting an eyebrow. "Aren't we taking the birds?"

"Not for a trip this short," said Eino. "We'll give the lovebirds a break. Besides, it's a good day for a stroll."

The two finished packing up the greatwings, and after a light breakfast, they said their goodbyes on the porch. Betta handed Eino a pouch of mushroom dumplings. "You boys be sure to come back now, you hear," she said, pulling Eino into a tight embrace. When he was close, she whispered in his ear. "And bring me some Brumanti liquor when you visit. I don't think I can take much more of this girl's cooking."

"Oh hush," whispered Eino back. "Stranian food is good once you get a taste for it."

Betta pulled back and shook her head. "Some things are just too broke to fix."

"It ain't too late to come back to the inn."

"Dilgaa forbid," said Betta with a smile. She cast a glance toward Joren. "Besides, I reckon you boys will want some privacy."

They set out for town, turning one last time to wave. As he turned his attention back to the dirt road, he found himself at a loss for words. He'd been anxiously awaiting this day ever since he arrived in Yel Mor. Together with Joren, they'd spent every day trekking into the mountains and growing the new inn. They even camped in the mountains for days at a time, spending long nights carving out rooms and putting together furniture. It was hard work, but with Joren at his side, he looked forward to every single day.

The chill in the air drew his eyes to the snowy mountaintops. It was late autumn now, and before long the snows would fall on the valley, reaching his new inn. He'd been rushing these past few weeks to complete his work before winter fully took hold.

"It's funny." Eino chuckled to himself. "If we get in the sky today, we'll be just about on my old schedule." He was looking forward to seeing his old friends again, although he wasn't excited at the prospect of explaining his absence over and over.

Joren looked up excitedly. "Does that mean we'll be able to visit all the same festivals?"

"Sure does," said Eino. He cast a sideways glance. "I didn't think you'd care about all that. I ain't never seen you at any of the festivals."

He looked down. "Honestly, I always wanted to go, but I was so worried about money that I never got to enjoy them."

"Well, just because you're bunking with me don't mean you get off of fishing duty," said Eino, playfully nudging him with his elbow. "But you and I are gonna have a lot of fun at Sarbakh this year!"

When they reached town, they found Fulko on a bench outside the tavern chewing on a large muffin. A half-grown greatwing perched on the roof. As soon as he spotted the pair approaching, he jumped to his feet and bowed. "It's good to see you again, Master Joren."

Joren grimaced. "Just Joren is fine, thank you."

The boy looked up, confused. "My apologies. I do not wish to disrespect you, Mast—" Fulko cleared his throat. "Joren."

"You can start calling me 'Master Eino' if you like," said Eino with a chuckle. He looked from side to side and peered into the tavern. "Ain't Vennick with you?"

Fulko shook his head. "He's back in Muna with Val and Leora. I wanted to make this journey on my own."

"Nice work, kid. I don't reckon I could've made that trek at your age. How are the others anyhow?"

"They're doing well. Both Vennick and Val are teaching at the Academy now. Leora's still a little too young to enroll, but she's due to be accepted next year," said Fulko. "Also, Vennick and Val are now engaged."

"Really? Well, congratulations!"

"It's true. The wedding is to be held in Muna some time in midwinter, and both of you are invited."

"Us and half of Itharos I bet!" said Eino. "I don't know if we—"

"We'd love to go," said Joren. "Of course, we'll need to get a present for them."

"Tough guy to shop for. What do you get the man who has every weapon?" Eino smiled, casting his eyes toward the mountains. "I reckon we'd better get going if we're gonna make the ceremony."

"Then let's get going." Fulko held his fingers to his lips and whistled. "Green! Come on, girl!"

"You named her Green?" Eino asked, peering up at the bird as she unfurled her long wings.

"Yeah. It's my favorite color."

"But she ain't green."

"So? Blue's not blue, and Red's not red."

Eino pursed his lips. "You ain't wrong."

"Shall we, then?" The boy started along the dirt path toward the mountains, but stopped when neither Eino nor Joren followed. "Aren't you coming?"

"Just wait a minute. We're taking the short way up." Eino blew his whistle, which made Green squawk. A few minutes later, Blue and Red crested the hill and glided down to meet them.

Eino tossed one of Betta's dumplings to Blue. The greatwing snatched it up and lowered herself. "Hop on, kid. You can ride up with me."

Fulko loaded his bags onto Blue's saddle and climbed on behind Eino. With a whoop and a tug on her reins, Blue flapped her wings and climbed into the sky. Joren rode Red close behind them, with Green chirping and swooping along the whole way into the mountain pass.

After a few minutes, Eino guided blue into a deep valley. When the worksite came into view, Fulko let out a gasp. "Whoa. That looks bigger."

"It is bigger." Eino called back, puffing out his chest. "Three floors in the cap this time. And a couple more cabins too." He'd finished carving out the insides of the main inn body and cabins, and he'd just completed work on the promenade and bridges the day prior. He'd also cut the mushrooms from their roots to test if they were ready to float, keeping them tethered with a few taut ropes. None of the driftcaps had fallen, and with the wind tugging at them, the mushrooms almost seemed eager to climb high into the sky.

One of the inn's newest additions was a driftcap built to serve as a roost for the greatwings. Both Blue and Red converged on it, settling into their nest in the hollowed out top. Below them was a newly built coop, and as Eino, Joren, and Fulko climbed down, they were greeted by a cacophony of clucking wool hens patrolling the driftcap's body for worms and other parasites.

Eino frowned and counted them. "Well cast me. Ol' Chandarre found himself some new ladies. I reckon I'm gonna need some more feed." He reached down to pet the rooster, but Chandarre pecked his hand instead. Eino clicked his tongue. "Just what am I gonna do with you?"

"Very impressive." Fulko looked around and gave an approving nod. He reached into his satchel and produced a glimmering green crystal roughly the size of his thumb. "I imagine you'll want me to embed this here?"

"Wow, Decrian crystal," said Eino, his voice reverent. He was entranced by the torrent of aura swirling beneath its flawless glassy exterior. Even with his limited grasp of auramancy, he could feel how much more powerful this core was than his old one. But even though he appreciated the generosity of the gift, Eino couldn't help but notice just how small the core was. With all of the tales he'd heard of the quality of Decrian crystal cores, he'd expected something at least a little bigger. After realizing he'd been staring, Eino shook himself loose of his trance. "But no, I reckon I'll put the core in the main body of the inn. Just like on the old one."

"Oh, this isn't the core," said Fulko. "It's just one of the minor crystals Val sent to help you better control the inn's aura in all of the side mushrooms." He reached back into his satchel and, with some effort, he produced a crystal as wide as his head and twice as tall. "This is the core."

Eino's eyes went wide, almost feeling as though he should avert his gaze. "Th-this is too much. Way, way, way too much," he stammered. "Ain't no way I can accept all this."

Fulko shrugged. "Val said you might say that. She also said to tell you that she didn't spend a jingle of her own money on it. She thought you might appreciate that these crystals were paid for by funds that were—and I quote—'affectionately borrowed' from her ex-husband's personal coffers."

Eino smirked. "Well, I can't rightly turn down a gift from a bishop, now can I?" With how strict Val had been, he never thought she'd be capable of such a grand heist, particularly from someone as dangerous as the Butcher Bishop. He made a personal note not to underestimate her.

"I can embed the core as well, if you'd like."

"Cast me, kid! Are you studying auramancy now too?"

"Only enough to get by. We'll still need Val's help to make sure everything's working properly, but I can keep the barrier up and running until we reach Muna."

They walked across the rope bridge to the main body and circled the promenade. Eino opened the door to the common room.

Fulko looked around, taking in the fireplace and the large round window across from it. "It's just like I remember."

"Trust me, it's even better." Much of the new inn was laid out like the last one, but he'd taken what he'd learned to make a few changes and upgrades. Together they walked to the panel in the wall labeled "Do Not Open."

Fulko glared at Eino. "You can't be serious."

"It was worth a shot," said Eino with a chuckle. He reached around to the side of the bookshelf and opened a hidden doorway down to a narrow staircase.

It led a short way down to a small alcove. "I'm gonna need someone to put an aura lock on this thing at some point."

"It should be fine for now." The boy set the core in the alcove and began drawing aura into his hands, tracing the edges of the crystal with his fingertips.

Eino looked over the boy's shoulder as he worked. "You need any help?"

"No, but this will take me a little while."

Eino stepped around Fulko and turned his attention to Joren, his fingers grazing his arm. "Then how about I show you the top floor?"

"So you're finally ready to show me what you've been working on up there?" Joren looked up excitedly.

Eino smiled. "Come on." He led Joren out to the common room, then up the stairs to the extended loft. They took their time with the climb, making their way past the area that would become Joren's workshop. The furnishings were sparse, with only a work table and a few vials of herbs dotting a shelf, but soon it would have everything he needed to not only do his apothecary work, but to guide Fulko as well.

Joren's face scrunched up as they made their way past the table. "I'm not entirely certain I'm ready to be a teacher."

"Don't say that. You're gonna do great." Eino patted his shoulder. "And just think, you won't have to take your own notes anymore."

Joren chuckled. "I doubt any of his tutors back in Muna made him take down their personal notes."

"Maybe, but you've got something them eggheads don't," said Eino. "You've got more experience being an apothecary than all of them put together. And you didn't have to bury your nose in some book to learn how to do it."

"There's still a lot I don't know." He looked up and smiled. "But maybe you're right."

"Of course I'm right. I'm always right." Eino puffed out his chest. "Just like I'm sure you'll love this."

At the top floor, Eino threw the doors open. He stepped aside, gesturing for Joren to come in. Joren looked around and gasped, dropping his bags. There was a broad window along one side, offering a panoramic view of the sky. Beside it was a doorway that led out to a small balcony. A few small windows circled the rest of the room, letting in plenty of light from the suns.

Against one wall was a wide, comfortable bed piled high with cushions and folded blankets. It was flanked by a pair of wardrobes, and there was a sturdy chest at the foot of the bed. Against the far wall was a stone fireplace with two chairs for a sitting area, and beside it was a desk. The decor was sparse, with only a few of Eino's maps hanging along the wall by his desk. But as they traveled, they'd make this space their own. Together.

"And the best part?" Eino stretched his arm above his head to touch the ceiling. "No more bonking our heads!"

Joren gazed around the room, the awe clear on his face. "It's amazing, Eino."

"Well, it's only the beginning." Eino grabbed his hand and tugged him to the balcony. He pulled him in close, his nose touching Joren's.

There was a sudden flash of aura all around them that made them both jump. They turned to look and saw a shimmering green bubble slowly materialize and envelop the entire worksite. The shimmering faded, leaving an almost imperceptibly transparent barrier.

"Mr. Eino? Master Joren?" a voice called from somewhere below. "I've finished with the core!"

"We'll be there in a second!" Eino called over the edge of the balcony. He turned back to Joren. "Guess it's high time to get the new and improved Driftcap Inn back in the sky!"

Joren gulped. "Are you sure we're ready?"

"Nope!" said Eino with a smile. "But sometimes you've just gotta jump."

Eino pulled out an aurastone from his jacket. With a drop of his aura, the locks on the inn's tethers popped open and released the inn. It slowly ascended into the sky, cresting the evergreens. Looking out across the top of the forest, Eino's heart fluttered as the horizon came into view.

Joren wobbled on his feet, clinging close to Eino for support.

Eino smiled. "You gonna be alright?"

"Yeah. I think so." Joren took a deep breath. "As long as I can count on you."

"Always," said Eino, as he pulled him into a kiss.

Continue on for a recipe for Hen's Nests. If you enjoyed this book, please consider leaving a review. For a **bonus chapter** and more recipes, sign up to my newsletter https://katevalentauthor.com/steeping-notes/

Recipe for Hen's Nests

This breakfast dish is a breakfast staple of The Driftcap Inn. Eino invented this dish one morning when inspiration hit while gathering eggs from the wool hens. It pairs well with a side of bacon, fruit, or both.

Hen's nests

- 4 cups vegetables

- 2 eggs

- 1/2 tsp salt

- 1/2 tsp pepper

- 1/2 tsp paprika

- 1/2 tsp garlic powder

- 1/2 tsp onion powder

- 4 tbsp olive oil (2 for the fry pan and 2 for the fritters)

- *1/2 cup all purpose flour

****Yogurt Dill Sauce**

- 2 tbsp plain yogurt (the tangier the better)

- A pinch of:

  - Garlic

  - Pepper

  - Salt

  - dill

- A spritz of lemon

Instructions

1: Grate or julienne various vegetables. Long strips work best. Cabbage, zucchini, potatoes, carrots, green onions, spinach, and other leafy greens all work well. Squeeze the water out of the vegetables.

2: Add the seasonings, egg, flour, 2 tablespoons of the oil, and mix. If the mix is too wet to hold together, add more flour.

3: Make the fritters by squeezing a handful of vegetables together. Create a hole in the center for the egg.

4: Add 2 tbsp of cooking oil to a fry pain and let it warm up.

5: Fry the fritters on each side for about four minutes each.***

6: When the nests are done, crack eggs into the pan and cook them to your liking (Eino prefers his yolks runny). Once done add them to the center of the nests.

7: Mix together the yogurt dill sauce.

8: Drizzle the sauce over the fritters and serve.

Notes:

*For a gluten-free version, white rice flour works well.

**For a dairy-free sauce, use mayo in place of yogurt.

***For a large batch, you can bake them on a baking sheet at 400 F/200 C. Crack the egg right in the nest and bake for eight minutes or until the egg is done to your liking.

About the author

Kate Valent is three cats in a trench coat masquerading as a writer. She writes all things fantastical, with tea, magic, and romance featuring heavily in her stories. Her history degree is put to use in her writing in ways that would only disappoint her professors. She lives in Pittsburgh, Pennsylvania with the love of her life. You can find out more on her website katevalentauthor.com